Those Questing Heroes

by

Stephen M. T. Greene

The Saga of the Enforcers

Those Questing Heroes

Cover Art by *Tina Lynn Stout*

The Wild Rose Press, Inc.
PO Box 708
Adams Basin, NY 14410-0708
Visit us at www.thewildrosepress.com

Publishing History
First Edition, 2026
Trade Paperback Print ISBN 978-1-5092-6382-0
Digital ISBN 978-1-5092-6383-7

The Saga of the Enforcers
Published in the United States of America

Dedication

This is for my brother Andrew, who also writes.

Chapter 1

The big metal doors of the Crooked Cantina opened like the jaws of a monster and let in the two Universal Marshals. Their eyes swept the gloom. Red, green, and black blood stained the dull white walls. The cantina occupied a designated space near the center of Hothtar, a frontier town on the criminocratic planet Darkania, in the Lokina Sector of the Milky Way Galaxy. None of the cantina patrons paid any attention to them.

"Have you ever seen such a loathsome place filled with so many foul creatures and vile minions in your life?" the shorter of the two Universal Marshals asked.

"No, faerieling," Enforcer Apparis, the Roc, responded, whose sharp beak looked ready to peck any patron stupid enough to lay a hand, paw, tentacle, pincer, or any other type of appendage on him. "They all look like birds of prey ready to swoop down on the unwary."

The two Universal Marshals appeared a distinctly striking pair. Apparis stood over seven feet tall, a living creation made by a combination of biosciences and biotechnologies, occult arts, and celestic fields. The purpose of his makers was to actually create a new Enforcer, and the Roc eventually and ultimately accomplished that. But the team of scientists, occultists, and celestists who originally made him died eight years ago in an earthquake soon after they completed their experiment. They left him trapped in a cryogenic tube until it malfunctioned and finally set him free to fulfill his destiny, almost a year after the quake. His tenure as a Universal Marshal reached six years now.

Apparis folded his white and electric-blue wings close to his powerful body. His large, keen, electric-blue eyes scanned the cantina like a macroscope, searching distant space for celestial objects. One look at his huge avian head gave the impression Apparis must be a hunting bird in being form, because it resembled that of a Bald Eagle. Talons extended very sharply from his huge hands and feet, deadly natural weapons to slash foes in mortal combat. "This nesting place of filthy worms isn't even fit for buzzards to scavenge through."

Benethor, the Elf-Enforcer, nodded in agreement. He stood only five feet tall, a slim figure with willowy limbs and long yellow hair. His blue eyes were lighter in shade than his towering companion and his facial features were finely chiseled, unlike his friend, whose were bluntly pronounced, except for one anatomical feature. Pointy ears protruded from the beautiful head of Benethor whereas his fellow Universal Marshal had no such visible organ to speak of. The Elf-Enforcer wore all white—tunic, tights, and moccasins. Belted around his trim waist hung an Elvin sword and a large pouch; strapped to his back, a full quiver of arrows and matching bow. His artificial garb was an obvious contrast to his giant comrade, who was naturally and thickly clothed in white and electric-blue feathers. Benethor had served as a Universal Marshal for eleven years. "Well, let's begin our seeking."

The Enforcers started to move through the many metal tables in the cantina, all occupied at present by a wide variety of creatures, both natural and artificial.

Gray and white smoke filtered through the somewhat stale air as some patrons puffed pipes and similar devices. The stone floor, though with an even surface, showed cracks in places. They went to the bar, and a male Eworkian bartender, a humanoid with four fingers, blue skin, and a black walrus-like mustache, greeted them.

"What'll you have?" the cantina keeper asked.

"For me, a Phoenix Fireball," Apparis said.

Benethor wrinkled his nose in disgust at getting a drink in the unsavory establishment. But he played along anyway. "Blue Moonbeam Fizz."

The bartender slid their beverages down to them. Apparis grabbed his tall glass, filled with a bright reddish-orange liquid bubbling like crazy, and downed it in one gulp. Benethor stared at the sparkling blue drink in another tall glass and seemed leery of swallowing as if it might be poisoned. Given the character of the place, the concern of the Elf-Enforcer over his refreshment was legitimate.

The Roc turned around and watched a fight break out between a big hairy Grizzla and an octopoid Molluskian. Both combatants exchanged heated words before they struck blows. The Molluskian tried to wrap his furry opponent in six tentacles like a mummy, but the Grizzla brushed aside the slender, flexible limbs. Then the Grizzla crashed both his giant hairy fists atop the soft, slippery head of the Molluskian and the octopoid alien crumpled to the floor in a slumbering heap. Apparis shook his head and faced the Elf-Enforcer, who still hesitated to consume his drink. The Roc made no comment on Benethor, just eyed the azure liquid in front of the smaller Universal Marshal. Instead, Apparis ordered another Phoenix Fireball.

Benethor sipped carefully at his beverage. Apparis had already swallowed his second drink. A three-eyed alien next to the Elf-Enforcer addressed the Universal Marshal after gulping a dark brown ale from a hexagonal stein.

"Hey, little Elf man, is that big avian beside you your hunting falcon?" The bulky being guffawed.

"I do not practice the sport of falconry," Benethor replied, offended by the unclean brute.

The slobbery alien burped. "How about giving me some coins from your pot of gold?"

Benethor imbibed a little more of his drink. "You're confusing me with a Leprechaun."

"Then what treasures can you offer me, you stinking Elf?"

Benethor smiled. "Only blessings from nature."

"Pah!" The ponderous creature rubbed his scaly hands together and breathed foully on the Universal Marshal. "What do you have in that pouch there?"

"My personal property." Much unpleasantness radiated from the scumbag to the magical senses of Benethor. The next moment, the alien licked his scaly lips and reached down to take the white pouch from his wide white belt. Instantly, the Elf-Enforcer whipped out his sword and stabbed its point against the ridged throat of the surprised being. The alien stopped his hand short of snatching the pouch from the Universal Marshal. "Take your hand away, vile animal, or taste the blade of my Elvin sword."

The unruly patron seemed to weigh the odds of blatantly challenging Benethor for possession of the mysterious pouch. Apparis appeared unworried about his fellow Universal Marshal being accosted by that dreg of the galaxy. The standoff ended with the alien withdrawing slowly from the busy bar and disappearing somewhere in the crowded cantina.

Benethor shrugged the incident off. Everybody else in the joint treated the matter as a regular occurrence and simply ignored it. Apparis had already dismissed it but would have come quickly to the aid of the Elf-Enforcer if it had been necessary.

The cantina band stepped up to the stage after a long break and began to liven the place up with an instrumental piece fast in tempo. Seven members formed the band, all from different alien species, each with a different musical instrument ranging from a rainbow-colored synthesizer to a double-arm guitar with twenty strings.

"Vulgar melody," Benethor remarked, preferring music on a classical level. Elvin melodies particularly fitted such high-quality tunes.

Apparis listened. "It's decent noise to enjoy. But birdsongs are better and more natural."

Benethor concurred wholeheartedly. A human barmaid passed by him, and he called to her. "Is the Slug here?"

"Not yet," answered the curvaceous blonde holding a tray full of various drinks. "But he should be here soon."

Five minutes later, Ajawbo the Slug arrived with his retinue of bodyguards and other personnel. Ajawbo was an elephantine slug-like being mottled gray and white. His undulating bulk rolled over the floor like blubbery meat being pushed across the slick deck of a space vessel engaged in hunting voyages. Huge, glossy black eyes bulged from his enormous round head, and a forked tongue occasionally darted out from his cavernous maw. His nostrils looked like twin air shafts regulating his breathing.

"An utterly repulsive creature," Benethor remarked as the Slug exchanged pleasantries with some of the cantina patrons.

"No ordinary bird could kill that giant worm," Apparis quipped. "Maybe a thunderbird or a gigantic roc could."

Both Universal Marshals waited until the Slug situated himself in his customary spot in the cantina, a ramped platform in the northwest corner of the place, not too far from the bar. Ajawbo put his retinue around him like a protective shield of living bodies. The Slug motioned, with a huge fatty arm, for the cantina band to play a song he enjoyed. It acceded to his wishes, and the lead singer, a small female alien, started to wail a rousing, fast tune, rocking back and forth to the beat. Backup voices in the band piped in during the chorus sections of the song.

The Roc and the Elf-Enforcer looked at each other briefly, then made their way to the Slug. When the two Universal Marshals got close enough to Ajawbo, an armed pair of hefty razorback guards jumped forward to place themselves between the Enforcer duo and their master. Ajawbo noticed the Universal Marshals after the cantina band finished its song and prepared for the next one.

Ajawbo addressed the pair of Enforcers. "What do you want from me, stranger beings?"

Benethor answered for them. "We seek knowledge of the Fellowship of Darkness."

Ajawbo paused before replying. "What do you wish to know about the Fellowship?"

"Their location," Apparis stated simply.

Ajawbo appeared to be thinking. "Why do you need such information, stranger beings? What use can it be for you?"

"We have important affairs to settle with the Fellowship," Benethor explained, fingering his pouch.

Ajawbo grumbled. "What kind of affairs?"

Apparis flapped his wings once, emphatically. "That is between us and them."

Ajawbo shook his head. He seemed to weigh their request. "I'm afraid I cannot accommodate you."

An unspoken exchange occurred between the two Universal Marshals. They responded together, "We insist on your help."

Ajawbo growled in agitation. "Who are you to demand anything from me?"

"By the authority of who we are and by the power vested in us from our leader," Benethor stated.

Ajawbo's eyes widened at that. "Just who are you, and who is your lord?"

Apparis gave the Slug a menacing glare. "You do not need to know."

Ajawbo spoke to the two razorback beings. "Guards, have these two fools leave my presence."

Both burly guards before the Enforcer duo raised their poleaxes in threatening gestures. Their hostile actions did not budge the Universal Marshals.

"Kill them!" Ajawbo ordered.

Both guards attacked them. Apparis stepped aside and caught a poleaxe. The Roc lifted its owner into the air and sent him crashing into the wall behind the Slug.

Then, Apparis threw the weapon to the floor.

Simultaneously with the Roc, Benethor somersaulted to the right side of the other guard and came up with his sword in hand. The Elf-Enforcer slashed the wide gut of the razorback being, who dropped to the ground with a bleeding midsection. Benethor finished him by cutting off his head.

Abruptly, the rest of the Slug's retinue surrounded him as protection against the danger from the Universal Marshals. Ajawbo seemed to be cursing.

"Hey!" one of the cantina patrons yelled, a lanky humanoid sitting at a table behind the conflict involving the Slug. "I know who that birdman is. I've seen him in action before. He's a peace officer of the Universal Federation of Planets!"

Someone then screamed, "Enforcers!"

The band stopped playing and all the patrons in the cantina rose up, some with weapons ready to strike. The two Universal Marshals backed away from the Slug and put the nearest wall behind them. Benethor yanked open his pouch so he could pull out its contents in a hurry when needed, then readied his bow. Apparis instantly parted his magnificent wings and stood in a fighting stance, arms out before him.

Both Enforcers knew they faced a cantina full of Criminals, except Ajawbo the Slug, who fitted the classification of a Villain. Fortunately, no Archvillains appeared among the evil mob. The odds seemed overwhelmingly against the two Universal Marshals, who obviously saw no way out of their dangerous predicament except by doing battle against all that sea of scum.

A feline-like alien leaped at Apparis from the left.

The Roc belted the creature away and a snake-like being flew at him next. Apparis raked the serpentine alien across the face with such great speed and force that the viperish fiend lost both eyes and most of his face before collapsing to the floor, writhing in agony. On the other side, Benethor cut down some patrons in lightning fashion with his bow, his arrows finding their marks swiftly in rushing bodies.

All the remaining Criminals charged the Federation peace officers as one unit. Benethor immediately released his bow and ripped a large red Elfstone from his pouch as Apparis stretched his wings to their fullest. As the mass surged at them, The Elf-Enforcer blasted powerful red beams from the Elfstone into the mass while the Roc oscillated his huge pennons at them with the awesome power of a true thunderbird at hurricane force. As if it slammed into an invisible wall, the foul swarm was pushed backward faster and faster, crashing into chairs, tables, drinking glasses, and other objects.

In the next moment, squads of Federation troopers raided the cantina and mopped up the motley mass of defeated Criminals. Apparis and Benethor ran after Ajawbo and caught him before the Slug snuck out the back way of the cantina. The trained soldiers rounded up everyone inside and made them all kneel.

The Federation troopers wore different colored unisuits to identify their ranks. Enlisted personnel dressed in golden unisuits. A sergeant among the skilled warriors in a green unisuit gave orders to the squads. As the two Universal Marshals returned to line Ajawbo with the other prisoners, the sergeant approached and saluted them.

"Well done," Benethor said to the warrant officer.

"What should we do with them, sirs?" the sergeant asked.

Apparis exchanged looks with his fellow Universal Marshal. "Take all these vermin outside, except the Slug. We want to interrogate the Villain."

"Yes, sir." The sergeant saluted the Roc. "You heard the Enforcer. Move these pathetic civilians outside, pronto."

In a moment, the two Universal Marshals began their interrogation of the Slug. Ajawbo looked calm under their silent glares, unimpressed by the fact that they were Enforcers.

Benethor broke the muted atmosphere. "As we said before, we seek the location of the Fellowship of Darkness."

"We are not interested in your evil organization on this planet," Apparis added. "Tell us what we want, and our departure from here will be swift and sure."

Ajawbo huffed. "Why should I help you? What profit is in it for me?"

"You get to keep your operation intact," Apparis said. "We Enforcers could have ended your business any time the Federation desired it."

The Villain took a deep breath. "You speak with truth. But if I told you what you wanted, the Fellowship could send me to the scumyard."

"If you don't tell us what we want to hear, we'll shut your evil operation down permanently," Apparis said. The Roc opened his beak and let loose a sonic boom that blasted a hole in the wall of the cantina right behind the Slug. "Your choices are quite limited."

The display of destructive power caused Ajawbo to hesitate. The Slug fell silent as if reconsidering his options. Finally, the Villain let out a torrent of unintelligible words before responding with, "The Fellowship of Darkness is searching the galaxy for an object of great power."

Benethor perked up. "What are they questing for?"

Ajawbo spilled it all. "The Fellowship is looking for Lordruingat, the Cube of Power."

That revelation utterly surprised the Enforcer duo.

"Lordruingat is a myth," Benethor said.

Apparis stated, "All myths and legends have a basis in fact."

Benethor stepped closer to the Slug. "Why would the Fellowship seek the Cube of Power when it is nothing more than a fairy tale?"

"One of the servants of a member of the Fellowship of Darkness found the place where Lordruingat is hidden away," Ajawbo explained. "But the servant was rather delirious when he related his story to the Fellowship, and they could not get a definite fix on the exact location. They ascertained that he spoke factly, that Lordruingat does indeed exist, so the Fellowship searches the galaxy for it."

The Universal Marshals finished the interrogation and left the Slug in the hands of the Federation troopers after calling for an escort. Both Enforcers waited until they were alone.

"We must inform the High Enforcer," Apparis stated.

Benethor nodded. "The Universal Marshals may be going on a quest of our own."

Chapter 2

Delveran walked toward the conference room of the Federation Department of Justice on the tenth floor of the Federationplex. Glowpanels lighted his way. On either side of him stood automatic doors to various chambers, no one going in or out of them at the moment. He was alone in the corridor.

The High Enforcer stood six feet tall with a lean frame. His green eyes focused on the automatic doors ahead of him, wondering why the department wanted to see the Grand Universal Marshal. He sported a trim mustache and curly black hair. He wore black—suit, shirt, belt, shoes, and a cape. The Zordrak Pentacle, a very powerful amulet made of iron and attached to a silver chain, hung around his neck. On it, eight white swords touched tips in a circle, ringed by twelve mystic signs in white, all surrounded in black.

Delveran stopped at the entrance to the chamber. He buzzed the intercom to the conference room on his left and waited for admittance. A male voice bade him enter, and the Sorcerer-Enforcer did.

Delveran strode up the aisle of the conference room. On either side of him sat rows of seats. Glowpanels in the ceiling lit the chamber. He approached the crescent table on a platform in the back of the conference room, where sat five officials of the Federation Department of Justice, all in purple robes and matching boots. Before them were control consoles. In a moment, he stood before them beside three armchairs.

Am I in trouble? Delveran thought. He did not like the look on their faces.

"Welcome, High Enforcer," Nolid Rax said, a male humanoid. "Take a seat."

"I prefer to stand," Delveran responded.

Nolid led this council before the Grand Universal Marshal. "As you wish."

Torina Keld, a female human, spoke. "How could this have happened? The escape of thousands of Archvillains from the Universal Prisonplex is unacceptable."

"Fortunately, no Criminals or Villains escaped from the Universal Prisonplex," Ioworth interjected, a male of the race of faerie.

"That is little consolation," Torina countered. She paused. "What are you doing about those escaped Archvillains, High Enforcer?"

Delveran sighed. "The Universal Marshals are searching for them and the Fellowship of Darkness."

"That is good to hear," Nolid said. "When can we expect some arrests of them?"

Delveran frowned. "I don't know. We are combing the galaxy for them, pursuing every lead. The Fellowship of Darkness needs a new place for their headquarters."

"Is the Archvillain organization a threat to the Federation?" Kaylor Maasa, a male alien, asked.

"They may become a threat," Delveran replied. "Especially if they recruit the thousands of escaped Archvillains to their side. If they joined together, they could become the next supreme evil."

"We cannot let that happen," Nolid remarked.

"Agreed," Delveran concurred.

Brianna Zendramus, a female humanoid, spoke. "It would be disastrous to the galaxy if they did. Lucky for us, the invasion of Tellus failed, and the enemy space fleet was destroyed. A trade-off for the success of the jailbreak of the Universal Prisonplex."

Torina snorted. "That not a good trade-off."

Nolid cut in. "It depends on how you view it."

"Yes," Kaylor agreed.

Delveran nodded. But he thought it lopsided in favor of the jailbreak.

"The escaped Archvillains may seek revenge against the Federation for their former incarceration in the Universal Prisonplex," Nolid said.

"And especially the Enforcers," Delveran added. "Since the Universal Marshals had arrested them to be imprisoned in it."

The five officials agreed with the Grand Universal Marshal on that.

"What about the leader of the Archvillain organization, Professor Magnemus," Kaylor said.

"The Scientific Being," Delveran finished for him.

Kaylor continued. "Would taking him out cause the Archvillain organization to disband since he formed it in the first place?"

"Possibly," Delveran answered. "Then again, another Archvillain could step forward and take his place."

"With Famine and Pestilence freed, they and War and the Grim Reaper could bring back the Four Horsemen of the Apocalypse to terrorize the galaxy once more," Torina stated.

"True," Delveran acknowledged. The Grand

Universal Marshal had been the one who had arrested Famine and Pestilence and had sent the two Incarnations to the Universal Prisonplex before he had become the High Enforcer.

"There is another matter requiring our attention," Kaylor said.

The five officials talked among themselves. Delveran crossed his arms and waited for them to address him again. They did soon.

"There has been a dramatic rise of space piracy in the galaxy," Brianna explained. "Ships of the Federation have fallen victim to these attacks. We need the Universal Marshals to investigate this and find out what is behind it."

"And to stop whoever it is," Kaylor added.

Delveran nodded. "I understand. Maybe an Archvillain or a group of them is responsible."

That did not please the officials. It certainly did not sit well with the High Enforcer.

"If an Archvillain or Archvillains is behind the increasing occurrences of piracy in the galaxy, then he, she, or they must be stopped," Nolid stated.

Delveran smiled. "I and my fellow Universal Marshals will get to the bottom of it."

Torina leaned forward in her chair. "We expect results from your efforts."

"Of course," Delveran responded.

"Is there anything you wish to bring up, High Enforcer?" Ioworth asked.

"Yes," Delveran replied. "I wish to recruit new beings to become Universal Marshals. It has been a while since we have."

The five officials talked among themselves for a bit.

Delveran uncrossed his arms.

"Your request is granted," Nolid said. "How many do you wish to add to the present number of Universal Marshals?"

"At least several," Delveran answered. "There are a few possible and potential candidates I know of. They will need to be interviewed."

"All right," Brianna said.

Delveran grinned. "Thank you."

"Is there anything else?" Torina asked.

"No," Delveran replied.

"You are dismissed," Nolid said.

Delveran bowed his head. The High Enforcer left the chamber.

Next, Delveran went to a turbolift and took it up to the forty-fourth floor. He walked down a corridor to the office of the head of the Federation Department of Foreign Affairs. Some beings went in and out of rooms on either side of him. A few he passed in the passageway. He reached the office and entered.

Delveran stopped before the desk of Drusilla, an elderly woman and humanoid, the personal secretary of the director. "Good afternoon, High Enforcer. Shall I announce you?"

Delveran smiled. "Yes."

Drusilla talked over the intercom. "Ma'am, the Grand Universal Marshal is here to see you."

"Send him in."

"Yes, ma'am." Drusilla looked up at the High Enforcer. "You can go in now."

"Thank you," Delveran said.

He entered the inner office. It featured fewer machines than the outer office. To the right of the desk hung a telescreen, off. Two armchairs sat before the desk.

Evarinia stopped looking at her computer notepad, seated in her office chair. Her hazel eyes sparkled to reveal her inner beauty, and her long chestnut hair and curvaceous body magnified her outer beauty. She wore a blue pantsuit with blue slippers. Like Delveran, she was human.

Evarinia put down her computer notepad on her desk, got to her feet, and embraced him. They kissed.

"How has your day been going?" Delveran asked.

Evarinia smiled. "It has been rather busier than normal. And yours?"

"I just came from a meeting with officials from the Federation Department of Justice." He informed her of what had transpired with them.

"I have received messages from governments of non-Federation planets about piracy," Evarinia said. "Too many incidents have occurred. Besides the stealing of goods, there have been killings, and females have been raped. In some instances, ships have been destroyed. Do you have any idea who is behind these?"

"Not yet. I will assign a force of Universal Marshals to deal with the matter."

Evarinia nodded. "The arrangements for our marriage ceremony are coming along."

"Yes. Our mating ritual will be a splendid day."

They embraced and kissed again.

"When will I see you again?" Evarinia asked.

"Tonight. I shall come to you at your place."

"Where are you going next after here?"

Delveran sighed. "I am going to pay a visit to the Warden at the Universal Prisonplex."

"Have your Universal Marshals captured any Archvillains yet?"

"Not yet. I am surprised that the Universal Marshals haven't made any arrests of the foul beings. Some Criminals and Villains have been apprehended. But I fear the Fellowship of Darkness have already recruited many of the Archvillains that had escaped after the invasion of Tellus."

Evarinia touched his chest. "The Archvillain organization remains a threat to the Federation."

Delveran agreed. "It is unknown whether or not the Fellowship of Darkness has found another planet for their stronghold."

"Have you tried divination to find out about that?"

"Yes. My mantic work has not yielded definite information about it. But I am certain that they will find a new world for their headquarters."

Evarinia smiled. "You could combine your magic powers with other Enforcers to find it in the galaxy."

"True. The last time I combined my magic powers with other Universal Marshals, we created a sending. It worked for a time."

"You could do another one."

Delveran shrugged. "Possibly. But the Fellowship of Darkness may be on guard against it after the last one."

They embraced and kissed again. Then Delveran left her office. He took a turbolift down to the first floor of the Federationplex. He went to the teleporter hall and got teleported to the Universal Prisonplex outside of the office of the Warden. In a moment, he touched the button on the intercom to announce his arrival.

"Come in," a male voice said over the intercom.

Delveran entered. Warden Thurjen Addarak sat at his desk. A telescreen appeared right of the Warden. Two armchairs sat before the desk, which had a computer on it.

Thurjen was a short, thin man, human, with brown eyes and a brown mustache bushy like his brown eyebrows. He wore a brown wardensuit with matching belt and boots. "The control room of the antipower cells is fully functional now."

"Excellent news," Delveran said.

"Now all we need is for your Universal Marshals to arrest Archvillains to be locked away in them."

"Yes."

"Still nothing on the Archvillain organization?" Thurjen opened a desk drawer and pulled out his pipe, a pouch of tobacco, and a lighter.

Delveran took a deep breath. "Nothing."

"They must be up to something. I can't imagine them not doing anything in the galaxy."

"I am certain they are recruiting new Archvillains to their cause. It is logical they would do so."

"Indeed. The question is are they big enough to threaten the Universal Federation of Planets."

"I don't believe yet. Eventually, they may if they could get all those Archvillains who had escaped from the Universal Prisonplex on their side."

Thurjen put a pinch of tobacco in his pipe and lit it. He puffed on it. "How many Universal Marshals do you have searching the galaxy for the Archvillain organization and its new base of operations?"

"Not enough. I have not heard a word from the Universal Marshals I have sent to discover their whereabouts. However, I should soon receive reports from them on the matter, one way or another."

"At least some of your Universal Marshals have arrested Criminals and Villains for incarceration in the Universal Prisonplex." Thurjen took another puff on his pipe.

Delveran sighed. "There is that. But I would feel much better if the Universal Marshals had apprehended some Archvillains for it. Then they could be interrogated about the Fellowship of Darkness."

Delveran finished talking with Thurjen. The High Enforcer left the Warden and went to the teleporter room of the Universal Prisonplex and got transported to the Justiceplex. He stepped off the large black telegrid in the teleporter room of the headquarters of the Enforcers and found Benethor and Apparis waiting for him. A black telescreen, off, hung on the wall behind the telegrid and teleport console, a control podium.

"What do you have to report?" Delveran asked.

Benethor spoke. "We have some disturbing news regarding the Fellowship of Darkness."

Delveran frowned. "To my office.

The High Enforcer led the Elf-Enforcer and the Roc to it across the long and wide hallway of the Justiceplex—a T-shaped structure—from the teleporter room. Glowpanels autoactivated in his office as they entered the chamber.

Delveran sat in his office chair behind his desk as the other two Universal Marshals sat in two of the armchairs before the desk. A large black telescreen, off, hung on the wall right of the Grand Universal Marshal. A storage cabinet, a computer, and a visual recorder for logs appeared across the room from the telescreen.

"What news do you have?" Delveran asked.

Benethor and Apparis told him about the Archvillain organization searching for Lordruingat. When they finished their tale, the High Enforcer let out a deep breath. They waited for him to speak.

"So the Cube of Power is real," Delveran said. "The Universal Marshals will have to go on a quest to find it first."

"Do you want us to be a part of the quest for Lordruingat?" Benethor asked.

Delveran paused. "Yes. Go to the teleporter room and beam Nazzar, Hulkeme, Kesharra, and Yevadne here. They will join you on the quest. Meet me in the briefing room."

"Will you have any other Universal Marshals join us later in the search?" Apparis asked.

Delveran thought about it. "I will send you reinforcements for the quest when I can."

The High Enforcer dismissed them to do the task he instructed them. Alone, he pondered the significance of the Cube of Power. Lordruingat could be an ultimate weapon used by the Fellowship of Darkness against the Federation. After a while, he left his office and headed for the briefing room.

Chapter 3

Downtown Hilaton bustled with activity. The city, located in the southeast region of the continent of Survarille, was the tenth-largest metropolitan area on Tellus.

Pedestrians crowded the walkways of Hilaton. Traffic flowed heavily in the city. It was late afternoon.

Customers went in and out of the many businesses in the area. Hilaton Park overflowed with people, a few with pets. The weather was sunny.

Two black vans parked in front of the Tunston Tower, the tallest building in downtown Hilaton. Out of the vehicles stepped five male humans and five male humanoids, all armed with automatic weapons. The leader of the group, Marthan Guile, a humanoid, also carried a blue briefcase.

The group of men entered the skyscraper. They crossed the lobby to the control desk. A guard, a human male, pulled out his revolver and got shot by one of the terrorists before he could fire his weapon. One of the bunch took the place of the guard. Marthan led the rest to an elevator that they took up to the twentieth floor.

After exiting the lift, Marthan led them to a suite. They busted into the chamber and took the people there hostage. The captives were lined up against a wall, cringed in fear of the Villain and the Criminals with him. The suite featured four desks with eight chairs and a long table.

"Stop your sniveling," Marthan said to the hostages. "Or we will shoot you." He put the blue briefcase on the table and opened it. Inside lay a photon bomb.

"Why are you doing this?" a captive asked the Villain, a female human.

Marthan grinned. "Because those in power must learn that we must start over again civilization. We have lost our way. Beings right now live in the dark ages. They must learn to see the light of reason once more."

"You're crazy," another hostage said, a male alien.

"Maybe," Marthan responded. "Maybe not."

Outside, the Hilaton police surrounded the building. One of the terrorists, a human male named Griffus, looked out a window to see them below.

"We have company, boss," Griffus said.

Marthan smiled. "Expected."

"Isn't there a vault here filled with riches, boss?" another terrorist asked, a male humanoid named Nasalah.

"Yes," Marthan replied. "It is filled with precious metals in the form of bars."

Griffus turned from the window. "Why don't we steal them, boss?"

"Because we're not here to rob the place," Marthan answered. "Though it is tempting to do so."

"Yeah," Nasalah said, sounding disappointed.

Marthan laughed. "This explosive here is our message to the Federation. And to the whole galaxy. It will level blocks in the downtown area."

****

On the street below, the Hilaton police kept bystanders away from the scene. But one male being joined the officers, who recognized him. He stood over six feet and wore a white unisuit with matching boots and a cape. They knew him as Nazzar, the Android-Enforcer. Not an ordinary automaton, but one with special powers built into his mechanical system.

"What is the situation here?" Nazzar asked the police captain, a male human named Driscoll. He explained it to the Universal Marshal.

"We have the place completely surrounded," Hardith Bay said, a police sergeant and male alien. "They are not going anywhere. They are on the twentieth floor, suite 2020."

Nazzar assessed the situation. "Have the terrorists made any demands?"

"No," Driscoll answered. "We are trying to communicate with them, but they have been silent."

Nazzar found that surprising. "Do you have men ready to move in on the terrorists?"

"Yes," Driscoll replied. "They wait for the word to be given to proceed."

Nazzar nodded. "Let me go in first. Wait twenty minutes, then send your men in."

"All right," Driscoll said. "Be careful."

Nazzar walked into the skyscraper. The Android-Enforcer strode over to the control station, where the terrorist behind it stood up and aimed his automatic weapon at the Universal Marshal.

"Halt," the humanoid male said to him, stepping from behind the control station. "Or I will shoot you."

Nazzar stopped twenty feet from the control station. Before the terrorist could fire his automatic weapon at the Android-Enforcer, the Universal Marshal shot laser beams from his eyes at it, and the man dropped his weapon. As the foul being tried to pick it up, Nazzar flew at him with jet boots, knocked him into a wall, and rendered him unconscious.

The Android-Enforcer found the dead security guard behind the control station. "Poor soul."

The Universal Marshal went over to the stairs and flew up them to the twentieth floor. When he reached it, he stopped flying.

Nazzar already learned that the terrorists held the hostages in the suite at the end of the corridor on the south side of the building. The Android-Enforcer did not know how many terrorists they were exactly or the number of hostages. He figured he needed to come up with a plan to save the captives without endangering them.

The Universal Marshal strode quietly down the hallway to the chamber where the terrorists and hostages were located. No one else walked the passageway. On either side of him stood doors to other rooms. Nazzar thought they did not have occupants in them at this time. He used his X-ray vision to look into some of them and confirmed his logical deduction.

Nazzar crept up to the double doors of suite 2020 and stopped before them. The entrance was locked. He put his left ear to the double doors and listened to the conversation on the other side with his super hearing.

"Is it time to arm the bomb, boss?" Griffus asked.

"I will set it for ten minutes," Marthan replied. "We don't want to prolong the inevitable."

"What about them?" Nasalah asked, pointing his gun at the hostages. "Should we shoot them now?"

"No," Marthan said. "Let them be blown apart by the explosive. They will also be martyrs to our cause."

Nazzar heard every word spoken. The situation became more dire. The Android-Enforcer knew he must act soon to save the captives and stop the photon bomb from detonating.

"It's a shame that we can't finish our prisoners off with bullets," Griffus said.

Nazzar stepped back from the double doors of the suite. The Universal Marshal fired laser blasts from his eyes and blew the double doors wide open. He rushed in.

"Kill him!" Marthan yelled.

The men of the Villain fired their automatic weapons at the Android-Enforcer. Bullets bounced off the body of the Universal Marshal. Hostages screamed.

Nazzar charged at the terrorist nearest him and disarmed the Criminal, then threw the fellow against a wall, knocking him out. He repeated the action with each of the remaining Criminals, moving very fast. That left only the Villain.

"Say goodbye, my hostages," Marthan said.

The foul being aimed his automatic weapon at the captives and started shooting. But Nazzar intercepted the bullets before they found their marks.

"What are you?" Marthan asked, his gun empty.

Nazzar grinned. "A superhero."

The Android-Enforcer disarmed the Villain, then sent the foul being flying into a wall, knocking him out. Next, the Universal Marshal turned his attention to the photon bomb. It still lay on the table, armed. Just then, Hilaton police entered the suite.

"Arrest them," Nazzar said.

Police officers cuffed the terrorists and escorted them down to the police wagon waiting outside. The freed hostages thanked the Hilaton police for their release.

Driscoll came up to the Android-Enforcer. "Can you disarm it?"

"Yes," Nazzar answered and did.

The Android-Enforcer handed the disarmed photon bomb to Hardith. The police sergeant handled it with care and took it away for evidence.

The freed hostages thanked the Universal Marshal for saving them. Then, they got escorted out of the suite by police officers. They would be giving statements to the Hilaton police.

"What will you do now?" Driscoll asked the Android-Enforcer.

Before Nazzar could answer, he got teleported to the Justiceplex.

Chapter 4

Flight 253 flew from the city of Vallaspar to the city of Callenovon in the northwest region of Survarille. Altogether the trip should last over two hours, now early afternoon.

The jumbo jet so far encountered no problems in the flight. It seemed routine. There was no turbulence, medical emergencies, and unruly passengers on board. Flight 253 was more than halfway to its destination.

Just then, the airplane encountered turbulence. The jumbo jet rocked, then flew through the air wildly like a bucking bronco, alarming the passengers. A stewardess, a female human named Aseji, spoke in the intercom to calm them down.

"Be at ease, folks. It is just a little turbulence. The plane will get through it."

The jumbo jet rode it out. Soon, the turbulence stopped. There was a sigh of relief from the passengers.

"See," Aseji said over the intercom. "Nothing to fear."

Another stewardess, a female humanoid named Issa, pushed a tray of snacks and drinks down the aisle. The passengers were a mixture of humans, humanoids, and aliens. Some of them took the nourishment offered.

In the cockpit, the captain, Kyle Redson, a human male, piloted the airplane. Across from him sat Hughan, a male humanoid and co-pilot. Behind them sat the third member of the flight crew, Yedsina, a female humanoid.

"Weather is pretty good now," Hughan said.

"Yes," Kyle agreed. "Steady as we go."

The jumbo jet continued on course. No other planes flew within its vicinity. The flight crew had flown together for five years.

Some passengers had headsets on, listening to music, audiobooks, or other material. Others watched different programs on miniscreens. Most of them just relaxed and enjoyed the flight.

A passenger, a male alien, asked a question of Issa. "How long before we reach our destination?"

"In about forty minutes," Issa responded.

The jumbo jet had been in service for seven years. There had been no mechanical issues with the airplane over that time. Maintenance crews kept it running smoothly. Its safety record had been excellent thus far.

One of the passengers, an elderly human male, grabbed his chest suddenly. Issa noticed what was happening and went to aid him.

"What is wrong?" Issa asked.

Aseji spoke on the intercom. "Is there a doctor on board?"

A passenger, a male humanoid, got up and hurried over to the sick man and Issa. "I'm a doctor—Doctor Fiant."

"Can you tell what ails him?" Issa asked.

"Looks like a heart attack or stroke," Fiant said.

Aseji already informed the cockpit of the situation. The doctor treated the sick man as best he could under the circumstances.

In thirty minutes now the airplane was scheduled to land at the Callenovon Airport. A male passenger, a human, started ranting about the end of days for the Federation. A flight marshal onboard restrained him, helped a little by two other passengers, both male humanoids.

Ahead, the jumbo jet encountered a thunderstorm. Flight 253 experienced a bumpy ride. Then, lightning struck the left wing of the airplane, and the engine caught fire. People screamed.

In the cockpit, Hughan radioed a mayday. The jumbo jet started losing altitude. Oxygen masks came down from the ceiling of the airplane. Passengers panicked.

The flight crew had a tough time controlling the jumbo jet. It kept losing altitude.

"We might have a crash landing, captain," Hughan remarked.

"Hold tight," Kyle said.

The airplane plummeted. Soon, it reached six thousand feet. Open ground stretched far below the jumbo jet.

Suddenly, the airplane stopped descending, and the fire went out. Outside, a gigantic figure of a male being held the jumbo jet in the air. It was Hulkeme, the Genie-Enforcer. The Universal Marshal featured purple skin, purple eyes, a purple beard, a purple ponytail, slanted eyebrows, and pointy ears. He wore all white—vest, pants, and wing-tip slippers.

"We're saved," Yedsina said.

"Who is that creature?" Hughan asked no one in particular.

Hulkeme spoke. "I will take you to your destination."

Everyone in the airplane heard him. Cheers erupted

among the passengers in relief. The Genie-Enforcer teleported himself and the jumbo jet to the Callenovon Airport.

At the Callenovon Airport, the Universal Marshal set the jumbo jet gently down on an unused runway. Then Hulkeme shrunk in size to nine feet tall as everyone on board the airplane got off by the emergency slide. Rescue personnel arrived on the scene after the flight crew contacted the control tower.

Everyone gathered around Hulkeme. Passengers stood in awe of the Genie-Enforcer.

"Thank you for saving us," Kyle said.

Hulkeme grinned. "You're welcome."

"Lucky for us you were there to help us," Hughan said.

The grateful passengers thanked the Genie-Enforcer for saving them. He acknowledged their gratitude. Then, the Universal Marshal vanished before their very eyes and got teleported to the Justiceplex.

Chapter 5

The party moved through the oasis of Tham Mashere in the southwest region of the continent of Mellenroel. Their travel went through a jungle with hot and humid temperatures. They heard bird calls. Above them shined in a blue sky the Tellusian sun, Kambec.

"Are we near the Nagizah Pyramid yet?" Nal Pollack, a human male, asked their guide.

"We're not too far away from it," Jai Malars, a male humanoid, answered. "Patience, my dear mister Pollack."

Nal turned to the humanoid woman walking behind him. "Have you ever been on such a journey before?"

"Yes," Kesharra, the Solar Being, replied. The Enforcer featured dark skin, brown eyes, and an Afro. She wore a yellow unisuit with matching boots and cape. Across her chest appeared the symbol of a sun. "The last time I ventured somewhere as such was three years ago."

The party numbered ten people. Kesharra was the only female among them. The Universal Marshal acted as a protector of the group. Her special powers resided on the scientific level of energy power.

Soon, they came upon a waterfall. It cascaded into a pool of water, fresh and clean. The party stopped for a rest break.

"The scenery is beautiful," Nal remarked.

"Indeed," Prace Ambers, a male humanoid, agreed.

Kesharra also concurred with that observation. It reminded her of her homeworld, Arala, in the Jujuwen Sector of the Milky Way Galaxy. Her birth planet was a member of the Universal Federation of Planets.

"We've rested long enough," Nal said. "Time to move it."

They resumed their journey. Bird cries were louder. The oasis of Tham Mashere featured a dozen waterfalls at least.

The party came upon a glade. Now they heard monkey chatter. Insect life droned. Ahead, an animal the size of a wolverine ran into view with red fur and a white muzzle. Then it disappeared in the brush.

"Do you think there will be wealth inside the Nagizeh Pyramid?" Gorbone, a male human, asked.

Nal grinned. "According to legend, it is filled with riches amassed over centuries by the Skandars. A humanoid race that vanished without a trace for some reason."

"What about the Bracelet of Altorak?" Villim Straus, a male human, asked. "If found, it could be used to raise the army of Altorak."

"That is the myth," Nal responded. "If used, it would also awaken the monstrous creature sleeping in the Nagizeh Pyramid."

"That is something we don't want to happen," Prace said.

Kesharra agreed. Their venture was risky. But the reward would be great. She did not care for the wealth rumored to be inside the Nagizeh Pyramid. The Universal Marshal was mainly concerned for the safety of the party.

They went through dense underbrush. They heard

cries other than bird calls, monkey chatter, and insect buzzing. The oasis became more alive with wildlife.

"Are there any dangerous animals in the oasis?" Prace asked their guide.

"Maybe jungle cats," Jai replied. "Possibly huge snakes."

Kesharra believed she could handle any dangerous animal in the oasis. On her homeworld she fought some before. The Universal Marshal hoped they would not encounter such threats.

The party emerged from the jungle. Before them stretched open space. In the middle of the expanse towered the Nagizeh Pyramid.

"See," Jai said. "I told you I could find it."

Prace smiled. "What a sight."

They started across the expanse. Before they could reach the Nagizeh Pyramid, the ground shook. Then it stopped.

"What was that?" Nal asked no one in particular.

Prace shook his head. "I have a bad feeling about this."

Suddenly, animated skeletons burst up through the earth armed with swords or spears. The party, armed, except for Kesharra, prepared to shoot the fleshless figures.

Kesharra stepped in front of the men. "Stand back. I will deal with them myself."

The men obeyed her. Kesharra waited for the skeletons to attack. They charged the party, screaming. The Universal Marshal counted twenty of the fleshless figures. Behind the Enforcer some of the men acted nervous. The Solar Being stayed calm and cool.

Kesharra fired solar blasts of yellow from her hands.

She destroyed the skeletons in short order. It impressed the men the way she handled the situation. *That takes care of that.*

"Wow," Nal said.

"Awesome," Villim remarked.

Kesharra turned to the men. "We can enter the pyramid now." *Inviting place.*

The party continued on. Finally, they entered the pyramid without any further incidents.

Flaming cressets provided light in the pyramid. They walked down stone steps and entered a vast chamber. In it stood statues.

"These sculptured figures must be representations of Skandar gods, heroes, and kings," Prace said.

Nal touched one of the statues. "Obviously."

"Hopefully, no one else is in here with us," Villim remarked. "We don't need any more company."

The rest of the party concurred with that. Jai led them out of the chamber down a corridor. Ahead, they heard a noise. It sounded like grinding.

The passageway opened into another large room. In it lay the wealth of legend. So much gold and silver.

"By God," Prace said. "We have struck it rich."

"How are we going to carry it out?" Villim asked the rest of the party.

"We'll have to go back and get transport for it," Nal answered. "There is so much here."

"A lot of cataloging to be done here," Prace remarked.

Jai held up a gold bowl. "This place may be cursed."

"Bull," Villim said. "This pyramid is full of treasure to be taken by those who find it."

Kesharra did not want any of the gold and silver

there. She hoped that the place was not under a curse. The Solar Being knew a few planets in the galaxy where they operated. Her home world was not one of them. *Curses should be taken seriously.*

"Is the Bracelet of Altorak in here among these piles of wealth?" Villim asked the rest of the party.

Nal grabbed a silver goblet off a heap. "Finding it in here would be difficult. Maybe it is in a different chamber."

"Could be other ones that have treasures as such," Prace said.

The party decided to look in other chambers. They went through another corridor and came upon another room with a gold chest on a stone podium.

"The Bracelet of Altorak must be in it," Nal said. "Open it."

Villim did. Inside the chest, it was empty.

"Someone has beaten us to it," Prace remarked.

A voice behind them spoke. "You're so right."

The party turned around. Twelve men, all humanoids, aimed their rifles at them except one. The man who spoke was their leader. In his hands lay the Bracelet of Altorak.

"Who are you?" Nal asked.

The leader smiled. "I am Khall Drome. These are my compatriots."

"You're not thinking of using the Bracelet?" Prace asked. "It is folly."

Khall laughed. "Whoever wears the Bracelet can control the army of Altorak."

"What do you intend to do with such control?" Villim asked.

Khall sighed. "Conquer all of Mellenroel."

Kesharra did not like the sound of that. The Solar Being could not use her special powers yet on their foes. She waited for the right moment to do so.

"If you please, follow me to the chamber to awaken the army of Altorak," Khall said. "Don't try anything. My compatriots will shoot you if you do."

Khall led them out of the room and down another passageway. His men split six in front of the party and five behind them.

They entered another chamber well-lit by flaming cressets. Khall halted them before a wall where a hole appeared. He put on the Bracelet of Altorak.

"For conquest," Khall said. He walked up to the wall and put his arm wearing the Bracelet in the hole. He turned it. "Now, the army of Altorak will be mine to command."

Kesharra feared the worse. The Solar Being sensed a presence awakening behind the wall. Khall pulled his arm out of the hole and stepped back. Everyone else did as well.

The pyramid shook for a few moments. Then, it stopped abruptly. The wall before them opened up. Behind it, a monstrous creature emerged. It resembled a half man and half crab.

"In the name of Altorak, I command you," Khall said. "What is your name?"

The monstrous creature answered. "I am Scorpittus. Who are you to command me?"

"Khall Drome, wearer of the Bracelet of Altorak."

"What is thy bidding?"

"Kill all these with me."

"You're betraying us?" one of the leader's men asked.

Khall grinned. "Nothing personal. The army of Altorak is mine to command alone."

Both groups of men, except Kesharra, fired their rifles at Scorpittus as he attacked them. The monstrous creature grabbed a man in his pincers and tore him in half. Then, another man got ripped in two. Bullets seemed to pass through the body of the monstrous creature with little effect. Scorpittus roared.

"Damn," Nal said. "What will it take for this thing to die?"

Kesharra fired solar blasts of yellow from her hands at Scorpittus. They made the monstrous creature rear on its hind legs and push backward. The Universal Marshal kept up the effort as the huge figure retreated from the onslaught by the Solar Being.

Khall aimed his rifle at the Enforcer. Before he could shoot Kesharra, Prace fired at him and wounded him in the chest. Khall fell to the floor.

"Can you destroy that monstrous creature?" Villim asked the Solar Being.

Kesharra paused. "Maybe. It is taking much just to keep him at bay."

The Solar Being sensed that the army of Altorak was being raised now. It rose from the desert east of the Nagizeh Pyramid, ready to march on civilizations and slaughter people. All it needed was orders from the wearer of the Bracelet of Altorak to do so.

"Get the Bracelet off him," Kesharra said.

Nal ran to Khall and removed the magical object from his arm. "What do you want me to do with it?"

"First, use the Bracelet to command the army of Altorak to disintegrate," Kesharra answered. She sweated a bit.

Nal put the Bracelet around his arm and spoke the command for it. The army of Altorak dematerialized, sensed by the Universal Marshal.

"Now what?" Nal asked.

Kesharra forced Scorpittus back into the space behind the monstrous creature. The terrible being tried to advance but still could not. Her solar blasts became heat rays of a hot sun and drained the life from him. The men already stopped firing their weapons.

"Command the Bracelet to help me fell Scorpittus," Kesharra said.

Nal did. The monstrous creature began to disintegrate until nothing remained of him.

Scorpittus roared one last time before being annihilated. The Universal Marshal stopped firing.

Khall coughed a few times. "I don't want to die like this." Then he expired.

Prace shook his head. "Damn fool. He gave his life for nothing."

"What do you want to do with the Bracelet?" Nal asked the Solar Being.

"We'll take it back to the Occultplex in Acropollon," Kesharra replied. "We can't leave it in the pyramid so someone else can find and use it."

"Okay," Nal responded.

The Universal Marshal led them out of the pyramid. All the men who had followed Khall surrendered to the Enforcer and her party.

Outside, they crossed open ground once more. Again, they entered the jungle. It took them three days to cross the oasis of Tham Mashere. In time, they arrived at the city of Mozempic, the second-largest metropolitan area of Mellenroel. Night fell.

Inside the Mozempic Museum, Kesharra and her party visited the curator, Yordic Wastrel, a humanoid. They showed him the Bracelet of Altorak.

"Magnificent," Yordic said, looking over the magical object. "Made of pure gold. What are you going to do with this?"

Before Kesharra could answer, she got teleported to the Justiceplex.

Chapter 6

Enforcer Yevadne, the Zephyr, stood with the army of Cammalain on the Sherean Plains in the Midwest region of Mellenroel. They faced another army, the Tauths, or Tauthans, across open ground. Beyond the plains to the west rose forestland. East of the plains stretched hills. North and south of the plains towered mountains. Kambec, the Tellusian sun, shined in a partly cloudy sky.

"These barbarians must be stopped here," Prince Xandermas said. His Highness was a young man, tall and dark-haired. He rode a white stallion.

"These butchers have caused enough harm," Captain Grollan remarked. He was a veteran of wars, older than the prince, on a bay horse. "I have seen what these barbarians can do."

Yevadne knew of the savage reputations of the Tauths. The Universal Marshal encountered them a few times previously in battle. Tall, she featured red hair and hazel eyes, light-skinned. The Enforcer wore a red unisuit with matching boots and cape. Her special powers resided on the scientific level of energy power.

A horn sounded from the enemy. The Tauths yelled battle cries. Some of them pounded their shields with swords. These had no effect on the army of Cammalain.

"Brutes," Captain Grollan said.

A horn blew from the army of Cammalain. Yevadne

could feel the tension in the air. The Zephyr readied herself to engage the Tauthans. She figured the coming battle would be real bloody. The Universal Marshal knew that the Tauths did not take prisoners and executed those still alive after a battle they won, merciless to their enemies.

The Tauths began to march toward the army of Cammalain, who responded by doing the same thing. The earth between them shrank in distance as they approached each other. Then, the Tauthans charged at the army of Cammalain, who did likewise. Soon, they clashed, and the battle began in earnest.

Yevadne shot the enemy with cyclone blasts and hurled Tauths high in the air to crash down on the earth so hard it killed them. Two Tauthans charged at her from front and behind. The Universal Marshal took to the air and flew above them. She created a tornado and wiped them out.

The battle roared on. Neither side could get the upper hand yet. The Tauths fought with such battle lust matched by the sheer determination of the army of Cammalain. Even the sloppy dress of the barbarians infuriated them.

A Tauthan with a spear tripped the white stallion of Prince Xandermas. His Highness fell to the ground and rolled to his feet. Tauths surrounded him in order to slay him. But before they could overwhelm him with numbers, Yevadne fired cyclone blasts from her hands and sent them flying from the prince.

"Thank you, milady," Prince Xandermas said.

Yevadne nodded. She fought side by side with His Highness. Captain Grollan dismounted from his horse and joined them. They fought with their backs to each other.

The tide of battle turned in favor of the army of Cammalain. Slowly, the Tauthans lost ground as their numbers dwindled.

A horn blared from the Tauths. It signaled a retreat. They fled from the battlefield as the army of Cammalain won the battle.

"Should we pursue them, Your Highness?" Captain Grollan asked.

"No," Prince Xandermas answered. "Let them go. We have given them a resounding defeat."

Yevadne agreed with the decision. Prince Xandermas and Captain Grollan remounted their steeds. A cheer rose from the men for the victory over the barbarians.

"Back to the castle," Prince Xandermas said. "We will celebrate our triumph over the enemy."

"What about our dead, Your Highness?" Captain Grollan asked.

Prince Xandermas frowned. "We will gather their bodies and burn them in honor."

The corpses of their fallen comrades were piled carefully into wagons on the hills behind them. Plenty of bodies filled the wagons. Some of the men prayed to gods for the souls of the deceased. Doctors treated the wounded.

Yevadne flew between the prince and the captain as they traveled east for Cammalain. The men were in a good mood.

"Milady, where are you from?" Captain Grollan asked the Zephyr.

"I am from the world of Sullanis," Yevadne replied. "It is a member of the Federation."

"What is your world like?" Prince Xandermas asked.

Yevadne thought a moment. "It has high technology. Sullanis is governed by a council of twelve members. It does trade in the galaxy."

Captain Grollan patted his horse. "Is there anyone else like you in your world?"

"No," Yevadne responded. "I am the only one with special powers."

The journey back to Cammalain Castle took several days. They reached it and made pyres to burn the bodies of their dead. Yevadne was silent like the rest as men lit the pyres with torches. The bodies burned to ashes.

After the funeral was over, they gathered in the great hall of the castle. They celebrated their victory over the Tauthans.

Prince Xandermas stood up to give a toast. "Hail to the victorious dead. May their spirits find peace in the Hall of Heroes."

A cheer rose up from those gathered. "Here, here!"

Yevadne drank a little and ate the feast given. The Zephyr recollected the history of her world when there had been war. Sullanis had been at peace for fifty generations now.

Prince Xandermas drank a few sips from his goblet. "Do you think the Tauthans will be back to fight us again, milady?"

"They may, Your Highness," Yevadne answered. "The Tauths live to fight. They want to conquer other people. Surrender is not in their vocabulary."

"If they come back," Captain Grollan said, "we'll be ready for them."

Yevadne believed that. The Zephyr thought the

Tauthans were like locusts. A threat to other lands in Mellenroel. The Universal Marshal hoped the Tauthans learned their lesson after being defeated but doubted it. She figured she might have to be in battle against the barbarians again.

"Do you have an army on your world?" Captain Grollan asked.

Yevadne smiled. "We do have armed forces on Sullanis, including space warriors."

"Have they seen much combat, milady?" Prince Xandermas asked.

Yevadne sighed. "Yes. All before Sullanis joined the Federation. Since then, my world has not seen any fighting."

"How long has your world been in the Federation, milady?" Captain Grollan asked.

"Fifteen years," Yevadne replied.

"How long have you been an Enforcer, milady?" Prince Xandermas asked.

Yevadne thought. "It has been eight years being a Universal Marshal. I was recruited by them."

"If I may ask, milady, do you have a mate?" Captain Grollan said.

The question did not bother Yevadne. "No. I am single."

Before they could ask her any more questions, the Zephyr got teleported to the Justiceplex.

Chapter 7

An hour later, Delveran entered the briefing room, a rectangular chamber. It was on the same side of the corridor as the teleporter room, near the front of the Justiceplex. The High Enforcer sat at the control console of the crescent-shaped table that stretched in the middle of the briefing room, directly facing the automatic doors. There were twenty armchairs around the table. Behind the walls hid hi-tech devices. Glowpanels in the ceiling lit the chamber.

Seated at the table with the Grand Universal Marshal were Benethor, Apparis, Nazzar, Hulkeme, Kesharra, and Yevadne. They waited for the High Enforcer to speak.

"The Fellowship of Darkness is searching for Lordruingat, the Cube of Power," Delveran began. "Therefore, I am sending you on a quest to find it. Other Universal Marshals will join you later. The Archvillain organization must not get their hands on it."

"Are there any clues to where it is hidden?" Kesharra asked.

Delveran shrugged. "What do we know of Lordruingat, Nazzar?"

The Android-Enforcer accessed the information from his internal files. "It is said that the Cube of Power has ulgnostic power, the fourth energy power above the other three—scientific, occultic, and celestic. Or simply called paramic, following physical, psychic, and primal."

"So it can dominate the other three below it," Yevadne said.

"Correct," Nazzar confirmed. "According to legend, it came first into existence. The other three followed in order."

"What else?" Delveran asked.

Nazzar accessed more information from his internal files. "There are stories of it being guarded by what are called Watchers on some remote planet in the galaxy. Other tales have it residing on other worlds."

"Do these Watchers also possess this ulgnostic power," Kesharra asked.

"Some stories say they don't, others limited," Nazzar answered. "It is said that their sole job is to protect Lordruingat from being taken from its resting place, so no one can wield the Cube of Power."

Benethor spoke next. "Are there any reports in the Federation archives of anyone looking for it?"

"Yes," Nazzar replied. "A few teams of scientists, occultists, and celestists have searched for Lordruingat. Some races in the Federation have looked for it. None ever came close to finding it."

"There must also be reports in the Federation archives of people not of the Federation who have sought it," Apparis stated.

"Yes," Nazzar responded. "Both good and bad. But none ever found it."

Delveran addressed the Genie-Enforcer, who sat on his immediate left. "Did anyone ever wish of you for the Cube of Power?"

"They did," Hulkeme replied. "My special powers

could not get a hold of it from its hiding place."

Benethor spoke again. "I heard that the Cube of Power operates like an Elfstone."

"No one knows how it operates for sure," Nazzar said. "Some tales say it functions like a Genie. Others say that it requires blood to bring it to life. Still, additional stories say it works like a computer."

"Who will lead the quest?" Yevadne asked the High Enforcer.

"Benethor," Delveran replied.

The Elf-Enforcer acknowledged the Grand Universal Marshal. "So be it."

Kesharra smiled. "May luck be with us on the quest."

"All right," Delveran said. "You shall begin the quest for the Cube of Power tomorrow. Nanomach will arrange a ship for you."

"Where do we start to look for Lordruingat?" Apparis asked the High Enforcer.

Delveran turned to the Roc. "Check the archives here first. Then go to the Libraryplex. You're dismissed."

The six Universal Marshals left the briefing room to begin the task of searching for the Cube of Power, leaving the High Enforcer alone. Delveran moved on to the next matter at hand: space pirates. He went to the computer room to see Nanomach, the Computer-Enforcer.

Chapter 8

Enforcer Falatar, the Lunar Being, rode a bullet train. It sped from the city of Erinvoq in the southeast region of Survarille to the city of Urdanth in the northeast region of the continent. The Universal Marshal relaxed and read a nonfiction book on physics.

The scenery the bullet train passed featured stands of trees and open plains. It was late afternoon. Plenty of passengers were on board the speedy transport. It was on schedule. Falatar liked taking the bullet train, his favorite mode of transportation. Usually, he traveled alone.

At the moment, the Universal Marshal was not on duty. He took some time off from work to unwind and enjoy a vacation. The last thing he did before taking one was bust a ring of Criminals who had stolen merchandise from hovertrucks in Erinvoq.

Falatar originated from the planet Triskelios in the Anordic Sector of the Milky Way Galaxy. His home world was an industrial planet. His father worked as an engineer and his mother headed a corporation, Tragus Corp. He was an only child and humanoid.

A conductor, a male human, walked down the aisle where his seat was. He stopped before the Universal Marshal. "Sir, the bar and eatery are open near the front."

Falatar looked up from his book. "Thank you."

The conductor continued down the aisle, talking to other passengers.

Falatar had been a Universal Marshal for seven years now. His special powers resided on the occultic level of energy power. He was the only one from his native planet with special powers. He remembered getting recruited by the Universal Marshals when they learned of his unique nature. Tellus served as his second home now. He visited Triskelios occasionally and saw his parents, who were very proud of him. The most striking thing about him was that he was an albino— short white hair, pink eyes, light-skinned. He wore a white unisuit with matching boots, belt, and cape.

Across the aisle from Falatar sat a male human with a briefcase cuffed around his wrist. *This guy is really acting nervous*, the Lunar Being thought. *Wonder if he expects trouble. Whatever is in that briefcase must be very important. Why is he traveling alone?* The Universal Marshal returned to reading his book.

The man introduced himself. "I am Poul Garridon."

"I am Enforcer Falatar."

"You're a Universal Marshal?"

"Yes. I see you're guarding that briefcase with your life."

Poul wiped the sweat from his brow. "I have critical documents in it. I must get to the Ballor Corporation with them."

Falatar grasped the situation now. "Why are you traveling alone? Should you not have some protection with you? An armed escort?

"I am traveling in secrecy. Bodyguards would draw attention."

Falatar nodded. "Are you worried someone is out to get those critical documents?"

Poul swallowed. "Yes."

"Who?"

"A rival corporation."

Falatar sighed. "Maybe you should have taken a different mode of transportation. Like going to a teleporter station."

Poul grimaced. "Erinvoq doesn't have one. I tried to get passage on a sky transport, but they were all booked."

"Well, the bullet train is a speedy transport anyway. It won't be long before you get to your destination."

Poul hugged the briefcase tighter. "In some ways, I wish I could have used a security detail for the trip. It would have made me feel safer."

"If you need a bodyguard," Falatar said, putting his book down on the seat, "I am willing to offer my services. No charge."

Poul smiled. "That is kind of you to offer. I accept."

They shook hands without another word.

Later, a commotion occurred in the passenger car ahead of theirs. From it, two male humanoids entered their passenger car, one bigger than the other. They strode down the aisle and passed people straight to Poul.

"All right, hand over the briefcase, mister," the taller one said to Garridon.

Falatar used his special powers and caused the two brutes to grab the sides of their heads. The Lunar Being drove them mad. Both men fell to the floor out cold. In shock, none of the other passengers reacted or said anything.

"What did you do to them?" Poul asked.

Falatar grinned. "I made them insane. They will be out for a while."

The conductor came back to their passenger car and beheld the two men on the floor. "What happened to them?"

"They tried to take this man's briefcase," Falatar answered. "So I rendered them unconscious."

"Who are you?" the conductor asked.

"A Universal Marshal," Falatar replied.

The eyes of the conductor widened. "We'll tie them up and deliver them to the authorities in Urdanth."

They bound both men with rope and put them in a freight car. The conductor went about his business. Falatar and Poul returned to their seats.

"There might be more of them," Poul said.

Falatar grabbed his book. "Possibly. Hopefully not."

After a while, Poul wanted to go to the bar and eatery on the bullet train. Falatar accompanied him. They ate a meal in the dining car. Both ate steak with a salad and rolls, plus drinks from the bar.

"You ever think about doing something else besides being a Universal Marshal?" Poul asked.

Falatar laughed. "Once, I wanted to enter the corporate sector and join my mother. But that changed when I learned I had special powers. So I became an Enforcer."

Just then, four human males armed with blasters entered the dining car. Falatar did not recognize them. They dressed like militants in army fatigues.

"I am Madarius, leader of the Red Line Faction. Everybody stay where you are. We are commandeering this train." He scared the passengers.

Falatar considered his options on taking them on. Too many people in the dining car. He decided it would be too risky to try something. The Lunar Being would bide his time and wait for the right opportunity to make his move.

"Make no mistake about it," Madarius said. "We are in charge. So no one try anything."

The passengers stayed silent and still. Madarius spoke to one of his men, and they left the dining car to go to the front car, where the engineer controlled the bullet train. That left two militants in the dining car to watch over the passengers.

"This is pretty easy," the taller of the two militants said. He aimed his weapon at a female passenger and pretended to shoot. She almost fainted.

The other one smiled. "No problem. We should join the rest of the guys in a while. Madarius planned this out well."

Falatar concentrated his special powers on the nearest militant. The man shook his head repeatedly from the effort of the Universal Marshal on him.

"Are you okay?" the other one asked.

"My head is killing me."

The militant fell to the floor unconscious. His buddy came over to him. Falatar then used a gravitic push on the one standing and sent him flying against the bar, knocking him out.

Falatar grabbed the blasters and handed them to two male passengers. "Keep them covered. I will deal with the other two militants."

The Lunar Being went to the front car of the bullet train. The Universal Marshal stopped outside the door to it. He looked in and saw Madarius talking to the engineer. The other militant started walking toward the Enforcer.

Falatar moved to the side as the fellow left the front car. The Universal Marshal grabbed him and flipped him to the floor, then knocked him out with a kick. He took the blaster from the man and charged in the front car.

Madarius raised his weapon. Before the militant leader could aim, the Lunar Being fired and shot the blaster from his hand.

"Hands up," Falatar said.

Madarius pulled an army knife from behind his back. He stepped closer to the Enforcer. "How about me and you settle this in combat, like men."

"All right, scum."

Falatar dropped his blaster. Madarius attacked him, swinging the knife. The Lunar Being evaded the strikes. The militant leader thrust the blade for his heart, but the Universal Marshal caught his arm and disarmed him. The Enforcer tossed aside the knife.

Madarius swung a haymaker for his temple. Falatar blocked the blow and cracked a backfist across his face. The militant leader reeled. The Universal Marshal followed that up with an elbow to the jaw, a knee to the stomach, and a throw to the floor.

"Damn you," Madarius said.

Falatar knocked him out with a punch. He turned to the engineer, who never moved from his spot. "Are you all right?"

"Yes. Just shaken a bit."

"Did they try to change the destination of this transport?"

The engineer sighed. "They wanted it to stop outside the city of Kenling ahead."

"Contact the Urdanth police," Falatar said, retrieving the blasters, "so they could be taken into custody."

"Okay."

Falatar got male passengers to help him and tied up

the four militants, who got put in the freight car with the other two men bound there. The six men were unconscious. The Lunar Being handed the two blasters to the conductor.

All the passengers sat in their seats again, nervous. Falatar picked up his book as Poul tried to relax. Before the Lunar Being could start reading it again, he got teleported to the Justiceplex.

Chapter 9

Agwennel, the Undine-Enforcer, walked around the cruise ship *Treasure* as it sailed for port in Acropollon. The water elemental was not on duty as a Universal Marshal at this time. Right now, the weather cooperated as it was sunny out, and passengers on board enjoyed the festivities.

Agwennel featured blue skin, long aquamarine hair, and azure eyes. She wore a blue robe with matching slippers. Her special powers resided on the occultic level of energy power. She featured the ability to turn into a being of water and control that element.

A few of the passengers waved to the Universal Marshal as she passed them by. People swam in the pool on board. Others played games.

When Agwennel reached port, she would return to duty. Her last assignment ended over a month ago when she arrested a Villain named Charl Bednard, busting his illegal export business on the island of Lunani. The foul being got sent to the Universal Prisonplex. His henchmen were incarcerated elsewhere.

In the Angranadan Ocean swam a school of blue-necked dolphins on the starboard side of the cruise ship. No seabirds in the sky. Agwennel could taste the salty sea air. The Universal Marshal breathed it in deeply.

The Undine-Enforcer lived in the water as her normal home, being a water elemental. She did have private quarters at the Justiceplex, like all the Universal Marshals, but she preferred her natural environment. She had served as a Universal Marshal for ten years now.

Agwennel thought about taking a dive into the pool on board, then considered jumping into the ocean. She decided against both for now. Instead, the Undine-Enforcer continued to walk on the decks of the cruise ship, noticing no trouble. She hoped it stayed that way.

The captain of the cruise ship, Melwyn, a female humanoid, greeted the Universal Marshal near the control room. Agwennel stopped to talk with her.

"Have you enjoyed the cruise so far?" Melwyn asked.

Agwennel let out a deep breath. "The voyage has been stimulating, captain. I take trips on boats whenever I can. Being a Universal Marshal usually keeps me busy."

"I would be honored if you dine with me at my table tonight. Say six."

Agwennel smiled. "It would be a pleasure, captain."

The captain returned to the control room. The Undine-Enforcer moved on and eventually stopped at the pool on board. She changed into a being of water and went into the pool. It felt good being in her natural environment.

Later, Agwennel got ready for supper. The Universal Marshal walked to the dining room on a lower deck. She spotted Melwyn at the captain's table near the middle of the chamber. The Undine-Enforcer sat on the immediate left of the captain. Melwyn introduced everybody at the table to each other.

For supper, fish was served with salad, potatoes, and fresh bread. For a beverage, there was red wine for the adults and milk for the children. People crowded the eating hall.

"I have heard that a few Enforcers have been accused of excessive force making arrests," Jorg Langwood, a male human and an investigative reporter, said.

Agwennel did not feel offended by the comment. "That is news to me. No Universal Marshal, to my mind, has ever abused his or her authority."

"There are rumors that there is corruption among your ranks," Jorg stated. "That the Federation Department of Justice turns a blind eye to it."

"Sweetheart, we really shouldn't be talking about such things at the dinner table," Nami Langwood, the wife of the investigative reporter, interjected.

Jorg ignored his mate. "How do you respond to the charges of corruption, Enforcer?"

Agwennel sighed. "There is no corruption among the Universal Marshals. We fight to preserve peace and justice in the Federation."

Jorg pressed the issue. "What about the story that the High Enforcer was in part derelict in his duty concerning the invasion of Tellus by the space fleet of the Fellowship of Darkness?"

"The Grand Universal Marshal performed his duty admirably in the face of such a threat," Agwennel responded. "His leadership is not in question. The Universal Marshals defended Tellus against the invasion with their very lives."

"The war for Tellus was not entirely without cost," Jorg countered. "In lives lost and the jailbreak of the Universal Prisonplex that freed thousands of Archvillains."

Everybody else around the table sat in shock at the words spoken by the investigative reporter. Criticizing the Universal Marshals amounted to attacking a sacred institution. Some of the people at the table felt Langwood was out of line but did not say anything about it. None voiced their opinion on the matter.

"It is natural that lives were lost in the war for our planet," Agwennel said. "The enemy was well-prepared and well-organized for the invasion. But Tellus did not succumb to it. Ultimately, the enemy failed to conquer us."

Jorg persisted. "And the jailbreak?"

"It is very unfortunate that Archvillains got busted out of the Universal Prisonplex," Agwennel responded. "The Universal Marshals tried to prevent it from happening but were not successful. Criminals and Villains did not escape, though."

Jorg shook his head. "What about the situation with Archvillains? What are the Enforcers doing about it? The Fellowship of Darkness?"

"The Universal Marshals are tracking Archvillains so we can recapture the foul beings who escaped," Agwennel replied. "The Enforcers are searching for the new stronghold of the Archvillain organization in the galaxy."

Melwyn chimed in. "Let us talk of more pleasant things. The discussion should focus on the cruise. Does anyone here have anything they wish to bring up?"

"I think it has been splendid so far," Nami said. "There is plenty to do aboard the ship. The islands we visited so far were nice."

"Captain," Rozz asked, a female humanoid, "when do we arrive in port in Acropollon?"

"We are due to arrive in four days," Melwyn answered.

"Then where does the cruise ship go, captain?" Nami asked.

Melwyn took a drink of wine. "The *Treasure* sails south to the port of Fiorgrad. The cruise ship will circle Survarille and stop at other ports, including a few islands. Then, the boat will sail north once we reach the east coast of Survarille. Our final destination is the port at Nadorvalla in the northeast region of the continent, south of Urdanth."

Jorg grumbled. He seemed to be consumed with work on board. Agwennel found his questions of the Universal Marshals bothersome, an insult to all the good the Enforcers do for the Federation in the galaxy.

After the dinner was over, Agwennel took a stroll on the deck where the pool was. She looked at the placid water in it. It reminded her of her homeworld of Aquavena in the Aquarian Sector of the Milky Way Galaxy. Her native planet was a water place.

The Undine-Enforcer walked away from the pool. She came upon two men, both humanoid, robbing a female human armed with knives. The victim screamed.

"Let her go," Agwennel said.

The taller of the two men grinned. "Looky here. Trying to be a hero. Listen, doll, we are taking what we want."

"So walk away," the shorter of the two men stated. "This doesn't concern you."

Agwennel sized the men up, both Criminals. "I'm not going to warn you again."

The taller man laughed. "You threatening us? Beat it."

The Undine-Enforcer acted. She turned into water and blasted them with aqua that sent both men reeling. They fell to the deck and dropped their knives.

Ship personnel ran onto the scene as the Universal Marshal stopped firing. She explained the situation to the ship security, and the two Criminals were taken before the captain.

"Put them in chains," Melwyn ordered.

The two foul beings were slapped in irons and escorted to an empty room. They were locked inside and a guard was stationed outside it. The two prisoners would be handed over to the authorities in Acropollon when the cruise ship landed at port.

Two days later, the *Treasure* experienced rough seas. The cruise ship got pummeled by waves. A ninety-foot one roared toward the boat.

Agwennel saw the huge wave. The Undine-Enforcer used her special powers and shrunk the wave before it could strike the vessel and do damage.

No further incidents occurred. The cruise ship arrived at the port in Acropollon. Passengers disembarked for shore. Police took the two prisoners into custody.

Before Agwennel got off the ship, she got teleported to the Justiceplex.

Chapter 10

Jeddriel, the Archangel-Enforcer, led the security detail for Representative Lonn Kurdak of the planet Byzantinia for the council hall connected to the Federationplex in Acropollon. There, the Federation Assembly would meet in session to debate matters.

Jeddriel stood a few inches over six feet with chestnut hair and hazel eyes, his brown and white wings folded against him invisibly. He wore brown—pants, a shirt, and shoes. Sometimes, he dressed in an ocher robe with matching boots, but not today.

The Universal Marshal took the assignment of guarding the politician, who was a male humanoid, by orders from the High Enforcer. The Federation Department of Justice requested of the Grand Universal Marshal that the Universal Marshals protect the representative. It was feared that another assassination attempt had been planned by enemies of Byzantinia. The first attempt had failed on Byzantinia during a rally, resulting in the death of the female assassin, shot by Byzantinian police.

The entourage of the representative was moderate in size. Besides Lonn, there was his personal secretary, Chimi Graton, and a bunch of other underlings. Plus the security detail. Everybody had been checked out of the party for security clearance.

Jeddriel swept his gaze around the avenue they took.

There appeared to be no danger at the moment, but the Archangel-Enforcer felt a bit uneasy.

"Representative," Chimi said, "the Namorean Representative wants to meet with you following the meeting in the assembly chamber."

Lonn frowned. "Did he say why?"

"He didn't specify the reason, sir," Chimi replied.

Lonn paused before answering. "All right. Set it up."

"Yes, sir."

Buildings towered on both sides of their path. Most of them housed businesses. The Byzantinian Representative had an office in the Federationplex, like all his fellow representatives. He also had a diplomatic residence in Acropollon, where they had come from for the coming assembly.

Downtown Acropollon bustled with activity. The Tellusian sun Kambec shined in a partly cloudy sky early afternoon. All kinds of being walked the streets of the Tellusian capital. People went in and out of businesses. The Acropollon Park overflowed with visitors. Heavy traffic moved in the metropolitan area.

The entourage arrived at the council hall. Already other diplomatic parties headed inside the enormous structure. They entered the immense building, led by Jeddriel, who felt a little better that they made it.

There was tight security around the assembly chamber. All the diplomatic parties found their reserved sections in the council hall. The Byzantinian delegation took their places in the section five rows up. Lonn sat before a control console.

Everyone waited for the Federation President to enter the assembly chamber. In the center of the council hall was his seat around a control station. Much noise permeated the place as many conversations erupted in it. The council hall featured a flat roof.

Finally, the Federation President entered the assembly chamber with his entourage. He was Sethremus, an alien from the planet Shanaboo. He wore a black robe and matching boots. Currently, he served nine years in his official position. His entourage sat in the control station reserved for them.

Everybody quieted down in the council hall. Jeddriel looked around at the delegates. He did not know any of them since he was not into politics. The Archangel-Enforcer wondered if any of the other representatives had received death threats—targets for assassination.

Sethremus cleared his throat. "Welcome to the assembly meeting, all. The first matter to be debated is peacekeeping missions for non-Federation planets."

The Hugnout Representative, a male alien named Cragor, touched the green button on his control console before him and buzzed to be heard. The Federation President recognized him to speak. "We should not have to provide security for worlds not members of the Federation. It is their responsibility to install protection for their own planets. Not ours. We could be entangled in affairs that are trouble."

The Zionia Representative, a male humanoid named Wolfert, interceded next. "I agree with my colleague. The Federation needs no more problems from outsiders. We have enough as it is."

"I disagree," Fath Yurric, a human male representative from the planet Redascant, said. "Some of us do trade with non-Federation planets."

The representative from the planet Yurgo, a female

alien named Jorica, chimed in. "We should not be trading with non-Federation planets at all. They should not concern us. Let them use their own security forces to keep the peace."

Voices erupted in talk among the delegates. Arguments ensued. It took some time for the Federation President to calm things down. Jeddriel felt a bit uneasy about the assembly.

"Is there anyone else who wishes to speak on the matter?" Sethremus asked.

Representative Hazwyn Mallakoth, a male humanoid from the planet Soltooine, buzzed to be heard next. "We should do a committee about the matter. Not be in a hurry to judge it. Further discussion is necessary before we make a decision."

"I second that," Izra, the Ansala Representative, a female alien, said.

An underling whispered in the ear of the Federation President. Sethremus nodded. "Is there any motion to disagree with forming a committee on the matter?" No one spoke up. "So be it. A committee will be formed to look into the matter further."

Jeddriel did not have an opinion on the matter. The Archangel-Enforcer had no interest in politics. Currently there were no peacekeeping forces at work by the Federation. That included the Universal Marshals being a part of them. In the past, there had been.

"The second item on the agenda is admitting new members to join the Federation," Sethremus said. "The planets Nayemen, Dorfina, and Wallanbee have made such requests. The floor is yielded to the Nayemen Representative first."

The Nayemen Representative, a male humanoid

named Fargus Threep, stood up. "Greetings to all the delegates here. My world has submitted the proper documents to join the Universal Federation of Planets. We offer friendship and diplomatic ties to it. Also, trade. Our world is peaceful and under a planetary government that believes in the rights of all citizens." He sat down.

Sethremus smiled. "The assembly will vote to admit Nayemen to the Federation."

The vote took place. Most of the representatives in the assembly voted in favor of Nayemen to join the Federation.

"It has passed," Sethremus said. "Nayemen is now a member of the Federation."

The representatives of both Dorfina and Wallanbee, the former a female human and the latter a male alien, gave their respective speeches on admission to the Federation. Then, the assembly voted in favor of the two worlds to become members of the Federation. It did not surprise Jeddriel, who had no homeworld to speak of in the galaxy. The Archangel-Enforcer originated from a higher plane than the physical one.

Sethremus moved on to the final matter for the assembly to debate on in this session. "Space pirates have become an increasing problem in the galaxy. Federation ships have fallen victim to them. Therefore additional protection by Federation forces is required for Federation ships traveling the galaxy."

Fath stood up. "Redascant ships are some that have been raided by these space pirates. Federation battlecruisers must be assigned to escort Federation ships to destinations in order to protect them from being attacked by them."

"I agree," Izra said. "A few of our own ships have

been boarded by these raiders. They must be stopped."

"Yes," Fargus interjected. "The situation is intolerable."

Hazwyn voiced a concern. "What about the Universal Marshals? Are they working on the problem?"

"They have been assigned to deal with the matter," Sethremus stated. "They will get to the bottom of it."

Voices rose again as the delegates talked among themselves. Jeddriel did not know until now that the Universal Marshals had been given the assignment of investigating the problem of space pirates. The Archangel-Enforcer wondered if he would be contacted by the High Enforcer to be on the force of Universal Marshals to deal with the matter.

Sethremus quieted the delegates down. "Is there any dissent about Federation battlecruisers being used to escort Federation ships on routes?" No one did. "Then the measure is passed. That will be all."

The assembly had no more business to attend to. Sethremus dismissed the meeting. The delegations began to file out. Jeddriel led the Byzantinian party from the assembly chamber.

"Where to, sir?" Chimi asked the Byzantinian Representative.

"Back to our residence," Lonn replied. "I will speak with the Namorean Representative there."

The trip back to the diplomatic residence occurred without any incidents. Chimi contacted the Namorean Representative to meet with the Byzantinian Representative later tonight.

The diplomatic residence resided in an urban area of Acropollon. It was an automated structure like the rest of the houses in the neighborhood. Three hovercars were parked in the driveway. A wired fence enclosed the backyard.

Inside Lonn prepared to eat dinner. Chimi and a few underlings joined him. Jeddriel did not eat while on bodyguard duty. The rest of the security detail left for the night.

In the middle of supper, the Archangel-Enforcer sensed unknown beings moving toward the house. "I detect a hit squad approaching, representative. About seven assailants."

"What do you want us to do?" Lonn asked.

Jeddriel considered. "Stay down. I will take care of them."

The Archangel-Enforcer rushed to the front of the residence, the living room. Unarmed, he dematerialized and went through the front door, his wings appearing once outside.

Seven shooters armed with blast rifles stopped at the sight of him. They began to fire. Jeddriel dodged their shots and flew into them, knocking them all to the ground. The Universal Marshal grabbed a blast rifle off one of them and fired the weapon at them while on the move. He killed the entire hit squad. Afterward, he dropped the blast rifle and went back inside the residence to the dining room, where the Byzantinian Representative and the others crouched.

"You can get up now," Jeddriel said.

Lonn sighed. "Did you get them all?"

"Yes," Jeddriel replied. "Call the Acropollon police."

Chimi did. In time, the authorities arrived along with the coroner. Jeddriel gave a statement to the Acropollon police, who recognized him. The bodies of the seven assailants got piled into a hoverwagon and carted off for the pathology department in downtown Acropollon. The Acropollon police left the area.

The Namorean Representative arrived to see the Byzantinian Representative. The main topic of discussion between them involved mining on the non-Federation planet of Borzai, an uninhabited world close, in space terms, to Byzantinia and Namorea. The two representatives agreed to share the mining of Borzai for its auradium.

The next morning, Lonn and his retinue traveled to his office in the Federationplex. Jeddriel wondered if the assassination attempts were over for the Byzantinian Representative. The Archangel-Enforcer needed to know who was behind them. Before he could start an investigation into the matter, the Universal Marshal got teleported to the Justiceplex.

Chapter 11

Enforcer Hashrah, the Turbobeing, got assigned to a commando unit for a rescue mission. The Universal Marshal featured long dark hair and amber eyes, dressed in a blue and white unisuit with matching boots and cape. She was humanoid and originated from the planet Asaturne in the Cygnus Sector of the Milky Way Galaxy. Her title earned respect from the eleven humanoid males in the commando unit, who followed her lead.

Their objective was to save ten hostages being held by the warlord Fangtu, a male human, on the island of Washubi, west of Survarille in the Angranadan Ocean. The Villain asked for two million credits from the Tellusian government for their release. It did not agree to his terms. A standoff occurred. The foul being told the Tellusian government he would execute the hostages one by one until the ransom was paid. Thus the formation of a rescue mission.

"Remember, we should land on the far side of the island," Hashrah said. "Not close to the fortress of the warlord." *I hope we don't get spotted. We have to be very careful.*

They flew in a sky transport around the back of the island. When it was time, the eleven commandoes jumped from the air vehicle wearing jet packs. Hashrah flew with them, not needing one.

The Turbobeing led them flying over the jungle

toward the island fortress of the warlord. Sunny weather greeted them. A flock of birds took to the sky from below, heading in the opposite direction. No aircraft flew in the vicinity.

The commandoes were armed with automatic weapons, grenades, garrotes, knives, and smoke canisters, plus ropes attached to grappling hooks. Hashrah did not carry any weapons, for she was one. Her special powers resided on the scientific level of energy power. On a few past assignments, she had been on rescue missions. So had the commandoes with her.

They approached the island fortress from a distance, keeping low. The Universal Marshal scanned the earth below them for the warlord's men. None appeared.

Hashrah stopped them to land in a clearing below. Once on the ground, the commandoes gathered around her. The fortress lay three miles south.

"Do we know where in the fortress the warlord is holding the hostages?" Baric Masters asked, a commando captain.

Hashrah answered. "Not exactly. We will have to search the island fortress room by room." *I hope they are all still alive.*

"Do we know how many men the warlord has?" Hyle Danforth asked, a commando sergeant.

"Fangtu has a large contingent of soldiers," Hashrah replied. "Well-armed."

"What about military vehicles?" Darwyn Mendel asked, the youngest of the commandoes.

Hashrah paused. "None. Nor do they have any fighter craft. But the island fortress is heavily guarded."

"That is expected," Baric remarked. "We'll have quite a time penetrating their defenses."

Vith Addis, the oldest of the commandoes, chimed in. "Do we make a frontal assault, or do we strike from the rear?"

"We will attack from behind," Hashrah replied. "Try to surprise them."

After finishing the discussion, they resumed flying in the air. The Turbobeing led them as they stayed down, not to be seen so easily.

They cautiously approached the island fortress. They spotted it from the rear, on top of a mountain. Below the precipice spread jungle. To climb the rocky height would take much effort. They soared just above the tangled vegetation, well below the rear of the island fortress. When they were near enough, they ascended to the roof of the stronghold.

They landed on the palace roof of the island citadel. The commandoes took off their jet packs. Hashrah led them across the roof to the front of the palace. They looked over the edge of the roof and spotted many soldiers below, milling around in a courtyard. In the center of the courtyard rose a water fountain. A stone wall circled from the palace to the other side of the courtyard, where stood a metal gate, open.

"They haven't noticed us yet," Hyle remarked.

Baric smiled. "That is a good sign."

They moved away from the edge and went to the rear of the roof. Taking their grappling hooks out, the commandoes dug them into the parapet. Secured, the eleven men used the ropes and climbed down to the rear windows of the palace. Hashrah hovered before one. Altogether they crashed through the glass and entered a corridor on the second floor of the palace.

Two soldiers noticed them and fired their automatic

weapons at them. The commandoes responded with gunfire and killed both.

"Search the rooms," Hashrah said. *The hostages have to be here somewhere.*

They began looking through rooms. More soldiers ran upstairs to intercept them. Hashrah shot turbo blasts from her hands at the enemy and slayed a number of men. The commandoes returned fire as they came under attack.

The Universal Marshal opened a door and found no one inside. Bodies littered the passageway, bleeding corpses of the enemy. Soldiers kept coming in waves. The Turbobeing and the commandoes took out soldiers nonstop.

"The hostages are not on this floor," Hyle said.

"To the first floor then," Hashrah ordered. *Where can the hostages be?*

The Universal Marshal led them down the stairs to the first floor. They met strong resistance from soldiers. Bullets wrecked things on the ground level—furniture and other fixtures, including paintings on the walls. The noise of gunfire pervaded the atmosphere.

Darwyn threw a grenade. The detonation sent soldiers flying, killing them. A bullet grazed the young commando in the left shoulder and caused him to drop to his knees. Two soldiers bore down on him. Before the men could shoot Darwyn dead, Hashrah came to his aid and blasted them with turbo fire, slaying the pair.

"Thanks," Darwyn said.

"How bad are you hurt?" Hashrah asked. *Got to be more careful there, soldier.*

Darwyn felt his left shoulder. "It's a superficial wound. It won't slow me down."

A bunch of soldiers stormed the palace, firing wildly. Hashrah shot turbo blasts from her hands and decimated them. *So many of them.*

As the others kept firing at the enemy, some of the commandoes kicked in doors to rooms. They discovered the chambers empty. Door to door, they went to try and find the hostages.

Two of the commandoes reached the front entrance to the palace. Soldiers charged at them. Baric and Hyle threw grenades at the men. Explosions sent soldiers flying and killed.

"The hostages are not on this floor," Vith said.

Hashrah turbo-blasted more soldiers. "They must be in the basement then."

The Turbobeing and the commandoes ran to the stairs leading to the sublevel. They encountered opposition. Soldiers shot at them, and they responded likewise. Hyle got nicked in his right hand, but not seriously.

The Universal Marshal led them to a room full of cells. Behind bars stood the hostages.

"Stand back," Hashrah said to the imprisoned six men and four women. The Turbobeing blasted the cell doors open with turbo shots and freed the hostages.

"Mission accomplished," Darwyn remarked.

"We have to get off the island first," Baric said.

Hashrah led them back the way they came. Soldiers still appeared to try and stop them from leaving. They fought their way for the stairs, the commandoes, and the Universal Marshal protecting the people they rescued. Soon, they went up the steps.

On the first floor, the soldiers attacking them thinned in number. Hashrah blasted a path through the enemy and cleared the way outside into the courtyard. Their goal now was to reach the airfield beyond the gate of the fortress, where the sky transport awaited them.

Fangtu appeared at the gate. The warlord held a bazooka. He aimed it at them and fired. The projectile zoomed toward them. Hashrah shot turbo blasts from her hands and destroyed it before it could reach them.

They fought their way to the gate. A couple of the commandoes threw grenades behind them and took out more soldiers. Hashrah disposed of the Villain with a turbo blast.

Hyle pushed the gate open. All of them rushed out of the fortress. The soldiers left in the courtyard numbered too few to stop them.

Ahead appeared the airfield. The sky transport sat in it, the ramp lowered. One by one, they climbed the ramp into the air vehicle. When everybody was aboard, they took off in the direction of Aquilitar, a city on the west coast of Survarille south of Acropollon, the capital of Tellus.

"That is the end of the warlord and his men," Vith said.

Baric grinned. "A force of landtroopers will be sent to the island to secure it."

In a while, they reached Aquilitar. They landed at the airtrooper base, where they were welcomed home.

Once Hashrah got off the sky transport, the Turbobeing found herself teleported to the Justiceplex.

Chapter 12

The same day, Delveran held another meeting in the briefing room with four other Universal Marshals. Earlier Nanomach located the four other Universal Marshals on Tellus and got them teleported to the Justiceplex. At the long table in the chamber sat Falatar, Agwennel, Jeddriel, and Hashrah.

Delveran sat before the control console again. "The Federation Department of Justice has given the Enforcers a new directive. It seems space piracy has dramatically increased in the galaxy. Federation ships have been targeted by space pirates more frequently."

"Is an Incarnation behind it?" Falatar asked the High Enforcer. The Lunar Being leaned forward in his chair.

"Possibly," Delveran replied. "You must find out if that is the truth."

Jeddriel spoke next, the wings of the Archangel-Enforcer invisible. "In the past, before I was a Universal Marshal, I had run-ins with pirates."

"In space?" Agwennel asked. The Undine-Enforcer was not in water form at this time.

"Both in space and on worlds," Jeddriel answered. "But I never encountered an Incarnation of Piracy."

"Which means there could be one," Hashrah said. The Turbobeing let out a deep breath.

"Yes," Delveran agreed. "There are plenty of Incarnations, both good and evil, in the universe."

Falatar leaned back in his chair now. "I have met some of them. But not an Incarnation of Piracy."

"I have met a few of them myself," Jeddriel interjected. "Both good and evil."

Delveran cut in. "There are records of Incarnations. Also, there are data concerning pirate activity and more in the galaxy. Check the information on them both."

"As you say, High Enforcer," Falatar said.

Agwennel voiced a question. "Are there any prisoners in the Universal Prisonplex that are pirates?"

"A few have been incarcerated," Delveran replied.

"We could interview them," Hashrah said. They all agreed with the Turbobeing on that.

Delveran looked at each of them. "You will have Federation battlecruisers to aid you on the assignment. I will send additional Universal Marshals to join you. Keep in regular contact with the Justiceplex."

"As you command, High Enforcer," Jeddriel said.

The Grand Universal Marshal dismissed them. He went to his office.

Chapter 13

Professor Magnemus was not pleased with the destruction of their space fleet. The Scientific Being was satisfied that the jailbreak of the Universal Prisonplex was successful. Thousands of Archvillains were freed from it to recruit for the Fellowship of Darkness.

Magnemus stood eight inches over six feet with a husky frame, dressed in a white lab suit, black lab belt, and black lab shoes. He fingered his long beard, thick and red like his fluffed-out hair. His violet eyes scanned the view screen before him as he stood on the bridge of his spaceship, the *Technokado*, as if searching the heavens for something.

Magnemus was a scientist. His field was biocreation, the science that dealt with the making of natural and artificial life. The bridge personnel manning the different consoles around him were biocreated minions of his.

Asearse entered the bridge from a turbolift. The Charybdian featured webbed hands and feet, pointy ears, smooth and flawless skin the color of the deep blue sea— the same shade as her eyes—with thin and slanted eyebrows. Her black hair fell past her shoulders. The black gown and black slippers she wore heightened her evil beauty. She wore a silver wristwatch from Earth.

"Professor," Asearse said, stopping behind him.

Magnemus turned around. "It is a shame that the

Complex is lost to us. The important work I did in it cannot be replaced. But the biolaboratories on board will suffice for biocreation experiments and other work."

Asearse smiled. "We have three new members for the Fellowship here waiting to see you. They are in the meeting room."

Magnemus nodded. "Let's go see them then."

The Scientific Being and the Charybdian took the turbolift down to the next level. They got off and headed for the meeting room. They passed automatic doors on either side of them to various chambers.

"Any word from our team searching for Lordruingat?" Magnemus asked.

"Nothing new to report," Asearse replied. "They are on another world questing for the Cube of Power."

"Which planet this time?"

"Taurora."

Magnemus recalled that the planet was a primitive world with low technology. He had never visited it.

They reached the meeting room and entered. Inside stood three Archvillains, two males and one female, behind a long table. At one end sat a control console.

Asearse introduced the first of the three to the Scientific Being. "This is Bulkan, the Blob."

Massive in form, Bulkan stood nine feet tall. His amber eyes were deep-set, his light brown hair short. He wore a tan unisuit with matching shoes. His special powers resided on the scientific level of energy power. The Blob was humanoid.

"It's great to be free again," Bulkan said. "The Universal Prisonplex was terrible to be in. I was wasting away until you busted me out."

Magnemus grinned. "Many Archvillains that had

been imprisoned there feel the same way. Welcome to the Fellowship of Darkness."

"How many of our kind are in it?" Bulkan asked.

Asearse answered the question. "There are now thirty-nine members in the Fellowship with the addition of the three of you. Our ranks are growing. There are still plenty of Archvillains out there to join it. Thousands."

"My talents will not go to waste then," Bulkan said.

"They won't," Magnemus agreed.

Asearse introduced the second Archvillain of the three to the Scientific Being. "This is Saryelle, the Scyllan. My twin sister."

Saryelle resembled the Charybdian. The Scyllan featured long black hair, pointy ears, webbed hands and feet, and smooth and flawless skin. However, her skin was sea green, the same color as her eyes. She wore a blue gown with matching slippers. Her special powers resided on the occultic level of energy power.

Magnemus was amused by the fact that they were twin sisters. "Welcome to the Fellowship of Darkness."

"I am grateful to be reunited with my sister," Saryelle said.

Asearse beamed. "As am I."

"Do you have any other family that are Archvillains?" Magnemus asked the Charybdian.

"No," Asearse replied. "Just my sister."

Magnemus turned to the Blob. "And you?"

"None," Bulkan said. "There is just me."

Asearse introduced the last of the three to the Scientific Being. "This is Foulbard, the Shocker."

Foulbard stood a few inches shorter than the professor. He featured long dark hair, gray eyes, and a short beard. The Shocker wore a black unisuit with matching boots and metal wristbands. His special powers resided on the scientific level of energy power, involving shock waves.

"Welcome to the Fellowship of Darkness," Magnemus said.

Foulbard smiled. "It's good to be a member of an organization of your own kind."

"Indeed," Magnemus remarked.

"Will we be going after the Enforcers to take them out?" Foulbard asked.

Magnemus frowned. "When our numbers are far greater than the Universal Marshals. Then we strike."

"When we do," Asearse added, "it will deal a mighty blow to the Universal Federation of Planets."

"I hear that you are seeking Lordruingat," Saryelle said.

"If we can get our hands on the Cube of Power, it will give us a great advantage over our enemies," Asearse stated. "Such power to command."

Bulkan spoke again. "Does the Fellowship have a base of operations in the galaxy?"

"Not at this time," Magnemus answered. "We were forced to abandon our last stronghold, the Complex, on Earth because of the Universal Marshals. We are looking for a new planet to call home."

"Is there any work you want us three to do?" Foulbard asked.

"One of you can help in the search for a planet to build a new stronghold on," Magnemus replied. "Asearse is already doing that."

Saryelle stepped around the table. "I volunteer to help my sister with it."

"Excellent," Magnemus said. He addressed the

Shocker. "You can join the team looking for Lordruingat."

"All right," Foulbard agreed.

Bulkan raised a hand. "And me?"

"You can help in our recruitment of other Archvillains to join the Fellowship," Magnemus said. "We need to do the job faster."

"Very well," Bulkan responded.

Magnemus left them after telling the Charybdian where he would be. He strode to the turbolift and took it up to the next level. After he got off, the Scientific Being walked down a corridor for Biolaboratory One. He passed two of his minions, a pair of robots, in the passageway. In a moment, he entered the chamber with lights on to simulate day.

Inside the large room flourished a new biome of a rain forest, scaled smaller than the one in the Complex he made in the demesne created by a realming device on Earth. He heard the squawking of birds and the chattering of monkeys, sweet music to his ears, in the trees. Night and day cycled in the chamber through devices. A small waterway flowed through the biome, which featured dense vegetation. A machine controlled rainfall in the rainforest.

Magnemus grabbed a handful of dirt and felt its grainy texture. He smelled its earthy odor.

Satisfied, he dropped his handful of earth. Next, he examined a small tree. Its dark brown trunk looked healthy to him as he touched it. It rose to twelve feet in the air.

"I must get samples of this biome for analysis," Magnemus said to himself.

The Scientific Being went to the edge of the small

waterway. Fish swam in a school in it. He spotted a large turtle in it as well. The professor nodded, happy the biocreation experiment progressed naturally without problems.

Magnemus left Biolaboratory One and headed for another chamber on the same deck. As he entered the room, the lights turned on automatically. He stood in Biolaboratory Two, which featured the biocreation of robots. About a dozen droids lined up in the room, unfinished. He strode over to the first automaton in line and removed its chest plate. The professor tinkered with it, seeing how much more work needed to be done to have the robot ready to function.

Someone buzzed outside the chamber. Magnemus told them to come in. Asearse walked into the room.

"What is it now?" Magnemus asked.

"The Universal Marshals have learned of our quest for Lordruingat and are searching for it themselves," Asearse answered.

Magnemus swore. "How did they learn about it?"

"From Ajawbo the Slug."

"That Villain has cost us the element of surprise. No matter. How many of our fellow Archvillains are on the team now looking for the Cube of Power?"

"With the addition of Foulbard, there are seven of them."

Magnemus sighed. "Increase the number on the team again."

"By how many this time?"

Magnemus thought. "Add three more for now. Later, others will join the team. We must beat the Universal Marshals in finding Lordruingat."

Asearse straightened her gown out unconsciously.

"Who do you want to be added to it besides the Shocker?"

"The Viper, the Hellcat, and the Cyclopean."

"All right."

Asearse left him and went to find the three named.

Magnemus pounded a fist on the robot before him. The new development of the Enforcers searching for the Cube of Power now made it a race to find it. He swore again. The professor went back to work on the droid, hoping his team would get to Lordruingat first.

Chapter 14

The space freighter traveled through space at sublight speed. Thome Jarret, captain of the vessel and a male human, sat in his command chair, bored with the routine of another cargo delivery to be done. This time, the ship headed for the planet Quillantas. It made runs to the industrial world regularly and kept a tight schedule. They left the planet Urias a day ago.

"Steady as she goes," Thome said.

The helmsman, Jakar Brann, a male humanoid, responded to the captain. "Aye, sir."

The view screen in front showed white dots that represented stars. No other ships appeared in their vicinity. The space freighter was the size of a battlecruiser and of the Federation.

Nylessa Portos, the second in command and a female humanoid, joined the captain on the bridge. "No trouble so far?"

Thome smiled. "Correct."

"What about any reports of space pirates in our sector?" Nylessa asked.

Thome turned his head to face her. "So far, I have heard no such activity in our area of the galaxy. I know Federation ships have been attacked by them in other quadrants."

"Where is our next cargo pick up after we're done with Quillantis?"

"The planet Nammis." Thome let out a deep breath. "The freight we will be transporting from it is mining equipment and medical material for the planet Gillago. Good paydays."

Jakar chimed in. "Should we set coordinates for hyperjump to Quillantis, captain?"

"Yes," Thome replied. "On my mark."

Before the space freighter could make the jump to hyperspace, two ships suddenly appeared and blocked its path. The cargo ship stopped before it could collide with the pair of unknown vessels.

"Space pirates!" Nylessa said.

The communications officer, Mellia Frond, a female human, spoke. "Captain, I have a message from the pirate ships."

"Play it," Thome said.

"Space freighter, you will not do anything unless you want to be destroyed. We are boarding. Do not resist."

"What do we do, captain?" Saegon Hyllac, a male human and chief engineer, asked.

Thome seemed to think about it. "We have little choice. If we fight back, some of us will surely be killed. We're not a battlecruiser. And we're unarmed."

"So we surrender?" Nylessa asked.

Thome sighed. "Yes. There is nothing we can do."

A boarding party of seven buccaneers teleported to the bridge of the space freighter from one of the pirate ships. The crew of the cargo ship did not put up a fight. The space pirates were armed with blasters and scimitars.

One of the buccaneers, a male humanoid with an eye patch, spoke. "We now control this vessel. Do as you're told, and you won't get killed. Our captain will be here soon."

The leader of the space pirates teleported to the space freighter from one of the corsairs. He was Captain Mahab, the Incarnation of Piracy. Tall, the Archvillain featured black hair, a long beard, and gray eyes. He wore a scarlet doublet with sleeves, black trousers, black boots, a black belt, and a scarlet tri-peaked hat. He was armed with a blaster and his scimitar of power. His special powers resided on the celestic level of energy power.

"Is the freighter secured, Mister Wyller?" Mahab asked.

The eye-patched buccaneer spoke. "Aye, captain. We took the vessel without a fight."

Mahab grinned. "Good." The foul being addressed the bridge crew of the space freighter. "Which of you is the captain of this vessel?"

"I am," Thome said.

Mahab stepped over to him. "What is your cargo?"

"Medical supplies, nonperishable food, and industrial machines," Thome answered without hesitation. He sweated a little.

Mahab nodded. "Mister Wyller, see to the transport of their goods to our vessels."

"Aye, captain." Wyller talked into his wrist commband with the pirate ships. "Begin teleporting the cargo from this freighter to our ships."

"What are you going to do with our cargo?" Thome asked the Incarnation of Piracy.

Mahab backhanded the freighter captain's jaw. "Don't talk unless I want you to."

Thome shut up after the sting to his cheek. His crew

was helpless to aid him.

"What do you want to do with the cargo ship, captain?" the space pirate Carreo, a male human, asked. He pointed his weapon at the chief engineer.

Mahab smiled. "We will let it go empty-handed to its destination. We have no use for the space freighter. Too bad it isn't a battlecruiser. That we could have used."

"The Federation will not be pleased that we raided another of their ships, captain," the space pirate Malargos, a male humanoid, said.

Mahab laughed. "I spit on the Federation. They cannot stop us from pirating their vessels. Let them try to end our raids on their ships."

"Will they send Universal Marshals against us, captain?" Carreo asked.

Mahab scoffed at that. "I would not be surprised if the Federation sends Enforcers against us. They may have already. But even the Universal Marshals will not stop us."

After a while, the stolen cargo was all teleported to the cargo bays of the pirate ships. The Incarnation of Piracy ordered his men back to the corsairs. With the pirates gone, the space freighter resumed its journey to Quillantis. There they would report to Federation authorities about the stolen cargo.

An hour later, on board the pirate ships, the *Jolly Mercer* and the *Jolly Capcorn*, Mahab and his men celebrated the successful raid of yet another space freighter and another blow to the Federation. In the mess hall of the *Jolly Mercer*, the Incarnation of Piracy drank a tankard of mead and ate a meal of wild boar with mixed vegetables and rye bread.

Mahab refilled his tankard and raised it. "Here is to the next successful raid."

His men cheered and broke out in song.

"Where next to do a bit of pirating, captain?" Wyller asked.

Mahab thought on that. "The Capricorn Sector of the Milky Way Galaxy. There are trade ships that need to be looted."

The celebration lasted three hours. Afterward, the two pirate ships engaged their superluminal drives and appeared at their destination.

On the bridge of the *Jolly Mercer,* Mahab sat in his command chair. The view screen before him showed space in the vicinity. His crew kept busy.

"Captain, we are on course for the planet Daffamark," Gaelor said, a male human.

Mahab used his special powers to locate a vessel near the quadrant they flew in. "Change course to intercept the trade ship ahead of us near the Sutara Nebula."

"Aye, captain," Gaelor acknowledged.

Soon the two pirate ships engaged superluminal drives again after they communicated with each other. When they returned to sublight speed, both corsairs appeared in front of a trade ship. The merchant vessel stopped, larger than the two pirate ships, the Sutara Nebula in sight.

Mahab ordered his men from both buccaneer vessels to board the trade ship. They encountered resistance. Armed droids with blast rifles shot at them in a wide corridor. The pirates fired their blasters at the charging robots. The Incarnation of Piracy called on the celestic power of his scimitar and slashed his way through the droids, whose weapons could not harm him because of his supernatural nature. His men rallied behind him.

The two pirate ships fired ion cannons at the trade ship and crippled it. Back in the merchant vessel, alien beings joined the fight, armed with blasters. Mahab blocked their shots, moving forward like a juggernaut. The Archvillain felled them with his blaster and his scimitar. He forced his way to the bridge of the trade ship, his men following him.

"Surrender!" Mahab ordered.

"Never!" Shakar, the leader of the alien beings, responded.

A droid with a photon spear took on the foul being. It swung its weapon at the Incarnation of Piracy. Mahab blocked the strikes, then slashed at the fighting robot. The droid parried his blows. Back and forth they went, neither gaining an advantage nor tiring.

The fighting robot thrust his photon spear at the Archvillain. Mahab dodged the attack and thrust his scimitar deep into the chest of the droid, which shook and collapsed to the floor. The automaton ceased to function.

Mahab removed his scimitar from the nonoperating droid, walked over to the leader of the alien beings, and pressed the point of his scimitar against the throat of Shakar. "Now surrender."

Shakar looked at his stunned crew. None of them could help him. "We yield."

Wyller came up to the Incarnation of Piracy. "The trade ship is secured, captain."

"Any casualties?" Mahab asked.

"A few of the men got wounded," Wyller replied. "Two deaths to report."

Mahab nodded. He took his scimitar and rammed it through the body of Shakar. The leader of the alien beings dropped dead on the floor.

"What do you want to do with the rest of his crew, captain?" Wyller asked.

Mahab removed the scimitar from the corpse of Shakar. "Kill them."

Wyller relayed the orders to the rest of the men. They slaughtered the surviving alien beings and deactivated the remaining droids. Then, they unloaded goods from the trade ship to the buccaneer vessels.

"Captain, what do you want to do with the merchant vessel?" Wyller asked as they left the bridge, filled with dead bodies now.

Mahab fingered his black beard. "Destroy it. It is of no use to us."

"Aye, captain."

After they left the trade ship and returned to the pirate ships, the buccaneer vessels moved a safe distance away from the merchant vessel. Both pirate ships blasted the trade vessel with ion cannons and it imploded in space.

The eyes of Mahab twinkled. The Archvillain seated himself in his command chair. The Incarnation of Piracy grinned. Then he laughed.

"Where to now, captain?" Wyller asked.

Mahab let out a deep breath. The Incarnation of Piracy felt very pleased with himself. "Back to our home base. We will take a break from pirating for a short while. Make plans."

Chapter 15

Draegor awoke from his hibernation. The leader of the Watchers, a male humanoid with white hair and white beard in a white robe and white shoes, awakened the others from their slumber as well, inside an inactive volcano. He lit his glow wand and walked down a passageway into a cavern and illuminated where Lordruingat rested on a rock stand. The Cube of Power shined electric blue, the size of a large ball. Some of the other Watchers entered the cavern.

"Someone tried to take it from here," Draegor said. "I sense this."

"Does your vision reveal who the culprit was exactly?" Garion asked, also a male humanoid, shorter than the leader, in a white robe and white shoes.

Draegor closed his eyes for a moment. "A minion of an Archvillain. He failed to remove Lordruingat from its place and the Cube of Power drove him mad in reaction to the theft attempt."

"It is still safe then," Farianne said, a female humanoid in a white robe and white slippers.

Draegor frowned. "No. I see two sides searching for Lordruingat."

"Who?" Garion asked.

"One is Archvillains of an organization called the Fellowship of Darkness," Draegor replied. "The other is the Enforcers of the Universal Federation of Planets.

Neither so far has found the specific location of Lordruingat."

"They must not succeed in their quest to obtain the Cube of Power, either side," Narwyn said, a female humanoid in a white robe and white slippers.

"Yes," Garion agreed. "It can alert us about any attempts to grab it."

Draegor nodded. "Down through the centuries, many have tried to get Lordruingat. All failed, including beings with special powers. These beings were blocked from discovering the resting place of the Cube of Power by it, though some came close."

"What should we do about the Archvillains and the Enforcers seeking it?" Farianne asked.

Draegor thought about it. "We must dissuade them from searching for it. If necessary, force them to give up the quest for Lordruingat."

"You mean kill them?" Narwyn asked.

Draegor sighed. "If it comes down to that, yes."

"We Watchers have never slain anyone before," Garion said.

"True," Draegor concurred. "But if desperate measures are needed, then taking lives will be done, sad as that may be."

Watchers talked among themselves. Now, there stood twenty of them in the cavern. They argued over killing beings to protect the hidden place of Lordruingat. Also, to save their own lives if they were threatened with death. The noise became too much, and the leader of the Watchers quieted everyone down.

"I will consult with the Cube of Power," Draegor said. He walked over to Lordruingat and placed his hands on it.

The other Watchers waited for him to receive instructions from the Cube of Power. It glowed more in his hands. Draegor closed his eyes and mind-melded with Lordruingat, in touch with its ulgnostic power. He stayed that way for a long time before releasing his grip on the Cube of Power.

"What did Lordruingat communicate to you, great leader?" Farianne asked.

Draegor sighed. "Its hidden location is paramount. We are to do what is necessary to maintain that. If we must kill other beings to ensure that, then slaying them is acceptable."

"As you say, great leader," Farianne said.

The rest of the Watchers would follow what Lordruingat required of them. None of them questioned what the Cube of Power commanded.

"There is another possible threat to finding Lordruingat," Draegor stated. "The Cube of Power has informed me of it."

Maloras, a male humanoid dressed in a white robe and white shoes, spoke up. "Who else may be seeking it, great leader?"

"Space pirates," Draegor replied. "So far they have no knowledge of the questing for Lordruingat. But one especially among them is gifted with second sight. He may have a vision of the Cube of Power."

"Who is this being you speak of, great leader?" Garion asked.

"The Incarnation of Piracy," Draegor answered. "They call him Mahab."

The Watchers all gathered together in the cavern around Lordruingat. They chanted before the Cube of Power, in tune with it. It showed them images of things in their minds. They saw quests for other sacred objects, none that compared to Lordruingat. The Cube of Power showed them beings, particularly those who previously searched for it and others with special powers who could possibly locate it. Pictures of planets popped into their heads—worlds that could provide clues to the whereabouts of Lordruingat.

"We must erase all traces that could lead to finding the Cube of Power," Garion said.

"Yes," Farianne agreed. "There must not be anything that can be linked to Lordruingat."

The chanting stopped. All the Watchers bowed their heads to the Cube of Power.

"We must beware some of the Enforcers and certain Archvillains looking for Lordruingat," Draegor said. "Especially those with special powers of a seeking nature. There are those on both sides who have the ability to find hidden treasures."

"Like Genies?" Narwyn asked.

Draegor turned to her. "Yes. One attempted to get Lordruingat with his wishful magic. The Cube of Power blocked the attempt."

"Certain races of faerie could succeed in seeking it," Maloras said. "Like Elves."

"True," Draegor confirmed. "They have powerful magic."

Seuron, a male humanoid in a white robe and white boots, chimed in. "Sorcerers would also have enough magic to do so."

"That applies to masters of the occult arts in general," Draegor clarified for him.

The Watchers filed out of the cavern. Draegor led them into another cavern, his glow wand still providing illumination. The space they were in featured stone benches in rows with a stone podium before the seats. Cressets stood around the chamber with glow stones in them. Draegor commanded the light rocks to shine, and it became bright enough to see in the cavern. He stepped behind the stone podium as the other Watchers sat on the stone benches.

"This meeting is called to order," Draegor said.

His fellow Watchers quieted down. All their eyes turned on him.

"We must make plans for the defense of Lordruingat," Draegor began. "The threat to the Cube of Power is great this time. Never has there been such danger to it."

"And to us," Farianne added.

Draegor nodded. "We will divide into two parties. The first will stay and guard Lordruingat. The second will leave this planet and go after the Archvillains and the Enforcers seeking the Cube of Power. Half of us in the first party, half of us in the second party."

"Which party will you lead?" Narwyn asked.

"The second one," Draegor answered. "Farianne will be in charge of the first party."

"We will guard Lordruingat with our very lives," Farianne promised.

The Watchers carried no weapons. They possessed, to a limited degree, ulgnostic power, unlike the Cube of Power, which contained an abundance of it.

"We have no arms," Garion said. "Do we make weapons?"

Some of the Watchers grumbled about that. They fell silent again.

"No," Draegor replied. "We possess enough energy

power to fight with. The Archvillains and the Enforcers seeking Lordruingat possess special powers on the three lower energy powers: scientific, occultic, or celestic. They are no match for us."

"But they may carry weapons to use against us," Maloras stated.

Draegor huffed. "That could be. But we are unfamiliar with arms they may have anyway. We have never used weapons before."

"Maybe we should start to learn how to use them," Narwyn said.

More grumbling among the Watchers. Some wanted to get weapons, and some did not. An argument erupted over the matter.

"Silence!" Draegor shouted. He restored order before it came to blows. "If there comes a time when we need to wield weapons, then we will do so. For now, we will not carry them."

"As you say, great leader," Farianne said.

The rest of the Watchers fell in line. Nobody complained further on the matter.

Draegor let out a deep breath. "Now, I will divide us into the two parties."

The leader of the Watchers divided them into two units of ten each. Garion and Narwyn got assigned to the party led by Draegor; Maloras and Seuron joined the party led by Farianne.

Draegor pulled Farianne aside. "Protect Lordruingat any way you have to. If my party fails to stop the Archvillains and the Enforcers, then it will be up to your party to prevent either of them from reaching the Cube of Power."

"As you say, great leader," Farianne responded.

"My party will not leave a trail to follow in search of Lordruingat," Draegor said. "If there is a choice in us finding and stopping the Archvillains or Enforcers first, it would be better if it were the Archvillains."

Farianne seemed perplexed. "Why?

"Because they are considered evil," Draegor replied. "The Enforcers are considered good. If Archvillains get their hands on Lordruingat, they would likely use the Cube of Power for destruction and do terrible things with it. If the Enforcers get their hands on it, they would likely use it for constructive purposes."

Garion came over to them. "We are ready to leave, great leader."

Narwyn joined them. "How are we going to leave this planet, great leader?"

"There are ships docked on this world," Draegor answered. "We will commandeer one. It will take us where we need to go."

The two parties said goodbye to each other. Draegor led his party out of the cavern and then out of the inactive volcano. The leader of the Watchers hoped they could stop the Archvillains and the Enforcers before it was too late.

Chapter 16

The six Universal Marshals went to the library in the Justiceplex. They started to research for Lordruingat, checking record discs for anything on the Cube of Power. The Enforcers found some information on it.

"It says here that Lordruingat may be sentient," Benethor said, reading the data on a record disc.

Hulkeme looked up from holding one. "That may be. It might explain why I could not use my special powers to bring it to me."

Kesharra chimed in. "I have here one possible planet Lordruingat may be on. It is called Vingrezza. It is in the Gemini Sector of the Milky Way Galaxy."

"What else about the world is mentioned?" Yevadne asked the Solar Being.

Kesharra checked. "There is very little known about the planet. It is not a member of the Federation. There is nothing to indicate if it is inhabited or not."

"Here is a planet the Cube of Power may be on," Apparis said. "It is not a member of the Federation but it is inhabited. The world is called Dellakor. It is in the Orion Sector of the Milky Way Galaxy. And is listed here as a magicratic world."

Nazzar spoke. "I think the planets we will find rumored to have Lordruingat on it will all be non-Federation ones. That seems logical."

"The Cube of Power could be anywhere in the

galaxy," Apparis said. "It might be on a world unheard of by the Federation."

"True," Nazzar agreed.

They searched through all the files in the library. When they were finished, they went to the teleporter room in the Justiceplex and beamed to the Libraryplex, an enormous structure in downtown Acropollon. They began searching through record discs in it. Other patrons looked through the files in the Libraryplex. Glowpanels lit the place.

"So far, how many planets have we found that could have Lordruingat on it?" Yevadne asked her fellow Enforcers.

Benethor sighed. "Just two. There must be more than that we should find here."

The Libraryplex featured ten floors of record discs. Personnel who worked in the place helped people out. There were booths where patrons could put record discs in reading devices to gain information. The place had a teleporter station connected to it annexed.

Three of the Universal Marshals sat at booths and read record discs. The other three looked in rows of stored files for anything related to the Cube of Power. Occasionally, the Enforcers got help from the Libraryplex staff.

"I have found another planet Lorduingat could be on," Nazzar said from his booth. On his right sat the Solar Being, and on his left sat the Elf-Enforcer, both in similar booths.

"What world?" Benethor asked the Android-Enforcer.

"The planet Natyrek," Nazzar replied. "Another nonmember of the Federation. It is designated as an automatic world, run by machines."

"I wonder how many planets there are said to have the Cube of Power on them," Kesharra voiced. She put a record disc in a reading device.

Benethor shook his head. "There could be a few. Then there could be many."

"If it is many, it could take a long time to search them all for Lordruingat," Kesharra said.

"An exhaustive quest," Benethor added.

Kesharra smiled. "I have found another candidate for the Cube of Power. The planet Targaris. In the Taurus Sector of the Milky Way Galaxy. It is inhabited by a race of aliens. Not a member of the Federation, of course."

The six Universal Marshals spent a considerable amount of time at the Libraryplex. They looked through file after file for anything on Lordruingat. There were record discs with stories of the Cube of Power, from it being used in a number of ways in the galaxy for different purposes to how it came into existence. One creation story of it said that God made it; another that advanced beings were responsible for it. There were tales of the Watchers that guarded it. Various sources describe how big Lordruingat was, what it looked like, and where its resting place was. There was also information on who searched for the Cube of Power, from scientists, occultists, and celestists to Incarnations, explorers, pirates, and others. Members of the Federation sought it; nonmembers of the Federation sought it. No one ever found it.

The six Universal Marshals finished looking through the record discs in the Libraryplex. They went to the teleporter station and teleported back to the Justiceplex. Afterward, they went to the briefing room again.

"We have much information on Lordruingat," Kesharra said.

Apparis spoke. "The question is how helpful is the data we found."

"I have organized it all in my internal file systems," Nazzar stated.

"How many worlds have been rumored to have the Cube of Power on them?" Benethor asked the Android-Enforcer.

Nazzar accessed the number. "At least eleven."

"What planet do we start looking for Lordruingat?" Kesharra asked the other Universal Marshals.

"It is a difficult choice," Apparis remarked.

Hulkeme chimed in. "Why don't we start with the first one we found named."

"That would be Vingrezza," Nazzar said. "In the Gemini Sector of the Milky Way Galaxy. Unknown if it is inhabited or not."

The other Universal Marshals agreed that Vingrezza should be the first world in their search for the Cube of Power.

"It is said that Lordruingat was used to battle the first supreme evil in the galaxy," Nazzar informed them.

"Against the Tree of Evil, Illdrasil?" Benethor asked. Elves had fought in the war against it. Over a thousand years ago.

"Yes," Nazzar replied.

Yevadne chimed in. "Was Lordruingat successful against the Tree of Evil?"

"There are stories that it was," Nazzar answered. "And there are stories that it wasn't."

The Universal Marshals remembered that it was the

original Enforcers who had ended the evil of Illdrasil. Not the Cube of Power. That led to the birth of the Universal Federation of Planets.

"What else?" Kesharra asked the Android-Enforcer.

Nazzar accessed data. "There is a tale that Lordruingat was used to create the Watchers that guard it."

"That is new," Apparis remarked.

"And there are stories that the advanced beings who made the Cube of Power are the Watchers," Nazzar stated.

Benethor shook his head. "Do these advanced beings have names?"

"A few tales allude to them having names," Nazzar replied. "There are several mentioned. Matyrion. Barryn. Avargos. Sagormone. Nedric."

"Anything else?" Yevadne asked the Android-Enforcer.

Nazzar checked his internal files. "There is a tale that a league of sorcerers created Lordruingat. To make a weapon of ultimate power."

"Wow," Apparis remarked. "That is a revelation."

"What about celestists?" Hulkeme asked the Android-Enforcer.

Nazzar accessed the information. "Yes. There is a story that a group of celestists made the Cube of Power. Something invincible to top everything else that they created."

"What about scientists?" Apparis asked the Android-Enforcer.

Nazzar checked his internal files. "Yes. A story of them experimenting with different energies in the universe. That they created in Lordruingat a new source of energy. Renewable. Unlimited. Sustainable."

"Are there tales of the Cube of Power being created by foul beings?" Kesharra asked the Android-Enforcer.

"Accessing," Nazzar responded. "Yes. There are tales of Lordruingat being associated with evil. One story is that pirates once owned it. Another claims black magicians. But there are equally tales of it being associated with good."

"Indeed," Benethor said.

Nazzar nodded. "Then there are tales of the Cube of Power being neutral. Neither good nor evil. It is unknown whether the Watchers are good, evil, or neutral. There are stories of them being any of the three."

"What about names for the Watchers?" Yevadne asked. "Any mention of them in tales?"

Nazzar accessed the information. "I have no names recorded for the Watchers, only that they have a leader. Nothing else."

"What about their number?" Apparis asked.

"Accessing," Nazzar said. "The number of the Watchers, according to tales, ranges from a dozen to over a hundred."

"Do they have any associations in the galaxy?" Kesharra asked.

Nazzar checked his internal files. "There are stories of Watchers interacting with other beings in the universe. Most tales say they never identified themselves to other people."

Two new Universal Marshals entered the briefing room. The first was Enforcer Danbarrack, the Rubber Being. Tall, he featured brown eyes, sandy hair, a short beard, and a willowy frame. He wore a blue unisuit and matching boots.

The second was Ursanne, the Norn-Enforcer. She featured long dark hair and gray eyes and wore a brown tunic with matching boots and belt.

"We've been assigned to the quest," Danbarrack said.

"Yes," Ursanne confirmed.

The other six Universal Marshals caught them up to speed. Much information to tell them.

Nanomach arranged for a ship to be given to the eight Universal Marshals by order of the High Enforcer. They went to the teleporter room of the Justiceplex and beamed to the Acropollon Spaceport.

The eight Universal Marshals found themselves at the northwest edge of the city. Docking Bays surrounded the launch field, open space, of the Acropollon Spaceport on its north, south, and west sides, while the terminal extended along its east side, marking its official boundaries. Its control tower rose in the center of its terminal. A number of spaceships parked in individual spots on the landing areas, a big rectangle.

Maintenance crews worked on stationary ships on the launch field. Cargo workers loaded and unloaded freighters. Other beings stood around vessels and conversed. None of the people and activity at the Acropollon Spaceport concerned the Enforcers.

The Universal Marshals went to Docking Bay Five. Benethor stepped forward and placed a hand on the touch panel for bioscanning, to the right of the hangar doors. The hangar doors slowly slid open in sound, permitting the Enforcers entry.

Inside Docking Bay Five parked the *Horizon*, a Federation battlecruiser. The large vessel was equipped with a teleport drive. Glowpanels in the high, wide ceiling lighted the place. Just inside the docking bay, a control panel was by the hangar doors. In the back of the covered and enclosed area were automatic doors to a storage chamber filled with maintenance equipment and other items. The ventilation system of the hi-tech hangar was on automatic control as filtered air circulated; automatic control had the normal temperature set at seventy degrees in the hi-tech hangar.

The *Horizon* was a rectangular battlecruiser with four legs supporting its heavy tonnage. It was a fine vessel, silver and sleek, one of a number of ships available to the Universal Marshals. It looked undamaged, needing no major or minor repairs.

The Universal Marshals went around the back of the ship and walked up its lowered ramp in single file, Benethor in the lead. Once inside the vessel Nazzar went to the control touchpad for the ramp and pressed the red square on it, raising the ramp closed.

They walked up a passageway to the front of the *Horizon*. Glowpanels lighted their way. On either side of them stood automatic doors to various rooms. When they entered the bridge, Benethor sat in the command chair. The other Enforcers sat at different stations. A rectangular view screen appeared before them.

"Turn on all systems," Benethor commanded.

Nazzar sat at the science console. "All systems on."

"Open the roof for us to leave," Benethor ordered.

"Roof opened," Danbarrack said from the station left in front of the Elf-Enforcer.

Benethor smiled. "Engage engines."

"Engines engaged," Danbarrack responded.

The thrusters fired. Soon, the *Horizon* lifted off and rose out of Docking Bay Five. It flew toward space.

"When we are far enough from Tellus," Benethor said, "set course for Vingrezza."

The ship left Tellus. When it was far enough from the planet, Danbarrack set the coordinates to engage the teleport drive. Soon the vessel telejumped from the Sagittarian Sector of the Milky Way Galaxy for the Gemini Sector of the Milky Way Galaxy.

Vingrezza orbited an orange sun as its second planet. There were eight worlds in its solar system. Vingrezza had two small moons. It was unknown whether any of the planets in the solar system were inhabited as those worlds were uncharted. Soon, the ship orbited Vingrezza.

"I think we should send down a small party first to explore Vingrezza," Nazzar said. "We don't know what we'll find on it."

"Suggestion accepted," Benethor agreed.

"Who should go?" Kesharra asked.

Benethor decided who would go. "Kesharra, Apparis, Ursanne, and Hulkeme will teleport down there. Be careful."

The Solar Being, the Roc, the Norn-Enforcer, and the Genie-Enforcer went to the teleporter room on board. Apparis set the coordinates and autoteleportist on the teleport podium as the other three stepped onto the telegrid. The Roc joined them. The autoteleportist engaged, and the four of them beamed down to the planet.

They found themselves teleported by a lake. Mountains rose around them to the north. To the south lay forestland. East and west of them stretched open ground.

"What beautiful scenery," Apparis remarked.

"Kind of a paradise," Ursanne said.

They heard no sounds. A gentle breeze blew from the south. They smelled nothing but fresh air. In the blue sky above shined the Vingrezza sun.

"Which way should we go?" Kesharra asked the other three.

"The direction of the forestland," Hulkeme suggested.

"Fine by me," Apparis said.

Kesharra and Ursanne agreed. They headed for the forestland.

The Universal Marshals reached the forestland. Now they heard bird cries. Insect life droned a bit. They stepped on and crunched sticks on the firm earth, which smelled tangy to them. The trees stood tall with thick canopies. The terrain was uneven.

They spotted wildlife. Small birds with purple feathers in the trees. A large creature that resembled a deer. Two small woodcats hunting for prey.

"Signs of animals is natural," Apparis remarked.

"The big question is are there any people on this world," Ursanne said.

Hulkeme used his special powers. "I don't sense any life forms that are intelligent beings here."

"This land may be untouched by civilization," Kesharra said.

"That may be a blessing," Ursanne commented.

They continued on. More wildlife appeared—an animal that resembled a cross between a porcupine and a wolverine, one like a small brown bear with a white snout, and a couple of squirrel-like critters.

"Can you sense anything unusual here?" Apparis asked the Genie-Enforcer

Hulkeme used his special powers again. "I detect nothing out of the ordinary. So far."

"I don't sense anything unusual either," Ursanne said.

They came upon a tree with claw marks on it. High up on its trunk.

"That does not bode well," Kesharra remarked.

"Whatever made those marks must be dangerous," Apparis stated.

The Universal Marshals resumed traveling. Nothing appeared to threaten them. More birds appeared among the trees, black owls in particular.

"This world seems peaceful enough," Ursanne said.

"Yes," Apparis agreed. "An uninhabited planet ripe for colonizing."

"Not necessarily a good idea," Kesharra stated.

They entered a clearing. So they stopped and took a break.

"This place may be ideal for Lordruingat to be on," Ursanne said. "It's not been encroached by civilization. Not colonized. Paradisical in nature."

"Easy for the Cube of Power to be hidden on," Hulkeme added.

"What are some of the types of planets Lordruingat is said to be hidden on?" Kesharra asked the Android-Enforcer.

Nazzar accessed the information from his internal files. "A few tales mention that the Cube of Power rests on planets untouched by beings. Other stories have it on worlds inhabited by primitive people. Several yarns have primitive people worship the Watchers and the Cube of Power."

"Are there tales of Lordruingat being on planets that

are more advanced?" Apparis asked.

"Yes," Nazzar answered. "Stories vary though as to what kind of world the Cube of Power is actually on."

"Finding Lordruingat is going to be very difficult," Ursanne remarked. "It is no wonder that no one has ever found it."

"Until recently," Apparis said. "That minion of the Scientific Being who discovered it by accident went mad. It is unknown who else is searching for the Cube of Power besides the Archvillain organization and the Universal Marshals."

"True," Nazzar agreed. "As far as the data about Lordruingat is concerned, others may be looking for it."

"The quest for the Cube of Power is very old," Ursanne added.

"There must be plenty of clues to where Lordruingat rests," Kesharra said.

Nazzar nodded. "Somewhere, there should be signs as to where the Cube of Power is really located. We simply must uncover them."

The Universal Marshals resumed their journey through the forestland. Eventually, they arrived at the southern edge of it. Before lay a valley with mountains towering on both sides. On the ground ahead they spotted an enormous footprint. They hurried to it and looked down at the impression.

"What could have made this imprint?" Kesharra asked no one in particular.

Nazzar studied it. "The creature that made this must be at least several hundred feet tall."

"This does not bode well," Apparis remarked.

They moved onward. The sky became partly cloudy. A flock of white-tailed birds flew overhead. The valley featured tall grass, uncut.

The mountains on either side loomed like sentinels watching the valley, featuring passes that the Universal Marshals could barely see. Nothing moved in sight on them.

They found more footprints in the valley. Immense but different.

"Gigantic creatures roam this world," Ursanne remarked.

"Let's hope we don't meet any," Kesharra said.

The valley ended at the edge of a sea. They stopped.

"Where now?" Apparis asked his fellow Enforcers.

At that moment, something huge rose from the sea. The enormous creature, reptilian in nature, featured plates sticking out its back and a spiked tail. It stood five hundred feet tall. The gigantic monster started for shore.

"Run," Nazzar said.

The Universal Marshals raced back up the valley. The gigantic monster chased them, moving slowly, taking big strides. It gained on them a little at a time.

Ahead of them, another gigantic monster appeared. It was bear-like, gray, and bellowed in challenge to the other enormous creature.

"We're trapped between them," Kesharra remarked.

"Head for the mountains," Nazzar said.

The Universal Marshals ran for the mountains on their right. In some places, the mountains looked steep; others not. Nazzar led the way as they climbed up the alpine terrain.

The gigantic monsters ignored them for the time being. Instead the enormous creatures clashed, coming together. Both tried to get the upper hand. Each attempted to bite the other.

"At least they're not paying any attention to us," Kesharra remarked.

"This planet seems to be dominated by gigantic monsters," Nazzar stated. "They must rule this world."

The gigantic monster that was reptilian swung its tail and connected with the head of the bear-like one, stunning the enormous creature, which shook its head. Seeing an advantage, the reptilian colossus plowed into the ursine titan and knocked it to the ground. The former tried to finish off the latter but failed as the bear-like thing whacked the reptilian colossus in the head a few times, then rolled to its feet. They engaged again, grappling with each other.

"What a battle they are fighting," Kesharra remarked.

The Universal Marshals stopped at the foot of a mountain pass. They watched the fight between the two behemoths rage on.

A gigantic bird, like a thunderbird, flew across the sky. The winged monster dove for the Enforcers.

Kesharra reacted by firing solar blasts from her hands at the enormous avian and knocking it from the air. The gigantic bird crashed into a peak and tumbled down to the valley floor. It righted itself and took off into the sky again, away from the Enforcers.

Hulkeme used his special powers. "I sense many gigantic monsters on this planet. I do not sense Lordruingat here."

"Maybe you can't sense the Cube of Power," Apparis said. The Roc addressed the Norn-Enforcer. "Do you sense anything?"

"I detect no life forms that are beings here," Ursanne replied. "I also cannot sense Lordruingat here. Only enormous creatures."

The Universal Marshals continued to search for the Cube of Power. As for the battle between the two gigantic monsters, they quit and went their separate ways. Eventually, the Enforcers decided to return to the ship. Hulkeme teleported them up to the vessel.

Chapter 17

Two more Universal Marshals joined Jeddriel, Falatar, Agwennel, and Hashrah for the assignment involving space pirates. The first was Enforcer Jarek, the Glad Sower, the Incarnation of Life. He stood four inches over six feet, with a thin build and long limbs. A white cloak wrapped his albino body with matching loafers on his long feet; a white cowl hid his face. The only visible part of the Universal Marshal was his hands with long fingers and short nails. He wielded a hoe of power. His special powers resided on the celestic level of energy power.

The second Universal Marshal was Enforcer Memfelice, the Psychic Being. She featured long sandy hair and blue eyes, tall for a female. She wore a white unisuit with matching boots and belt. Her special powers resided on the occultic level of energy power.

The six Universal Marshals met in the library of the Justiceplex. They looked at the history of pirates in the galaxy, finding plenty of information on the subject, discs with much data.

"It says here that there is a home base for pirates in the galaxy," Falatar said.

"Does it have a name?" Agwennel asked the Lunar Being.

Falatar checked. "Yes. It is simply referred to as the Retreat."

"Does it say where this place is located?" Memfelice asked the Lunar Being.

Falatar checked again. "It indicates a swampy world but nothing about what sector it is in of the galaxy. On a planet called Nashotah."

"Piracy has been a problem in the galaxy for thousands of years," Jarek stated. The Glad Sower scanned what was on a disc in a reading device. "There are indications that there is an Incarnation of Piracy."

"What about a name for the foul being?" Hashrah asked the Glad Sower.

Jarek checked. "There is one reference to that. The name of Mahab."

"Have you ever encountered the Incarnation of Piracy?" Jeddriel asked the Glad Sower.

"I have crossed paths with pirates," Jarek answered. "Not with Mahab directly, if he exists. I have also saved the lives of people who were injured in raids by buccaneers. Even arrested a few pirates."

Some of the Universal Marshals apprehended pirates previously on planets and in space. Buccaneers were imprisoned in the Universal Prisonplex, Criminals and Villains. No Archvillains, though. It had been a while since an Enforcer arrested a pirate to be put away in the Universal Prisonplex. The last to do it was the Glad Sower.

Memfelice put a new disc in a reading device. "Here is something interesting. It says here that pirates in the galaxy have a council overlooking piracy in the galaxy."

"How many constitute this council?" Falatar asked the Psychic Being.

"Twelve," Memfelice replied.

Hashrah spoke after ejecting a disc from a reading

device. "Does it give the names of the members of this council, past or present?"

Memfelice checked. "No."

"Anything else?" Falatar asked the Psychic Being.

Memfelice checked. "It says here that the Incarnation of Piracy leads the council. But it also says the council votes to decide who leads it."

"Tellus has never had a pirate problem," Jeddriel remarked. "But other worlds in the Federation have."

"That includes the planet Earth," Jarek said. In the past, the Incarnation of Life visited it.

"Should we talk to the pirates who are imprisoned in the Universal Prisonplex?" Agwennel asked her fellow Universal Marshals.

"It's not a bad idea," Falatar said. "Maybe we can glean something from them."

Jarek nodded. "Possibly that the Incarnation of Piracy really exists."

"There is nothing in these records that indicates Mahab interacted with other Archvillains," Jarek said.

"Unfortunately, there are no Archvillains imprisoned in the Universal Prisonplex we could speak with," Jeddriel added.

Memfelice spoke. "The Archvillain organization might know of the Incarnation of Piracy."

"True," Jarek agreed. "It's even possible the Fellowship of Darkness might have tried to recruit Mahab."

"Or the Incarnation of Piracy may already be a member of the Archvillain organization," Jeddriel said.

The Universal Marshals left the library in the Justiceplex and went to the teleporter room. They beamed to the Libraryplex in its teleporter station. The

Enforcers looked through discs for further information on pirates, especially the Incarnation of Piracy. Other patrons used the Libraryplex. Staff was on call.

Hashrah got a disc and put it in a reading device. "It says here that the pirate council is made up of members from different planets. When one dies, another buccaneer takes their place."

Falatar looked through another disc in a reading device. "It says here that the home base of pirates on Nashotah, the Retreat, was established by the Incarnation of Piracy."

"On this disc, it reads that piracy started with the Incarnation of Piracy and spread throughout the galaxy," Agwennel said. "It began before the first supreme evil reigned in the galaxy. It coincided with the terror campaign started by the Four Horsemen of the Apocalypse—the Incarnations of Death, War, Famine, and Pestilence."

"It is surprising that the Universal Marshals never encountered the Incarnation of Piracy over the centuries we have existed," Memfelice stated.

Jarek chimed in. "We may have seen the handiwork of Mahab because of the pirate activity in the galaxy. Plenty over a thousand years."

"The Incarnation of Piracy would certainly have many followers who are pirates in the galaxy," Jeddriel remarked. "They must worship him as some kind of deity."

"There should be records of incidents with Mahab by beings in the Federation and not in the Federation.," Hashrah said.

Falatar leaned back in his chair. "People must have seen the Incarnation of Piracy when they were raided by pirates. But how would they recognize what Mahab looks like? If he dresses like any other pirate, it would be hard to distinguish him as the Incarnation of Piracy."

"Here is an interesting bit," Hashrah said. "Mahab has a pet parrot named Starly."

"That is not unique," Jarek countered. "Other pirates on worlds have had pet parrots. It does not distinguish him from any other pirate."

Memfelice took out a disc from a reading device and put another one in. "We have found nothing that indicates what makes Mahab different than all other pirates in the galaxy other than he is the Incarnation of Piracy."

The Universal Marshals finished their search through the record discs in the Libraryplex. They went to the teleporter station of the place and beamed back to the Justiceplex. The six Enforcers went to see Nanomach. The Computer-Enforcer gave them the latest news on piracy in the galaxy.

The High Enforcer assigned the six Universal Marshals a fleet of ships to deal with the problem of piracy. They went to the teleporter room of the Justiceplex and beamed up to the Federation battlecruiser, the *Constellation*. Altogether, there were five vessels for the Enforcers to use in the mission of dealing with space pirates so far.

The Universal Marshals stood on the bridge of the *Constellation*. Captain Soberyn Tal, a humanoid, commanded the ship. Bridge personnel kept busy.

"Where to?" Soberyn asked the Enforcers.

"The last place a raid by pirates took place," Jeddriel answered for them. "The Omicron Sector of the Milky Way Galaxy."

"Mister Dolle," Soberyn said, "set coordinates for the Omicron Sector and prepare to engage the teleport drive."

The helmsman obeyed the orders given. "Ready, captain."

Soberyn addressed the communications officer behind him at her station. "Telia, tell the other ships our destination, to follow us, and be ready to engage their teleport drives."

"Yes, captain," Telia, a human female, responded. "Message received."

Moments later, the five ships engaged their teleport drives and telejumped from the Sagittarian Sector of the Milky Way Galaxy to the Omicron Sector of the Milky Way Galaxy.

"Scan the vicinity for any other vessels in the area," Soberyn ordered the science officer.

"Scanning," Nymeron, a male alien, responded. "No other ships in sensor range, captain."

The *Constellation* and the other four Federation battlecruisers traveled at sublight speed through the quadrant. On the view screen in front of the bridge white dots shined in clusters, representing stars. Nothing appeared out of the ordinary.

"What are you looking for in particular?" Soberyn asked the Universal Marshals.

Jarek replied for them, "Any signs of piracy, like abandoned ships or vessels with no survivors on them."

"Do you expect we will encounter pirate ships in battle?" Soberyn asked the Enforcers.

"Sooner or later, we should expect to engage them in a fight," Jeddriel replied for them. "They have been very active in the galaxy lately."

"We're hoping to find their home base, the Retreat, eventually," Hashrah said.

The five Federation battlecruisers traveled through the sector looking for any signs of piracy or pirates. They passed through a solar system with seven planets, none of them inhabited. They searched for any trail of their quarry.

"Captain," Nymeron said, "sensors detect a ship ahead."

"What kind of ship?" Soberyn asked.

Nymeron scanned further. "A freighter. It is just listing there."

Soberyn addressed the communications officer. "Contact the ship, Telia."

Telia obeyed his orders. She tried to communicate with the unmoving vessel. "No response, captain."

"Checking for life forms onboard," Nymeron said. "Readings indicate bodies on the ship. But no life signs."

Soberyn turned to the Universal Marshals. "What would you like to do about it?"

Falatar answered for the Enforcers. "Teleport us to the ship. We can check it out."

"All right," Soberyn responded. He contacted the teleporter room of the *Constellation* on his command chair over the intercom. "Ready to beam over a party to the other vessel."

The Universal Marshals left the bridge. They took a turbolift down to Deck Three. They exited the turbolift and walked down a corridor to the teleporter room. At the control podium stood teleportist Rammen Shar, who set the coordinates for them to beam over to the still vessel.

"Ready to teleport you," Rammen, a male human,

said.

The Enforcers stepped onto the telegrid. Rammen teleported them to the freighter. They materialized on the bridge of the ship. Instead of finding anyone alive on the bridge, they discovered corpses. They checked the bodies.

"This one died by a stabbing weapon," Falatar said, looking over the remains of a male humanoid slumped at a station. "Likely a sword or something else."

Hashrah turned over a body slumped at another station. "This one died from a blaster shot of some kind. Death was instantaneous."

"This appears to be the handiwork of pirates," Jeddriel remarked.

All the corpses on the bridge died from either a stabbing weapon or a blaster shot of some kind. The Universal Marshals confirmed this after examining each corpse.

"Let's check the rest of the ship," Agwennel said.

The Enforcers left the bridge and went down a passageway. Other bodies lay in the corridor, killed like those on the bridge. They entered and searched different rooms on the freighter, but the results were the same: more corpses.

The Universal Marshals entered the cargo bay of the freighter. The chamber was empty of goods. Pirates cleaned the ship out. They found no bodies in the cargo bay.

"The pirates were thorough," Falatar remarked.

"Left no survivors," Memfelice added.

The Enforcers exited the cargo bay. Hashrah contacted the *Constellation* on a telecommunicator band around her wrist and informed the captain of what they'd found so far. Then, the Universal Marshals searched the freighter a little more.

"The freighter personnel wielded no weapons in their defense against the pirates," Jarek remarked. "There are none on board. No armory to speak of."

"Clearly, the freighter was ambushed," Hashrah pointed out. "Unknown how many pirate ships were involved."

"The main tactic of the pirates," Jeddriel added. "Surprise."

The Universal Marshals entered the sick bay of the freighter and found a few more bodies, the ship's doctor and a nurse among them.

"Poor souls," Jeddriel muttered.

The Enforcers left sick bay. As they traversed another passageway, they heard some strange sounds. They wondered where the noises were coming from.

"Behind us," Jarek said.

Coming up behind them crawled robotic spiders, many of the mechanical creatures.

Hashrah fired turbo blasts from her hands at the droid arachnids and destroyed them. Agwennel changed into water and shot aqua beams at them, wiping them out. Memfelice used her psychic power of pyrokinesis and burned them.

"It's a booby trap left by the pirates," Falatar remarked. The Lunar Being used his special power of a gravitic push to slam into the robotic spiders.

Jarek swung his hoe of power into them and smashed the mechanical creatures to pieces. Jeddriel used his special powers to blast the droid arachnids apart. It took a while before the Universal Marshals stopped the robotic spiders.

Hashrah talked into her telecommunicator band. "We're ready to beam back."

The Enforcers teleported back to the *Constellation*. After they materialized in the teleporter room, they returned to the bridge.

"What should we do about the freighter?" Soberyn asked the Universal Marshals.

Jeddriel replied for them. "Contact the Federation on Tellus. Tell them to send a battlecruiser to tow the ship back to the planet. The authorities can deal with it."

"All right," Soberyn responded. He addressed the communications officer. "Send a message to the Federation on Tellus about the freighter. Relay the coordinates for the vessel."

"Yes, captain," Telia said.

The Enforcers told the captain what happened on the freighter. They gave him a full report.

The *Constellation* and the other battlecruisers waited until a ship came to tow the freighter back to Tellus. Afterward, they continued on course through the quadrant.

"The pirates don't usually take hostages," Hashrah remarked.

"They may recruit other beings to join them," Falatar said. "New blood."

Jeddriel agreed. "They didn't leave any traces on that freighter."

"There must be other worlds in the galaxy where pirates congregate," Agwennel stated.

"True," Jarek said. "We will have to visit some of them to find answers to questions we have about the space pirates. Like exactly where Nashotah is in the galaxy."

"And learn that the Incarnation of Piracy does exist," Memfelice added.

"I believe he does," Jarek said. "The increase in piracy in the galaxy seems to me to indicate it as such."

The *Constellation* entered another solar system. There were ten planets in it. The sun of the solar system was a yellow star.

Soberyn addressed the science officer. "Any inhabited planets in this solar system?"

Nymeron checked the bridge computer. "Yes, captain. The fourth planet. It is called Taratheon."

"What else do you have on it in the computer banks?" Soberyn asked.

Nymeron accessed the information. "Taratheon is a colonial world inhabited by a race of humanoids. Not a member of the Federation. It has been visited in the past by Federation members."

"Anything about pirates on it?" Soberyn asked.

"Looking," Nymeron replied. "Yes, captain. Piracy exists on it. To a fair degree."

Soberyn turned to the Universal Marshals. "Do you want to go down to Taratheon to see what you can find out about space pirates?"

The Enforcers discussed it among themselves. In the end, they came to an agreement on the matter.

"We would like to teleport down to the planet," Jeddriel replied for them.

"All right," Soberyn said. He addressed the helmsman. "Put us in orbit around the planet a safe distance away."

"Yes, captain," Dolle responded.

The Universal Marshals left the bridge again and headed for the teleporter room. Once inside the chamber, they stepped onto the telegrid. Rammen set the coordinates for them to beam down to a seaport. Moments later, they appeared at their destination.

The Enforcers stood outside the city limits of the place, in the clearing of some woods. No one was around. They got their bearings and walked out of the forest into the seaport.

Ships docked at the seaport. Other vessels left and sailed for the open sea. Ships were being loaded, unloaded, or repaired. People went about their business. The weather was fair under a partly cloudy sky. A breeze blew from the south.

A male humanoid dressed in colonial wear greeted them just outside the dock. "I am Samychel. Can I help you?"

"Possibly," Jeddriel replied for them. "We need to speak to someone about your piracy problem."

"Then you need to speak with the constable," Samychel said. "You will find his office in Tralagar Square. In the center of town."

The Universal Marshals thanked him. They walked through the city, heading for Tralagar Square. People glanced at them. Some of the inhabitants rode coursers, animals that resembled shaggy horses but bigger. There were vendors on the streets as well, selling items from food to trinkets and everything else in between. Children also played in spots, along with dogs.

"This seems like a pleasant place," Memfelice remarked.

"The citizens show no fear of us," Falatar stated.

In time they reached Tralagar Square. In the middle of it rose a stone fountain with water cascading in a pool. A few people tossed coins into the water and appeared to be making wishes. Buildings in the seaport were made of wood and stone. Some windows were open.

The Universal Marshals found the constable's office. A sign hung over the door. They entered the building.

Six people worked in the place behind wooden desks. A few citizens talked with the deputies of the constable, who occupied a separate room in the office.

A deputy came up to them. "Can I help you?"

"We wish to speak with the constable," Falatar answered for them.

"About what?"

"Piracy," Memfelice replied for them.

The deputy seemed to eye them with suspicion. "Who are you?"

"We are Universal Marshals of the Universal Federation of Planets," Jeddriel stated.

The deputy left them and went to speak with the constable. The constable, Silas McCree, rose from his chair and went to the Enforcers.

"Constable," Jarek said.

Silas frowned. "I have heard of you. What about piracy do you want to know?"

"Have you ever been raided by pirates from outside your world?" Agwennel asked.

"We have been victimized by buccaneers whom we have never seen before," Silas replied.

Falatar voiced the next question. "Did you hear the name of a pirate called Captain Mahab?"

Silas grimaced. "Yes. He and his men attacked ships on the sea. Looted what they could. Killed a few people."

"When did they raid you last?" Memfelice asked.

"About a fortnight ago," Silas answered. "Are you

going after them?"

"We have been assigned to stop them," Hashrah responded for them. "So far, we have only encountered their handiwork in the galaxy. Sooner or later, we will find them."

"What is so special about Captain Mahab?" Silas asked.

"He is the Incarnation of Piracy and an immortal," Jeddriel said. "He has many followers who are pirates. He is their god. He has been operating as a pirate as such for centuries."

The Universal Marshals finished talking with the constable and left his office. Hashrah contacted the *Constellation* on her telecommunicator band. The teleportist beamed them back up to the battlecruiser. They went to the bridge.

"Learn anything from the people of Taratheon?" Soberyn asked the Enforcers.

Falatar sighed. "Not much. Mahab and his men raid worlds besides spaceships."

"Does he have a preference to whom or what he raids?" Soberyn asked.

"They seem to pillage wherever they please," Memfelice answered. "They are not particular who they raid."

"They may loot at random," Hashrah added. "There is no certain pattern to their raids."

Soberyn addressed the helmsman. "Take us out of orbit."

"Yes, captain," Dolle responded, a male alien. "What course should we set?"

Soberyn turned to the Universal Marshals. "What is our next destination?"

"The planet Amaekar," Hashrah said.

Soberyn addressed the helmsman. "Make it so."

"Aye, captain," Dolle responded.

The *Constellation* and the other four battlecruisers engaged their teleport drives and telejumped from the solar system they were into another one. The trip was instantaneous.

"Captain," Nymeron said. "The scanners have detected a ship in sensor range."

"Identify it," Soberyn ordered.

Nymeron complied. "It's a battlecruiser of some kind. It may be a pirate ship."

Soberyn leaned forward in his command chair. "Increase speed to intercept it."

"Yes, captain," Dolle responded.

Before the five Federation ships could catch the unknown vessel, it disappeared from sight.

"Captain," Nymeron said. "The strange ship is no longer in sensor range."

"Rats," Soberyn muttered. He turned to the Universal Marshals. "What is significant about Amaekar?"

"It is said that pirates congregate to the world," Jeddriel replied for them. "We may gain knowledge about piracy in the galaxy, particularly about Mahab."

Soberyn addressed the helmsman. "Put us in a safe orbit around Amaekar."

"Yes, captain," Dolle responded.

The *Constellation* orbited the planet. All four of the other Federation battlecruisers waited a safe distance from the inhabited world.

The Enforcers left the bridge and went to the teleporter room. Rammen beamed them down to

Amaekar. The Universal Marshals did not know what to expect from their visit to the planet.

Chapter 18

Onboard the *Slaughter*, the ten Archvillains gathered in the meeting room. They sat at a long table. At the control console at one end of the table sat the leader of the group, Sumerlin, a black magician. He stood over six feet tall with hazel eyes and blond hair, dressed in blood red—shirt, pants, belt, shoes, and a cape.

"The Enforcers know of our quest," Sumerlin said.

Xigan, the Behemoth, pounded the table with a fist. He towered over nine feet tall, massive in build, with sandy hair and blue eyes, dressed in a brown unisuit and matching boots. "Fish swallow! How did they learn of our quest for the Cube of Power?"

"Now it is a race to find Lordruingat," Darlesse, the Hellcat, remarked. She was the cousin to Lethesis, the Wildcat. Her long red hair cascaded past her shoulders, and her brown eyes were flecked with gray. She wore a pink unisuit with matching slippers.

"This is something we don't need," Ripgarth, the Cyclopean, stated. He stood over ten feet tall with a heavy build and chestnut hair. In the center of his forehead protruded an amber eye. He wore a dun-colored outfit, including boots.

"We cannot let the Enforcers beat us to Lordruingat," Tajana, a Sphinx, agreed. She featured short dark hair, brown eyes, a lion's body on two feet, and brown wings folded at present. She dressed in a white tunic, leather sandals, and a white and black kerchief.

"We should have a head start on them," Daggermash, a Manticore, said. He stood over seven feet tall with rust-colored eyes, a lion's mane, and a scorpion's tail, dressed in tan clothes. "They must have learned about it only recently."

"The question is, what do they know about Lordruingat that we don't," Namina, a Siren, interjected. She featured long black hair and gray eyes, wearing a black gown and matching slippers. "They may know a lot more than we do."

"So far, our own efforts to find the Cube of Power have yielded nothing," Amyrielle, the Echidnan, remarked. She sported long silver hair and gray eyes. She wore a silver dress with matching shoes.

Gnashboros, the Viper, spoke. "It's not a good sign that the Universal Marshals also are seeking Lordruingat." He stood over six and a half feet tall, with black eyes, green hair, and a slim build. He wore green clothes—trousers, a shirt, and shoes.

"The Enforcers are going to be a problem for us," Foulbard, the Shocker, said. "We certainly cannot let them stop us."

"They may cross our path and force them to fight us, especially if both of us find the Cube of Power at the same time," Sumerlin stated. "They have more resources than us to find the location where the Cube of Power rests."

"Unfortunately, true," Darlesse agreed. "Our research to find the exact spot where Lordruingat is has yielded little useful information."

"How many planets have we searched so far for the Cube of Power?" Foulbard asked his fellow Archvillains.

Tajanna answered the question. "The count at the moment is six. It is a riddle where Lordruingat is in the galaxy."

"Maybe no one is meant to find it," Daggermash said. "It has been hidden in the galaxy for thousands of years."

"Some of the members of our Fellowship have tried to have visions of where the Cube of Power can be found," Sumerlin stated. "None of them can get an exact reading on where it can be found."

"Have you tried?" Darlesse asked the black magician.

Sumerlin grimaced. "Yes. But my mind's eye can't seem to pinpoint its resting place. It's like a fog is blocking my second sight."

"I don't think Lordruingat is on a Federation planet," Xigan said. "It must be on a non-Federation world."

"That seems logical," Ripgarth agreed. "If it were on a Federation planet, it would have been found already."

"What planet should we go next to find the Cube of Power?" Namina asked the black magician.

"We have a number of worlds to choose from," Sumerlin replied. He sighed. "I think I would pick the planet Lanndar."

"Why?" Namina asked.

"Because it is said that the planet has secret chambers filled with hidden treasures on it," Sumerlin answered. "One of them chambers may hide

Lordruingat."

The black magician dismissed them. They returned to the bridge of the ship and plotted a course for Lanndar. The android helmsman engaged the teleport drive and the *Slaughter* telejumped to the solar system, where the planet orbited a yellow sun as its third world.

"Should we land on the planet or teleport a party down?" Darlesse asked the black magician.

"We will land on Lanndar," Sumerlin replied. "First, we'll turn on the stealth mode of the vessel to hide us from sight."

The black magician ordered the helmsman to engage the cloaking mechanism of the ship. The android obeyed, and the *Slaughter* became invisible.

"What kind of world is Lanndar?" Xigan asked the black magician.

"It is an Earth-like planet," Sumerlin answered. "On the same scientific level with the Terrran world. But on a higher occultic level and celestic level than Earth."

The *Slaughter* approached Lanndar at sublight speed and entered its atmosphere. No planes in their vicinity. Just a morning sky of blue.

"Where do we put down exactly?" Gnashboros asked the black magician.

"On the continent of Garamon," Sumerlin replied. "In its central region, where digs are going on for hidden treasures, particularly of power. Maybe Lordruingat."

The *Slaughter* descended for a plateau beyond the digging sites. It landed quietly in the area of fairly level high ground on four huge legs. The ten Archvillains left the ship by a ramp lowered in the middle of the unseen vessel. They took with them equipment like ropes and holograph devices to camouflage their physical appearances and weapons like blasters and blast rifles.

The Archvillains walked down a slope until they reached even ground. Then they activated the holograph devices and they appeared as ordinary humans to the Lanndarians, a race of humans. Soon, they entered the digging sites.

Lanndarians worked on at least two dozen spots. Men dug in places in numbers. Hot temperatures made them sweat. Some men, overseers, directed the efforts of their fellow Lanndarians, barking commands. The labor was painstaking.

Sumerlin addressed an overseer. "Have much luck?"

The Lanndarian, Barryn, turned to the black magician. "Not much. We found a couple of minor treasures, though."

"What are their worth?" Sumerlin asked.

Barryn snorted. "Ancient artifacts that would bring a fair sum."

Sumerlin nodded. "Looking for anything in particular?"

"Yes," Barryn answered. "A large, strongbox filled with objects of great power. The Chest of Alefford."

Neither the black magician nor the other Archvillains ever heard of it before. Their knowledge of such things on Lanndar was minimal.

"Are you looking for something in particular yourselves?" Barryn asked the Archvillains.

Sumerlin smiled. "Yes. We seek Lordruingat, the Cube of Power. Have you ever heard of it?"

"I have," Barryn replied. "A sacred object of tremendous power that by some accounts is said to be guarded by spirits. It is rumored to be the special weapon of a divine king who was gifted with magic. There is a story that it is in the Chest of Alefford."

"What other objects of power are in it?" Sumerlin asked.

Barryn let out a deep breath. "One is the Sphere of Corabrey. It is said to capture souls and imprison them. Originally used by an evil practitioner of the black arts."

"Fascinating," Sumerlin remarked.

"Another is the Lamp of Caladdin," Barryn said. "With it, you could make wishes come true."

Sumerlin laughed. "Just how many objects of power does this Chest of Alefford contain?"

"It ranges between a half dozen to a dozen items," Barryn responded. "No one knows for sure."

Darlesse spoke up. "Are there riches buried at these sites? Not just objects of power?"

Barryn nodded. "The wealth of the Fomorian kings is said to be buried in huge chambers here. So far, we have not found the riches. But we are making progress though, slowly."

"Good," Daggermash muttered.

A Lanndarian worker brought another ancient artifact to the overseer. It was a vase, blue and white. Barryn looked it over.

"A major find?" Sumerlin asked the overseer.

"Perhaps," Barryn answered. "I date it back to the fifth Fomorian dynasty."

The Archvillains left the overseer and explored the digging sites. A few of the foul beings used their special powers on the area to see if they could pick up anything.

"I feel the presence of spirits here," Sumerlin said. "Hiding something."

"Yes," Tajanna agreed. "I sense power emanating from objects in spots."

They found a place to dig. Ripgarth fired a blue beam from his eye and blasted a hole in the sandy earth. The Cyclopean stopped when he revealed an antechamber underground.

"Something is down there," Daggermash remarked. "I detect it."

"What?" Foulbard asked.

Daggermash frowned. "I'm not certain exactly what it is."

Sunlight spilled into the antechamber. It shone on an empty space.

Xigan and Ripgarth tied ropes around their waists to anchor them. Foulbard and Gnashboros climbed down the ropes first. Sumerlin and Namina followed. The black magician lit a torch with red fire from his hand for more light.

They spied an opening to a main chamber and entered in single file.

In the center of the chamber rested a golden chest on a platform. Spirits guarded the large strongbox, supernatural beings in white. They appeared not friendly.

Gnashboros grinned. "The Chest of Alefford."

"How do we get passed the spirits?" Namina asked her fellow Archvillains.

Sumerlin stepped forward. "Leave that to me." He handed the torch to Foulbard.

Foulbard, Namina, and Gnashboros stepped back. The black magician moved closer to the strongbox. Spirits circled it. They growled at the Archvillain.

"Do you speak?" Sumerlin asked the spirits.

A male spirit did. "It is forbidden to take the Chest of Alefford from its resting place. Go now before you face your doom."

Sumerlin smiled. "I'm afraid we can't do that. We need to look in the Chest for something important."

"No," a female spirit said. "The Chest must not be opened."

"Why?" Sumerlin asked.

Another male spirit answered. "The magical objects within are too dangerous in mortal or immortal hands. They must never be wielded again."

"I see," Sumerlin said.

Another female spirit spoke. "Now leave this place."

Sumerlin breathed deeply. He spread his arms. In an instant, he made a red shield of occult fire.

The spirits seemed surprised by the action of the black magician. They attacked the Archvillain. His red shield of occult fire repelled them. The other three foul beings watched the fight, not aiding the black magician.

"*Scoresu spiritus nal chem erudis*!" Sumerlin intoned. He hammered the spirits with magical firepower. "*Fin hajah gruu minos dal nechee*!"

The spirits screamed. One by one, they disappeared until none remained. The black magician ceased his red fire of occult energy.

"Well done," Namina remarked.

"Where did they go?" Foulbard asked the black magician.

Sumerlin grinned. "I banished them."

The four Archvillains went to the Chest of Alefford. Sumerlin opened the Chest. Inside rested a bunch of objects. None resembled a cube.

"Wow," Gnashboros muttered. He picked up a crystal globe. "The Sphere of Corabrey."

"Indeed," Sumerlin said. "Tool of a sorcerer."

Namina grabbed the next magical object. "The

Lamp of Caladdin. I wonder if it would work, if it could bring Lordruingat to us."

"Try it," Foulbard said.

"All right," Namina responded. "How does this thing work?"

"Invoke it by speaking your wish," Sumerlin said.

Namina nodded. "Bring me Lordruingat, the Cube of Power."

The Lamp glowed in her hands. But nothing materialized.

"It appears it cannot grant that specific wish," Gnashboros remarked. "Lordruingat will not allow that to happen."

"It was worth a try," Foulbard stated.

Other objects lay in the Chest. Sumerlin picked up a silver bell from it. The black magician rang the bell and it sounded loud—very loud. It almost made the Archvillains cover their ears.

Foulbard retrieved a golden horn from the large strongbox. "What does this do?"

Sumerlin sensed the power from it. "I believe it calls on hordes of the dead to serve the blower of the horn."

Namina took a jeweled goblet from the Chest of Alefford. "What power does this have?"

Sumerlin closed his eyes and felt the drinking vessel. "It is the Cup of Immortality. It gives everlasting life."

Foulbard reached into the strongbox and pulled out a gold ring. The Shocker examined it. There were markings etched on it. "Wonder what this does."

"Put it on your finger and find out," Sumerlin said.

Foulbard shrugged. He slipped the gold ring on his right index finger. It made him disappear.

"A ring of invisibility," Sumerlin remarked.

Foulbard took off the ring and reappeared. "Fascinating."

"Should we leave the Chest here or take it with us?" Gnashboros asked the other three Archvillains.

"We will take it with us," Sumerlin said. They agreed with him.

They carried the strongbox from the main chamber to the antechamber. Foulbard tied a rope around the Chest of Alefford. Then Xigan and Ripgarth hauled it up to the surface. After that, Sumerlin, Foulbard, Gnashboros, and Namina climbed the ropes back to the top.

Landarrians, including Barryn, gathered around the Archvillains. There were gasps of astonishment among the Lanndarians.

"You found the Chest," Barryn remarked. "We can handle it from here."

Sumerlin shook his head. "Sorry. But we're taking it with us."

"You cannot," Barryn said. "It belongs to us."

Daggermash grinned. "Not anymore."

"Give us the Chest, and we will not harm you," Barryn responded.

The Archvillains deactivated their holographic devices and showed their true appearances. It caught the Lanndarians by surprise. The foul beings were outnumbered by the Lanndarians by at least a hundred to ten. The Lanndarians were armed with shovels and pickaxes.

"Take it from them," Barryn told his fellow Lanndarians.

The Lanndarians attacked the Archvillains, who

defended themselves. Ripgarth shot a blue beam from his eye and knocked out Lanndarians. Sumerlin blasted them with red fire from his hands and charred them. Darlesse leaped and stomped them to death. Foulbard sent shock waves against them and blew them apart. Namina sang a Siren song and drove them mad. Xigan smashed them with his fists. Tajanna and Amyrielle used blasters and killed them, while Daggermash and Gnashboros fired blast rifles at them and slayed them.

The Archvillains wiped out all the Lanndarians. Bodies littered the sandy earth.

"Fools," Gnashboros remarked. "Thought they could take us."

Some of the Archvillains laughed. The foul beings took the Chest of Alefford back to the ship. Once onboard, the *Slaughter* took off and left the planet.

Chapter 19

The Enforcer Quest gained two more Universal Marshals assigned to it by the High Enforcer. The Federation battlecruiser *Deliverer* teleported the pair from it to the *Horizon*.

The first Universal Marshal was Enforcer Milantheus, Father Time. The Incarnation of Time resembled an old man with long white hair and a long snowy beard with blue eyes. He wore a white robe and leather sandals. In his hand, he carried his hourglass of power.

The other Universal Marshal was Idyllion, the Nuclear Being. He stood over six feet with maroon eyes, maroon hair, and chiseled features. He wore a maroon unisuit with matching boots and belt.

The ten Enforcers met in the briefing room of the *Horizon*. Apparis sat before the control console on a long table.

"Vingrezza is a hostile world full of, and ruled by, gigantic monsters," Benethor remarked. "It seems unlikely that it would have Lordruingat hidden on it. Our first search of the planet yielded nothing."

The Universal Marshals tried using the ship's sensors to see what it could detect on Vingrezza. The effort resulted in finding no sentient beings on the planet or signs of civilization. No power sources either.

"Should we conduct a further search of the world?"

Yevadne asked her fellow Enforcers.

"No," Nazzar said. "I don't think it will do any good."

Benethor frowned. "Agreed."

"What planet do we go to next to look for the Cube of Power?" Kesharra voiced for them.

Benethor thought about that like the others. "Dellakor, the magicratic world."

"That planet would seem more suited to have Lordruingat than Vingrezza," Danbarrack stated.

"Yes," Benethor agreed. "Races of faerie are the dominant species on the world. Magic rules it."

"A place with magical objects certainly," Hulkeme added.

"And maybe Lordruingat," Apparis said.

The meeting adjourned. The *Horizon* set a course for Dellakor, located in the Scorpio Sector of the Milky Way Galaxy. Moments later, the ship engaged its teleport drive and telejumped to the quadrant. Then, it activated its cloaking mechanism. Soon, it orbited the planet, third from its yellow sun, about the size of Tellus. It ran on automated control.

The ten Universal Marshals went to the teleporter room and beamed down to the surface. They found themselves in a glade. Above them, wispy clouds floated in a blue sky. Bird cries reached them.

"Which way should we go?" Yevadne asked her fellow Enforcers.

Ursanne sensed in different directions. "I feel the presence of a village south of us."

"All right," Benethor said. "We shall head that way."

They traveled through forestland south. The tall

trees featured light brown bark, serrated. In a while, they emerged from the wooded area. They encountered animal life along the way, such as some deer with white tails and natural creatures that resembled wolverines.

To the west of them, they spied mists. They avoided the condensed vapor clouds. To the east ranged mountains. Ahead stretched open ground.

"Lovely scenery," Kesharra remarked.

Ursanne stiffened. The other Universal Marshals noticed it.

"What is it?" Danbarrack asked the Norn-Enforcer.

Ursanne sensed. "We have company coming from the mists. On foot."

"Do you feel they are hostile?" Nazzar asked.

Ursanne answered in a moment. "Yes."

"Defensive positions," Benethor said.

The Universal Marshals formed a defensive ring. From the mists emerged faerie beings that sported tusks, armed with spears, swords, and spiked clubs. They charged at the Enforcers, yelling a battle cry.

Benethor pulled the red Elfstone from his pouch on his belt. When the enemy was within range, the Elf-Enforcer blasted the attackers with the red Elfstone. Kesharra fired solar beams from her hands into them as Yevadne did with cyclone shots. Apparis flapped his wings at them in hurricane force and sent them flying. Idyllion let them have nuclear blasts from his body and knocked them over. Nazzar fired laser beams from his eyes and struck them.

The fight did not last long. The Universal Marshals routed the attackers and sent them into retreat back through the mists.

"Onward to the village," Benethor said.

The Enforcers resumed the journey. No more incidents occurred. Eventually, they arrived at the village, which consisted of stone huts. Its inhabitants consisted of faerie beings with yellow skin, dark hair, and pointy ears. The adults stood taller than Benethor. Children played in the village. Dogs ran around.

An elder came up to them. "I am Najoseth, leader of this clan. Who be you, strangers?"

"We are Universal Marshals from the Universal Federation of Planets," Benethor answered for them.

People in the village gathered around the Enforcers. The inhabitants were awestruck at the sight of them, curious about them.

"Why are you here?" Najoseth asked.

Apparis replied for them this time. "We seek an object of power."

"What object?" a female villager asked from the crowd around them.

Hulkeme answered the question. "Lordruingat, the Cube of Power. Do you know of it?"

Najoseth frowned. "I know of a number of magical objects that exist. But I do not know this Lordruingat by sight. Perhaps it goes by another name."

"Is there anyone else we could ask about it?" Benethor asked.

"Maybe the Wise Ones in a city might know of it," Najoseth responded. "They have greater knowledge of such matters."

The Universal Marshals talked among themselves for a bit. They came to an agreement.

"What is the closest city?" Apparis asked the elder.

"That would be Farlaw," Najoseth replied. "To the west. Three days journey from here."

"Thank you," Yevadne said.

Najoseth spoke with the other elders of the village. "Will you stay the night? We cannot offer much in hospitality."

The Universal Marshals discussed the offer among themselves. They all agreed.

"We would be delighted," Kesharra said.

The villagers treated the Enforcers as honored guests. A few of the villagers started a fire in the center of the place. Everyone gathered around it. They all ate a meal of some kind of fruit and soft bread, washed down with fresh water.

A village elder named Elysa told the first tale around the fire. Her story featured heroism by two of her kind—brothers—who slayed a terrible monster to save the village. Other elders told other tales, rousing stories of love, friendship, family, hardships, and miracles.

Villagers asked the Universal Marshals to tell tales of their own. Benethor entertained them with a yarn about Elves in a war against the first supreme evil the Universal Marshals fought. It spellbound the villagers. The Elf-Enforcer related another tale about magic and adventure, the birth of Elfstones. After he finished, Kesharra related a story of an adventure she experienced on Tellus, a gripping tale. Then Hulkeme spoke about him saving the lives of people on an airplane.

Villagers pressed the other Universal Marshals to tell stories. Nazzar talked of his last assignment, where he rescued hostages. Danbarrack related a tale of an arrest he made of a Villain. Ursanne spoke about her people, Norns, and what they did in the universe. Apparis gave an account of his creation. Milantheus told of his being an Incarnation and what it specifically entailed.

Yevadne related the tale of a battle she fought in on Tellus. And Idyllion mentioned a story of how he apprehended a bunch of Criminals who stole merchandise on the planet Harbold.

After a while, everyone retired for the night. The Universal Marshals slept in a large hut near the middle of the village. Nothing disturbed them.

In the morning, the Universal Marshals broke fast with the villagers. They asked questions of the Enforcers about the Federation. Dellakor was not a member of the Federation, and the villagers wondered how their world could join it. The first requirement for that was a planet must have a global government, which Dellakor did not have.

"Our world has many clans and individual cities," Najoseth said. "Politics differ region by region. Unfortunately, we are not a united world."

Benethor smiled. "Maybe one day you will be."

Najoseth nodded. "I have hope for that."

The Universal Marshals said their goodbyes to the villagers and went on their way. They crossed fertile plains. A brown and white rodent stopped digging and watched them pass, then resumed burrowing. In the sky, a flock of large blue birds flew overhead. They spotted a herd of bison-like creatures foraging on the open grounds north of them. A breeze from the south felt cool to them. The azure sky was cloudless.

"That village was quaint," Kesharra remarked.

"Yes," Benethor agreed. "Filled with good people."

The Universal Marshals traveled due west. A couple of miles later, they came upon a lake. They went around it. Halfway past it, bubbles appeared in the large body of water. They stopped at the sight of that.

"What is making them bubbles?" Idyllion asked no one in particular.

"Fish probably," Yevadne said.

The Enforcers got a closer look at the lake. The bubbles moved closer to them. Suddenly, tentacles rose from the large body of water and attacked them. The Universal Marshals defended themselves against the squid-like thing.

Nazzar fired laser beams from his eyes at the monster. Kesharra shot solar beams at the huge creature as Benethor used the red Elfstone against it. In time, they drove the squid-like thing back into the lake, and it submerged.

"This planet has dangers to be wary of," Benethor remarked.

"We must keep our eyes open," Apparis agreed.

Three miles later, the Universal Marshals arrived at a forest. They entered the wooded area and spread out. Bird cries reached their ears. It sounded like a cacophony. A black rabbit hopped into view ahead.

"Cute," Yevadne remarked.

Then, a white wolf pounced on the rabbit and killed it. The fierce animal carried the carcass in its jaws and ran away.

"Predator and prey," Apparis remarked.

The Universal Marshals traveled through the forest in two days. Before them stretched rolling plains now. They started across the open grounds. The sun shone in a partly cloudy sky above them.

A herd of black-tailed deer ran across their path ahead. In the sky flew a green-tailed hawk, which squawked. Little wind blew.

Eventually, they reached their destination. The city

of Farlaw spread out for miles in all directions. They entered it and walked a busy street with pedestrians going in and out of houses and tall buildings. Citizens watched them coming, curious about them.

"Where should we go in here?" Kesharra asked her fellow Enforcers.

"We need to speak with some of its people," Hulkeme stated.

Soon, they entered a market. Merchants sold a variety of goods, particularly magic items.

The Universal Marshals stopped before a vendor selling a bunch of different trinkets.

"Excuse me, sir," Benethor said, "where can we find the Wise Ones here?"

The vendor, a short and plump man, answered momentarily. "In the great palace, in the center of Farlaw. You are new to our city."

"Yes," Benethor responded. "Thank you."

Sellers hawked their wares on either side of the Universal Marshals in rows. The Enforcers continued on and passed through a residential district. Children played in the streets. Finally they came to the palace, a large structure.

"Impressive," Yevadne remarked.

The Universal Marshals walked up to the palace doors. Two men in uniforms guarded the entrance to the place. The Enforcers halted before them.

"Who are you and state your business," the taller guard said.

"We are Universal Marshals, and we wish to speak with the Wise Ones," Benethor replied for them.

The two guards talked between themselves.

"Wait here," the shorter guard said. He went inside

the palace. Ten minutes later, he returned. "Follow me."

The shorter guard led them inside. He led them through a vast hall to a huge chamber in the north wing of the palace. In the large room, at a table piled with scrolls, maps, and books stood a Wise One, a middle-aged man with a brown mustache dressed in a blue robe and black shoes. The huge chamber featured lavish furnishings.

"Guard, leave us," the Wise One ordered.

The man left. The Universal Marshals admired the palace.

"I have been expecting you," the Wise One said. "I am Garaland."

"How do you know we were coming?" Nazzar asked.

Garaland smiled. "I saw you in a vision. You come from another world."

"Yes," Danbarrack confirmed. He introduced himself and the other Enforcers.

"What do you seek?" Garaland asked.

Benethor answered the question. "Lordruingat, the Cube of Power."

"Ah," Garaland said. "You believe it is here on my world."

"Possibly," Apparis responded.

"We are questing for it," Benethor added.

Garaland nodded. "There are stories of such a magic object on Dellakor. Tales vary as to where it is. Some say it is in the Skanspear Mountains, guarded by the Latrojans. Others that it is the forests of Harrowing Deep watched by the Woodmen."

"Has anyone ever tried to find it?" Kesharra asked.

Garaland frowned. "Yes. But none have ever

succeeded in the search."

"We need to find it before the Archvillain organization called the Fellowship of Darkness does," Hulkeme said.

Garaland's eyes widened. "Evil ones."

"Yes," Benethor confirmed. He fingered his pouch of Elfstones.

"I have foreseen them as well," Garaland said. "Terrible foes with powers."

"Yes," Ursanne acknowledged for them.

Garaland paused. "Very well. I will help you in your quest. I will gather a party together and lead you to the places where your magic object might be. We will leave at first light tomorrow. Tonight, you will be my honored guests at the palace."

"Thank you," Benethor responded.

Garaland showed them to a large room to rest for the night in the south wing of the palace. In the evening the Universal Marshals joined Garaland in the dining hall of the palace. The chamber filled to capacity. Many sat at the long tables. Servers piled food and drink on the tables before everyone.

Garaland stood up and raised a glass of blue wine. "May I have your attention? Tonight, we have honored guests to feast with us from a land far away. Let us toast to their good health and prosperity."

"Here, here!"

Everybody, including the Universal Marshals, raised their glasses and drank the sweet beverage. The main course for the evening meal was roasted pig with brown bread, black rice, buttered onions and turnips, and apple cobbler. Laughter and conversation echoed in the dining hall.

Diners at the tables asked questions of the Universal Marshals. The Enforcers answered them amiably. Servers brought forth dessert in the form of cake pieces, chocolate with vanilla frosting. Some diners ate white melon slices.

Four hours later, the Universal Marshals retired for the night. The rest of the diners left the dining hall and exited the palace on their way home. A few retired to bed chambers in the palace.

In the morning, Garaland fetched the Universal Marshals. He led them outside the palace where riders waited. Steeds were given to the Enforcers. Only Hulkeme declined a mount and would walk distances. Pack horses carried supplies.

"Onward!" Garaland said.

The Wise One rode in front with the Universal Marshals. People of Farlaw watched them go, and some in the crowd cheered them. It was like a parade.

"Where are we destined for first?" Benethor asked the Wise One.

"To the forests of Harrowing Deep," Garaland replied.

The party left the city and traveled south. Good weather accompanied them.

"How far to Harrowing Deep?" Benethor asked the Wise One.

"Five days," Garaland replied.

Before them rolled fertile plains. They spotted ground rodents burrowing in the earth west of them. The small animals watched them go by and showed no fear of the party.

"What about these Woodmen?" Ursanne asked the Wise One.

"They are said to guard the forests of the world," Garaland answered. "Not to let anyone harm the trees by fire or axe. If anyone tried to harm the woods, the Woodmen would strike back and bring doom to the offenders."

Yevadne voiced a question. "Do the Woodmen have a leader?"

Garaland nodded. "The Woodmen are led by the Forester. No one knows his name. It is said you can hear him sing in forests."

Ahead of them rose a range of grassy hills. Soon, they climbed the gentle slopes. A soft breeze blew from the east.

On the first night, they camped on the hills. In the evening sky stars shined along with a silvery moon. They rested in peaceful surroundings. They ate supper.

"There appears to be no war on your world at the present time," Milantheus remarked to the Wise One. Father Time held his hourglass of power in one hand and shook it.

"It has been a generation since we had one," Garaland said. "It ended with the destruction of a dark lord named Mordwrath."

Benethor addressed the Wise One. "Do you Wise Ones ever gather in council?"

"Every year, we hold the Great Meeting in a different city each time," Garland responded. "We speak of many things. This year, we will meet in Farlaw in three months."

The next morning, they ate a small breakfast before they took off. A cloudier sky greeted them. They traveled at a steady pace.

"What is your world like?" Garaland asked the

Universal Marshals.

Nazzar explained it to the Wise One. His fellow Enforcers interjected comments in his narrative at points about Tellus, a planet very different from Dellakor.

"Could my world join your Federation?" Garaland asked.

"It is possible," Nazzar replied. "But the first requirement is your planet must have a global government, which at this time it doesn't have."

Garaland frowned. "Unfortunately, true. Maybe in the future, we might."

The second day of their journey was also uneventful. That night, they made camp again on the grassy hills. In the evening sky, a shooting star streaked across the heavens.

"A good sign," Garaland remarked.

The next morning, they ate a quick meal and then resumed their journey. A cloudless sky greeted them this time. The weather felt much warmer.

In the afternoon, they left the grassy hills and ventured through wilderness terrain. Stands of trees appeared here and there. A stream meandered north. Bare mounds sparsely dotted the landscape. Birds sang in trees. Insects buzzed. It looked as if nature came alive.

"Does this area have a name?" Benethor asked the Wise One.

"No," Garaland responded. "Travelers are known to go through it occasionally."

The party made camp again. They got drinking water from the stream after the Wise One pronounced it safe to drink. They ate a light supper.

The Universal Marshals asked questions of Garaland about the Wise Ones, who lived in cities around Dellakor. To the Enforcers they sounded like part mage, part scholar, all wisdom figures. They ruled their world but not as a global government. Elders led villages, Wise Ones to a minor degree.

In the morning, after breakfast, they started out again. The temperature felt a little cooler. They trekked through the wilderness terrain carefully, exploring the natural environment. A red moose ran across their path. On a tall tree to their right, a yellow squirrel climbed.

"How far does these wilds extend?" Kesharra asked the Wise One.

"All the way to Harrowing Deep," Garaland answered.

Apparis voiced a question. "Are there any villages near here?"

"No," Garaland replied. "This wilderness is uninhabited."

The party camped another night in the wilderness terrain. So far, the journey had been pleasant. No dangers arose to threaten them. But they knew the real test would be in Harrowing Deep.

The next morning, after they ate breakfast, it started to rain, a light drizzle. Some of the riders grumbled. The downpour lasted into late afternoon. Then, the sun broke through the clouds.

Ultimately, they reached their destination. Forests of Harrowing Deep spread out before them. It seemed peaceful at the edge.

"We shall camp here for the night," Garaland said. "We will enter Harrowing Deep in the morning. Best not to chance it in the dark. Light no fires."

The party ate supper in silence. No sound emanated from Harrowing Deep. It was as if the forests were asleep.

Apparis kept a watch. The Roc felt no need for sleep. Later, Benethor joined him.

"I dislike this quiet from the forests," Benethor said.

Apparis agreed. "We know not what dangers we will face in there."

"I could use the blue Elfstone in my pouch to seek what we are searching for in Harrowing Deep," Benethor stated. "But I fear its magical power would be detected by the denizens in the forests."

Apparis nodded. "Maybe you should use it as a last resort."

Benethor shrugged. "Aye. There is a small chance that Harrowing Deep will willingly yield Lordruingat if the Cube of Power is in there in truth."

"I anticipate a fight over it if it is in there," Apparis said.

Benethor concurred. "Maybe we could make a deal for it if it is in there."

"That, to me, is a longshot at best."

"Any way you look at it, it is going to be difficult to get it."

The night passed without incident. In the morning, they ate breakfast. They took their time to prepare to enter Harrowing Deep. The weather stayed good.

"All right," Garaland said, "let's move out."

The party started the trek into Harrowing Deep. They heard the screech of a bird ahead, the only sound other than the footfalls of the horses. Nothing else stirred at the moment.

Trees towered over them as they went through the forests. Timbers of dark brown bark with large canopies. The firm ground seemed to be rich earth.

Benethor grabbed the red Elfstone from his pouch and used it to detect danger. The magic rock did not glow to indicate any liability or exposure to harm or death. "So far, no threats from anything."

"No trouble?" Apparis said. "That is a good sign."

The party continued on without incident. Soon, they reached knolls with trees spread out. Patches of grass covered the small hills.

"It seems so quiet now," Yevadne remarked.

"I sense a presence in Harrowing Deep," Ursanne said.

That alarmed the party. They halted at the order of the Wise One.

"Is the presence you feel benevolent or malevolent?" Danbarrack asked the Norn-Enforcer.

Ursanne closed her eyes and reached out with her feelings. "Neutral at the moment."

"We must be careful then," Garaland said. "Onward."

The party resumed the journey. A few insects droned. A flock of white birds squawked ahead of them on the ground, and at the sight of the party, took off. Next, they encountered an orange bear, not too large, that ran off before they got too close to it.

"I sense the presence getting nearer," Ursanne stated.

"Be on your guard," Garaland warned.

The red Elfstone glowed in Benethor's hand. Suddenly, Woodmen surrounded the party, which stopped. Riders armed themselves.

"Don't make any sudden moves," Nazzar advised. "We don't want to provoke them."

The Woodmen did not attack the party; they just

stood there as if waiting for someone or something to show up. They also seemed to be sizing up the party.

"A presence is approaching us," Ursanne said.

A tall figure emerged from the trees, carrying a crook. A male figure with white hair and a snowy beard in a green robe stopped in front of Woodmen. He addressed the party.

"I am Madrik the Forester. You have intruded in Harrowing Deep. Go and return whence you came. No harm will befall you if you leave now."

"We cannot leave yet," Garaland responded for them. "We search for an object of power."

Madrik snorted, and his white eyes widened. "What is it you seek?"

"It is called Lordruingat, the Cube of Power," Benethor replied for them.

Madrik shook his head. "There is no object as such in these forests. The only power alive in Harrowing Deep is mine."

Ursanne reached out with her feelings through Harrowing Deep. "I do not sense any object of power in the forests. Only the presence of the Forester and the Woodmen."

"Have you ever heard of Lordruingat?" Benethor asked the Forester.

Madrik paused. "I have heard of the Cube of Power. But you are looking for it on the wrong world."

Ursanne suddenly sensed something else. "There is something you're not telling us."

Madrik turned to the Norn-Enforcer. "You may be envisioning life energy emanating from acorns in birth pods."

Ursanne seemed unsure about that. "Lordruingat

could be hidden from your sight in Harrowing Deep."

"No," Madrik responded vehemently. "I know these forests one end to another in all directions. Nothing escapes me in Harrowing Deep."

Hulkeme spoke up. "Let me try." The Genie-Enforcer used his special powers and tried to find the Cube of Power in the forests and teleport it to them. No success.

Madrik's nostrils flared. "Return to your place of origin. There is nothing for you here."

"Is he lying?" Danbarrack whispered to the Norn-Enforcer.

Ursanne sensed the truth. "Not that I can tell."

The Wise One, some of his men, and the Universal Marshals talked among themselves on what to do. They reached an agreement shortly.

"We would like to explore Harrowing Deep more," Garaland said.

Madrik shook his head. "You may not. It is forbidden."

"Give us leave to, and we won't harm any of the trees and animals in the forests," Garaland countered.

Madrik stomped his foot. The Forester raised his crook. "Woodmen, attack!"

The party defended itself. Garaland threw exploding powder from a bag on his saddle and blew up Woodmen. His men fought with swords or battle-axes.

Benethor blasted Woodmen with the red Elfstone. Kesharra fired solar beams from her hands and devastated them. Yevadne blew them apart with cyclone winds. Apparis shot sonic blasts from his beak to score on them. Nazzar damaged them with laser rays from his eyes.

Idyllion sent nuclear blasts from his body and shredded them. Hulkeme tore them limb from limb. Danbarrack stretched and tangled them up. Ursanne used her special powers and blinded them. Milantheus froze them in time with the help of his hourglass of power.

The battle lasted awhile. In the end, the Woodmen retreated. Madrik disappeared.

"How far should we search through Harrowing Deep?" Garaland asked the Enforcers.

Benethor answered the question. "Not too long." The other Universal Marshals agreed with him.

The party searched through the forests in rapid fashion. They wanted to get it done quickly. They feared another assault from the Forester and the Woodmen. None manifested.

The party took another two days to look through Harrowing Deep. Their search turned up nothing. So they changed direction and headed north for the Skanspear Mountains. They left the forests behind and traversed rolling plains under sunny skies.

"Tell us about the Latrojans," Yevadne asked the Wise One.

Garaland took a deep breath. "It is said they are a fierce people. They hunt in the mountains abundant with mountain sheep and other animals. Stories have them not wandering from the heights to visit other lands."

"Do people from other lands ever visit them in the range?" Kesharra asked.

Garaland tilted his head toward the Solar Being. "There are a few tales as such."

"Have Wise Ones ever ventured into the mountains to speak with them?" Benethor asked.

Garaland appeared to think about that. "Yes. I

personally have never done so. The Wise One Maratell is said to have spoken with them at length."

It took them three days to reach the Skanspear Mountains. They made camp below the rocky heights for the night. The atmosphere in the party was better than their time in Harrowing Deep. They ate supper in a cheerful mood.

"Do the Latrojans have Wise Ones of their own?" Yevadne asked the Wise One.

"They have practitioners of magic, it is said," Garaland replied. "It is unknown how good they are. I believe they could match Wise Ones in cities. It is also said they have an oral tradition and not a written one."

The next morning, after breakfast, they started the climb up the Skanspear Mountains. Rugged terrain greeted them. The peaks of the alpine region towered over them like rock sentinels watching them.

The party entered a mountain pass. Ahead, they encountered a flock of mountain sheep. The grass-eating animals featured thick, fleecy coats of white. Rams of the herd sported big curved horns. The herbivorous creatures moved out of their way to let them pass.

"Are there any predators in these mountains?" Apparis asked the Wise One.

"Yes," Garaland responded. "Mountain cats and rock bears. Both very dangerous. There may be other ones as well."

The party later came upon a tarn. They took a break and refilled waterskins from the small mountain lake. Afterward, they resumed their journey, and a few miles later, reached a canyon. The deep valley with steep sides made some of the riders feel uncomfortable.

"I sense no danger here," Ursanne said.

Benethor pulled out his red Elfstone from his pouch. It did not glow, indicating no danger either. He put the magic rock back in the small bag. "All clear."

The canyon wound through the mountains like a snake through grass. They began walking down the deep valley with steep sides and kept alert for anything. For the moment, the weather felt cool. No animals appeared in sight.

The party took a while to cross the canyon. It seemed quiet. Nothing disturbed them so far.

"The Latrojans will speak with us frankly," Garaland said. "They will talk truthfully with us. They are an honest people."

The trip through the canyon ended with the ground rising now. They went through another mountain pass. It led them to a glen, and they crossed the narrow valley into mountain forests. Still no signs of danger.

The party camped the night on the northern edge of the timberland. They heard a mountain owl hooting, hidden in the trees. No sound of insects or other animals reached them at the moment. The Roc and the Elf-Enforcer kept watch.

"This reminds me of my homeworld a bit," Benethor said.

Apparis folded his wings against his body. "My memory extends far back to the facilities where I was created. Partly in ruin when I awoke from my long slumber."

The Elf-Enforcer stiffened. His sharp hearing picked up noise from a distance.

"What is it?" Apparis asked.

Benethor moved his head in the direction east. He pulled the red Elfstone from his pouch. "Something is coming."

The two Universal Marshals woke up the camp. They explained the situation to the other Enforcers and the rest of the party.

"Can you identify what is coming our way?" Garaland asked the Elf-Enforcer.

"Not exactly," Benethor answered. "Whatever it is, it is big."

The party waited for the coming lifeform. Out of the dark sprang a rock bear, over eighteen feet high, with dark brown fur. It roared as it attacked them. The huge carnivore sent two men flying with swipes from its large paws.

"Get back!" Nazzar said to the men fighting the ursine creature. They obeyed him.

The Universal Marshals defended the party. Kesharra shot solar beams from her hands, Nazzar laser beams from his eyes, and Benethor blasted from the red Elfstone at the rock bear. Their combined attacks kept the huge carnivore at bay.

Apparis sent sonic blasts from his beak at the ursine creature. The strikes added firepower to what had already hit the rock bear and knocked it over. Finally, the overwhelming shots from the Universal Marshals killed the huge carnivore.

"It is a shame we had to slay the beast," Benethor said. He put the magic rock back in the small bag.

"It was either us or the rock bear," Garaland stated. "It attacked us out of instincts."

Benethor frowned. "We invaded its territory."

Nothing more was said about the rock bear. In the morning, they ate a quick breakfast and continued on their way. They left the carcass of the huge carnivore to rot or be eaten by scavengers.

"Where are the Latrojans said to live in these mountains?" Danbarrack asked the Wise One.

"Stories tell us they reside deep in the heights," Garaland replied. "There are tales of a mountain in the shape of a skull that is a gathering place for them."

The party left the forests and traveled on uneven terrain open and grassy. Four miles later they spotted another tarn west of them. At the small mountain lake a huge feline, gray with yellow spots, drank from it.

"Mountain cat," Garaland remarked.

"Will it charge us?" Yevadne asked.

Garland paused. "I don't think so. But if it is hungry, it might."

The mountain cat looked in their direction. It chose not to attack them and bounded away around the tarn.

"Guess it wasn't hungry," Yevadne remarked.

Seven miles later the party stopped. Before them rose the mountain in the shape of a skull.

"What do we do now?" Danbarrack asked the Wise One. "Should we enter that place or what?"

"No," Garaland answered. "The Latrojans will find us. We will wait here for them."

Less than an hour later the Latrojans emerged from the skull mountain. They approached the party and halted twenty feet from the party. Dark-skinned and dressed in furs, the Latrojans bore spears.

One of the Latrojans stepped forward and spoke. "I am Wututu, chief of the Latrojans. Who are you and why do you come to us?"

Garaland did the talking for the party. "We are searchers looking for an object of power."

"What great magic do you seek?" Wututu asked.

"Lordruingat, the Cube of Power," Garaland answered.

Wututu conferred with some of his fellow Latrojans. "That which you seek is not among us. You must look elsewhere for it beyond these mountains."

Garaland frowned. "Do you have any idea where we should look?"

"No," Wututu replied. "The great magic you seek is not in our lore."

Garaland spoke with the Universal Marshals. "We thank you for talking with us. We will be on our way."

"Go in peace then," Wututu responded. He touched his chest.

The party left the area and turned east. Eventually, they descended from the Skanspear Mountains and entered the jungle. They camped for the night.

The Universal Marshals talked among themselves. The rest of the party slept.

"What planet do we search for Lordruingat next?" Kesharra asked the Android-Enforcer.

"Natyrek," Nazzar replied. "The machine world."

The search for the Cube of Power on Dellakor yielded nothing. A great disappointment to the Enforcer Quest. Finished on the magicratic world, Hulkeme teleported up the Universal Marshals to the *Horizon*. The ship engaged the teleport drive and telejumped from the Scorpio Sector of the Milky Way Galaxy to the Canubus Sector of the Milky Way Galaxy.

Chapter 20

Delveran prepared to interview three new recruits
for the Universal Marshals. He went to the training room
in the Justiceplex on its short stem at its north end. The
candidates for the positions of Enforcers waited for the
High Enforcer there.

The first recruit to be hired for the Universal
Marshals was Nazerock, to be known as the Gnome-
Enforcer. The earth elemental stood four feet tall with
brown eyes and a dark beard, dressed in a beige outfit
and matching boots. His special powers resided on the
occultic level of energy power, able to control the
movements of the earth.

The second recruit to be hired for the Universal
Marshals was Faragorn, known as the Cosmic Ranger.
He stood over six feet tall with black hair and hazel eyes,
dressed in brown—tunic, trousers, belt, and boots. He
carried a special weapon with him, a sword of power
named Thothbreaker.

The third and final recruit to be hired for the
Universal Marshals was Lorraym, known as the
Siroccon. She stood four inches under six feet with long
auburn hair, green eyes, and a beautiful body, dressed in
a tawny tunic and matching slippers. Her special powers
resided on the scientific level.

"So far, you have passed the tests for becoming
Universal Marshals," Delveran said. "You are to be

applauded. Now I need to ask you some questions. How much have you each fought evil in the universe?"

Faragorn answered first. "On my homeworld of Terraconia, my people waged war against a dark lord named Malemarnack and his evil forces. We defeated the foul being and his vile minions after a long campaign."

Delveran let out a deep breath. "Did you slay Malemarnack?"

"Yes, with Thothbreaker," Faragorn replied, patting his sword of power in its golden scabbard. "The deed was done in his black fortress."

"Have you lost anyone close to you to evil?" Delveran asked.

Faragorn nodded. "Fellow rangers. Brave men who gave their lives to preserve good."

Delveran addressed the Gnome-Enforcer next. "What evil have you fought?"

"Terrible creatures of the night on different worlds," Nazerock answered. "I have traveled the galaxy doing good where I could."

"Did you ever band with others to take evil out?" Delveran asked.

"At times, mostly with other faerie folk," Nazerock replied. "Elves, Dwarves, and others as such. I also teamed up with fellow elementals to stop evil."

Delveran turned to the Siroccon. "What evil have you fought?"

"Invaders to my homeworld of Hugaea," Lorrraym responded. "The people where I come from are a simple people. We welcome strangers if they are friendly toward us."

"You have lost people close to you against evil," Delveran stated.

Lorraym grimaced. "Yes. Especially those who were very dear to me."

Delveran remembered that Terraconia and Hugaea were members of the Federation, the former for six years now, the latter for three years now. The homeworld of the Gnome-Enforcer, Ringgor, was not a member of the Federation—yet—a native planet with faerie beings as the dominant species.

Delveran asked the three recruits about their family history. Faragorn told the High Enforcer about some of his relatives serving as rangers—his uncle and father in particular. Lorraym mentioned especially about her mother and grandmother, who were medicine women. Nazerock had no family by blood—given the fact that he was an elemental—but there were other Gnomes in the universe.

"Now you need to prove yourselves in the training room," Delveran said. "You will engage holographic foes in combat to test your mettle."

"Do we go one at a time?" Lorraym asked.

"No," Delveran responded. "You will fight together as a unit. You will be tested for single engagements as well as teamwork."

The High Enforcer went to the control booth of the training room. He sat in a swivel chair. He touched a button and spoke on the intercom to the training room. "Are you ready?"

"Yes," Faragorn answered.

"Set," Lorraym replied.

"Go ahead," Nazerock said.

The holograph of a jungle appeared in the training room. Sounds of birds could be heard. The three recruits stood in open space and readied themselves to fight in the daytime.

In the jungle, beastly beings yelled and charged them, armed with battle-axes. Faragorn pulled Tothbreaker from its sheath and met one foe head-on. The Cosmic Ranger dodged a blow and slashed with his sword of power at the gut of his opponent and opened him up. Fast, he cut the head off of the beastly being and killed him. Then, he clashed with his next armed assailant and dispatched him quickly.

Lorraym shot heat rays from her hands and blasted a beastly being. Her foe flew from her against a tree and got impaled on a limb. She spun around to face her next opponent. Flying in the air, she flew circles around him at great speed and made him dizzy. The Siroccon then rammed into him and sent him crashing into another tree, unconscious.

A beastly being bore down on Nazerock. The Gnome-Enforcer turned into smoke, and his foe went right through him. He rematerialized, shook the ground under his larger opponent, and sank his assailant into the earth. Another beastly being roared and charged Nazerock. The Gnome-Enforcer used his special powers and lifted his foe in the air, then brought his assailant down hard and snuffed the life from him.

"Form a circle with our backs to each other!" Faragorn said.

The three recruits made a defensive ring. More beastly beings charged them. The Cosmic Ranger parried a strike by an attacker, then sliced his leg off. He moved in and finished him off. Lorraym made a heat ball and blasted it through the chest of another opponent. Nazerock opened the earth beneath two of the enemy who fell to their deaths.

The trio disposed of every beastly being that came at them. Finally, the training exercise was over. The holographic scene vanished. Delveran left the control booth. The High Enforcer clapped his hands.

Faragorn sheathed his sword of power. "How did we do, High Enforcer?"

Delveran smiled. "You did very well. Both as individuals and as a team. I welcome you as new Universal Marshals."

"Are we going to get our first assignments now as Enforcers?" Lorraym asked.

"When something comes in, you will get your orders," Delveran said. "Right now, you can relax. You have been assigned individual quarters in the Justiceplex."

The High Enforcer gave them each a set of antipower handcuffs. They each went to their private chamber in the Justiceplex. Delveran walked into the computer room of the headquarters of the Universal Marshals to get updates from Nanomach about the Enforcer Quest and the search for space pirates.

The computer room was a square chamber on the same side of the corridor as his office, near the back section of the Justiceplex. Glowpanels in the high ceiling autoactivated as soon as he stepped into it, casting bright light. A lone computer stood in the middle of the chamber. Control consoles ringed the lone computer with swivel chairs before them, their seats padded with black synthon, their shiny frames of golden omnimetal.

Delveran sat at one of the control consoles. "How is the Enforcer Quest faring?"

"So far, they have searched the planets Vingrezza and Dellakor for Lordruingat," Nanomach answered.

"Neither world has the Cube of Power on it. They are now searching the planet Natyrek for it."

"What information do you have on Natyrek?"

"Accessing," Nanomach responded. "It is an automated world ruled by machines. Not a member of the Federation. No living beings inhabit it at present."

Delveran leaned back in the swivel chair. "Any records of evil on the planet?"

"No. Data on Criminals, Villains, or Archvillains are nonexistent concerning it."

"What about its makers?"

"Working." Nanomach paused. "Those who built the machines on Natyrek apparently abandoned the planet."

"Could the machines have risen against its makers and exterminated them?"

"Possible. It is a mystery as to what actually happened to them."

Delveran let out a deep breath. "Next item. What is the report of the Universal Marshals assigned to find the space pirates?"

Nanomach whirred. "The Enforcers on the assignment to find them found a pirated ship with no survivors. They visited the planet Taratheon and gathered a little information on pirates. Now they are going to the pirate world Amaekar."

Delveran spoke with Nanomach further about other Universal Marshals on different assignments. No arrests had been made about Archvillains. The High Enforcer wondered if the Fellowship of Darkness found a planet for a new base. He was also concerned about how many Archvillains the Archvillain organization had recruited now.

Chapter 21

The Universal Marshals beamed down to Natyrek. They found themselves teleported inside an automated factory. Robots worked in the place, going here and there. None of the droids paid them any attention. Yet.

"What are they making?" Yevadne asked the Android-Enforcer.

"Other automatons," Nazzar replied.

"What for?" Danbarrack asked.

Nazzar computed an answer. "It looks like they are building an army."

"It seems as if they plan to invade some world," Ursanne said.

"The question is which one," Hulkeme added.

The Universal Marshals watched machines build robots. It happened on an assembly line.

"I sense no living presence here," Ursanne remarked. "Only machines."

"What could have happened to their makers?" Yevadne asked the Android-Enforcer.

Nazzar shrugged. "There are several possible scenarios about that. Their makers could have abandoned them. The machines could have risen up against their makers and terminated them. Invaders off-world could have wiped out their makers. A plague could have killed their makers. It is a big mystery as to what happened to their makers."

The Universal Marshals explored the automated factory. Robots went about their business, apparently unconcerned about the visitors among them, programmed to build their forces.

"They are efficient in their work," Nazzar remarked.

The Universals Marshals walked the floor of the manufacturing facility and admired the precision in which robots were built. Production lines continued nonstop and worked around the clock.

The Universal Marshals halted when a silver robot came up to them and addressed them. "What are you doing here, sentient beings?"

"We are looking for something," Nazzar said.

The robot beeped. "What is it you are looking for?"

"Lordruingat, the Cube of Power," Kesharra replied.

The robot beeped again. "That does not compute. There are no objects of power on our planet. Just machines."

"Lordruingat may be hidden from you on your world," Benethor countered.

"That is not logical," the robot responded. "You should leave. This place is not for sentient beings."

"I think we will search your planet for Lordruingat," Nazzar said.

The robot turned to the Android-Enforcer. "You are a machine, like us. Why are you with sentient beings? You should not be with them."

"I have my orders," Nazzar responded.

"Whose orders?" the robot asked.

"From the High Enforcer," Nazzar replied.

The robot seemed perplexed. "What planet are you from?"

"Tellus," Nazzar answered. "Capital of the

Universal Federation of Planets."

The robot shook his head. In a moment, he sent out a signal. "If you will not leave, then we will take you prisoner."

A bunch of robots marched toward them, armed with blast rifles. The Universal Marshals took stances to defend themselves.

"Do not resist," the robot warned them. "You will be taken to cells."

"I don't think so," Danbarrack said.

Kesharra shot solar beams from her hands at the droids before they could use their weapons. Benethor pulled his red Elfstone from its pouch and fired at the robots, blasting them apart. Yevadne let loose cyclone winds and scattered the automatons. Apparis opened his mouth, and sonic blasts shredded the walking machines. Nazzar fired laser beams from his eyes and dismantled droids. Idyllion exploded nuclear blasts from his body and annihilated robots. Hulkeme used his special powers and lifted automatons in the air to crash them on the floor to pieces. Milantheus froze walking machines in time. Ursanne used her special powers and tore droids to pieces. Danbarrack stretched, grabbed two robots, and smashed them together.

More droids armed with blast rifles flooded the area. The Universal Marshals decimated their numbers. Their robot attackers came in waves as if endless. The automatons fired their blast rifles at the Enforcers, and their laser shots got deflected by Hulkeme and frozen in time by Milantheus.

The robot who had spoken to them beeped repeatedly. "Surrender peacefully, and we will not harm you!"

The Universal Marshals did not surrender. They kept wiping out droids one after another. The Enforcers fought long and hard, outnumbered by the automatons.

"Aim for the assembly lines and shut them down!" Nazzar shouted.

Milantheus used his special powers of time and stopped the production of robots. Nazzar, Benethor, Kesharra, and Idyllion fired at the assembly lines and destroyed them with their individual weapons: laser beams, red Elfstone, solar rays, and nuclear blasts.

The robot speaker threw up his arms. "No!"

Finally, the waves of armed droids ceased. Mechanical parts littered the floor.

"Now you surrender to us," Nazzar told the robot speaker. "What are you called?"

"NRJ7."

"Do you surrender?" Ursanne asked.

NRJ7 seemed dejected. "We yield to you."

"Good," Apparis said. "Now then. Have you ever heard of Lordruingat?"

"Yes," NRJ7 admitted. "A weapon of great power, it is told. It is written that our makers created the Cube of Power to put in an ultimate droid. But no robot has ever seen such a device. It may be stored somewhere on our planet. Records of it are scarce."

"Our sources indicate it may be on your world," Ursanne said. "We researched it and came up with a number of possibilities of where to find it."

"Why do you wish to find it?" NRJ7 asked.

Danbarrack answered the question. "Because the Archvillain organization, the Fellowship of Darkness, is looking for it. They must not get their hands on it. If they do, they could use it against the Federation."

"When was the last time living creatures visited your world?" Benethor asked.

NRJ7 computed a response. "It has been centuries since sentient beings came here. There are records of that. Our planet is an isolated world."

"Have you ever been visited by Archvillains?" Apparis asked.

NRJ7 seemed confused by the question. "What are Archvillains?"

"Foul beings with special powers like us," Kesharra replied.

NRJ7 beeped a few times. "There are records of such individuals having visited us long ago. But not recently."

"The Fellowship of Darkness may not be aware of your world," Benethor stated.

"Logical," NRJ7 agreed. "We know of the existence of other planets in the galaxy populated by sentient beings. We do not know of any planets in the Milky Way like ours. Do you know of other worlds like ours in the galaxy?"

Nazzar accessed the information internally. "None in my files. But droids do exist elsewhere in the galaxy."

NRJ7 seemed disappointed by that. "Follow me. I will show you where are storehouses are. Maybe the Cube of Power is in one of them."

The Universal Marshals followed NRJ7 to the storehouses. The first one held robots like small tanks, not activated. The second one kept parts for walking robots. The third one stored components for computers.

"How many storehouses do you have?" Kesharra asked the droid.

"On the entire planet, over three hundred," NRJ7

replied.

"That is a lot," Danbarrack remarked.

The fourth storehouse they checked held a cube, metallic and orange. It rested on a stand in the middle of the place.

"It can't be that easy," Yevadne said.

NRJ7 touched the cube. "Behold the ur-spark."

Ursanne sensed the object before them. "I feel the power of this cube. But not on a supernatural level. Neither occultic or celestic or another."

"A scientific one, then," Nazzar said.

"What is the purpose of the ur-spark?" Apparis asked the droid.

NRJ7 paused for a moment. "The cube is put in the chest cavity of a superior battle robot and gives the machine unlimited power. It is said to make the droid invincible."

"Has it been used by any robot on your world?" Benethor asked the droid.

"No," NRJ7 answered.

"So it has never been tested," Nazzar said.

"Correct," NRJ7 responded.

"Could there be more than one cube on your planet?" Ursanne asked.

"It is possible," NRJ7 replied. "But I don't know of any other one besides the ur-spark."

The ur-spark did not operate. NRJ7 tried to make it work but failed. With permission from the droid, Nazzar attempted to ignite the cube but was unsuccessful.

Benethor pulled a yellow Elfstone from his pouch. "Let me see if this will work."

The Elf-Enforcer shot a golden beam from the yellow Elfstone into the ur-spark. At first nothing happened. Then the magic rock lighted it up. But the effect lasted a short time.

"At least we know it responds to power," Nazzar remarked.

Hulkeme used his special powers to find Lordruingat on the planet. No luck.

The search through the storehouses on Natyrek took a week. They did not find another cube. Instead, they found only things that pertained to machines not of the ur-spark, like spare parts for robots and various droids such as protocol ones.

Finished on Natyrek, Hulkeme teleported them up to the *Horizon*. Next they would search the planet of Targaris. The ship engaged its teleport drive and telejumped from the Canubis Sector of the Milky Way Galaxy to the Taurus Sector of the Milky Way Galaxy.

Chapter 22

The *Slaughter* arrived in the Thorrean Sector of the Milky Way Galaxy. The ship approached the planet Verkemia, a feudal world. It engaged its cloaking mechanism and entered the atmosphere of the biosphere. Verkemia was not a member of the Federation and orbited a yellow star as its fourth planet.

The vessel flew for the surface of the feudal world. Verkemia possessed five continents. The dominant species on it was a human race. There was no global government on it.

The *Slaughter* landed in a glade of a forest some distance from the nearest civilization. The Archvillains gathered in the meeting room of the ship. Sumerlin sat at the control console of the long table.

"What is known of this world?" Xigan asked his fellow Archvillains.

Ripgarth answered the question. "On a scientific level, it is primitive. On the occultic level, it is progressive. On the celestic level, it is poor."

"What else?" Darlesse voiced.

"The Verkemians have no mechanical transports," Ripgarth replied. "They ride beasts."

"What of their technology?" Daggermash asked.

"Their technology rates low compared to modernized ones," Ripgarth replied. "Their weapons are not of a photonic nature. They wield swords, spears, lances, battle-axes, war hammers, and so on. They are medieval."

"But they do have occult practitioners in their midst," Sumerlin said.

"Are they as powerful as you?" Tajanna asked.

Sumerlin smiled. "They may have masters of magic like me. We will find out when we explore this world."

"What is the closest habitation to us?" Gnashboros asked.

Sumerlin checked by manipulating the control console before him. "Several days from our present position, east."

The meeting adjourned. They left the ship without blasters and blast rifles. The black magician figured they would not need such arms. His fellow Archvillains agreed with him.

They entered timberland and walked through the trees. They heard birdsong. The air felt warm. They carried holographic devices with them to disguise their true appearances.

At night, they camped in the forest. Night sounds varied from hoots and squawks to howls and roars. The noises did not bother them. Nothing could really threaten them as far as they knew.

Sumerlin sensed the feudal world. He could not feel Lordruingat on the planet. Not surprising. The black magician closed his eyes and dozed off.

The Archvillains got up at dawn. Shortly, they headed east again. Thus far, they'd faced no danger.

The Archvillains stopped when they spotted riders coming toward them. Knights in shining armor bore down on them. The mounted riders, over a hundred, halted when they reached the foul beings. One addressed them in their holographic forms.

"I am Sir Barwyck, knight of the bronze eagle banner. Who are you, and what is your business?"

Sumerlin answered for them. "We are travelers from afar. Our business is our own."

"Are you soldiers?" Barwyck asked. "Mercenaries? Barbarians?"

Tajanna replied for them this time. "We are seekers of magical objects."

Some of the knights laughed. They seemed to think the Archvillains joked. A few of their mounts pawed the ground.

"So you are wizards then," Barwyck said.

"Not exactly," Daggermash responded.

"Except myself," Sumerlin interjected.

Barwyck turned to the black magician. "We have no need for new wizards. There are plenty around. You would be more useful if you were soldiers."

"Are you at war?" Darlesse asked.

Barwyck sighed. "There is much fighting happening. Lands are being fought over. We are sent to secure our borders."

Amyrielle spoke up. "We are not interested in your territory. Your fighting does not concern us."

"You should be concerned," Barwyck stated. "Your party could be attacked by our enemies. You look like you need protection from them."

Foulbard chortled. "We don't need your protection. We can defend ourselves if necessary."

Some of the knights laughed at that. The Archvillains in their holographic disguises did not appear to be capable of battle, unarmed.

Barwyck snorted. "What is your destination?"

"The city just east of here," Namina replied.

"That is our home of Grayrock," Barwyck said. "I will give you an escort to there."

Sumerlin smiled. "That is kind of you."

Barwyck picked out twenty knights assigned to the Archvillains, not pleased having an escort. The foul beings accepted the offer without argument. Barwyck and now eighty knights rode on. The remaining twenty took positions around the Archvillains.

A knight introduced himself to the Archvillains. "I am Sir Gillamore. Come with us, please."

The Archvillains followed the mounted warriors for Grayrock. A few of the foul beings preferred to fight the knights but restrained themselves. They left the forest and crossed open ground now.

"Where do you hail from?" Gillamore asked the Archvillains.

Ripgarth answered the question for them. "From different worlds. Mine is Akeltia, a place partly more advanced than this one."

Gillamore patted his sword. "Do you have knights on your world?"

Ripgarth frowned. "No. But we do have warriors. We also have wizards. And monsters."

"Monsters?" Gillamore repeated. "We have a few here on the lands. Occasionally, we have to slay one."

"My world is more advanced than his," Foulbard said in comparison to the Cyclopean's. "Technology is on a greater level. But we do have soldiers. No monsters, though."

It took them two days to reach Grayrock. The escort led them into the city. A high wall of stone encircled the municipality. People went about their business in the place, some staring at the Archvillains, strangers in their midst. Children played in the streets. Merchant shops lined an avenue to their right, people going in and out of them. It was midday.

"Is there anyone you wish to talk to here?" Gillamore asked the Archvillains.

Sumerlin answered for them. "Yes. We would like to speak with any wizards or scholars here."

"We will take you to the Guild of Wizards," Gillamore said. "They might be able to help you."

The horsed knights led them to a huge structure in the middle of Grayrock. It stood three stories tall, oblong in shape. Water issued from a fountain before it. Right of the fountain stood a lone tree, tall and white.

"We part here," Gillamore said. "Inside this place, you will find those you wish to speak with. Farewell."

The mounted warriors took off back the way they came. Their horses trotted off, and the Archvillains proceeded to the large wooden doors of the building. Sumerlin grabbed the knocker on the left door and pounded it.

The left door opened, and a short, old man appeared, dressed in a gray robe and matching boots. "What do you want?"

"We wish to speak with some of your guild members," Sumerlin replied for them. "Who are you?"

"I am Syrell, the doorkeeper. Wait here. I will speak with one of the masters."

Syrell left the door open as the Archvillains stood there for a time. Finally, Syrell returned and ushered them inside. A tall fellow of middle age with a bald pate and wearing a red robe and leather shoes greeted them and introduced himself.

"I am Veragoth, leader of the guild. Are any of you wizards?"

"I am," Sumerlin said. The black magician introduced himself and the other foul beings with him.

"This way," Veragoth told them, motioning with his right hand.

The Archvillains followed the wizard. A set of stairs climbed ahead of them. To their left and right extended hallways to rooms. Veragoth led them up the steps.

They reached the third floor. Veragoth took them to a large chamber in the east wing of the building. They passed a few guild members who hurried on their way.

Inside the big room stood a huge wooden table in the center with a dozen chairs around it. Shelves of books rose along the walls. Magic paraphernalia, like an armillary sphere and alchemy equipment, rested on the west side of the large chamber. In the back of the big room hung a large window.

The Archvillain sat in the chairs. On the table lay books, scrolls, drawings, and maps.

"What is it you wish?" Veragoth asked the foul beings, standing.

Sumerlin answered for them. "We search for Lordruingat, the Cube of Power."

Veragoth frowned. "I do not recognize the name of the magical object. But it may be called something else here."

"You ever hear of Watchers?" Xigan asked.

"Yes," Veragoth replied. "They guard places. Others protect magical objects. A few serve evil sorcerers. Some lie in wait, like in lakes, to attack people."

Namina voiced the next question. "What knowledge

do you have of any things of power on your world?"

Veragoth seemed to think a moment. "There is the tale of a sacred relic of such power in the Castle Ullmark. There are stories of it being found, but no one has ever retrieved it from the place. It is said to be guarded by sentinels or knights and rumored to be in the possession of a powerful wizard."

"Where is Castle Ullmark?" Gnashboros asked.

Veragoth looked at a map on the table. "North of here. It would take a week to reach it."

"Are there any settlements along the way?" Foulbard asked.

"Yes," Veragoth said. "A few towns and a couple of villages."

The Archvillains spoke with Veragoth for a while. He knew only of a few magical objects on Verkemia, including a magic lantern and a sword of power. Afterward, the foul beings said goodbye to the guild leader. They proceeded to leave Grayrock for Castle Ullmark.

The Archvillains could feel the stares of the citizens of the city on them. It bothered not the foul beings. They emerged from the city and turned north.

The Archvillains journeyed over hilly terrain. Behind them, horsed knights entered Grayrock. The foul beings traveled on foot. A flock of green birds flew overhead in a partly cloudy sky, honking. The air felt cool.

Several hours later, the Archvillains descended a valley with stands of trees. In the middle of the depression nestled a village. The foul beings made for it.

The villagers gathered around and greeted the Archvillains, children among the inhabitants. Homes in the settlement were made of wood with thatched roofs. The size of the village was large, and in the center of it sat logs for seats with a firepit.

An elderly male with a crook stood before the Archvillains. "I am Aloras. Welcome to our humble abodes."

"What place is this?" Tajanna asked.

"The village of Shady Howe," Aloras replied. "Do you wish to stay the night?"

The Archvillains talked among themselves about that. They made a decision.

"Yes," Sumerlin said. "Thank you for your hospitality."

Soon evening fell. The Archvillains joined the villagers for a communal dinner in the center of the settlement. For supper the inhabitants served the foul beings a venison stew with carrots and onions in it, along with barley bread, red melons, and cold water to drink.

A young woman named Lasansa asked the Archvillains the first question. "Where are you from? You are strangers to these lands."

"We hail from far, far away," Daggermash answered. "From different worlds."

A middle-aged man named Namikken spoke up next. "Why are you traveling through our realm? What is your destination? Is there something you seek?"

Sumerlin responded for the foul beings. "We are on our way to Castle Ullmark. There is a prize there we wish to get."

An elderly woman named Terianne entered the conversation. "Castle Ullmark? It is a haunted place inhabited by shades of the dead. The living stay away from it. The thing you seek is forbidden to remove from its resting place."

"Has anyone in your village ever been there?" Foulbard asked.

"There are stories of a few of our people visiting it," Aloras said. "They never returned."

The warning to stay away from Castle Ullmark would not be heeded by the Archvillains. The villagers feared for the lives of the foul beings, who shrugged it off, feeling like they could handle any dangers or threats from the place. Later, everyone retired. The Archvillains stayed in a guest hut for the night.

"These villagers are primitive," Ripgarth remarked.

"Their concern for us is touching," Darlesse said.

The Archvillains slept until just after dawn. They broke fast with the villagers before they continued on their journey. The whole settlement saw them off.

The Archvillains left the valley and climbed rugged hills. Small stands of trees dotted the verdant landscape. The weather this morning felt much warmer as a cloudless sky hung over them. Animal life teemed in the territory, from gray-tailed deer to black squirrels.

"Have you ever used any magical objects before?" Darlesse asked the black magician.

Sumerlin smiled. "I have possessed talismans. Right now, I don't have any magical objects with me."

"Do you think the villagers are right about Castle Ullmark?" Amyrielle asked the black magician.

Sumerlin laughed. "I wouldn't be surprised. There is some truth in what they told us."

"Can you sense this sacred relic?" Xigan asked the black magician.

Sumerlin tried. "I feel the presence of a power ahead of us. It could be the magical object told about or a living being or spirits of the dead. I cannot get a definite fix yet."

The Archvillains descended the rugged hills onto flatlands. A little later, they passed by a small lake. Blue ducks paddled on its placid surface.

The sky became partly cloudy. Soon, they entered a forest. Tall trees with dark barks towered over them like wooden giants watching them. Dusk arrived as they walked through the timberland, unafraid of anything that could harm them. White owls hooted on branches.

"We'll camp here for the night," Sumerlin said.

The Archvillains made camp. They took turns taking watch, Ripgarth first. Nothing occurred while he kept an eye out.

Foulbard took the second watch. During the night, he heard howls of wolves. The lupine creatures sounded a bit distant from them, not a threat at this time. In the sky, a half-moon shined among clusters of stars.

When Nashboros took the third watch, the wolves sounded much closer. The Viper awoke his companions, and they formed a defensive ring. Soon they saw huge gray wolves slavering, gray eyes glowing.

The lupine creatures attacked them. Ripgarth fired a blue beam from his eye and killed wolves. Sumerlin shot red fire from his hands and fried them. Foulbard blasted them apart with shock waves from his hands. Namina sang a song and drove them mad. The Archvillains repelled the lupine creatures repeatedly until the wolves scattered and disappeared in the night.

The next morning, the foul beings resumed their trek for Castle Ullmark. The attack last night by the wolves unfazed them. They went through the forest at a quick pace.

It took the Archvillains two days to clear the timberland. Next, they climbed a mountain range and traveled through narrow passages. This part of their journey took three days to traverse the alpine region. Now, they crossed a marsh covered with green reeds and pools of water. It was slow going through the swampy tract.

"I remember once seeing corpses in a marsh like this one," Sumerlin said. "Warriors who died in battle."

"I don't care for this low wetland," Darlesse complained. "It's soggy and gross."

It took the Archvillains a day to cross the marsh. They began to ascend to higher ground, hilly terrain. When evening fell, they made camp. The weather felt cooler.

"Do you still feel the presence of a power ahead of us?" Tajanna asked the black magician.

Sumerlin sensed it. "Yes. It is getting stronger the closer we approach it."

The night passed uneventfully this time. After dawn, they continued on.

By midday, they arrived at their destination. The hilly terrain gave way to flats, where towered Castle Ullmark. The fortified dwelling appeared menacing to the Archvillains. They hurried over the open ground to the large, imposing house, which featured three towers. No one greeted them when they passed through an open gate and entered the courtyard of the place.

"This is spooky," Amyrielle remarked.

Castle Ullmark featured gargoyles, grotesquely carved figures, and silent watchers. They seemed to follow the movements of the Archvillains.

"This place appears deserted," Foulbard said.

Sumerlin sensed the surroundings. "I feel the presence of a living entity here. Hiding from us. Waiting."

"I don't like the sound of that," Foulbard interjected.

The Archvillains walked up to the main door of the castle. Ripgarth pushed it open. The foul beings entered the fortified dwelling.

Windows let in sunlight, curtains drawn. Before them rose a wide set of stairs. They stood in a vast hall with a high ceiling. In the main living room of the castle sat a piano with a bench.

"Which way?" Darlesse asked the black magician.

Sumerlin closed his eyes for a minute. "Up the stairs."

As the Archvillains began climbing the stairs, they suddenly heard a male voice.

"You are intruders. Go back. You are unwelcomed here. You have been warned."

"Show yourself," Xigan said.

The voice wailed. It did not scare the Archvillains.

"Coward!" Ripgarth shouted.

The Archvillains heard chains rattle. Next, they heard clanking sounds.

"What is making that racket?" Daggermash asked no one in particular.

The foul beings stopped on the stairs. The clanking sounds grew louder. Then, phantom knights appeared clad in suits of armor, armed with swords, battle-axes, and maces, at the top of the stairs and at the bottom of the steps. The Archvillains defended themselves.

Foulbard blasted apart a wave of phantom knights with shock waves below them. Ripgarth fired blue beams from his eye and Sumerlin shot red fire from his hands and blew apart the ghostly warriors at the top of the stairs. An endless surge of minions charged the Archvillains. The foul beings kept taking apart the phantom knights, who did not speak or utter any sound.

Finally, the assault ended with no more ghostly warriors to fight. The voice spoke again.

"You will pay for this!"

"I think not," Sumerlin responded for them.

The voice wailed again. "There is only death here for you."

"Go back to the shadows where you belong," Namina said.

The Archvillains resumed climbing the stairs. They reached the next floor and found two corridors, one going each way. On the walls hung tapestries. The hallways appeared deserted.

"Which passageway do we take?" Darlesse asked the black magician.

Sumerlin sensed both directions. "The one on the right."

The Archvillains took the corridor the black magician suggested. Locked doors appeared on either side of them. The foul beings tried to open a few, but they remained closed. At the end of the hallway, they halted before a locked door.

"I sense something inside this chamber," Sumerlin said.

Xigan smashed the locked door before them. The door flew open. In the center of the room, on a stand, lay a giant diamond. The brilliant precious stone glowed.

"I feel power emanating from that," Sumerlin said.

"It isn't Lorduingat," Tajanna remarked. "Doesn't even resemble the Cube of Power."

The voice spoke again. "Do not take that diamond."

"Should we take it?" Gnashboros asked the other Archvillains.

The foul beings agreed that they should. They escaped from Castle Ullmark with the huge crystal carried by Ripgarth. Nothing stopped them from fleeing the fortified dwelling. They heard the voice wail in defeat.

"Back to the ship," Sumerlin said.

The Archvillains returned to the *Slaughter*. They searched Verkemia no more for Lordruingat. The Cube of Power existed on another planet they figured. They needed to decide what world to visit next to search for it.

Chapter 23

The *Horizon* orbited Targaris, the fourth planet from its sun. Hulkeme teleported them down to the surface. The Universal Marshals found themselves on a plateau. It rained. They climbed down the broad, elevated tract of flat land, getting soaked.

"The nearest settlement is south of us," Nazzar said. "The Targarisians are an alien race with advanced technology. Their planet is not a member of the Federation."

"Has anyone in the Federation ever visited this world?" Yevadne asked.

Nazzar accessed the information from his internal files. "On record, a few members of the Federation have been here. An attempt was made to establish a colony on Targaris."

"Does it still exist here?" Danbarrack asked.

Nazzar checked his internal files again. "It is unknown what happened to the colony. After a time, communication ceased between it and the Federation. No one has found out why so far."

The downpour stopped after a while. Ahead of them stood structures. They approached a tall building and stopped at its closed entrance. Idyllion tried to open it, but it refused to accommodate them.

"Let me do it," Hulkeme said. The Genie-Enforcer used his special powers and got the entrance to admit them. The sliding door closed behind them.

The Universal Marshals stood in a wide corridor, deserted. Poor lighting illuminated the passageway. They listened and heard nothing.

"Where is everybody?" Apparis asked no one in particular.

Benethor turned to the Norn-Enforcer. "Can you sense anything?"

Ursanne tried. "I feel the presence of living beings in the area. They may be hiding from us."

Benethor pulled the red Elfstone from his pouch. "Better be prepared to fight."

The Universal Marshals walked down the corridor. They came to double doors that opened automatically and let them into a chamber. The room appeared to be a lab. Vertical tubes contained small lifeforms—aliens—in solutions, and a rack of test tubes held specimens. In a corner, vials of chemicals stocked shelves. Other equipment lay on a long table.

"Someone was experimenting on creatures," Kesharra remarked.

"Biocreation work," Nazzar added.

The Universal Marshals found drawers full of discs by a computer, which operated. Nazzar grabbed a disc and slid it into the computer. A female voice began to speak from the machine.

"The DNA of the aliens here is extraordinary. They have twenty-seven pairs of chromosomes. We spliced the cells of them to see their genetic makeup. The aliens breathe oxygen like us. We discovered that they lay eggs for reproduction. So we gathered some of their eggs and watched them hatch. We need to find out if males fertilize eggs or if the process is asexual."

Nazzar removed the disc from the computer and put in another one. The narration continued on from the previous disc.

"The aliens are as big as we are. Their egg incubation periods last about a month. Their growth rate is faster than humans. We have to be careful how we handle them. They are unpredictable and dangerous. Already, we have lost three lives because of them. So far, we have been unable to communicate with them. A language barrier exists between us and them. We do not know how they speak to each other. Maybe they use telepathy. Anyway we experiment on them further to see what we can learn. They are unlike any alien species we have ever come across."

Nazzar removed the disc from the computer and put it back in the drawer where he found it. The drawers contained a total of over a hundred discs, unmarked.

"Should we take some of the discs back to the ship?" Yevadne asked the other Enforcers.

Benethor answered the question. "Not now. Maybe later."

The other Universal Marshals agreed with the Elf-Enforcer. They left the lab and continued on down the hallway. In the walls of the passageway appeared holes in them.

"These holes look like they were made by blaster fire," Nazzar said.

Benethor studied the burnt markings. "A battle occurred here." The Elf-Enforcer spotted dried blood farther on the floor of the corridor, black and red. "Both sides suffered casualties. No indication who won the fight."

The Universal Marshals stopped at a prison room to

their left. Inside the chamber lay the corpse of an alien. The dead creature featured a slim build, long limbs, and a triangular head with three eyes on a long neck. They entered the prison room.

"Poor thing," Kesharra said. "It died in captivity."

Danbarrack interjected a thought. "Could it have committed suicide?"

"Possibly," Nazzar answered the Rubber Being. "There are no signs of a struggle."

The Universal Marshals left the chamber and resumed the trek down the corridor. Soon, they came to a junction. Hallways appeared in two directions.

"Which path we should go?" Milantheus asked the other Enforcers.

Nazzar turned to the Norn-Enforcer. "Can you detect which way should we take?"

Ursanne sensed the passageways. "I feel a presence ahead in the right corridor. Nothing in the left one."

The Universal Marshals took the right corridor. The lighting improved as they strode cautiously down the hallway. After they walked a ways, they found another body—human. He was alive but mortally wounded, and he opened his eyes at the sight of them.

"Who are you?" Benethor asked the man.

"My name is Doctor Hyle Kaiser. Who are you?"

Apparis answered him. "We are Universal Marshals."

"Enforcers?" Hyle said. "If you come to rescue us, you're a bit late."

"We are not here to save you," Nazzar responded. "Our mission is a different one."

"What is your mission?" Hyle asked. He coughed a few times.

"We are on a quest to find Lordruingat, the Cube of Power," Benethor replied. "Do you know of it?"

Hyle coughed again. "I have heard of it. You think it may be on this planet?"

"Yes," Benethor said.

"We have never come across its location on this world," Hyle responded. "Only an alien species."

Kesharra spoke. "What happened to the rest of your people?"

"They were killed by the aliens in a fight," Hyle replied. "The aliens spray a green mist from their mouths that proves fatal."

"We need to heal you," Benethor said. The Elf-Enforcer reached into his pouch and pulled out an orange Elfstone.

Hyle coughed up blood. "I am dying. Let me go in peace."

Before Benethor could use the magic rock in his hand to heal the doctor, Hyle expired. The Elf-Enforcer closed his eyes and put the orange Elfstone back in the pouch. "Rest in peace, Doctor Kaiser."

"There might be other survivors here," Yevadne said.

"Can you sense any of them?" Nazzar asked the Norn-Enforcer.

Ursanne closed her eyes and tried. "I don't feel the presence of any living humans. But I do feel the presence of aliens."

The Universal Marshals left the corpse of the doctor and continued on. Ahead, they came to an elevator. The Enforcers took it down to a sublevel. They got off the elevator and proceeded through another corridor. Holes appeared in the walls of the hallway.

The Universal Marshals reached a chamber with large eggs in it. No aliens were around.

"Could they be ready to hatch?" Kesharra asked the other Enforcers.

Ursanne sensed the eggs. "I feel that they are."

Benethor pulled out the red Elfstone from his pouch. "We may be in for a battle ourselves with the aliens."

Suddenly, an egg hatched. Out came an alien baby. It saw the Enforcers and flew at them. Benethor used the red Elfstone and destroyed the small creature.

"We better get out of here," Nazzar said.

The Universal Marshals heard shrieks. More eggs started to hatch. Benethor used the red Elfstone and torched them all.

"The Targarisians are aware of our presence," Ursanne said.

The Universal Marshals fled back the way they came. Shrieks echoed from everywhere. They reached the elevator as aliens charged at them from the corridor. Before the enraged creatures could get them, the elevator zoomed upward.

The Universal Marshals got off the elevator and ran up the passageway they had previously used. Shrieks sounded all around them.

Aliens charged at them up the hallway. The Enforcers defended themselves. Nazzar fired laser beams from his eyes and slayed them. Apparis opened his mouth and shot sonic blasts that killed them. Benethor used the red Elfstone to fell them. Idyllion fired nuclear rays from his hands and decimated them. Yevadne shot cyclone blasts and wiped them out.

The Targarisians kept coming at the Universal Marshals in waves. The Enforcers destroyed them as fast as possible. The aliens seemed endless in number.

A Targarisian leaped from an adjoining passageway at Hulkeme. The Genie-Enforcer caught the alien in midair. It opened its mouth and sprayed a green mist at the Universal Marshal. He used his special powers and blew the stuff back at it. The green mist choked it and he hurled the deadly creature back down the hallway it came from.

The Universal Marshals fought their way outside the large structure. It drizzled. More aliens charged at them outside.

"There are too many of them," Milantheus remarked. Father Time used his special powers and froze a bunch of aliens like living statues caught in time.

"Take us back up to the ship," Benethor told the Genie-Enforcer.

Hulkeme obeyed. The Universal Marshals teleported to the *Horizon*.

On board the vessel, they went to the briefing room. Nazzar sat at the control console of the long table.

"The chances of Lordruingat being on Targaris seem very small," Idyllion remarked. "The planet is overrun by the aliens."

"I agree," Benethor said.

Yevadne voiced an obvious question. "Should we continue to search this world for the Cube of Power?"

"Where else would we look for it on the planet?" Kesharra asked.

Ursanne sensed Targaris. "I cannot feel any unusual power emanating from the world. If Lordruingat is down there, it must be shielded from detection."

Hulkeme used his special powers. "My magic does not work in trying to bring us the Cube of Power. Every time I try, I meet resistance. The object is beyond me."

"My Elfstone that seeks things cannot find it either," Benethor said. "The power of Lordruingat blocks the magic of my Elfstone from pinpointing its resting place."

Ursanne frowned. "Then we should move on to the next world where the Cube of Power might be."

Benethor turned to the Android-Enforcer. "Where shall we go next?"

Nazzar accessed his internal files. "The next planet we should search for Lordruingat is Moromont. It is an advanced world inhabited by a race of humanoids."

The Universal Marshals went to the bridge of the *Horizon* and plotted a course for Moromont. When they were ready, the ship telejumped from the Taurus Sector of the Milky Way Galaxy to the Scorpio Sector of the Milky Way Galaxy.

Chapter 24

The six Universal Marshals found themselves outside a settlement that also served as a port. They made their way into the town during daylight in fair weather. They spotted ships that sailed tied up at docks. Outside the city limits, spacecraft took off and landed. Beings from various races populated the municipality and also visited the settlement.

The Enforcers walked streets bustling with activity. Merchant shops dealt with customers. So did a tavern and other businesses, including a brothel. Vendors sold their wares.

"This reminds me of some places on Tellus," Falatar remarked.

"It is jumping, that is for sure," Hashrah said.

Agwennel twitched her nose. "Where should we go first?"

"One of the merchant shops," Jarek suggested.

The Universal Marshals entered a merchant shop that featured clothing. The owner, a rotund human with a bald pate in a sparkling blue robe and matching shoes, greeted them.

"I am Cully Branstrom, the proprietor of this establishment. Are you looking for anything to wear for a special occasion or normal dress?"

The merchant shop displayed many articles of clothing, from medieval wear to space garb, stocked to capacity. The business, large in size, held no interest to the Enforcers.

"We seek information," Memfelice said.

Cully narrowed his eyes at them. "Who are you?"

"Universal Marshals," Jeddriel told him.

Cully sweated a little. "Enforcers? How can I help you? I'm only a simple businessman."

"We are interested in pirates, in particular, the space variety," Jarek said.

"What do you want to know?" Cully asked, grabbing a purple doublet off a table stacked with them of different colors.

Hashrah answered the question. "Have you sold any of your merchandise to space pirates?"

"Yes," Cully replied. "But I do business with all kinds of people."

"Have you ever heard of Mahab?" Agwennel asked.

Cully grimaced. "I know the name. But I have never had any business transactions with him. However, I may have sold goods to men who serve under his command."

"When was the last time you made a sale to space pirates?" Memfelice asked.

Cully paused as if to remember. "Three days ago."

The proprietor could not help them much. So the Universal Marshals left his store and headed for the tavern, the Mighty Boar, two streets down from the merchant shop. The absence of children on the streets they noticed.

Two drunk humanoids came out of the tavern and almost bumped into the Enforcers. A big sign over the door depicted a wild boar, and the name underneath looked inviting. They entered the huge establishment packed with all kinds of beings. Serving maids brought food and drink to tables. Laughter could be heard, and loud conversation echoed in the joint. Several males played a game of darts. Some smoked pipes in the tavern.

"This place is filled with riffraff," Falatar remarked.

"It probably is the best spot to gain information that we need," Jarek said.

A tall human with a mustache served drinks at the bar. The Universal Marshals found a table to sit at. A serving maid, humanoid, came over to their table.

"I am Lillia. What can I get for you?"

Jarek answered for them. "A round of ale to start. What food do you have?"

"Venison stew and fish stew, wheat bread and oat bread, yellow cheese, eggs and bacon, and berry pie for today," Lillia said.

Falatar ordered for them. "We'll try three bowls of your venison stew and three bowls of your fish stew with slices of wheat bread and oat bread."

Lillia went to the kitchen to place their order. A fight broke out between a male alien, tall and gray, and a male faerie, tall with dark hair. Both combatants pulled out knives and circled each other. They stabbed and slashed at each other, looking for openings to inflict wounds. Patrons in the tavern cheered and booed them on.

"Barbaric," Hashrah remarked.

The tall human with the mustache got between the two combatants. "No fighting is allowed in here. If you have to settle it, take it outside."

The alien and the faerie stopped their fight. They put away their knives and went to separate tables.

"That was short-lived," Jarek said.

Lillia brought them their food. It smelled delicious. Steam rose from the bowls of venison stew and fish stew.

They dug in.

"This fish stew tastes very good," Hashrah commented.

Falatar smiled. "So does this venison stew."

"All the customers in here may be pirates," Memfelice stated.

"I would not be surprised," Jeddriel said.

The patrons playing darts gambled on the game. One male human shouted out the scores of the participants. After every throw, more bets got placed.

Falatar turned his head to watch the game. "I remember when I tried darts. It was before I became an Enforcer."

"Did you wager on the outcome of the contest?" Agwennel asked the Lunar Being.

"I did a little," Falatar replied. "I got pretty good at it."

Jeddriel swallowed a piece of oat bread. "Care to try your hand at it again?"

Falatar grinned. "Maybe. But what would I wager if I did?" He ate a chunk of wheat bread.

"What about information?" Hashrah asked. "If you would win, they would answer your questions."

"What do you think?" Falatar asked the rest of the Universal Marshals.

"It might be a good idea," Memfelice said.

"Then again, maybe not," Jarek interjected.

Falatar got up. "I'll try my hand at it. Maybe I could gain some information by winning."

The Lunar Being went over to the three men who played darts. None of the three males could get a bulls-eye. They stopped the match when he interrupted their game.

The tallest one, a male humanoid, spoke. "I am Viccard. Who are you?"

Falatar introduced himself. "Mind if I join you?"

"Are you any good?" Viccard asked.

Falatar grinned. "I was pretty good at it."

The shortest man, a human, talked next. "My name is Juless. This other bloke here is Bambar."

Bambar nodded in acknowledgment. He was a humanoid.

"Okay, stranger," Viccard said, "what will you wager?"

"If I win, you answer my questions," Falatar replied. "If you win, I pay you fifty credits."

"So you want information," Viccard said. "You're on."

Falatar smiled. "You can go first."

Viccard tossed a dart and got a twenty. Juless threw next, and the dart landed on ten. Bambar shot next and scored a fifteen.

"Not bad," Falatar remarked.

The Lunar Being aimed, and his dart flew to get a bulls-eye. The three men took their turns next and failed to hit the target in the center spot. Falatar managed to strike three more bulls-eyes. The three men did not get one bulls-eye between them.

"You win, stranger," Viccard said. "What do you want to know?"

Falatar glanced at his fellow Universal Marshals before answering. "About Mahab. Is the Incarnation of Piracy real?"

"Captain Mahab is an actual person," Viccard replied. "No one messes with him. He is the head of all pirates. To serve under him is a privilege."

"Where can he be found?" Falatar asked.

"We don't know," Juless answered. "Why do you want to cross paths with him?"

Falatar hesitated to answer. "Me and my friends have business with him."

"If you're not pirates," Bambar said, "what are you?"

Falatar smiled. "That I cannot tell you."

"Why not?" Juless asked.

Falatar sighed. "It isn't in our best interests for you to know."

"Is there anything else you want to know?" Viccard asked, exasperated.

"Yes," Falatar replied. "Where is the Retreat?"

"The Retreat?" Bambar repeated. "Only pirates can know its location."

"Why?" Falatar asked.

"Because it is the code," Viccard explained. "For a pirate to tell one who is not a pirate means death to both."

"So you cannot tell me," Falatar said. "No one can help us in this matter."

"True," Bambar confirmed.

A serving maid, a young humanoid, dropped a tray of drinks when she saw the Lunar Being. "I recognize you. You're an Enforcer."

That drew the attention of all the customers, all pirates. Suddenly, they rose from their seats and drew weapons, swords, or blasters. The other Universal Marshals got to their feet as well.

"You're an Enforcer," Viccard said. "Your kind is not welcome here."

Falatar shook his head. "We don't want any trouble."

"Well, you got trouble," Bambar spat. "You Universal Marshals put away some of our friends. The only way you're getting out of here is as corpses."

All the pirates attacked the Universal Marshals, who defended themselves, outnumbered. Only the serving maids and the owner of the tavern did not join the assault on the Enforcers.

Falatar hurled a gravitic push and knocked down a bunch of pirates. Then the Lunar Being used his special powers and drove attackers mad, and they dropped their weapons, grabbing their heads in pain.

Hashrah fired turbo blasts from her hands and took out buccaneers fast. The Turbobeing unleashed turbo rings that landed around the necks of assailants and choked them unconscious. She dodged a sword swing from a pirate, kicked him in the chest, and sent him reeling.

Agwennel changed to water. Blaster fire from buccaneers did not damage her and went through her. The Undine-Enforcer unleashed a big wave of water from her form and wiped out more pirates.

Jarek swung his hoe of power and felled buccaneers. The Incarnation of Life acted like the Incarnation of Death, his opposite, wanting to spare them the grave but forced to take their lives. A pirate slashed at him with a sword. The immortal Enforcer blocked the blow and cracked him on the head with his supernatural weapon, killing him.

Memfelice used her special powers to strike at them. First, she used psychokinesis and hammered buccaneers between the ceiling and the floor and slayed them. Next, the Psychic Being used pyrokinesis and charred more of them to ashes. Then she blew heads off pirates. Three of them charged her, wielding swords. The Universal Marshal levitated in the air and telekinetically hurled objects in the tavern at them and took them out.

Jeddriel materialized a flaming sword in his hand. His wings appeared. A bunch of buccaneers came at him, yelling, armed with scimitars. The Archangel-Enforcer swung his divine weapon and broke the blades of the ordinary swords of his attackers. Then he slashed through them and slaughtered them.

After a while, the pirates were all defeated. None of the buccaneers were left standing. Most had been killed in the fight. The survivors lay on the floor, a few conscious.

"We did not want to do this," Falatar said. The Lunar Being stood over a sprawled Viccard, who still breathed. "You and your kind gave us no choice. Do you wish to say anything?"

Viccard coughed up blood. "You will not get anything more from me."

Falatar shook his head. "What a shame."

Viccard smiled. "When Mahab hears about this, he will come for you. Your lives are forfeit. He will show you no mercy."

"We expect him to respond to our wasting you," Jarek said. The Glad Sower wiped the blood from his hoe of power with a cloth he found.

The owner of the tavern came over to the Universal Marshals. "My place is wrecked. Who is going to pay to fix it?"

"Find some investors, like fellow merchants," Jarek said. "Or ask the surviving pirates here to ante up."

"Too bad we couldn't get any more information," Hashrah stated.

"No use staying here any longer," Falatar interjected.

The Universal Marshals left the tavern. They beamed up to the *Constellation* and went to the briefing room.

"Where should we go next?" Agwennel asked the other Enforcers.

"The penal colony on the planet Falcora," Jarek said. "Their prisons are filled with pirates."

The *Constellation* set coordinates for Falcora. It and the other four battlecruisers telejumped from the Omicron Sector of the Milky Way Galaxy to the Lambdan Sector of the Milky Way Galaxy. In time, they arrived at Falcora, the third planet in its solar system with a yellow star.

The Universal Marshals beamed down to the surface of the planet. They did not know what to expect on this world. It had been a while since a Federation vessel visited it.

Chapter 25

In the training room, Delveran gave the three new Universal Marshals, each a pair of antipower handcuffs. "Keep them on you at all times."

"Do you have an assignment for us yet?" Faragorn asked. The Cosmic Ranger attached the nondynamis binders to his belt.

"Not yet," Delveran replied. "But be ready for one when it comes."

"I looked forward to some action," Lorraym said. The Siroccon smiled.

"Our first assignment will be special," Nazerock said. "It will initiate us as Universal Marshals."

The addition of three more Enforcers brought their total to eighty-sixth now. Delveran felt the Universal Marshals should recruit more because of the number of Archvillains that existed in the galaxy. The High Enforcer knew that the foul beings greatly outnumbered the Universal Marshals. So far, no Archvillains had been apprehended for the Universal Prisonplex. That fact bothered him much.

The three new Enforcers were assigned private quarters in the Justiceplex. There were more individual chambers left unoccupied, plenty of room for additional Universal Marshals.

Delveran would ask the Federation Department of Justice for the Enforcers to recruit even more beings to join the ranks of the Universal Marshals. He felt that the number of Enforcers might be inadequate to handle the sheer number of Archvillains that roamed the galaxy. He wondered how many members now comprised the Fellowship of Darkness, the Archvillain organization that could threaten the Federation if it got all those escaped Archvillains to join it, becoming the next supreme evil. He sensed that it did not have enough of the foul beings yet to take on the Federation. That was small comfort to him.

The three new Universal Marshals practiced in the training chamber in the meantime. They wanted to be sharp when duty called. Delveran admired their dedication to the Enforcers. He figured soon they would get their first assignments.

Nanomach kept the High Enforcer informed of and updated on current events. The Computer-Enforcer informed him of the progress being made by the Enforcer Quest and the Universal Marshals assigned to deal with the space pirate problem. The High Enforcer reported to the Federation Department of Justice on what happened in both matters.

Delveran sat in his office when Evarinia came to him. He got up, and they embraced and kissed. He told her of the news so far concerning the Enforcer Quest and the Universal Marshals dealing with the space pirate issue.

"I am still getting complaints from non-Federation worlds about raids by space pirates," Evarinia said.

Delveran sighed. "The Universal Marshals are doing everything we can to stop them. It will take time to find them and end the raids."

"You are worried that the Archvillain organization

may find Lordruingat first."

"Yes. The Cube of Power could be a great weapon for the Fellowship of Darkness to use against the Federation. It is unknown how Lordruingat works other than the Cube of Power can dominate the three levels of energy power below it."

Evarinia smiled. "You need a break. Let's have dinner."

Delveran grinned. "All right. Where?"

"My apartment."

Delveran told Nanomach over the intercom where he would be going. The High Enforcer and Evarinia went to the teleporter room of the Justiceplex and beamed to her apartment. She made them dinner, and he offered to help. For supper, they ate steaks with mashed potatoes and gravy, salads with a spicy dressing, rye bread, and redberry pie for dessert. For their beverage they drank blue wine from a vineyard in the west coast region of Survarille. They sat at her dining room table and consumed their meal.

"Have you ever thought of retiring from the Universal Marshals?" Evarinia asked.

Delveran swallowed some of his food. "Yes. There are times when I wonder how long I should be an Enforcer. There are things I miss doing."

"Like what?"

"Traveling to other worlds in the galaxy. There was a time when I visited worlds. What about you?"

"There are moments when I think of leaving my official position. I do love the work. When I do retire I will miss it."

After dinner, they went to her bedroom and made love. Delveran stayed overnight at her place. Evarinia slept well. But the High Enforcer experienced nightmares. He woke from them in a sweat, yelling. That awakened her.

"Bad dreams?" Evarinia asked.

Delveran wiped his face with a hand. "Yes."

"What did you dream?"

Delveran took a deep breath. "I saw Archvillains killing Universal Marshals. The foul beings attacked the Justiceplex and destroyed it."

"Could it be you looked into the future?"

Delveran knew that referred to oneiromancy, divination by dreams. "Possible. I may have foreseen what is to come."

Evarinia put an arm around his shoulders. "When was the last time you did as such?"

"It has been several months since I foresaw the future in my dreams. The last time was during the invasion of Tellus."

They went back to sleep. In the morning, they ate breakfast. Then they went their separate ways, her to her office in the Federationplex and him back to the Justiceplex.

Delveran entered the computer room of the Justiceplex. He stood before Nanomach. The Computer-Enforcer worked, surrounded by control consoles, in the middle of the chamber.

"Any news from the Enforcer Quest?" Delveran asked.

Nanomach checked his memory banks. "They have searched four worlds so far for Lordruingat. The planets Vingrezza, Dellakor, Natyrek, and Targaris. They did not find the Cube of Power on any of them."

"What world are they heading for next?"

"Moromont."

"What information do you have on it?"

"It is a planet inhabited by a race of humanoids."

"How does it rate?"

"On the scientific level, advanced. On the occultic level, nonexistent. On the celestic level, nonexistent."

"They have high technology then."

"Affirmative. Moromont is not a member of the Federation."

"Have any Federation members ever visited the world?"

Nanomach checked his data files. "There are records of visitation by Federation members. Not that many."

"Does the Federation consider Moromont for possible membership?"

"Affirmative. But the planet has not requested to officially join the Federation."

Delveran wondered why. "What else about the world?"

"It has not fought a war in over five centuries. Unknown why."

Delveran changed the subject. "Any news from the Universal Marshals on assignment after the space pirates?"

Nanomach checked his memory files. "They visited the planet Amaekar. It is known as a place where pirates gather. The Universal Marshals have learned that the Incarnation of Piracy does exist."

Delveran was afraid of that. "Have they learned his name?"

"Mahab."

"What else?"

"Pirates in the galaxy have a homeworld where they

meet. It is simply called the Retreat."

Delveran smoothed his mustache. "Any news of foul beings apprehended for the Universal Prisonplex?"

Nanomach checked his computer banks. "Universal Marshals have arrested eight Criminals and two Villains for it today."

"No Archvillains?"

"Affirmative."

Delveran felt dismayed that no Archvillains had been caught by the Universal Marshals for the Universal Prisonplex yet. He figured sooner or later, the Enforcers would apprehend some of the foul beings for incarceration in it. The Federation Department of Justice would not like the fact that no Archvillains had been caught for imprisonment. The High Enforcer wondered why the arrests of the foul beings eluded the Universal Marshals. Where were all those Archvillains hiding in the galaxy? The only one the Enforcers had any leads on was the Incarnation of Piracy.

Delveran also wondered if the Fellowship of Darkness found a new planet for its base. The High Enforcer deduced that the Archvillain organization had grown bigger by recruiting more and more of its kind. He'd already assigned Universal Marshals to find the Fellowship of Darkness. No word from those Enforcers about any signs where the Archvillain organization existed now. The High Enforcer felt frustrated at the lack of progress concerning Archvillains.

"Warning!" Nanomach said. "I detect drones coming toward the Justiceplex."

Delveran spoke in the intercom. "All Universal Marshals to the roof of the Justiceplex for an attack against us. Nanomach, initiate defenses for our headquarters."

"Affirmative," Nanomach acknowledged.

Delveran got to the roof of the Justiceplex. Faragorn, Nazerock, and Lorraym joined the High Enforcer.

Ion cannons rose up from the roof of the Justiceplex. They fired at armed drones flying toward the headquarters of the Enforcers and blew them apart. The sky was clear in the early afternoon.

Delveran shot green fire from his hands at drones and destroyed them. Lorraym unleashed heat beams from her hands and knocked out more of them. Nazerock used his special powers to explode the machines. Faragorn charged at them and slashed them to bits with his sword of power.

The battle lasted until all the drones were destroyed. All that remained were metal pieces of the machines. The ion cannons returned to their compartments in the roof.

"This is the work of the Fellowship of Darkness," Delveran said.

Now, it was more urgent to find the Archvillain organization. It had launched a bold attack on the Universal Marshals. Would the foul beings do it again?

Chapter 26

The ten Archvillains met in the meeting room on the *Slaughter* again. Sumerlin sat at the control console.

"What planet do we next search for Lordruingat?" Tajanna asked the black magician. The Sphinx voiced the question on everybody's mind.

Sumerlin leaned forward in his chair. "We have a choice of several worlds to look for the Cube of Power according to our present data. They are Marakis, Hydroconia, Barexy, and Wolcoth."

"What do we know about them?" Gnashboros asked the black magician. The Viper intertwined his fingers.

Sumerlin checked the information through the control console. "Marakis is a postapocalyptic world. It is dominated by a race of humans. It suffered a cataclysmic event in the form of a nuclear war."

"That does not sound promising to find Lordruingat there," Amyrielle remarked. The Echidnan shook her head.

Sumerlin continued. "Hydroconia is a water world. The dominant race on it is an aquatic people. It does have a race of land dwellers who are human. There is a symbiotic relationship between the two. On the scientific level, they are progressive. On the occultic level, they are below average. On the celestic level, they are nonexistent."

"It seems like a possibility for the Cube of Power to

be there," Foulbard said. The Shocker originally came from a planet of humanoids, Durtania. From it, only he possessed special powers.

Sumerlin resumed. "Barexy is a primitive world with low technology. That makes them, on the scientific level, below average. On the occultic and celestic levels, they are nonexistent."

"That also seems like a possibility for Lordruingat to be there," Xigan stated. The Behemoth pounded fists together.

Sumerlin let out a deep breath. "The last world is Wolcoth. It is an industrial world. On the scientific level, it is progressive. On the occult level, it is below average. On the celestic level, it is low."

Darlesse entered the conversation. "So which planet do we go to first to search for the Cube of Power?" The Hellcat pushed a lock of her red hair from her face.

"Why don't we visit them in the order they were spoken about," Ripgarth said. The Cyclopean blinked a few times.

"Does anyone object to that?" Sumerlin asked.

Daggermash chimed in. "I don't think it matters what order we visit the planets." The Manticore shrugged.

"We may have to look through all of them to find Lordruingat," Namina said. The Siren wanted to break out in song.

Sumerlin nodded. "Then we shall visit them in order spoken about."

The meeting adjourned. They went to the bridge of the ship and plotted a course for the planet Marakis. The *Slaughter* engaged its teleport drive and telejumped to the Madune Sector of the Milky Way Galaxy.

The vessel approached the solar system where Marakis orbited a white sun as its fifth planet with two moons. It slowed to sublight speed and prepared to land on the postapocalyptic world. Satellites orbited Marakis but were inoperative. The ship sped down through the atmosphere and set down in a glade. The open space in the forest could have accommodated more than one vessel.

The ten Archvillains left the ship, its autodefenses on. They headed south through a dense timberland. They heard nothing, and the air smelled stale but breathable.

"Did this planet suffer a nuclear winter?" Darlesse asked the black magician.

"For a time," Sumerlin answered. "The world is healing still from it."

The Archvillains encountered no animal life. It seemed too quiet. Nothing impeded their trek through the trees. In the sky, the sun shined at its zenith in a clear sky.

The Archvillains exited the forest three hours later. Before them stretched flatlands. In the distance, they spotted ruins. They headed for the destroyed buildings.

"This planet appears dead," Foulbard remarked.

"It seems to have no signs of life at all," Tajanna agreed.

The Archvillains arrived at the ruins. They walked down an avenue of destroyed buildings on either side of them. On the ground lay skeletons of beings.

"The nuclear war that doomed this world has many victims," Sumerlin said.

Suddenly, they heard cries. It seemed to come from all around them. The Archvillains formed a defensive ring.

"There is life after all here," Darlesse remarked.

From the ruins, survivors of the nuclear war, dressed in rags and armed with makeshift weapons, attacked the foul beings. They came from all directions.

Ripgarth fired a blue beam from his eye and wasted assailants. Sumerlin shot red fire from his hands and burned them into ashes. Namina sang, and her voice drove them mad, grabbing their heads and falling to the ground. Foulbard unleashed shock waves and decimated them. Daggermash stung them with his scorpion tail and killed them. Darlesse did flying stomps and slayed them by caving in their chests. Xigan smashed them with his fists and felled them. Tajanna, Amyrielle, and Gnashboros cut them down with blasters.

Their attackers soon quit and fled back into the ruins. The Archvillains stopped fighting. None of the foul beings were hurt or received any wounds. The cries from the survivors ceased, and it became quiet again.

"The battle was not much of a test for us," Darlesse remarked.

"If Lordruingat is here, it must be hidden away," Ripgarth said.

Sumerlin sighed. "This was once a thriving city. Not anymore. Marakis must be a world of nothing but destruction."

The Archvillains came upon wrecked cars. None of the vehicles had skeletons in them.

"Nothing was spared in the nuclear war," Foulbard remarked.

The Archvillains continued on. All around them stood more ruins. Mile upon mile of destroyed buildings. A pack of dogs appeared and ran away from them. The gray sky created a somber atmosphere.

Ahead of them, a cab drove toward them. That surprised the foul beings. It stopped in front of them.

"You shouldn't be out here," the cabbie said, middle-aged. "Dangerous folk are around."

"Who are you?" Sumerlin asked.

"I am Clent. We need to get inside before night falls. That is when the savages are at their worst."

"Where is there a safe place?" Darlesse asked.

Clent smiled. "Follow me. I will lead you to safety. This way."

The Archvillains followed the cab as it drove slowly down the street. Dogs barked. No other animal life could be seen or heard.

Clent took them to an oblong-shaped building surrounded by a fence. He opened the fence and stopped the cab before the undamaged structure, then got out of the car, closed the fence, and led the foul beings inside the place.

"Are there other survivors like you?" Tajanna asked the cabbie rhetorically.

"Yes," Clent answered. "Here and there. Spread out across the globe. Survivors of the Great War that devastated our world."

"How did the conflict start?" Foulbard asked.

Clent paused. "With an arms race. Both sides wanted to have more weapons than the other. Then, armies invaded other countries to claim territories. That led to all-out war and eventually the use of nuclear weapons."

None of the Archvillains never even experienced being in a nuclear war. Or ever faced genocide.

"Where do you come from?" Clent asked the foul beings.

"From different planets," Xigan replied for them.

Clent's eyes widened. "Why are you on our world?"

"We seek an object of power," Ripgarth answered.

"Is it nuclear in nature?" Clent asked.

"No," Sumerlin said. "We seek Lordruingat, the Cube of Power. Do you know of it?"

Clent shook his head. "Former governments on our world experimented with different power sources, trying to make new weapons. They may have succeeded, I'm not sure."

The cabbie led them down a corridor with doors on either side. Other people appeared, including children. None of them spoke.

"How do you survive?" Namina asked.

"We have stockpiles of food in the basement," Clent said. "The supply won't last forever. We never venture out at night because of the savages."

"Do you have weapons?" Daggermash asked.

"Actually, we do," Clent replied. "Guns and knives. Makeshift clubs."

The Archvillains remembered that the savages that attacked them did not carry guns.

"Do you have a leader among you?" Gnashboros asked.

"We have a council," Clent answered. "Do you wish to speak with them?"

"Yes," Sumerlin said.

"I will take you to them then," Clent responded.

The cabbie took them down a wide hallway to a large chamber. In the big room sat five people in armchairs in an arc. Other people stood or sat on the floor.

"Welcome, strangers," an elderly man said. "My

name is Majorah, Leader of this council." He introduced the other four members of it, two middle-aged females named Urlessa and Luperra and two middle-aged males named Sedwyn and Rymane.

The Archvillains introduced themselves. More people came into the large chamber to see the foul beings.

"Where do you come from?" Majorah asked the Archvillains.

"They come from different planets," Clent answered for them.

That caused a commotion in the big room. The council spoke among themselves.

"You come from space?" Urlessa asked. "How did you come to our world?"

"We flew in a spaceship," Darlesse replied.

That caused more of a commotion in the large chamber. The council spoke among themselves again.

"Have you come to help us?" Rymane asked.

"Not exactly," Foulbard answered.

"Then why are you here?" Majorah demanded.

"They seek an object of power," Clent answered again for the foul beings.

That brought shouts from people in the large chamber. The council argued among themselves. The Archvillains appeared unfazed by the conversation exploding around them.

"Did we make a mistake coming here?" Darlesse asked the black magician.

Sumerlin held up his hand. The other Archvillains wondered the same thing as the Hellcat. The council restored order.

"What object of power do you seek?" Majorah

asked the Archvillains.

Ripgarth answered this time. "Lordruingat, the Cube of Power."

"We know of no such object," Luperra said. "Is it nuclear?"

"No," Sumerlin responded.

"If such a thing existed, it would likely be in some government facility, probably military," Sedwyn stated.

Foulbard laughed. "That would seem logical."

"Why do you believe it is on our world?" Majorah asked.

"Our data indicated it might be on your planet," Xigan replied.

The council talked among themselves again. People gathered around the Archvillains as if to prevent them from leaving.

"Why do you seek this Lordruingat?" Urlessa asked the foul beings.

"We have need of it," Amyrielle replied.

"Is it some kind of special weapon, this Cube of Power?" Rymane asked.

"It could be used as such," Ripgarth admitted.

The council talked among themselves again. The Archvillains did not feel threatened by the people around them.

"I don't know how we can help you find this Lordruingat," Majorah said. "We have no knowledge of any special weapons. Of where they would be kept exactly."

"Where is your closest government facility?" Foulbard asked.

"That would be the Scalese military base outside of town west of here," Majorah replied. "Do you intend to go to every government building just to find the Cube of Power?"

"We will search through whatever facilities we can," Darlesse answered for the Archvillains. "As many as we can."

The council spoke among themselves once more. People around the Archvillains backed away.

"Then farewell and good luck in your search," Majorah said. "Beware of the savages."

The Archvillains said their goodbyes and left the building. The foul beings headed for the Scalese military base. People watched them go.

Down the street, they walked with more ruins on either side of them. Some of the wrecked buildings were small, and others large. Among the destroyed structures were hi-rise buildings, houses, businesses, and other facilities.

The Archvillains were not worried about the savages, who were no match for them. More dogs appeared and barked at the foul beings. The canines did not attack them but instead ran off. It took a while for them to reach their destination.

The Scalese military base still stood but its buildings had been damaged. They entered the place. They found skeletons of enlisted personnel here and there. The grounds featured wrecked tanks, jet planes, and other military transports.

Xigan put his hands on his hips. "Which structure do we enter first?"

Sumerlin used his special powers. "I sense something in that building."

The Archvillains went to what looked like a bunker. Left of its door hung a key pad.

"This needs a special code entered to get inside it," Foulbard said. The Shocker tried to open the door, but it would not budge.

Ripgarth stepped forward. "Let me try." The Cyclopean fired a blue beam from his eye and blasted the door open.

"That worked," Tarjanna remarked. The Sphinx led them inside.

The Archvillains entered the bunker. They found themselves in a large chamber with huge containers filled with explosive or incendiary material.

"Bombs," Sumerlin said. "Atomic, hydrogen, and cobalt. Stored for use in a war already over with." The black magician touched a container. "They are not armed to go off yet."

The Archvillains found a desk with many papers on it. Among the papers were written orders, plans for new missiles, and other documents.

The Archvillains left the bunker and searched through other buildings. One was a mess hall empty of diners with a large kitchen. Another was an office complex. A third was a big garage where two jeeps had been worked on and a tank.

"This whole scene is horrific," Namina remarked.

"Should we head back to the ship?" Daggermash asked the other Archvillains.

"We might as well," Amyrielle said.

They turned to the black magician. He frowned. All around them was nothing but death and destruction.

"We shall return to the ship," Sumerlin stated.

The Archvillains started back for the *Slaughter*. It took a while. On the way back, they encountered more savages who charged them, but the foul beings drove

them off. Once inside the ship—it was night outside—
they went to the briefing room again.

"It is going to be hard to search through every
government building or military base to find
Lordruingat," Foulbard said. "We can assume that they
all suffered damage in the nuclear war of the planet."

"Marakis has experienced much misfortune,"
Sumerlin remarked. "The survivors here cannot help us.
They are simply struggling to exist."

"Where do we look next on the planet?" Darlesse
asked the black magician.

"The world has five continents," Sumerlin said. "We
already tried using ship's scanners to find any trace of
Lordruingat on the surface, but to no avail. It is unknown
how many possible places on Marakis might hold the
Cube of Power."

"What about your sensing it?" Namina asked.

Sumerlin took a deep breath. "I have already tried
several times. I felt the presence of people but no objects
of power other than bombs. Marakis is essentially a
wasteland."

"We could be wasting our time here," Gnashboros
interjected. "It seems to me that this postapocalyptic
world is not a likely place for Lordruingat now."

"What do the rest of you think?" Sumerlin asked.

Amyrielle chimed in. "I agree with the Viper. A
devasted planet is not a good choice for the Cube of
Power to reside on."

"To my mind, Lordruingat may be on a planet that
is uninhabited," Xigan said. "Except for the so-called
Watchers."

Darlesse spoke up again. "I think the Viper and the
Echidnan are right."

"There is the possibility that the Cube of Power may have been on this world but was taken off it because of the nuclear war," Ripgarth said.

Sumerlin conceded that point. In the end, they decided not to search Marakis anymore for Lordruingat, figuring it was not on the planet. They plotted a course for Hydroconia. The *Slaughter* engaged its teleport drive and telejumped to the Aquarian Sector of the Milky Way Galaxy.

Chapter 27

Delveran used his special powers and looked into the future. He stood in his private quarters, alone. In his vision, he saw the Fellowship of Darkness finding a planet to call their new base of operations to replace the Complex on Earth. He could not specifically identify this world, but he saw the Archvillain organization on it.

The High Enforcer left his chambers and went to his office. He checked his messages. There were three of them. He played them. The first was from Admiral Allabar of space troopers, an alien.

"High Enforcer, do you need more battlecruisers to help deal with the space pirate problem?"

Delveran stopped the recordings and called the Admiral on his control console. "Admiral, I may need more ships to handle the matter of the space pirates. Have any Federation members requested an escort from military vessels to protect them against possible attack from space pirates?"

Allabar answered momentarily. "Yes, High Enforcer. Plenty of requests. We can only accommodate some of them. So far, no space pirates have attacked escorted ships."

"All right. Keep me informed of any new developments."

"Yes, High Enforcer."

Delveran played the second message. It was from

Hughus Mantock, a senior official from the Occultplex.

"High Enforcer, when your Universal Marshals find Lordruingat, will you bring it to the Occultplex for study? Or will you give the Cube of Power to the Scienceplex or Celestoryplex instead?"

Delveran stopped the recording again. He called the senior official on his control console. "It has not been decided yet what we will do with Lordruingat if the Universal Marshals get a hold of the Cube of Power before the Fellowship of Darkness. The decision on what to do with it is going to be rendered by the Federation Department of Justice."

"Have your Universal Marshals made any progress in finding Lordruingat?" Hughus asked after a pause.

Delveran let out a deep breath. "So far, the Enforcer Quest has pursued leads regarding finding it. No luck in locating it yet. I sensed that the Archvillain organization had not found it either thus far. I will keep you abreast of any news from the Enforcer Quest."

"Thank you, High Enforcer. If the Occultplex could be of any service, let us know."

"All right." The communication ended.

Delveran played the third message. It was from Warden Thurjen Addarak. He leaned back in his chair.

"High Enforcer, we have a situation in the Universal Prisonplex. Prisoners have rioted. They refuse to return to their cells. A few prison guards have been taken hostage. They want to discuss terms."

Delveran stopped the final recording. The High Enforcer contacted Nanomach on the intercom and told the Computer-Enforcer he would teleport to the Universal Prisonplex. He left his office, entered the teleporter room of the Justiceplex, and beamed to the office of the Warden in the Universal Prisonplex.

Thurjen sat before his desk. A telescreen, off, hung on the wall to the right of him. "I was expecting you." The Warden was a short, thin man with cropped brown hair and a bushy brown mustache like his brown eyebrows. He featured close-set brown eyes, and he looked comfortable in a brown wardensuit with matching belt and boots.

"What has happened lately?" Delveran asked.

Thurjen cleared his throat. "The prisoners have threatened to kill their hostages unless their demands are met."

"Has anyone been killed?"

"No."

"Is the situation contained?"

"Yes. The prisoners are in the courtyard under the watchful eye of prison guards in the guard towers."

Delveran frowned. "Have the prisoners requested to speak with anyone in particular?"

Thurjen sighed. "Yes. They want to speak with me and you."

That surprised Delveran. He did not figure out why the prisoners wanted to speak with him. It was obvious they would want to speak with the Warden.

"Let's go see what they want," Thurjan said.

Delveran nodded. They left his office and went to a guard tower which overlooked the courtyard. Below, prisoners milled around. The High Enforcer counted three hostages held by the inmates. The prisoners wore orange jumpsuits and black shoes, a mixture of various races. Prison guards were dressed in one-pieced suits—blue tops and black bottoms—with boots, belts, and helmets, all black. Simple blasters in black holsters and stun batons rested on opposite sides of their belts. Like the inmates, they were a mixture of races. The weather was sunny.

Thurjen grabbed a bullhorn from a prison guard. The Warden spoke into it. "I am here, and so is the High Enforcer. What are your terms?"

A male prisoner, a humanoid named Laso Rupp, a Villain, shouted up to them. "First, we want better food to eat. No more just slop."

"And your second demand?" Thurjen asked.

Laso smiled. "We want to be outside in the courtyard more often."

Thurjen turned to the High Enforcer. "Their terms seem reasonable so far."

"Yes," Delveran agreed. He wondered what the prisoners still wanted from the Grand Universal Marshal.

Thurjen addressed the prisoners again. "What else do you want?"

"More things to do inside this prison," Laso replied. "Like a telescreen to watch programs. Discs to read material. Games to play. A weight room."

Thurjen turned to the High Enforcer again. "Everything they have asked for to this point appears legitimate. Nothing out of the ordinary."

Delveran sighed. "Ask them what they want from me."

"Okay." Thurjen spoke through the bullhorn again. "What do you wish of the High Enforcer?"

"For him to use his influence with the justice department to have retrials of some of us," Laso answered. "There are those of us innocent of the charges that had been filed against us. Miscarriages of justice. We deserve to have our criminal records expunged by the Federation Department of Justice."

Their demand surprised the Warden and the High Enforcer.

Thurjen raised an eyebrow. "You should have lawyers filing for appeals."

"Some of us are already doing so," Laso responded.

"I'm not certain how much influence I have with the Federation Department of Justice," Delveran said. "Their lawyers should be contacting me directly if they think I can be of assistance."

Thurjen nodded. "We will consider your terms. Release your hostages."

"Not until you agree with our demands," Laso responded.

"Very well," Thurjen said. "We will get back to you."

The Warden and the High Enforcer left the guard tower after giving back the bullhorn to a prison guard. They went back to Thurjen's office and sat down.

"All the things they asked for could be granted," Delveran stated. "None of their demands are beyond agreeing with."

"We should make plans on rescuing the hostages," Thurjen said. "Freeing them may be difficult. Any ideas?"

Delveran thought. "Possibly. We could swap the hostages with Universal Marshals."

"They might go for it," Thurjen responded. "Which Enforcers do you have in mind?"

Delveran smiled. "The three new ones we recruited for the Universal Marshals. Nazerock, a Gnome. Faragorn, the Cosmic Ranger. And Lorraym, the Siroccon."

"Do you think we should agree with their terms?" Thurjen asked.

"Only as a last resort," Delveran replied. "Propose the swap first."

"All right. If it fails, do we make a rescue attempt?"

"Yes."

Delveran and Thurjen left the Warden's office and returned to the guard tower. A prison guard handed the bullhorn again to the Warden.

"Have you agreed to our terms?" Laso asked.

Thurjen spoke in the bullhorn. "We propose we swap your hostages with three Universal Marshals."

"No," Laso responded. "We keep the hostages until our demands are met."

Thurjen frowned. "Very well."

The Warden handed the bullhorn back to the prison guard. Thurjen and Delveran went back to the Warden's office and sat down again.

"How do we rescue the hostages?" Thurjen asked.

"We teleport Universal Marshals and heavily armed prison guards into the courtyard where the hostages are being held," Delveran answered. "Have heavily armed prison guards on the guard towers. Set the blast rifles of all the prison guards involved in the rescue attempt for stun."

"Sounds good," Thurjen commented. "We have a plan."

The High Enforcer went to the teleporter room of the Universal Prisonplex and had the teleportist there at the control console, a male humanoid, beam Nazerock, Faragorn, and Lorraym to the facility. The Warden got half a dozen prison guards, heavily armed with blast rifles, for the rescue attempt. Prison guards on the guard towers got heavily armed with blast rifles.

"What are we to do?" Lorraym asked the Grand Universal Marshal.

"You and a contingent of prison guards will be teleported into the courtyard to save the three hostages the prisoners have," Delveran replied. "Avoid killing the inmates if you can. Number one priority is to rescue the hostages."

"Understood," Faragorn responded for the three Enforcers.

The three Universal Marshals and the six prison guards stepped onto the telegrid. Ready, the teleportist beamed them into the courtyard near the spot where the three hostages were held. It caught the prisoners by surprise.

Lorraym shot heat rays from her hands and blasted prisoners off the three hostages. Faragorn used the butt of his sword of power and knocked out inmates. Nazerock used his special powers and shook the ground beneath the feet of prisoners to make them fall. The prison guards fired their blast rifles and stunned inmates to drop onto the earth unconscious.

The three Universal Marshals, six prison guards, and the three hostages got beamed back to the teleporter room. The hostages were unharmed by their short captivity.

The prisoners in the courtyard got herded back into their cells by prison guards heavily armed with blast rifles. The inmates hung their heads in dejection.

"We will have to rotate prisoners for the courtyard in the future," Thurjen said.

"What about their requests for things?" Delveran asked.

"I will look into that," Thurjen replied.

Delveran, Nazerock, Faragorn, and Lorraym were teleported back to the Justiceplex. The High Enforcer gave the other three Universal Marshals a joint assignment. They took a battlecruiser to search the galaxy for the planet where the Fellowship of Darkness would build a new stronghold. The Grand Universal Marshal foresaw it.

Chapter 28

Professor Magnemus worked on an android on a long table in Biolaboratory Three onboard the *Technokado*. The Scientific Being opened the head of the automaton. He removed some microchips from it and replaced them with other microchips. Around the chamber rested inoperative other androids. A storage cabinet stood in one corner of the room.

"You should function correctly now," Magnemus said. Before he could turn on the android, someone buzzed him outside the biolaboratory. "Come in."

Asearse entered the chamber. "We have recruited more of our kind for the Fellowship. Another fifteen have joined our ranks."

Magnemus grinned. "Excellent. Our organization is growing significantly. That makes our total membership now fifty-four."

"Do you wish to speak with our new recruits?"

"Yes. What is the latest report from our team searching for Lordruingat?"

Asearse straightened her black gown. "They have searched the worlds of Lanndar, Verkemia, and Marakis for the Cube of Power. No luck in finding it. Now they will search the world of Hydroconia."

Magnemus ran a hand through his red beard. "What about our drone attack on the Justiceplex?"

"It failed."

Magnemus frowned. "Not surprised. What about our members looking for a new planet to build our new base on?"

"They have not yet found an ideal world for it."

"Disappointing. Let's go see the new recruits."

Magnemus and Asearse left Biolaboratory Three and headed for the hall. On their way, they passed droids in the corridor. They took a turbolift down to the next level, got off, and soon entered the hall. Inside waited the fifteen new recruits for the Fellowship of Darkness.

Magnemus was pleased about the recent additions to the Archvillains organization. The professor looked them over. He welcomed them. "Our Fellowship has increased significantly. Eventually, we will outnumber the Universal Marshals when we get enough members."

"What are you doing about the Enforcers in the meantime?" Malotharios, the Leviathan, asked. The Archvillain stood ten feet tall with intense blue eyes and a massive build, dressed in a gray unisuit and matching boots.

"We are considering our options," Magnemus replied. "We already have tried to destroy their headquarters with a drone attack but were unsuccessful. Right now, we have a team searching for Lordruingat."

"The Cube of Power?" Nelessa, the Lamian, said. The Archvillain stood a few inches under six feet with long red hair streaked with white strands. Her yellow eyes shined like twin suns. She wore a yellow pantsuit with black spots on it and matching shoes. "I thought it was just a myth."

"It isn't," Magnemus responded. "If we could get our hands on it, it could be an ultimate weapon we could use against the Federation and the Universal Marshals."

"I know of this legend," Barakhar, the Galactic Cavalier, interjected. He stood six feet, four inches tall, with sandy hair and hazel eyes. He wore a special suit of armor, brown, armed with a sword of power. "I myself quested for it once. Supposed to have power beyond anything in the universe."

"Unfortunately," Asearse said, "the Enforcers are also looking for it."

That caused a commotion among the new recruits. Some said they wanted to be assigned to the search for Lordruingat. A couple verbalized it was a waste of time. The professor restored order before it got out of hand.

"I heard that the Fellowship is looking for a planet to build a new stronghold on," Sunryu, a Tengu, stated. The Archvillain featured red skin, long black hair with a ponytail, and wings, standing under six feet tall. He wore a green robe and matching footwear. The foul being was armed with a *katana* and a *tanto*, a double-edge knife.

"True," Magnemus confirmed. "We were forced by the Universal Marshals to abandon our last fortress on Earth. So we are searching for a suitable planet for our base of operations."

"Got any worlds that are candidates for that?" Tomemene, the Boogieman, asked. Greenish-brown moss covered the body of the Archvillain. He featured greenish-brown eyes and stood over seven feet tall.

"There are several planets that might do," Magnemus answered. "We have Fellowship members working on it."

"What do you want us to do?" Laferral, the Creature, asked. Green scales covered the Archvillain, who stood over six feet tall with emerald eyes.

"Some of you will be assigned to help find a planet

to build our new stronghold on," Magnemus replied. "A few of you will try and recruit more of our kind for our organization. Asearse will handle who will be assigned where."

"What about the quest for the Cube of Power?" Naselena, a vampire, asked. Tall, she featured pale skin, long black hair, dark eyes, and leathery wings. She wore a black tunic and matching slippers.

"At this time, we will not increase the number of the team searching for it," Magnemus answered. "But that may change if needed."

Asearse assigned five of the new recruits to join the Archvillains looking for a suitable planet to build their new stronghold on. She put seven other foul beings to try and get even more Archvillains to become members of the Fellowship of Darkness.

Magnemus left the hall and encountered Orlin, the Grim Reaper, in the passageway. The Incarnation of Death stood six feet, four inches tall, thin in build, and long of limb. A black cloak wrapped his jet-black body with matching loafers on his long feet; a black cowl hid his face. The only visible part of the Archvillain was his jet-black hands with long fingers and curved nails. He carried his shiny scythe of power with him.

"You have news about the Incarnation of War?" Magnemus asked.

Orlin touched the blade of his scythe. "Yes. I have convinced Vidarius to join our Fellowship."

"Excellent. Have you talked yet with the Incarnation of Pestilence?"

"I will speak with him next. Try to convince Jallar to join us."

Magnemus nodded. "What about the Incarnation of

Famine?"

"I will speak with Sallor after I speak with Jallar."

"Good. Our ranks must continue to grow."

That brought the membership of the Archvillain organization to fifty-five. Orlin went on his way for a meeting with the Incarnation of Pestilence. Magnemus took a turbolift to the bridge of the ship. Minions of the professor sat at and operated the control consoles. Glowpanels in the ceiling lighted the bridge.

Asearse entered the bridge. "We have found a few more worlds to consider building our new stronghold on."

Magnemus turned to her. "Which planets?"

"The worlds of Vitarra and Murron."

"What is known about them?"

Asearse gathered her thoughts. "Vitarra is a desert world. There are sand monsters on it. The dominant race of the world is humanoids. They mine the spice called Florenze on it."

Magnemus frowned. "That does not sound promising. What about Murron?"

"It is a forest world. Indigenous creatures are the dominant race. Not known for technology."

Magnemus smiled. "That sounds better. Seems more compatible a place for a new base of operations."

"What world do you want our next destination to be to check out for our new stronghold?"

Magnemus debated with himself on the matter. "Set a course for the planet Imperius. We will start there."

"After that?"

"The planet Golgoth. Then Murron."

Asearse relayed the orders to the helmsman, a male cyborg. The *Technokado* engaged its teleport drive and telejumped from the Nadune Sector of the Milky Way Galaxy to the Leonine Sector of the Milky Way Galaxy.

"Engage the stealth mode," Magnemus commanded.

The navigator, a female android, cloaked the ship. Soon, the vessel reached Imperius.

"Do we land on the world or teleport a party down there?" Asearse asked the Scientific Being.

Magnemus considered. "We will send a party down to the planet to explore the possibility of making it a home for a bigger Complex."

"Who do you want in the party?"

"You lead it. Take with you your sister, Bulkan, Sunryu, and Barakhar."

Asearse left the bridge and took a turbolift down two levels. She gathered the other four members for the party and equipment for it. They headed for the teleporter room on the ship.

A male clone sat at the control console in the teleporter room. He beamed down the five Archvillains to the planet.

"Which way?" Bulkan asked the Charybdian.

"East," Asearse replied.

Imperius orbited its sun as its fourth planet. The party traveled over rolling plains. Nothing appeared in view, no life forms or dwellings. A few wispy clouds floated in the blue sky above them. Little wind blew.

"What do we know of this world?" Barakhar asked the Charybdian.

"It has low technology," Asearse answered. "The dominant race here is human. There is an empire on this world."

The Archvillains continued on. They came upon a

herd of wilderdeer, red and white in color, ruminant swift-footed animals, the males having antlers. At the sight of the foul beings, the four-legged animals dispersed.

After walking a few hours they spotted a settlement. A city with buildings made of stone and no gate or walls around it. They entered it. The place teemed with people. Merchants sold their wares in a marketplace, and children played in the streets. The Archvillains caught the attention of the townspeople. A coliseum ahead of the foul beings arose.

A middle-aged man came up to them. "I am Pontes. Are you here for the games?"

"Games?" Saryelle repeated.

"Fifty-four days of them," Pontes said, straightening his white robe out and wearing sandals. "The new emperor has proclaimed them in honor of his recently deceased father."

"What kind of games are there?" Sunryu asked.

Pontes grinned. "Archery tournament. Knife throwing contest. Chariot racing. Fights with weapons. Wrestling matches. A broad range of them. The city of Harmine welcomes you."

"It would be interesting to see these games," Barakhar remarked, patting his sword of power.

"You are strangers here," Pontes stated. "Any of you interested in participating in the games, or are you just spectators?"

"If anything, we would be spectators," Asearse responded.

"Do you gamble on games?" Pontes asked.

"Not usually," Bulkan answered for them.

"When do these games begin today?" Barakhar

asked.

Pontes grinned. "Soon. People are filing into the coliseum now."

"We would be interested in seeing the games," Asearse said. The others agreed with her.

Pontes motioned for them to follow him into the coliseum. They did. A crowd entered the stadium, packing it. Pontes found them a place to sit about midway up.

After everyone sat, a middle-aged man dressed in a brown robe and sandals stood up in the reserved box for the emperor and his entourage and held up his hands. His name was Callador, and he spoke in a loud voice.

"Welcome to the twenty-second day of the games. First up, we will have an archery tournament."

Men set targets for the participants. Ten archers vied for the title of best bowman. The Archvillains knew of a Universal Marshal called the Great Archer.

When ready, the bowmen shot arrows into the targets. The crowd cheered. All the archers scored bullseyes in their first attempts, so the targets were set farther back in distance. They fired again, and this time, seven out of the ten hit bullseyes. That eliminated three from the tournament. The targets were placed farther back again, increasing the distance more. Now, four out of the seven hit bullseyes. That dismissed three more from the tournament. Again, the targets were pushed farther back, increasing the distance. This time, two out of the four remaining bowmen hit bullseyes. Two more of the archers were eliminated from the tournament. The targets were set farther back. One of the two remaining bowmen hit a bullseye as the other barely missed it. The winner of the tournament was an archer named Thebis from the region of Galileus.

"That was moderately entertaining," Saryelle remarked.

Next up, wrestling matches. Two men squared off with a referee officiating. The first match ended with a pinfall. The next match featured two more wrestlers from different provinces than the first contestants.

"I have seen such matches before," Bulkan said.

One wrestler performed a hip toss on his opponent and scored a point. Back and forth the match went as each man executed grappling techniques on the other. The contest ended with one man outscoring the other five to four.

The wrestling matches lasted awhile. There were thirty-two contestants. The final match featured a wrestler from the province of Calladonia and another from the province of Vitaly.

Both men looked to be lightweights. They wrestled, deadlocked in points, three to three. Finally, the man from Calladonia pinned the man from Vitaly to win the championship. The crowd roared its approval.

"Should we leave now?" Sunryu asked the Charybdian.

"I think we have seen enough," Asearse replied.

The Archvillains said their goodbyes to Pontes and left the coliseum. Outside the large structure personal guard to the emperor halted them. A crowd gathered around them.

"You are strangers to these parts," the captain of the personal guard remarked, a man named Silleus. "Where are you from?"

"From places far, far away," Barakhar answered for them.

"Come with us," Silleus said.

"Why?" Saryelle asked.

Silleus gripped the handle of his sheathed sword. "So we can know your true identities."

Sunryu drew his *katana* from its belt. "I don't think so."

The personal guard drew their weapons. There were twelve of them. They outnumbered the Archvillains two to one.

"Take them," Silleus ordered his men.

The Archvillains defended themselves. Asearse and Saryelle produced water, blasted the personal guards with aqua, and wiped them out. Sunryu and Barakhar killed two of the men, each with their blades. Bulkan bellyflopped atop one fellow and crushed him with his massive frame. The fight lasted short.

"That will teach you to mess with our kind," Barakhar stated.

The Archvillains hurried out of the city before any more personal guard could stop them. No one got in their way as they fled west.

"Now where?" Barakhar asked the Charybdian.

"South," Asearse answered.

The Archvillains made their way to a province called Naomar. There, they beheld an arena where gladiators fought, the main attraction of the area. The lord of the province was Lescorpius, who made the matches.

"I don't think this planet is right to build a stronghold on," Bulkan said.

"I tend to agree," Barakhar said.

The other Archvillains thought the same way. So they contacted the ship with a telecommunicator around

245

the wrist of Asearse and got teleported back to the *Technokado*. They made their report to the Scientific Being.

"Set a course for Golgoth," Magnemus ordered the helmsman.

"Yes, sir," the male cyborg responded.

The ship telejumped to another part of the Leonine Sector. It maintained its stealth mode. The vessel made orbit around Golgoth, the third planet from its yellow sun. Magnemus sent the same party down to the world that had visited the surface of Imperius.

The sky was a gray overcast, threatening rain. The party traversed hills and headed north.

"What is known of this planet?" Bulkan asked the Charybdian.

"It is gothic," Asearse replied. "Much different from Imperius."

The Archvillains traveled a bit before they came in sight of a settlement. They entered another city. Its architecture was more advanced than Harmine. The buildings featured high pointed arches, steep roofs, windows large in proportion to the wall space, and lace-like ornamental carving. People dressed differently than on Imperius—women in long dresses and men in dark suits. The dominant race on Golgoth was human.

People walked the streets. Some traveled by horse-drawn buggies. Policemen patrolled beats. Citizens stared at them.

"These people appear more sophisticated than on Imperius," Barakhar said.

"Technologically, they are more advanced than those on that world," Asearse pointed out.

Saryelle chimed in. "This world may be right for a

stronghold to be built on than Imperius."

"Aye," Barakhar agreed.

"There are no empires on Golgoth," Asearse added.

The Archvillains took in the sights. No one threatened them. They stopped a male pedestrian and asked him the name of the city. He told them it was Gloommar.

"Any place here we should stop at?" Bulkan asked the other Archvillains.

"We have no money to spend," Asearse stated. "That leaves out any restaurants, taverns, and hotels to frequent."

"What about libraries?" Saryelle asked.

Asearse turned to her sister. "This city might have one."

The Archvillains asked a female pedestrian if Gloommar had one. It did. They went to it.

Inside the library, a large facility, shelves of books dominated the space. With the help of a female librarian, the Archvillains found history books of Golgoth. They read passages from the material, getting to know the planet. Unlike Imperius, Golgoth experienced little war. The society of this world tended to be peaceful. It contained four continents, all inhabited. Democratic governments ruled them.

"This planet seems a good candidate to build a new stronghold on," Bulkan remarked.

Asearse agreed. "Definitely a better choice than Imperius."

"But is Golgoth overpopulated?" Saryelle questioned.

"That may make it less attractive to consider for a base of operations," Bulkan said.

"Nevertheless we will put it on the list for possible sites for a new stronghold," Asearse stated. "The professor will make the final determination on which world to construct a better Complex."

The Archvillains left the library after a while reading about Golgoth. They found a spot where no one was looking and telecommunicated with the *Technokado*. The foul beings got teleported back up to the ship.

The five Archvillains met the Scientific Being on the bridge. They gave him their reports on Imperius and Golgoth. Magnemus ordered the helmsman to engage the teleport drive and teleport them to the quadrant where Murron resided. The male cyborg obeyed and the ship telejumped from the Leonine Sector of the Milky Way Galaxy to the Cygnus Sector of the Milky Way Galaxy.

The ship, cloaked, established orbit around the forest world. Murron circled its yellow sun as its fourth planet. The party of five Archvillains went to the teleporter room and beamed down to Murron.

The forest world featured tall trees. Timberland miles around. The planet teemed with life, animals especially. They heard birdsong and the drone of insects around them. The sun above them reached its zenith in a blue sky.

"This world seems so placid," Sunryu remarked. "My kind would love it. Especially the trees."

"It has no cities," Asearse said. "It is not polluted. Technology is absent here."

"What about sentient races?" Bulkan asked.

"The indigenous creatures here are primitive," Asearse answered. "We don't know much about them other than they're tribal."

The Archvillains walked in an eastern direction. They spotted an animal that resembled a gazelle, which ran at the sight of the party. Then, a forest cat crossed their path and took off south. A little later, they passed a small lake.

The Archvillains came upon a village in the trees. They hid themselves from sight and observed the inhabitants, who were furry beings short and armed with primitive weapons. A fire burned in a pit. The foul beings watched the indigenous creatures in their daily routines, posing no threat to the Archvillains. After a while, they left the area, and the furry beings did not notice them.

The Archvillains explored Murron. When they were done, they got themselves teleported back up to the ship. Magnemus met them in the meeting room. They gave their report to the professor.

Magnemus thought about the planets on his list to build a bigger Complex on. The Scientific Being considered which world seemed suited best to have a base of operations on. He heard enough reports on the planets they explored to decide the issue. "We will construct a new Complex on Murron. It is very suitable for us. No governments to interfere with us. Not populated with modern societies."

Magnemus touched a button on the control console before him and a holographic image appeared of a new Complex. The Scientific Being went over the building of a bigger stronghold with them.

Chapter 29

The Universal Marshals beamed down from the *Horizon* to Moromont. They found a computerized world. Cybernetics, biosciences, and biotechnologies dominated the planet. People had microchips in their hands and their heads. The citizens could plug into machines and do a variety of things, such as download information or data in their brains and control androids with their consciousness connected to them as surrogates.

"Moromont is too dependent on machines," Idyllion remarked.

"Where should we start to look for Lordruingat here?" Milantheus asked the other Enforcers.

Nazzar answered. "A place of science."

The Universal Marshals stopped a male and a female pedestrian on a street corner. Their names were Radolf and Nefitir respectively.

"Where is the nearest institute of science in this city?" Nazzar asked the pair.

"There is the Netaflix Institute a few blocks from here," Radolf replied.

The Universal Marshals thanked them and walked to the place. People went in and out of buildings. Citizens rode in automated vehicles that drove themselves. There was no pollution. The ten Enforcers entered the Netaflix Institute of Science.

Inside the institute, people were attached to computers. A male scientist came up to them in a white labsuit and white boots.

"I am Doctor Hymus. How can I help you? Do you wish to connect to computers?"

The Universal Marshals talked among themselves. Finally, they reached a decision.

"I will bond with a machine," Nazzar said. The Android-Enforcer was the only one of the Universal Marshals that could.

Nazzar sat in a chair by a computer. Hymus connected cords to the positronic brain of the Android-Enforcer. Information began pouring into his memory cells. He looked for Lordruingat in the data flooding his positronic brain.

After a while, the connection ended. Hymus detached the cords from the positronic brain of the Android-Enforcer. Nazzar got to his feet.

"Get anything about the Cube of Power?" Apparis asked the automaton Universal Marshal.

"I found references to power cubes," Nazzar answered.

"Why are you looking for power cubes?" Hymus asked.

Danbarrack spoke up. "We are searching for one in particular. Lordruingat. Have you heard of it?"

"Yes," Hymus said. "We have a number of power cubes. Technological devices for different purposes."

"Do you know where Lordruingat is?" Kesharra asked.

"Not offhand," Hymus responded. "Why are you looking for it?"

"We need to find it before the Fellowship of

Darkness does," Ursanne explained. "Foul beings who would use it for destruction. Archvillains."

"Just who are you?" Hymus asked.

"We are Universal Marshals from the Universal Federation of Planets," Yevadne replied.

"I have heard of you," Hymus said. "I am familiar with Archvillains."

"Can you help us?" Benethor asked.

Hymus sighed. "I will try. Don't know if we will find this Lordruingat, though."

The doctor led them to a room where a power cube operated. It was large in size and purple. Its chief function involved maintaining energy to power the computers in the institute.

Hymus pointed at the power cube. "What about this?"

"No," Nazzar responded. "Lordruingat does not operate on a scientific or physical level. It is beyond the three basic energy powers." The Android-Enforcer explained them to the doctor.

"I am not familiar with the occultic or celestic levels," Hymus said. "Only with the scientific one. Our power cubes all operate on energy power of the physical."

"Then it is unlikely the Cube of Power is on Moromont," Danbarrack remarked.

"Sorry I'm unable to help you," Hymus said.

The doctor led them out of the chamber. The Universal Marshals said goodbye to him and left the Netaflix Institute of Science.

Outside, a bunch of police officers, twelve in number, waited for them. The police officers were armed with stun batons. A crowd of people watched what would transpire.

"You need to come with us," a police sergeant said.

"Why?" Benethor asked.

"Because you aren't microchipped," the police sergeant replied. "All citizens must be."

"We aren't citizens of your planet," Danbarrack responded. "We don't need to be microchipped."

That surprised the police officers and the crowd. The police officers talked among themselves. It caused a commotion in the crowd.

"You still must come with us," the police sergeant insisted. "You will need to be interrogated."

"No, I think not," Apparis said.

The police officers readied to use their stun batons. The Universal Marshals prepared to defend themselves.

"You leave us no choice," the police sergeant said. "We will use force to subdue you and take you in for interrogation."

The police officers moved in on the Universal Marshals, who did not want to hurt them. Benethor pulled the red Elfstone from his pouch and blasted them and they all flew backward on the ground. Kesharra shot solar beams from her hands and kept them lying on the pavement. Hulkeme used his special powers and disarmed the police officers by magically taking away their stun batons.

"Yield," Benethor said.

The police officers were dumbfounded. So was the crowd.

"We yield," the police sergeant responded.

Danbarrack smiled. "Good. By the way, we are in law enforcement like you."

Hulkeme magically gave back their stun batons. The

253

police officers put them back in their belts.

"Now, we must leave you and return to our ship," Nazzar said.

The Genie-Enforcer teleported the Universal Marshals back to the *Horizon*. They went to the bridge and sat at stations. Manual control of the vessel resumed.

"What planet do we visit next to search for Lordruingat?" Kesharra asked the other Universal Marshals.

"Farrago," Benethor answered from the captain's chair.

They plotted a course for Farrago and engaged the teleport drive. The ship telejumped from the Scorpio Sector of the Milky Way Galaxy to the Libra Sector of the Milky Way Galaxy.

Chapter 30

Draegor and the other Watchers with him chartered a ship, the *Galactic Star*. The crew of the vessel set a course for Caramax, a Federation planet in the Pisces Sector of the Milky Way Galaxy—a democratic one. None of the Watchers had ever ventured out of their homeworld before.

"This is so new to us," Garion said.

The Watchers sat in a briefing room of the ship. A black telescreen hung on the wall across from the automatic doors. A control console lay before Draegor.

"What is our mission, great leader?" Narwyn asked.

Draegor composed himself. "We are to find the Enforcers and the Archvillains searching for Lordruingat and stop them. If also necessary, Mahab and his space pirates."

"Finding them all will be a chore," Sorhea said, a female humanoid dressed in a white robe and matching slippers. "How do we track them all down?"

"We will find the trails they leave behind," Draegor replied. "Sooner or later, we will encounter them. Our paths will cross. It is inevitable."

"What about others who are not them that have searched for the Cube of Power?" Garion asked. "Could they help the Enforcers or Archvillains or space pirates in their quests for it?"

Draegor frowned. "There have been none who had

searched for Lordruingat that had any real clues to its whereabouts who could help them. Many before them have tried but have never come close. Except for that one minion of an Archvillain who did reach it. But that was an anomaly."

The Watchers talked among themselves. Shortly, Draegor restored order.

"There must be those among the Enforcers and the Archvillains who have the third eye capable of seeing where Lordruingat is at," Narwyn said.

"Yes," Draegor agreed. "They have made attempts to find the Cube of Power. Also, by other means. But none of their efforts have succeeded thus far."

"Can they use special powers to ultimately find Lordruingat?" Garion asked.

Draegor sighed. "Possible. But the Cube of Power shields itself from detection. Yet it is unknown if such beings could ultimately discover the resting place of Lordruingat. We cannot take any chances. The Cube of Power must be protected at all costs."

"How much do we know about the Enforcers and Archvillains?" Narwyn asked.

"Not much," Draegor answered. "We don't know which Enforcers or Archvillains are searching for Lordruingat. Nor do we know the extent of their special powers. But none of them have such abilities on the ulgnostic level like the Cube of Power or our limited ones."

'So find out as much as we can about them," Garion said.

"Yes," Draegor agreed. "We must learn which ones have special powers on the scientific level, the occultic level, and the celestic level. All below the ulgnostic level."

The leader of the Watchers dismissed them. They each went to private quarters. The ship traveled through hyperspace and would arrive at Caramax in five hours.

The *Galactic Star* reached the planet and began a descent to the surface. The Watchers gathered together outside the shuttlecraft bay. After the ship landed they disembarked from the vessel in a spaceport. They left the spaceport and entered the city of Amounjaro.

Traffic flowed heavily in the metropolis. Speeder cars, trucks, and buses zoomed along. The air smelled clean. Some people walked. The Watchers took in the sights.

"Where do we go here, great leader?" Narwyn asked

"A library," Draegor replied. "A place of information."

The Watchers got directions to the library from a male citizen, a human. They took a speeder bus to the public building. The trip went fast.

Inside the library, a very large structure, they looked for material on the Enforcers and Archvillains. They found holograms of nonfiction books on the subject matter. Sitting at a table they read all the information on the two groups.

"Here it says the Enforcers, the Universal Marshals, are a branch of the Federation Department of Justice headquartered on the planet Tellus," Garion said. "They have been waging war for over a thousand years against evil."

"Anything about specific Enforcers?" Narwyn asked.

Garion read through the material. "There are names of past Enforcers here. They have a leader called the

High Enforcer, or Grand Universal Marshal. According to this, the current one is Delveran, also known as the Sorcerer-Enforcer."

"What about Enforcers at present," Narwyn asked.

Garion checked. "There are eighty-six serving currently. This volume has been updated."

"Anything else?" Sorhea asked.

"The Enforcers vary in race and power level," Garion answered. "Some are scientists, some are occultists, and some are celestists. The same applies to Archvillains."

"That might be useful to know," Narwyn said.

Garion found something else. "Several months ago, Tellus was invaded by a space fleet under the command of Archvillains. It freed the Archvillains imprisoned in the Universal Prisonplex on Tellus outside the capital of Acropollon. The space fleet was destroyed with the help of Federation forces."

"It means that Archvillains outnumber Enforcers in the galaxy," Draegor surmised.

"Correct," Garion responded. He went through another holograph of a nonfiction book. "There is a list here of Archvillains in the universe. Among them are Incarnations. A number of them."

"What about Incarnations who are Enforcers?" Sorhea asked.

"Yes," Garion answered. "There are a few that are."

The Watchers also found material related to them and Lordruingat. Planets that might have the Cube of Power on it. What the Watchers are like. Stories of quests for Lorduingat. They felt flattered that archives existed of them and the Cube of Power.

Dreagor decided it was time to go. They left the

library. Since there was nothing else to do on Caramax, they returned to the *Galactic Star*.

Later, the ship took off. Next heading: the planet Scamoria, in the Pisces Sector of the Milky Way Galaxy, a member of the Federation. The vessel engaged its hyperdrive and traveled through hyperspace. The journey lasted three hours.

The *Galactic Star* landed on Scamoria at the Dumalin Spaceport on the northern outskirts of the city of Dumalin. Other ships landed and took off from the spaceport. The main terminal and control tower rested on its southern side.

The Watchers climbed aboard a hoverbus and went into the city. Heavy traffic flowed as all kinds of hovervehicles sped along. Tall buildings rose everywhere. Sunny weather greeted the day. Clean air circulated the aristocratic world.

The Watchers got off the hoverbus at a library. They entered the public facility and searched for material on the Universal Federation of Planets, the Enforcers, foul beings—particularly Archvillains—and anything related to them and Lordruingat. They found record discs on the subject matter.

The Watchers sat at tables with reading devices. They put record discs in the machines.

"It says here there are currently 1,390 planet members of the Federation," Garion said. "The Federation is over 1,007 years old."

Narwyn read a disc. "It says here that Illdrasil, the Tree of Evil, was the first supreme evil. It was destroyed by the Enforcers. The original members of the Universal Marshals numbered twelve. After the destruction of Illdrasil, the Federation was born. The planet Tellus was colonized, and the Federation and the Universal Marshals made their headquarters there."

"There is some information on Lordruingat here," Sorhea stated. "It says that the Cube of Power was created by aristocratic beings to consolidate their power on some world called Quinnox."

"There is plenty of data on foul beings here," Narwyn said. "Divided into three evil classes. Criminals, Villains, and Archvillains. There are stories about some of them trying to find Lordruingat. Even a tale of foul beings creating the Cube of Power for nefarious purposes. This led to their own destruction because they could not handle such power."

"Are there any indications what planet where Lordruingat is actually on?" Draegor asked.

"No, great leader," Garion answered. "No records of our world regarding the Cube of Power. But there is a reference to our planet but not in connection to Lordruingat."

"Should we erase the reference to our world on these discs, great leader?" Sorhea asked.

Draegor thought. "It is likely that other planets have mentioned in files the name of our world. To erase the information would draw suspicion. We cannot go to every planet and delete the data on our world. Therefore, we shall just stop the Enforcers and the Archvillains searching for the Cube of Power."

"That is a wise course," Garion remarked.

"It is simplified," Narwyn added.

The Watchers finished what they were doing. They left the library and roamed the city for a while before returning to the *Galactic Star*.

Chapter 31

The six Universal Marshals went to the prison in the city of Bothham, also a seaport. They introduced themselves to the Warden, Vinius Malcon, a tall male humanoid. Prison guards watched the prisoners, all in jail for piracy.

The stone structure of the prison appeared dark. It rested near the Gasborus Sea, housing over 300 pirates. There also stood a gallows, the wooden framework with nooses for hanging pirates. Today, there would be executions of some scheduled.

In the office of the Warden, the Universal Marshals talked with him. Vinius sat behind a wooden desk. On the wall hung pictures of famous pirates who had been captured.

"What can I do for you?" Vinius asked the Enforcers.

Falatar answered the question. "We wish to speak with some of your prisoners."

Vinius raised an eyebrow. "Why?"

"Because we need information about certain issues concerning piracy," Jeddriel replied.

"What issues?" Vinius asked.

"There has been a dramatic increase of piracy in the galaxy," Hashrah responded. "We need to know more about Captain Mahab, the Incarnation of Piracy. As well as the planet that is the home base of pirates in the galaxy called the Retreat."

Vinius frowned. "I don't know if any of the prisoners would want to help you. Their incarceration here is a sad lot. But if you wish to speak with a few of them, I can arrange it. Starting with those on death row. In two hours, we will be executing some pirates."

The Universal Marshals agreed. The Warden summoned prison guards who escorted him and the Enforcers down to the cells where pirates waited for execution. Five prisoners were scheduled for hanging. Their cells were dank.

"Inmates look alive," Vinius said. "There are Universal Marshals here who wish to speak with you."

A pirate, a male human lying on a bunk, roused himself to sit up. "What ye be wanting with us?"

"We want to ask you some questions," Memfelice answered for the Enforcers. "What is your name?"

"I am Myjohn. Former first mate of the ship *Black Diamond* under the command of Captain Qeeqig. What do ye want to know?"

"Tell us about Mahab," Agwennel replied.

"The Incarnation of Piracy?" Myjohn said. "He leads a fleet of ships to raid and pillage in the galaxy. His is the ultimate command among pirates. No one dares oppose him."

"Where is the Retreat?" Jeddriel asked.

Myjohn laughed. "No pirate can answer ye about its location. It would be death to them if they reveal its whereabouts."

"You're already on death row," Falatar pointed out.

Myjohn snorted. "I won't tell ye where the Retreat is and break the code."

"I admire your loyalty," Hashrah remarked. "But

you could do some good by telling us where the Retreat is. Even save lives."

"Telling you won't save me life," Myjohn responded.

"Nor any of the rest of us," another pirate added, a male humanoid.

"And you are?" Hashrah asked.

"Gibbus. I once had the honor to serve under the command of Captain Mahab. He is very clever. But he does not tolerate any insubordination. His word is law among pirates."

"He has broken the law," Jeddriel said.

Gibbus smiled. "Your law. His is the only law among pirates."

The Universal Marshals could not get any more information out of the prisoners. So they left the inmates on death row and went to other cells holding other pirates. The Enforcers questioned them but could not get any information from them because they refused to say anything useful.

"We have learned very little about Mahab and the Retreat from the prisoners," Falatar remarked.

"It was expected that they would not help us much," Jarek added.

The Universal Marshals went to the gallows to witness the executions for today. A crowd gathered for the event. The day turned cloudy.

Prison guards escorted the five prisoners for execution to the gallows. The Warden oversaw the hangings. People in the crowd booed the pirates—four males and one female. Prison guards lined up the inmates on the gallows and put the nooses around their necks.

A priest stepped forward. "May the Almighty have

mercy on your souls."

The Warden spoke to the prisoners. "If any of you wish to say something, speak now."

None of the pirates said anything. Vinius signaled to the executioner, a male humanoid, to pull the lever. Beneath the pirates, the trap doors opened, and they were hung. The crowd cheered.

"What a ghastly sight," Jarek remarked. The Incarnation of Life shook his head.

"That is the right word for it," Jeddriel agreed.

Later the Universal Marshals joined the Warden for supper at his residence, not far from the prison, along with a few officials. They ate a meal consisting of a meat stew, sourdough bread, mixed vegetables, and melons with orange wine to drink. They sat in a large dining room.

"I have been Warden now for ten years," Vinius stated. "It is a pretty good work and pays well."

An official, a male humanoid named Skyliss, chimed in. "The Warden has done an excellent job. No one has escaped from the prison. There have been no riots either. For the most part, the inmates behave themselves."

Another official, a male human called Hengar, spoke up. "So you're Universal Marshals. How long have you been Enforcers?"

"Eight years," Falatar replied.

"Eleven years," Jeddriel answered.

"Seven years," Hashrah responded.

"Ten years," Agwennel said.

Jarek recalled his time of service thus far. "Fourteen years."

Memfelice figured hers. "Six years."

"What did you do before you became Universal Marshals?" Vinius asked.

Jeddriel took a drink of orange wine in a goblet. "I was fighting evil before I became an Enforcer. God commanded me."

"What are you?" Hengar asked.

"An archangel," Jeddriel replied. "I am known as the Archangel-Enforcer."

"I am called the Lunar Being," Falatar stated. "I am from the planet Triskelios. The only one with special powers from my world. I worked for the Callatech Observatory as an astronomer assistant before I became a Universal Marshal."

"Are you a doctor of astronomy?" Vinius asked.

"No," Falatar answered.

Memfelice talked next. "I am referred to as the Psychic Being. I was a psychic, helping people. I gave them guidance. Police from my world of Parabola used my services to help solve crimes. Also, to find people. Now I use my special powers for the Universal Marshals."

"I am the Turbobeing," Hashrah said. "I was in the military on my planet of Nathebes before I joined the Enforcers."

"I am an Incarnation," Jarek stated. "The Incarnation of Life. Always have been."

"You're an immortal," Skyliss said.

"Yes," Jarek confirmed.

Agwennel chimed in. "They call me the Undine-Enforcer. I am a water elemental. I am from the world of Aquavena. Sometimes, my kind is invoked in magic."

Just then, they heard a loud boom. They stood up and heard it again. Outside, they ran. The booms continued. A male human, a prison guard, dashed up to them from the prison.

"What is it?" Vinius asked the prison guard.

The prison guard caught his breath. "We're being attacked! Pirate ships are firing on us, especially the prison. They are trying to free the inmates."

The Warden, the prison guard, and the Universal Marshals ran for the prison. People in the street panicked and scrambled for cover as the pirate ships from the sea pounded the city with cannon fire.

They reached the prison. Pirates from the ships landed and went to free their kind from the penal facility. Other buccaneers terrorized the citizens.

Pirates spotted them and charged at them armed with swords. Hashrah fired turbo blasts from her hands and knocked pirates down. Agwennel manifested water from the air and sent buccaneers flying. Jeddriel materialized a flaming sword and clashed with pirates as Jarek fought with his hoe of power. Memfelice used her psychic power of psychokinesis and flattened buccaneers. Falatar employed his gravitic push to take out pirates.

After the Enforcers dispatched pirates, they, the Warden, and the prison guard entered the prison. The cannon fire from the pirate ships continued, damaging structures and particularly the prison. More pirates from the corsairs freed their kind from the cells.

"This is a disaster," Vinius remarked.

Pirates with swords and pistols attacked them. A couple of buccaneers shot at them with their guns. Memfelice psychically stopped the bullets from reaching them. Falatar used his gravitic push and slammed pirates into the wall. Agwennel produced water from out of the air and crashed a wave into buccaneers and wiped them out.

Escaped pirates ran out of the prison. Hashrah fired turbo blasts from her hands and took out more pirates. They dodged buccaneers shooting pistols at them. A cannon ball struck a wall of a cell with a pirate imprisoned. It freed the buccaneer, and he fled.

"The city garrison is engaged in fighting pirates," Vinius said. "But our defenses aren't holding up well enough. Too many prisoners are escaping. It will be difficult to round up the fleeing inmates."

The prison emptied of prisoners. The Universal Marshals and the Warden hurried to the docks. In the bay, seven pirate ships sailed. The vessels kept firing cannons.

"How can they be stopped?" Vinius asked the Enforcers.

Memfelice used her power of pyrokinesis and torched a pirate ship. The buccaneers onboard doused the flames after throwing buckets of water on the blaze. A cannonball flew their way, and Falatar employed his gravitic push to stop the projectile from hitting them.

Agwennel made a tidal wave on the bay and smashed it into a pirate ship, which caused it to sink. The other corsairs sailed out of the bay after having accomplished their mission.

"This is a sad day," Vinius remarked.

"I'm sorry we couldn't have done more to stop the pirates," Jarek said.

"What will you do now, Warden?" Jeddriel asked.

Vinius seemed to consider that. "We will have to hunt down the pirates all over again. Rebuild the prison and other parts of the settlement where damage was done."

The Universal Marshals took their leave of the Warden and got teleported back up to the *Constellation*. They went to their individual quarters and rested for a while. Later, they would decide what to do next.

Chapter 32

"Should we plot a course for the planet of the Retreat, captain?" Gaelor asked.

Mahab relaxed in his command chair on the bridge of the *Jolly Mercer*. "Not yet. There is a prison ship in this sector carrying prisoners. We will attack the vessel and see if we can recruit some of them as pirates."

"Aye, captain," Gaelor said.

"Are there any other ships to raid in this quadrant, captain?" Wyller asked.

Mahab grinned. "Yes. We will get our plunder from them."

Malargos checked sensor readings. "There is a vessel ahead of us about a hundred kilometers distance, captain. Another freighter."

"Splendid," Mahab said. "Carreo, contact the *Jolly Capcorn* and tell them we are intercepting that freighter."

"Aye, captain," Carreo responded.

The two pirate ships engaged superluminal drives to cut off the space freighter. They succeeded in halting the cargo vessel.

Mahab led a raiding party to the teleporter room and beamed over to the space freighter. The captain and crew of the cargo vessel put up a fight. The Incarnation of Piracy and his men battled them.

"Yield or die," Mahab said to their foes.

The captain and crew of the cargo vessel fire blasters at the Incarnation of Piracy and his men, who returned fire. Mahab swung his scimitar of power and sliced through foes to their deaths. The fight lasted longer than what the Incarnation of Piracy wanted. In the end, the space pirates emerged victorious over the captain and crew of the cargo vessel.

A few of the crew of the space freighter remained alive. Their captain did not survive.

"What do we do with the prisoners, captain?" Wyller asked.

Mahab cut off the head of one of them. "They are of no use to us. Kill them."

His men obeyed and slaughtered the remaining members of the crew of the cargo vessel. Then, they transported the goods from the space freighter to the two pirate ships.

"What do you want to do with the space freighter, captain?" Wyller asked.

"Destroy it," Mahab replied.

After the goods from the cargo vessel got plundered, the Incarnation of Piracy and his men returned to their ships. The *Jolly Mercer* and the *Jolly Capcorn* put a safe distance between them and the space freighter. The pirate ships opened fire with ion cannons and destroyed the cargo vessel. Nothing remained of it.

"Where next, captain?" Gaelor asked.

"Set course for the prison ship," Mahab ordered. The Incarnation of Piracy already used his special powers to sense where it flew in the sector. He relayed the coordinates to Gaelor.

The two pirate ships engaged their superluminal drives and tunneled through space. They intercepted the prison ship and blocked its path. The prison ship halted and refused to yield to the pair of corsairs.

"They are putting up quite a resistance," Mahab said. "Fire ion cannons and knock out their engineering section."

"Aye, captain," Carreo responded.

The *Jolly Mercer* fired ion cannons and damaged the engines of the prison ship. It could not engage its hyperdrive or go at sublight speed.

"Take out its weapons systems," Mahab ordered.

"Aye, captain," Carreo responded.

The *Jolly Mercer* targeted its weapons systems and disabled them with the ion cannons.

"Prepare for boarding," Mahab said.

The Incarnation of Piracy led a raiding party to the teleporter room and teleported over to the prison ship. They met resistance from the prison ship. Prison guards and crew fired blasters and blast rifles at them. The buccaneers returned fire. A melee ensued.

Mahab swung his scimitar of power and slashed foes and felled them. A prison guard struck at the Incarnation of Piracy with a stun baton to render him unconscious. But the blow did not affect Mahab, who shrugged it off. His immortal form was impervious to blaster fire and stun baton strikes.

The Incarnation of Piracy and his men made the prison guards and crew of the prison ship retreat. Soon, the buccaneers overwhelmed the opposition and ended the fight.

"We have rounded up the survivors, captain," Wyller said.

"Good," Mahab responded.

"What should we do with them, captain?" Wyller

asked.

Mahab grinned. "Kill them."

The men of the Incarnation of Piracy obeyed him and butchered the survivors. Next, Mahab went to the sections of cells where prisoners languished. The first section of cells held a dozen inmates, all dressed in orange jumpsuits and black shoes.

"What is your name, and what are you in for?" Mahab asked an inmate, a male humanoid and a Criminal, sitting on a bunk.

"I am Mitana. My crime is armed robbery."

Mahab nodded. "How many counts?"

Mitana stood up. "Eleven."

Mahab smiled. "Impressive. How do you feel about becoming a pirate?"

"It sounds wonderful," Mitana responded. "Better than being a prisoner."

Mahab turned to Wyller. "We can use him. Open the cell."

"Aye, captain," Wyller responded. He touched buttons on the keypad to the cell and opened it.

Mitana walked out of his cell. He stretched his arms. "Freedom again."

"Wyller will see to it you are dressed appropriately and armed," Mahab said. "Welcome to my world."

The Incarnation of Piracy went to the next cell. Inside it stood an alien, a Villain.

"What is your name, and what are you in for?" Mahab asked.

"The name is Horvatis. I am in for being the head of a crime syndicate."

"A gangster," Wyller remarked.

"Where planet did you operate from?" Mahab

asked.

"Voltaira," Horvatis answered.

Mahab had never heard of the world. "How large was your operation?"

"Large enough," Horvatis replied. "My reach extended beyond my planet."

Mahab appeared not impressed. "Did the Universal Marshals bust your operation?"

Horvatis sighed. "Yes. The authorities of my homeworld enlisted the aid of the Enforcers to take down my operation. I lost everything. My wife and youngling were also taken into custody."

"That is a shame," Wyller remarked.

Mahab sighed. "How do you feel about becoming a pirate?"

"I never imagined becoming a buccaneer," Horvatis answered. "I wouldn't know how to be one."

"You could learn to be one," Mahab responded.

"Yes," Horvatis agreed.

Mahab turned to Wyller. "How many men do we lose on this raid?"

Wyller counted on his fingers. "Four, captain."

"We will need to replace them," Mahab said. He addressed the Villain again. "Would you be interested in becoming a pirate?"

"I don't know of what service I could be to you," Horvatis responded.

Mahab grinned. "We could find a niche for you."

"I have never wielded weapons before," Horvatis admitted.

"You could be trained in them," Mahab said. "We can turn you into a genuine pirate. What do you say?"

Horvatis seemed to consider the proposal. "I accept

your offer."

"Are your wife and youngling on board the prison ship?" Mahab asked.

Horvatis nodded. "They are in another section of the vessel."

Mahab turned to Wyller. "Release him."

Wyller touched the buttons on the keypad to the cell and opened it. The Villain walked out of the cell.

Mahab addressed one of his men. "Help Horvatis find his imprisoned family on board and free them."

"Aye, captain," Cauldar, a male human, responded.

Mahab interviewed a number of the prisoners aboard the prison ship. The Incarnation of Piracy recruited altogether half a dozen of the inmates to join the pirates. He ordered all the inmates to be set free. Those who would become buccaneers teleported back to the *Jolly Mercer* with him and his men. The rest of the freed prisoners took the prison ship and set out for parts unknown.

On the bridge of the *Jolly Mercer,* Mahab sat in his command chair. The Incarnation of Piracy felt pleased with himself.

"Where to, captain?" Gaelor asked.

Mahab let out a deep breath. "Set a course for the Retreat."

"Aye, captain," Gaelor responded.

The two pirate ships engaged their superluminal drives and tunneled through space. In a while, they disengaged their superluminal drives and entered the sector where the planet of the Retreat was located. Other pirate ships were in the area. They all orbited the planet and beamed down buccaneers to the surface of the swampy world.

Mahab led a party of his men to the huge structure of the Retreat. All around him stood tall trees with brown moss on them. Birdsong echoed in the air. Large reptiles swam in the waters of the planet. The air smelled of a pine-like scent.

Mahab and his party of men entered the huge structure of the Retreat. Fellow pirates greeted them and bowed to the Incarnation of Piracy, who grinned. Mahab stopped outside a large hall and told his men to wait there. Then, the Incarnation of Piracy entered the great chamber.

Inside stood an immense table of wood. Around it sat plenty of chairs. The walls looked bare. Mahab took his place at the head of the table. Many pirate captains joined him, both male and female.

"This meeting comes to order," Hollis said, a male human, captain of the *Jolly Rogue*.

All the other captains fell silent. Mahab waited for the first topic of discussion to begin, not interrupting the proceedings.

"The first order of business is the Universal Federation of Planets sending Universal Marshals after us," Hollis stated. "The Federation has battlecruisers searching the galaxy for us. They seek to find the Retreat."

Burrina, a female humanoid, captain of the *Jolly Natron,* spoke. "They will never find our home base. They must not find it. Or learn where it is."

"We may have to battle Federation forces," Larcan, a male alien, captain of the *Jolly Mark*, interjected. "Sooner or later, we will be confronted by them."

"It seems unavoidable," Gastov, a male humanoid, captain of the *Jolly Feral*, added.

Darwinona, a female human, captain of the *Jolly Pearl*, chimed in. "We must strengthen our defenses for the Retreat."

"Here, here," Jayondu, a male alien, captain of the *Jolly Dodger*, agreed.

Hollis addressed the Incarnation of Piracy. "What do you say, captain?"

Mahab answered momentarily. "We must be prepared in the event that Federation forces discover the location of the Retreat. I foresee the Enforcers will do that eventually. They cannot be ignored."

"Do we send some of our ships to intercept the Federation battlecruisers then?" Larcan asked the Incarnation of Piracy.

"Not yet," Mahab replied. "We have time to make plans for that eventuality. We must be ready when that happens."

The other pirate captains talked among themselves. Mahab observed their reactions. Hollis quieted them down.

"The Universal Marshals are not to be trifled with," Borgan, a male alien and captain of the *Jolly Vishon* said. "They are a real threat to us. In the past, they have jailed a number of our kind. Brother and sister pirates losing their freedom. Corsairs confiscated. Loot taken."

"We must immediately put together a fleet of our ships and be ready to do battle with Federation forces," Javondu stated. "We should not wait for them to attack us first."

"That would be wise," Darwinona remarked.

"Prudent," Larcan agreed.

The pirate captains talked among themselves again, except for the Incarnation of Piracy. He waited for them to calm down.

"We have to decide what ships will make up our fleet to fight the Federation battlecruisers," Gastov pointed out. "There have to be enough vessels for it."

"Our leader will decide which corsairs will comprise the fleet," Borgan stated.

All the other pirate captains turned to the Incarnation of Piracy. He would decide which vessels would comprise their fleet.

"I will think it over which of our ships will make up the fleet," Mahab said. "I will need a little time to decide."

The other pirate captains did not press him on the issue further.

Hollis cleared his throat. "Next order of business. On the penal colony on the planet Falcora, pirate ships attacked the prison there, holding members of our kind. The corsairs freed many prisoners. But there were Universal Marshals there who fought fellow buccaneers. The Enforcers did not stop the jailbreak."

"Good news," Jayondu remarked.

"There are other penal colonies imprisoning our kind," Hollis said. "Should we consider attacking them in order to free fellow pirates?"

The pirate captains debated the issue among themselves. Mahab said nothing on the matter yet. Hollis quieted everybody down again.

"I say we attack the penal colonies holding our kind prisoner and swell our numbers," Borgan stated. "It's a disgrace to be imprisoned for piracy."

"Our kind are mistreated in prisons holding them," Larcan said. That was the opinion of all the pirate captains, including the Incarnation of Piracy. "They need to be set free."

Mahab spoke again. "We can plan to raid the penal colonies holding our fellow pirates. But it should wait until we deal with the Federation forces and the Enforcers first."

All the other pirate captains agreed with him. The Incarnation of Piracy sat back in his chair.

"What about prison ships?" Darwinona asked the others. "Some of our kind are imprisoned in them."

Mahab leaned forward in his chair. "Recently, I led a raid on one. We freed the prisoners on it. I also recruited half a dozen of them to serve me."

This was news to the other pirate captains. They talked again among themselves. Some of them voiced concern about the matter. Others favored attacking prison ships to free their kind and increase their numbers.

Mahab interrupted the argument over the matter. "When the time is right, we can raid prison ships and free members of our kind and recruit others to our side. But it should also wait until we have dealt with the Federation forces and the Universal Marshals."

At last, the other pirate captains agreed with the Incarnation of Piracy. They moved on to the next order of business.

"Altogether, we have accumulated much plunder from our raids on all kinds of freighters, trade ships, and other vessels," Hollis said. "This includes those of Federation planets. They are arming themselves against us. Some are now getting military escorts to protect them from us. Recently, a few pirate ships have been damaged in their attacks on such vessels. One corsair, the *Jolly Darklin*, was destroyed by Federation battlecruisers."

"No survivors?" Borgan asked. "What about the

captain of the buccaneer vessel, Strayman?"

"Killed," Hollis answered.

Larcan pounded a fist on the table. "We must avenge the destruction of the *Jolly Darklin* and the death of Captain Strayman."

"Here, here," Jayondu seconded.

Hollis held up his hands. "We will. When the time is right."

The other pirate captains turned to the Incarnation of Piracy. Mahab nodded.

"Now, about the black markets," Hollis said. "Our profit margin is up for the last quarter. We are raking in more significant amounts of money."

"Very good," Mahab remarked.

"Most of the loot we are selling on the black markets has increased in price," Hollis stated. "I see this trend continuing."

The other pirate captains cheered that. Mahab smiled.

"There is another new matter that has been brought to my attention," Hollis said. "It involves a thing called Lordruingat."

Mahab raised an eyebrow. "The Cube of Power?"

"What is this object?" Gastov asked.

The other pirate captains turned to the Incarnation of Power. They had never heard of Lordruingat. But the Archvillain did know about the Cube of Power.

"Lordruingat is said to be the greatest power in the universe," Mahab explained. "It contains energy power beyond the other three."

The other pirate captains did not understand what the Incarnation of Piracy referred to. They gave the Archvillain bewildered looks.

"What are the other three?" Darwinona asked.

Mahab leaned back in his chair. "They are called scientific, occultic, and celestic, in order from lowest to highest in level. My special powers reside on the celestic one."

"Why bring up this issue?" Larcan asked the captain of the *Jolly Rogue*.

"Because the Enforcers are looking for it," Hollis told them. "Also, his kind." He pointed at the Incarnation of Piracy

"You mean Archvillains," Mahab said.

Hollis nodded. The other pirate captains erupted in talk again. This new development displeased them. They argued over it.

"Calm down, everybody," Hollis shouted. "Order. Order."

The other pirate captains quieted down. The Incarnation of Piracy appeared busy with thoughts on the subject.

"Should we be searching for this Lordruingat?" Burrina asked.

Larcan pounded a fist on the table again. "If the Universal Marshals find it first, they could use it against us."

"So we should search for this Cube of Power ourselves," Jayondu voiced.

"Make it a weapon for us to use against our enemies," Gastov added.

Mahab came out of his reverie and joined the discussion. "I will try to sense where Lordruingat is in the galaxy."

The Incarnation of Piracy closed his eyes and tried to feel where the Cube of Power was located in the galaxy. The other pirate captains watched him in anticipation. None of them spoke a word while the Archvillain concentrated on discovering its hidden presence.

Mahab opened his eyes. "I cannot see where Lordruingat is. It is veiled from my second sight. Not unexpected. It appears no one with special powers is able to discern where the Cube of Power is hidden."

Some of the pirate captains swore. A few pounded the table with a fist. Others shook their heads.

"The question still remains," Jayondu said. "Should we ourselves search for this Lordruingat?"

"I say we should," Darwinona interjected.

Larcan spoke. "I don't agree. It seems to me to be a waste of time."

The other pirate captains argued over the issue. Mahab considered whether they should or should not look for the Cube of Power. Finally the other buccaneer leaders turned to the Incarnation of Piracy for a decision on the matter.

"We have no resources to begin a search for Lordruingat," Mahab said. "No clues to what world it is on. The Cube of Power has been hidden for millennia from all. Others have tried to find it but failed. That includes those of my own kind, Archvillains. It is said in some tales about Lordruingat that beings called Watchers guard it."

Gastov snorted. "You're saying we should not search for the Cube of Power then."

"The odds against finding Lordruingat are too great," Mahab stated. "What would make us think we have a chance of discovering where it is hidden if everyone else failed to do so."

The other pirate captains agreed with his point. None of them could argue what the Incarnation of Piracy said. The Archvillain settled the matter.

"So we will not search for it," Jayondu muttered.

"Looks that way," Borgan added.

A few of the pirate captains grumbled. Mahab laughed.

"Our primary concern is to strengthen our defenses here against Federation forces and the Universal Marshals," Hollis said. "And to put together a fleet of ships ready to do battle against their battlecruisers."

Some of the pirate captains looked forward to fighting the Federation forces and the Enforcers. Mahab felt uneasy about the coming battles against the two that he knew would inevitably happen. Hollis dismissed the meeting.

Mahab left the hall. Outside, his men milled around.

"How did it go, captain?" Wyller asked the Incarnation of Piracy.

Mahab sighed. "We discussed a number of topics. Including a surprise matter."

"What one, captain?" Carreo asked.

"It is of no consequence," Mahab replied. He told them about other subjects discussed at the meeting.

"What do we do now, captain?" Wyller asked.

Mahab smiled. "We do a bit more of pirating."

The Incarnation of Piracy and his men got teleported back up to the *Jolly Mercer*. They set a course for the Capricorn Sector of the Milky Way Galaxy.

Chapter 33

The *Slaughter* established orbit around Hydroconia. It engaged stealth mode to make it invisible. The ten Archvillains beamed down to the surface of the planet, which circled its yellow sun as its third world. Eighty percent of Hydroconia was water.

The Archvillains headed west. Stands of trees surrounded them. In the clear blue sky above them flew a flock of white birds going south. They walked through tall grass, verdant and supple, for a while. Then the common wild growing vegetation shortened, signs of having been grazed by herbivore animals.

The Archvillains encountered no danger to them. The natural environment seemed quite peaceful. The sun reached its zenith.

"What is in this direction?" Darlesse asked the black magician.

"A city filled with humans," Sumerlin replied. "We shall see what we can find out about Lordruingat."

"I think this planet is a favorable possibility where the Cube of Power is," Foulbard remarked. The others tended to agree with the Shocker.

In an hour, the Archvillains arrived at the city. People flooded its streets. Strange animals also roamed the place. Buildings featured domed roofs copper in color.

The Archvillains stopped a male and a female

pedestrian, who wore costumes like most of the citizens. To the foul beings it looked like the city celebrated something.

"What is the name of this city?" Tajanna asked the pair of Hydroconians.

"Nabylon," both said in unison.

"Why are you dressed up?" Namina asked the next question.

"It is Liberation Day," the male human answered. "We celebrate it every year."

"What is it about?" Gnashboros asked the two Hydroconians.

The female human replied this time. "We mark the day when we gained our freedom from the Killic Empire. This is our twentieth anniversary."

The Archvillains wondered if the Universal Marshals had helped the Hydroconians in their fight for liberation. They did not ask the human couple about that. The two Hydroconians went on their way.

The Archvillains made their way to a building bigger than other structures in the city. They climbed steps and entered.

Inside, they found tiered seats with members in different colored robes and footwear sitting. The foul beings learned the building housed the senate of the land dwellers of Hydroconia. They addressed one senator, a middle-aged man in a red robe, who spoke.

"I am Senator Capollo. You are strangers to our world."

"Yes," Sumerlin responded for the Archvillains.

"How can I help you?" Capollo asked.

"We are looking for something," Daggermash replied for the Archvillains. "We wish to talk with someone here who may help us."

"What is it you seek?" Capollo asked.

Amyrielle answered the question. "An object of great magic called Lordruingat. The Cube of Power."

Capollo frowned. "I have never heard of it. I cannot help you."

"Is there anyone who can?" Ripgarth asked.

Capollo seemed to think about it. "Maybe scholars."

"Where can we find these scholars?" Xigan asked.

"Their headquarters is three buildings behind this structure," Capollo replied.

The Archvillains thanked him for his help. They left the senate building and strode behind it for the scholar house. They passed two smaller structures—an eatery and a recreation center—before they entered the home of learned men and women.

An elderly man in a white robe greeted them. "I am Quasarin. Head of the House of Scholars. How may I be of service?"

"We need help to find an object of great magic," Amyrielle said. "Lordruingat, the Cube of Power. Do you know of it?"

Quasarin's eyes widened. "I have heard of it. There are many stories about it."

"What can you tell us about it?" Darlesse asked. "Especially its whereabouts."

"Why do you seek it?" Quasarin asked.

"We need to find it before our enemies get their hands on it," Sumerlin replied.

Quasarin seemed perplexed. "You believe it is on my world."

"Possibly," Foulbard said.

"There are many stories about it," Quasarin stated.

"It is said to be guarded in a special place, like a mountain retreat by holy men or a forest house where a powerful being has a library of forbidden knowledge."

"What about the water dwellers on your planet?" Darlesse asked.

"The Jungans?" Quasarin said. "There are tales of them possessing it. None know for sure."

Gnashboros spoke. "You mention a mountain retreat. What mountains?"

"The Great Alps," Quasarin answered. "They are north of here."

Namina chimed in. "What about the forest house? Which forest?"

"It is said to be in the Great Forest," Quasarin replied. "It is south of here."

The Archvillains thanked the old scholar for his help. They left the scholar's house and got teleported back up to the *Slaughter*. The foul beings discussed in the meeting room what to do next.

Later, the Archvillains beamed down to the foot of the Great Alps. They climbed the range and entered a mountain pass. A herd of mountain deer migrated east, to the right of them. Overhead, an alpine hawk flew in a clear blue sky as the sun neared its zenith. The weather felt warm.

Ahead of the Archvillains, they spotted a tarn. They stopped at the small mountain lake. No aquatic animal life swam in it or paddled with feet on its surface. They continued on.

The Archvillains reached the mouth of a valley. Sumerlin halted them. The black magician closed his eyes and sensed in all directions.

"Well?" Darlesse asked.

Sumerlin gathered his thoughts. "I feel the presence of people north of us. The mountain retreat is ahead of us."

"Can you sense Lordruingat?" Tajanna asked.

"No," Sumerlin answered. "A veil is blocking my second sight from seeing it."

The Archvillains descended into the valley. Overhead, a flock of mountain geese flew south. The verdant elongated depression featured no animals in it or dwellings.

The Archvillains left the valley and ascended a peak. They reached a path that circled the mountain with a pointed summit. The narrow walk led to a stone bridge, a huge pair of doors on the other side. They crossed the stone bridge and stopped at the closed entrance.

"How do we get inside?" Daggermash asked the black magician.

Suddenly, the huge doors opened. A group of bald men in woolen robes and boots greeted them. The holy men numbered seven. Their leader spoke.

"I am Barazal. Why have you come to us?"

Amyrielle answered the question. "We seek an object of great magic called Lordruingat."

Barazal talked to the others with him. "We do not know of it."

Sumerlin read the thoughts of the holy men. "I can feel you are hiding something. Guarding something powerful."

"What is in our possession cannot be taken from here," Barazal stated. "It is forbidden for outsiders to even see it."

"What is it you have?" Foulbard asked.

"We cannot tell you," Barazal responded. "Only our

order is allowed to know what the sacred piece is."

The Archvillains talked among themselves. The holy men waited for the foul beings to speak again.

"We insist you show us this object," Darlesse said.

Barazal shook his head. "No. Please leave. We have nothing further to talk about."

The Archvillains looked angry. Instead of departing, they attacked the holy men. Foulbard shot shock waves at them and sent them flying. More holy men appeared. The foul beings moved forward against them. Ripgarth fired a blue beam from his eye and knocked down more of them. Sumerlin shot red flames from his hands and fried some. Darlesse leaped and stomped on the chest of one, killing him. Daggermash stung a few with his scorpion tail.

The Archvillains proceeded toward the hidden treasure guarded by the holy men. Their opposition to the foul beings appeared weak. The Archvillains slaughtered the holy men without conscience. In time, they reached the special chamber where the hidden object resided.

"There it is," Namina pointed out.

On a stone podium rested a tome. The learned book featured gilded lettering and a gold clasp. Two holy men protected it. Xigan took care of them and killed them with blows from his fists.

"All this for a religious volume," Gnashboros spat.

Sumerlin picked up the tome. The black magician undid the clasp. He read the first few lines of the learned book. "This is useless. I sense nothing in here that could be of help to us."

"Destroy it then," Darlesse voiced.

Sumerlin dropped it to the stone floor. The black magician shot red fire from his hand and burned the volume to ashes.

None of the holy men survived. The Archvillains left the mountain retreat. Once outside, they got teleported back up to the *Slaughter*. They later retired for the night.

The next morning, the Archvillains beamed down again to Hydroconia. They materialized in the Great Forest. Small birds chirped in the trees. Forestchucks—stocky, burrowing animals—in their path scattered. Twigs snapped under the feet of the foul beings as they walked. The air smelled fresh.

"I hope this time we have better luck," Ripgarth remarked.

The trees towered over the Archvillains and featured dense crowns. A partly cloudy sky above them hid the sun at times. A few insects droned.

The Archvillains walked for over two hours. No sight of the forest house yet. Only the sounds of nature played for them. No carnivore animals appeared to threaten them. They spotted tree squirrels dashing up trees, cute creatures with reddish-brown fur. A stream meandered to their left. In the flowing body of water, silver-scaled fish swam along with mud turtles.

A small snake, orange and blue, crossed their path. Xigan stomped it to death.

Another hour later, the Archvillains found the forest house. It looked made of stone and appeared average in size. Smoke rose from a chimney. The foul beings stopped a moment.

"I sense a powerful entity in there," Sumerlin said.

From around the corner of each side of the forest house, a huge canine came toward them. Both massive dogs, brown with white streaks on broad chests, growled at them. Then the animals barked.

From the forest house, a man emerged. Tall, he sported a short white beard and a white ponytail, dressed in a white robe and matching shoes, holding a staff. His purple eyes focused on them. The male humanoid spoke.

"Greetings, strangers. I am Amorbeus."

The pair of huge canines moved toward the Archvillains. Amorbeus commanded them to stay. Both massive dogs obeyed his command and sat. The animal names were Gasha and Killa, both males.

"I rarely have company these days," Amorbeus said. "Would you like to come into my abode?"

The Archvillains followed him into the forest house. Both huge canines came behind them.

Inside, a fire burned in a stone fireplace. Over the fire hung a pot with a stew cooking. In the kitchen stood a long wooden table with eight wooden chairs around it. An oven appeared before a wall. Cupboards were filled with stored food.

"Make yourselves at home," Amorbeus told them.

In the next room, books filled a library with a wooden table surrounded by five wooden chairs. Beyond that was a bedroom. Windows in the forest house were closed at the moment. Both massive dogs lay down on the bedroom floor.

"So you have always been alone here," Foulbard stated.

Amorbeus smiled and leaned his staff against a wall. "Yes. Would you care for some food?"

Some of the Archvillains would eat. Gnashboros, Namina, Daggermash, Darlesse, and Foulbard would sample his fare. They sat at the wooden table while the others stood.

Amorbeus got wooden bowls, silver spoons, and a wooden ladle from a cupboard. He scooped stew into the wooden bowls and placed one with a silver spoon before each of the foul beings who'd decided on a meal. He retrieved dark bread from a cupboard, placed the baked good on an oval dish, and set it on the wooden table.

"Delicious," Gnashboros said after swallowing some stew. The Viper tore off a piece of dark bread and ate it.

"I know you have come to see me for a reason," Amorbeus said. "What is it you wish to see me about?"

Sumerlin answered the question. "We seek a special object. Lordruingat, the Cube of Power. Do you know of it?"

"I have not heard that name in a long time," Amorbeus replied. "The last time it was mentioned by a group of occultists from another world seeking it. They asked for my help. As far as I know, they never found it."

"We have been searching for it for a while," Tajanna said. "From planet to planet. We have not found it yet."

Amorbeus frowned. "There are many stories about Lordruingat. I have heard so many tales about the Cube of Power being on different worlds, from members of the Universal Federation of Planets to non-Federation ones. Of being guarded by powerful ones called Watchers, ranging in number from six to six thousand. With so much information on Lordruingat, it is hard to decipher which is true and which is false."

"What else do you know about the Cube of Power?" Sumerlin asked.

"I know it is said to contain energy power on the ulgnostic level," Amorbeus answered. "There is the story

291

that gods made Lordruingat to augment their power. Another tale concerns that the Creator created the Cube of Power for a benevolent purpose."

Darlesse swallowed a bite of stew. "What benevolent purpose?"

"To help spread divine love in the universe," Amorbeus replied.

That was new to the Archvillains. They knew there were some things they had never heard about Lordruingat. Some true and some false.

Amorbeus continued. "There is the story of a group of scientists building the Cube of Power as a weapon that could destroy worlds. Also a tale with such a weapon being in the hands of an evil empire in the galaxy."

"Do you know of any planets that could be where Lordruingat is that we have not heard of?" Ripgarth asked.

"What worlds have you searched for the Cube of Power?" Amorbeus asked.

The Archvillains told him what planets they had already been to in order to find Lordruingat. Amorbeus heard of all of them he informed them.

"Can you tell us of any other planets the Cube of Power might be on?" Foulbard asked.

Amorbeus appeared to think on that. "Offhand, I know of a few other worlds said to be the resting place of Lordruingat. One is the planet Cubeon. Have you ever heard of it?"

"No," Amyrielle answered for them.

"It is an ice planet that supports life adapted to cold," Amorbeus said.

"Where is it located?" Xigan asked.

"In the Heltheon Sector of the Milky Way Galaxy,"

Amorbeus answered. "The sixth planet in its solar system."

The Archvillains made a note of it. Those of the foul beings eating finished their meal.

"Any other worlds you might know of besides Cubeon?" Namina asked.

Amorbeus nodded. "Barexy."

"That planet we heard of," Foulbard said.

Amorbeus raised a bushy eyebrow. "Wolcoth?"

"Heard of that planet as well," Foulbard said.

"What about the planet Oseeria?" Amorbeus asked.

Darlesse spoke. "That we have never heard of. Where is it located?"

"In the Libra Sector of the Milky Way Galaxy," Amorbeus answered. "It is the third planet in its solar system."

Sumerlin changed the subject. "What do you know about the Jungans?"

"The water dwellers?" Amorbeus said. "They do not much interact with land dwellers. Their kingdom is underwater. They do keep secrets."

"Could they be hiding Lordruingat?" Tajanna asked.

"It is possible," Amorbeus replied. "But I think it unlikely."

The Archvillains thanked him for his help and hospitality. They left the forest house and got teleported back up to the *Slaughter*. The foul beings got breathing apparatuses for underwater and returned to the planet.

Sumerlin sensed where the underwater kingdom of the Jungans was located. The Archvillains put on the breathing apparatuses for underwater and dove into the water near a peninsula. Down they went to the shield bubbles where the Jungans lived. The water dwellers met them as they penetrated a shield bubble and pockets of air.

The Jungans were alien beings with floppy ears and long snouts. Armed Jungans halted them as they approached a throne. An elderly Jungan sat on the throne, flanked by two others standing. He spoke to the Archvillains, who removed their breathing apparatuses.

"I am Chibotta king of the Jungans. Why have you invaded our sanctuary?"

"We seek an object of great magic," Amyrielle said.

Chibotta shook his head, and spittle flew from his lips. "What object?"

"Lordruingat, the Cube of Power," Sumerlin answered.

"You think we have it," Chibotta stated.

"Maybe," Foulbard said.

Chibotta laughed. "Who told you we might have it?"

"Some of the land dwellers," Gnashboros responded.

Chibotta shook his head again, and spittle flew from his lips once more. "This object you seek is not in our possession. You have wasted your time coming to us."

Sumerlin sensed the Jungans hid something. The black magician tried to pinpoint its location. "You have something valuable down here. I feel its presence."

Chibotta swore. "You have worn out your welcome here. Return to the surface."

"We would like to see this artifact you have," Darlesse said.

"That is out of the question," Chibotta responded.

"Why?" Sumerlin asked.

Chibotta rose from his throne. "It is a sacred relic of my people. Not for land dwellers to see."

"We insist," Ripgarth said.

Chibotta snorted. "Guards, escort them out of here."

Jungans, armed with pikes, motioned with their weapons for the Archvillains to leave the shield bubble. The foul beings did not budge. Instead, they attacked. Foulbard blasted guards with shock waves and hurled them backward. Ripgarth fired a blue beam from his eye and knocked guards down. Sumerlin shot red fire from his hands and burned guards.

More armed Jungans appeared and charged the Archvillains. The foul beings defended themselves and took them out. Darlesse leaped and did a flying stomp to one. Xigan, who towered over the Jungans, smashed them with his fists. Daggermash stung guards with his scorpion tail.

The Archvillains grabbed Chibotta after knocking aside the two Jungans beside him. More armed Jungans ran toward the foul beings.

"Stop!" Sumerlin shouted.

The armed Jungans halted. They did not know what to do. Their king was held captive by the Archvillains.

"Drop your weapons, or we will kill him," Sumerlin said.

Chibotta grimaced. "Do as they say."

The armed Jungans dropped their weapons to the floor of the shield bubble. None of them made a move against the foul beings.

"You will take us to see your sacred relic," Sumerlin said to the Jungan king.

Chibotta nodded. He directed them to a connecting shield bubble, and they penetrated it. The Jungan king led them through several more shield bubbles until they reached a stand with an oblong object that glowed blue.

"So this is it," Gnashboros remarked.

"Not Lordruingat," Tajanna muttered.

Daggermash swished his scorpion tail. "A great disappointment we did not find the Cube of Power."

"I told you it was not in our possession," Chibotta said.

The Archvillains took the Jungan king back to the throne room. The Jungan guards made a wide path for the foul beings.

"We will be leaving you now," Sumerlin said.

The Archvillains put on their breathing apparatuses and went through the shield bubble back into the water. They swam up to the surface. Once on dry land they got teleported up to the *Slaughter*.

The Archvillains retired. The next day, they went to the meeting room on the ship.

"What planet should we search next for Lordruingat?" Foulbard asked the black magician.

"Cubeon," Sumerlin replied. "It is the nearest world."

The *Slaughter* engaged its teleport drive and telejumped to the Heltheon Sector of the Milky Way Galaxy. They hoped to have better luck on Cubeon.

Chapter 34

The *Horizon* established an orbit around Farrago, the fourth planet in its solar system. The Universal Marshals teleported down to the unknown world. They found themselves in a city apparently deserted.

"I don't like this," Yevadne said.

"Where is everyone?" Danbarrack asked no one in particular.

The Universal Marshals walked down a deserted street. Only abandoned cars appeared. No bodies in them.

"Something must have happened to the inhabitants," Idyllion remarked.

"The question is what," Apparis said.

Buildings stood, none damaged. Local businesses were open but had no customers. The Universal Marshals entered a store that sold hardware. They checked it out. Plenty of goods stocked shelves. Nobody was behind the cash registers.

"This is strange," Ursanne remarked. The Norn-Enforcer picked up a can of red paint. She put it back after looking at it.

The Universal Marshals left the store and entered a record one. Many albums were in stock. Also CDs. Nobody behind the counter.

"At least they had taste in music," Kesharra quipped.

"Yes," Milantheus agreed. Father Time picked up an album. He did not know what kind of music was on it.

"This is spooky," Benethor remarked. The Elf-Enforcer wondered if the record store had nature music.

The Universal Marshals left the business and continued down the street. A gun shop appeared on their right. They entered the place and found unsold weapons. Besides guns, there were also knives. There were automatic weapons, shotguns, handguns, and other types of firearms. No one behind the counter here either.

"Could there have been a global war on this planet?" Yevadne asked her fellow Enforcers.

"I don't think so," Nazzar said. "There is no evidence so far to support such an event."

"Something must have happened to the people," Kesharra stated. "How could they have all disappeared?"

Hulkeme spoke. "Maybe they fell victim to an alien invasion."

"That is a possibility," Danbarrack agreed.

The Universal Marshals knew of alien invasions that had wiped out worlds. If an alien invasion did decimate the people of Farrago, where were the invaders? Also, there were no signs of animal life in the city, not even birds. It seemed all life on the planet had been exterminated.

The Universal Marshals came upon an apartment building. They decided to go inside.

The ten Enforcers opened doors to apartments. No one lived in them. They found baby strollers in a few of them and toys. All the apartments appeared deserted. They went up to the next floor.

The apartments on the second level were empty. In one, there was a table with cards on it, as if people had been playing. In another room, a TV was on, but there was only static on the screen. A third had shelves of books to read.

The Universal Marshals went up to the third floor. Same thing. No one lived in the apartments.

"This is disturbing," Ursanne remarked.

Benethor shook his head. "Whatever happened on this world, it must have been cataclysmic."

The Universal Marshals went up to the fourth floor. In one apartment they heard a noise from a closet. They opened it and found a young woman, blonde, sitting on the floor.

"Please don't hurt me," the young woman said, in a yellow dress and matching slippers.

Yevadne knelt. "We are not going to hurt you. What is your name?"

"Christa."

"Do you know what happened to your planet?" Kesharra asked.

Christa answered momentarily. "Plague."

That was a possibility the Universal Marshals had not considered. The young woman was clearly scared.

"A plague wiped out the people of your world?" Ursanne asked.

"They are not dead," Christa replied.

"What do you mean?" Danbarrack asked.

"They are zomboids," Christa answered.

Zombies. That surprised the Universal Marshals.

"The Walking Dead," Benethor remarked.

"They die, and then they come back to life," Christa stated. "They attack those not infected and pass on the plague to their victims, who become zomboids."

Apparis voiced the next question. "Are there other

survivors besides yourself?"

"Yes," Christa replied. "We are scattered here and there."

"Can the zombies be killed?" Apparis asked.

"If you cut off their heads, they die," Christa replied. "They can also be burned."

"Where are the zombies?" Idyllion asked.

"Outside the city," Christa answered. "They will come soon."

That sounded awful to the Universal Marshals. Of the Enforcers, only Benethor ever encountered zombies before.

"Is there a safer place than this apartment building?" Milantheus asked the young woman.

"No place is safe," Christa responded.

"Is there a more guarded structure in the area?" Nazzar asked.

Christa seemed to think about it. "There is the grand hotel. It is surrounded by a fence. I can take you there."

"I think that would be a good idea," Benethor said. "A more defensive place."

Christa led the Universal Marshals out of the apartment building. They headed east. More deserted structures on either side of them. More abandoned cars on the streets. Still no sign of animal life.

In time, they reached the grand hotel. It towered before them with a chain-link fence around it. A few abandoned cars appeared on the grounds. They stopped.

In the partly cloudy sky, the sun began setting. Shadows started to appear.

"What are you?" Christa asked the Enforcers.

"We are Universal Marshals," Apparis replied for them.

Christa's eyes widened. "Why are you here?"

"We are on a quest for Lordruingat, the Cube of Power," Benethor answered. "Do you know of it?"

Christa frowned. "I have never heard of it. Is it a weapon?"

"Not exactly," Nazzar said. He explained it to the young woman.

"And you think it is on my world?" Christa asked.

"A possibility," Danbarrack said.

Christa shook her head. "I don't know where it would be on my world. Unless it is a secret government project."

"You have armed forces on your planet?" Yevadne asked.

"There are military installations on my world," Christa replied.

"Where is the nearest one?" Kesharra asked.

"South of here," Christa answered. "The Jocoon army base."

Nazzar voiced the next question. "Where is the nearest institute of science?"

"North of here," Christa responded.

On the scientific level, Farrago was progressive. On the occultic level, the planet was below average. On the celestic level, the world was nonexistent. Zombies normally resided on the occultic level, invoked by magic usually, but not always.

"Does your world have any occult shops?" Benethor asked.

Christa frowned. "Magic stores? Very few."

The zomboids of Farrago had not been created by magic. The Universal Marshals wondered what kind of plague resurrected dead bodies on this world. They would tell certain Federation departments on Tellus about the problem on Farrago when they returned to the Federation capital after they completed their quest.

Christa led them inside the grand hotel. They crossed open ground and entered the towering structure. All seemed quiet.

They found themselves in the lobby. It was empty. No guests and no hotel personnel. Behind the counter keys to rooms lay in slots.

"This place has a casino," Christa said.

The Universal Marshals were not interested in gambling. The grand hotel contained thirty floors. The ten Enforcers figured that the rooms would be all empty. Christa led them to the spacious kitchen. She flipped on the lights.

Food and drink stocked refrigerators, cupboards, and a storage room. Christa opened a refrigerator and grabbed a cold soda. She unscrewed the cap and drank the pop.

"Do you know how long this plague has been around?" Ursanne asked the young woman.

Christa swallowed more of her beverage. "At least three months."

"Not long," Danbarrack remarked.

The Universal Marshals did not eat or drink anything from the kitchen. Christa led them back to the lobby after turning off the lights.

"Should we check some of the guest rooms in the hotel?" Hulkeme asked his fellow Enforcers.

"We'll probably find nothing," Milantheus said.

The Universal Marshals talked among themselves about the issue. They decided not to bother looking in guest rooms. They would have to get the keys to them.

Dusk came. They all went outside. Coming toward the grand hotel walked zomboids. The creatures, in tattered clothes, looked ravaged by the plague that had claimed Farrago.

The Universal Marshals acted. Benethor pulled the red Elfstone from his pouch and blasted zomboids apart with it. Kesharra shot solar blasts from her hands and destroyed them. Idyllion fired nuclear blasts from his hands and annihilated some. Apparis opened his beak and let loose sonic blasts that decimated the foul-smelling creatures.

"There are so many of them," Hulkeme remarked. The Genie-Enforcer picked up an abandoned car and smashed zomboids to pieces.

Milantheus used his special powers and froze them. Nazzar fired laser beams from his eyes and slayed zomboids, including the ones Father Time rendered motionless.

The zomboids kept coming. The Universal Marshals mowed them down like a scythe cutting blades of grass. Terrified, Christa stayed behind the Enforcers, letting them kill the abhorrent creatures.

"This world must have a population in the billions," Ursanne said.

Wave on wave, the zomboids came at them. The Universal Marshals wiped out each one. Finally, the waves stopped for a moment.

"More of them will come," Christa stated.

"That is not good," Yevadne said. "We can't keep fighting them."

Danbarrack turned to the young woman. "Did scientists on your planet try to figure out what caused the plague?"

"Yes," Christa replied. "It isn't known if any of them succeeded. They tried treating the victims of the plague to cure them."

"So they worked on an antidote," Danbarrack remarked. "That is encouraging. Maybe we will find answers at an institute of science. Possibly the antidote they were working on."

Just then, more zomboids came staggering toward them. The Universal Marshals resumed killing the creatures, who moved slowly and growled.

"I have not slayed so many zombies before," Benethor said. The Elf-Enforcer had done so occasionally but not in great numbers at a time.

The Universal Marshals knew Christa feared being turned into a zomboid. They protected her from harm. None of the zomboids got past the Enforcers. The young woman felt safe in their company.

Again, the waves stopped. On the ground lay many destroyed zomboids, piled up.

"I don't sense anymore of them in the area," Ursanne said.

Benethor put the red Elfstone back into his pouch. "Let's go back inside the hotel."

In the hotel, they rested for the night. The next morning, they left the hotel and headed north for the institute of science.

A sunny day greeted them. No clouds in the blue sky. To their surprise a flock of birds flew overhead south, the first sign of animal life on the planet.

It took them forty-five minutes to reach the institute of science. A sign on the front read: *GASTRON INSTITUTE*. They entered the facility without a problem.

They walked down a corridor. On either side stood closed doors. They stopped at a lab.

In the lab, they found scientific equipment. A bunch of test tubes rested on a table. Also a stack of notebooks with writings in them. Nazzar grabbed one and read it.

"What does it say?" Yevadne asked the Android-Enforcer.

"It says that they were making progress on finding a cure for the plague," Nazzar said. He turned a page. "They were experimenting on zomboids to try and change them back. They were partially successful."

"What does the last entry in it say?" Danbarrack asked.

Nazzar turned to the last page in the notebook. "They were being overrun by zomboids. They were forced to flee the institute."

"Anything about where they were going?" Apparis asked.

"They tried for a safe haven further north of here," Nazzar replied. "Toll Island."

"I know where that is," Christa chimed in.

The Universal Marshals and the young woman checked another lab. Two zomboids were strapped down on tables, growling. More scientific equipment in the chamber.

"Should we just leave the creatures here?" Kesharra asked her fellow Enforcers.

"We cannot set them free," Danbarrack stated. "They are a menace."

Benethor drew his Elvin sword from its scabbard. "It's a shame I have to do this. But it's necessary." The Elf-Enforcer cut off the heads of the two zomboids, resulting in the death of the pair of creatures. "May they find peace."

Christa seemed shocked by what the Elf-Enforcer had done. She got over it quickly and apparently understood the necessity of it.

The Universal Marshals and the young woman went to other rooms in the institute. None of the doctors in it stayed behind. They found only scientific equipment not used in a while. After searching through enough chambers, they left the place and headed south for the Jocoon army base.

Christa voiced a question to the Enforcers. "Could this Lordruingat you had mentioned to me cure people?"

"It's unknown what the Cube of Power could do," Danbarrack answered for them. "Little is known about it. Much information we have come across about it. So many stories of it."

Christa acted disappointed about it. She asked no more questions on the subject. The young woman instead questioned them on other things, like where they were from.

"The Universal Marshals are headquartered on the planet Tellus," Nazzar told her. "We are a branch of the Federation Department of Justice. We are led by the High Enforcer, Delveran."

"Could your Federation help my world?" Christa asked. "Help find a cure for the plague?"

"We will contact the Federation authorities to help with your blight after we return to our ship," Benethor answered for the Universal Marshals. "Doctors can be assigned to it to find the antidote for the condition suffered by your people. The Federation has done it before."

"Thank you," Christa responded.

The Universal Marshals and the young woman encountered no zomboids on the trip to the military installation. Once they arrived, the sun reached its zenith. Military vehicles sat there unused for a while, like jeeps and tanks. They found no bodies. The army base appeared deserted.

"Did your military fight the zomboids?" Ursanne asked the young woman.

Christa held back tears. "Yes. My father is in the army."

"What rank?" Danbarrack asked.

"A colonel." Christa seemed to reminisce about that.

"Was he stationed here?" Yevadne asked.

Christa shook her head. "He was stationed across the sea at the Dellic army base."

The Universal Marshals and the young woman looked through the barracks. They found made and unmade bunks. Playing cards were scattered on one bunk.

"It appears the soldiers abandoned the army base after being overrun by sheer numbers of zomboids," Danbarrack remarked.

"They may have escaped in army helicopters," Kesharra said. "There are none on the army base."

The Universal Marshals and the young woman searched through other buildings on the military installation. In a house they found a journal by an army captain. Nazzar picked it up off a nightstand in a bedroom.

"Any reference to the zomboids in its entries?" Danbarrack asked the Android-Enforcer.

Nazzar read some out loud. "It says here the soldiers battled the creatures. Wave on wave, they came at them.

307

Day and night. No one knows how the plague started in the first place, but it quickly spread. Soldiers began to get infected by the zomboids. Finally, the orders came down for the surviving soldiers to abandon the army base and head for safer ground. They took army helicopters to Toll Island."

"Where is Toll Island?" Apparis asked the young woman.

"It's east of here, about twenty miles from the seaport of Washcaw," Christa replied.

The Universal Marshals and the young woman left the house. As they exited the military installation, zomboids appeared.

"They're like a swarm of locusts," Kesharra remarked. "Unending."

The Universal Marshals battled the shambling creatures. Benethor pulled the red Elfstone from his pouch and destroyed them. Kesharra shot solar rays at them and blew them apart. Idyllion did the same with nuclear blasts from his hands as Nazzar sliced them to pieces with laser beams from his eyes. Apparis let loose sonic blasts from his beak and decimated them.

Christa hid behind the Universal Marshals. She could not fight back against the zomboids. The Enforcers kept her out of harm's way.

The Universal Marshals dispatched the last of the zomboids. On the ground lay the destroyed corpses of the diseased creatures.

"Where next?" Ursanne asked the Elf-Enforcer.

"The seaport of Washcaw," Benethor replied. He addressed the Genie-Enforcer. "Take us there."

Hulkeme teleported them to the city. It appeared deserted. Boats docked in the harbor with no one onboard them. A few craft were missing in spots.

"It appears some survivors may have taken boats to escape the zomboids," Danbarrack remarked.

Ursanne closed her eyes to sense the area. "I feel no survivors here. But I detect some did flee in the craft."

"Can you sense Lorduingat on the planet?" Nazzar asked the Norn-Enforcer.

Ursanne tried. "I don't feel the presence of the Cube of Power on this world."

Just then, zomboids appeared and staggered straight at them. The Universal Marshals destroyed the grotesque creatures—Kesharra with solar blasts, Nazzar with laser beams, Idyllion with nuclear fire, Apparis with sonic shots, and Benethor with the red Elfstone. This time there were not as many waves of the zomboids. More corpses on the ground.

"This world is full of death," Milantheus remarked.

"Where next?" Yevadne asked the Elf-Enforcer.

"Toll Island," Benethor answered.

Hulkeme teleported them to the piece of land surrounded by water. They materialized before a settlement. From it emerged some people armed with guns, survivors.

One middle-aged man spoke, "I am Doctor Jannus. How did you get here?"

"We teleported," Benethor answered for them.

Jannus exchanged a few words with those with him. "You're not infected."

"No," Benethor responded. "We visited Gastron Institute and read some of your notebooks on the plague."

"You're not from our planet," Jannus said.

"Correct," Nazzar confirmed.

Jannus talked more with those with him. "Why are you here?"

"We seek an object of power," Apparis stated.

"What exactly?" Jannus asked.

"Lordruingat," Nazzar answered. "The Cube of Power."

Jannus conversed further with those with him. "Never heard of it. You believe you will find this thing on Farrago?"

"It is a possibility," Idyllion said.

"But now we don't think so," Kesharra added.

"Just who are you?" Jannus asked.

"We are Universal Marshals from the Universal Federation of Planets," Nazzar replied for the Enforcers.

A young woman from the group of survivors spoke. "I am Deirdre. Can you help us with this plague?"

"We will notify the Federation about your problem after we return to our ship," Apparis said. "Federation doctors will be assigned to it to help you find a cure."

"Do you know what caused the plague?" Idyllion asked.

Jannus shook his head. "It is a mystery how it started. Many theories have been put forth on that. No one has been able to figure it out."

The Universal Marshals stayed the night. Christa would remain with the other survivors. The next morning, the Enforcers said goodbye and returned to the *Horizon*. They contacted the Federation on Tellus and explained the situation. The appropriate officials would handle it.

Chapter 35

The *Slaughter* made orbit around Cubeon. The planet suffered an ice age, a preternatural winter. It was inhabited by humanoids who had adapted to the cold conditions, like other lifeforms.

The Archvillains bundled up and took a shuttlecraft down to the surface. It landed before a mountain range. The foul beings stepped out of the shuttlecraft and walked toward the snowy peaks.

"This seems like an unlikely place for Lordruingat to be on," Namina said.

"Aye," Ripgarth agreed.

Gnashboros spoke. "The Cube of Power could be on any planet. There are no clues to what kind of world it could be hidden upon."

The Archvillains reached the foot of the mountain range and stopped. It snowed lightly. Fluffy clouds blocked the sun from sight.

Sumerlin closed his eyes and sensed Cubeon. After a few minutes, he opened his eyes. "I don't feel the presence of Lordruingat. But I do feel the presence of people."

The Archvillains spotted a pass among the snowy peaks. They decided to take it. The foul beings climbed. Snowfall got heavier.

The Archvillains walked a path through the mountains. In some places, the snow was deep.

Suddenly, the foul beings heard a rumbling. An avalanche tumbled toward them. They put their backs against a mountain. The mass of snow engulfed them. The wind whistled through the snowy peaks.

The Archvillains dug their way out. Sumerlin melted the snow with red fire from his hands. They managed to get clear of the white stuff.

"That was dangerous," Tajanna remarked.

"We have to be more careful," Gnashboros stated.

The Archvillains continued on. They wound their way through the mountains slowly. At one point, they came upon tracks.

"Wonder what creature made these," Darlesse said.

Foulbard bent down and touched the tracks. "Whatever made them, it may be unfriendly." He stood up again.

The Archvillains moved on. The snowfall lighted a bit. No other signs of life.

The foul beings came upon more tracks. Then they heard a roar. Followed by a chorus of more howls that echoed through the mountains. They halted.

"What is making that racket?" Namina asked no one in particular.

Sumerlin closed his eyes. "I feel the presence of creatures coming toward us." The black magician opened his eyes.

Soon, the creatures appeared. They were huge, covered in white fur, with long fangs and white eyes. They charged the Archvillains.

Sumerlin shot red fire from his hands at the creatures. Foulbard blasted them with shockwaves. Ripgarth fired a blue beam from his eye at them. Namina sang a song that drove them to cover their ears.

The Archvillains repelled the creatures, who ran away back the way they came. The foul beings heard roars again. They took a defensive stance and waited for another attack.

The creatures charged again at the Archvillains. This time, some of them threw rocks at the foul beings. Sumerlin destroyed the large masses of stone with red fire. The creatures retreated again as they could not penetrate the defenses of the foul beings. They did not return to assault the Archvillains.

"This world must hold many dangers," Amyrielle remarked.

"Finding Lordruingat could be costly here," Daggermash interjected.

The Archvillains resumed their trek. A while later, they found a cave.

"Should we investigate it?" Xigan asked the black magician.

Sumerlin took a deep breath. "We'll check it out."

The Archvillains entered the cave. They found bones of animals and beings in it.

"Those creatures we fought may be carnivorous," Foulbard said.

The Archvillains left the cave. Snowfall stopped. They continued on.

Fluffy clouds still blocked the sun from sight. The temperature felt a little colder. The wind whipped around them, making it chilly.

Sumerlin suddenly stopped. The other Archvillains halted.

"What is it?" Namina asked the black magician.

"I feel the presence of someone coming toward us," Sumerlin responded.

The Archvillains waited. Soon, a male rider on a four-legged beast approached them. He halted the large animal before the foul beings and spoke.

"I am Clemmoth. You are strangers to this planet."

"Yes," Sumerlin responded for them. "Do you live around here?"

Clemmoth patted his white beast on the neck. "Not too far from here. Do you wish to accompany me back to my place?"

The Archvillains talked among themselves. They agreed to go with him.

"Splendid," Clemmoth said. "Follow me."

Clemmoth led them east. In a couple of hours, he brought them to the bottom of the mountains. They stood before an open door, huge. Inside, they went. Other humans greeted them.

"Welcome to our settlement," Clemmoth said. "Would you care to freshen up for a meal?"

"That would be nice," Darlesse responded for the Archvillains.

The foul beings freshened up. Then, Clemmoth escorted them to a mess hall. They sat at an immense table with humans. Not too long their hosts served them food and drink.

A woman across from Tajanna spoke. "I am Ghirah. Where do you come from?"

Xigan answered the question. "From different worlds."

"We encountered huge creatures on our travel through the mountains," Sumerlin said. "We fought them off. Do you know what they are?"

"You were attacked by the Yeti," Clemmoth replied. "They are very dangerous and unpredictable."

"Are they carnivorous?" Foulbard asked.

"Yes," Clemmoth answered. "They have never attacked us here."

The food and drink looked good. The Archvillains relished the meal.

An elderly man entered the conversation. "My name is Lakadri. Why are you on our world?"

Sumerlin told them. "We are seeking an object of power. Lordruingat. Do you know of it?"

"You believe it's on our planet?" Lakadri asked.

"Maybe," Darlesse responded.

"I have never heard of it," Clemmoth said.

Lakadri cleared his throat. "I know of the Cube of Power."

"How?" Foulbard asked.

"I was once a member of a scientific team that searched for it in the galaxy when I was younger," Lakadri explained. "We searched high and wide for it. Never found it."

"Did you search Cubeon for it?" Foulbard asked.

Lakadri sighed. "No. But I don't believe it is here. Yet there is a small chance it could be hidden on this world."

"Did you ever want to search Cubeon for it?" Namina asked.

"Yes," Lakadri replied. "Never got around to it."

The meal lasted until late evening. Clemmoth showed the Archvillains to chambers where they could rest up.

The next morning, the Archvillains ate breakfast with their hosts. Machines regulated the temperature in the settlement, keeping it warm inside. The settlement featured many chambers deep into the mountains.

"How long have you been searching for Lordruingat?" Lakadri asked the Archvillains.

Sumerlin answered the question. "For a while now. What do you know of the Cube of Power?"

"I have heard many stories of it," Lakadri replied. "Found a number of references to it in research. It's said to be able to defend itself from harm."

"How many planets did your scientific team look for it?" Darlesse asked.

Lakadri fingered his chin. "I would say at least thirty. We searched for it on all kinds of worlds, including my native planet."

Tajanna spoke. "Which is?"

Lakadri smiled. "Aggamorah."

"What did some of your research reveal?" Foulbard asked.

Lakadri seemed to think about that. "One source said that Lordruingat is hidden on a desert world called Nirobi. Another indicated it's hidden on a tropical planet named Fuscia. There are references to being heavily guarded by sentinels, either living beings or otherwise."

"Did your scientific team visit those worlds to search for Lordruingat?" Ripgarth asked.

"No," Lakadri answered. "We stop short of doing that."

Gnashboros chimed in. "Where are they located?"

Lakadri jogged his memory. "Nirobi is in the Cygnus Sector of the Milky Way Galaxy. Fuscia is in the Orion Sector of the Milky Way Galaxy."

The Archvillains made mental notes of that information. Two more planets to look for the Cube of Power. Their search for it, so far, proved fruitless.

"I know of others who have searched for

Lordruingat," Lakadri said. "My scientific team shared information with some of them, especially an occultic team and a celestic team. They had no better luck finding it than we did."

"What useful data did they give your scientific team?" Foulbard asked.

Lakadri let out a deep breath. "We learned of the names of other worlds where the Cube of Power might rest that had not been searched. So my scientific team checked them out. We found nothing. After that we continued a little longer in our search for Lordruingat before we gave up."

"Anything else you can relate about the Cube of Power?" Amyrielle asked.

"One story about Lordruingat was that a messiah— a great teacher and spiritual master--from a primitive world wielded it to heal people. It is said that he traveled the galaxy to cure beings."

"Interesting," Sumerlin remarked.

Lakadri continued. "Another tale has it that spiritual masters guard the Cube of Power and use it to enlighten people. To get them on the spiritual path for their souls to ultimately reach the upper spirit worlds of God and be with the Creator."

None of the Archvillains were on the spiritual path. The closest of the foul beings to one was Sumerlin. The black magician knew of a few spiritual masters.

Lakadri resumed. "There are stories of religious orders that protect Lordruingat, ranging from Nayugi monks to Camazon priests. Also a tale of a group of female oracles on an island on some planet that use the Cube of Power to help them utter divine pronouncements."

The Archvillains learned new things about Lordruingat from the elderly human. Much of what he told them they never heard of before. How much was useful was unknown.

Everyone finished breakfast. The foul beings talked among themselves in private to decide what to do next.

"Should we continue searching for Lordruingat on Cubeon?" Darlesse asked the other Archvillains.

"I vote no," Daggermash voiced.

"Same with me," Tajanna said.

In the end the Archvillains decided not to search for the Cube of Power anymore on Cubeon. The foul beings would leave the ice planet and look for it on another world. They had a choice of where to go next.

The Archvillains returned to the shuttlecraft after saying their goodbyes to their hosts. It took them back to the *Slaughter*. They went to the meeting room once onboard.

"Where do we search for Lordruingat next?" Xigan asked the other Archvillains.

"We should travel either to Nirobi or Fuscia," Sumerlin said.

"Which is closer?" Ripgarth asked the black magician.

Sumerlin operated the control console before him. He accessed the bridge computer from there. "Nirobi."

After the meeting, the foul beings went to the bridge. They set course for the desert world. The *Slaughter* engaged its teleport drive and telejumped from the Heltheon Sector of the Milky Way Galaxy to the Cygnus Sector of the Milky Way Galaxy.

The ship established orbit around Nirobi, the second planet from its sun. The Archvillains went to the teleporter room and teleported down to its surface. They went from the cold weather of Cubeon to the hot temperatures of Nirobi.

Miles of sand dunes stretched in all directions. They headed south. In the sky shined the yellow sun with no clouds. No wind blew.

The Archvillains traveled a ways before mountains appeared. They stopped. Behind the foul beings, they heard a noise. At first, it sounded low and distant. Then, it increased in volume as whatever made it came closer and closer.

Sumerlin sensed whatever approached them. "I feel the presence of some kind of sand monster coming our way."

Through the sand, something enormous tunneled. The immense creature dived like a dolphin in water. It sported flippers along its elongated body with black eyes on the sides of its huge head and a wide mouth.

"What do we do?" Darlesse asked the other Archvillains.

"Into the mountains!" Sumerlin yelled.

The Archvillains ran for the mountains. They reached the rocky heights before the sand monster could get them. They fled through a narrow crevice.

The immense creature crashed into the mountains. It could not get them. It roared in frustration.

The Archvillains stopped running. They heard a thumping sound, steady in beat. The sand monster turned away from the mountains and headed for the source of that noise, west of them.

"What is making that racket?" Darlesse asked no one in particular.

Sumerlin closed his eyes and sensed the area. "I feel

the presence of beings in the vicinity." The black magician opened his eyes.

The Archvillains went back the way they came. They walked out of the narrow crevice. Before them stood people in desert suits, armed with blades crescent in shape.

"You make too much noise, and it attracts the sandwhales," a middle-aged man said. "I am Amathis, leader of the Nafreemen. Who are you? You are strangers to our world."

The Archvillains introduced themselves. Afterward, the Nafreemen talked.

"We should take them prisoner," a female Nafreemen stated.

"That is not a good idea, Amyrcella," a male Nafreemen countered.

Amyrcella snorted. "Why, Arakhar?"

"Because they look like they could fight back," Amathis interjected.

Sumerlin interrupted the conversation. "We mean you no harm."

"Where are you from?" Amyrcella asked.

"We come from different planets," Foulbard answered for them.

"Why are you here?" Arakhar asked.

"We seek an object of power," Ripgarth replied. "Lordruingat, the Cube of Power."

A heated discussion occurred among the Nafreemen. They argued until Amathis quieted them down. The foul beings said nothing and waited.

"We don't recognize the name Lordruingat," Amathis said. "Perhaps it's called something else."

"Possible," Sumerlin conceded.

Amathis put his weapon away in his belt. "Anyway, you will come with us to our hold."

Sumerlin nodded. The Archvillains followed the Nafreemen across the sand east. In a while, they reached more mountains. Up through a pass, they traversed that led to a cavern. Inside, more Nafreemen greeted them.

"This hold is one of many," Amathis told the Archvillains. "We have caches of water at all of them."

That made sense to the Archvillains. Water would be a valuable commodity on a desert world.

"We are at war with House Gapylos," Amathis said. "They are from another world."

The Archvillains had never heard of House Gapylos. They were unaware of a war on Nirobi.

"Why are you fighting with them?" Tajanna asked.

Amathis let out a deep breath. "Because they mine the spice Carrinol and certain minerals on our world. They are a threat to our existence. And they disturb sandwhales, who attack more frequently because of the noise their machines make."

The prospect of finding Lordruingat on Nirobi seemed dimmer to the Archvillains. They did not want to get involved in the conflict on the planet. But if the Cube of Power rested on the desert world, they might get caught in the middle of the war.

Sumerlin tried to sense Lordruingat on Nirobi. The black magician felt the presence of those who belonged to House Gapylos on the planet. But not the Cube of Power.

The Archvillains talked in private. Amathis and the other Nafreemen waited for the foul beings to finish conversing among themselves.

"We cannot get involved in this war," Amyrielle

voiced. "It's not our fight."

Gnashboros chimed in. "I agree. But if Lordruingat is here, we may have to choose sides in the conflict just to find it."

"Where would we look on this world for the Cube of Power?" Foulbard asked his fellow Archvillains.

Darlesse spoke. "Could it be in one of their holds?"

"There is the possibility that House Gapylos might have Lordruingat," Xigan interjected.

The Archvillains debated the issue a little longer. Finally, they decided what to do.

"My friends and I will help you fight House Gapylos," Sumerlin said. "It may have the Cube of Power. Where are they headquartered?"

"Their fortress is south of here," Amathis replied. "You plan to raid them?"

"We will sneak in and see if they have Lordruingat," Sumerlin answered. "Also, take out their leaders and some of their men."

Amathis' eyes widened. "How will you get into their fortress? It's heavily guarded."

"We simply teleport into their citadel," Daggermash replied.

The Nafreemen did not know what teleportation was. Sumerlin explained it to them. They offered to send warriors to help with the raid. The foul beings accepted it.

Word spread to other holds. The Nafreemen amassed an army. The raid would take place when they were all ready.

The Nafreemen hid in the sand as the Archvillains teleported into the fortress. The foul beings took out guards and lowered the shield protecting the citadel.

Nafreemen poured into the place.

An alarm sounded. Soldiers of House Gapylos responded to the attack on the fortress. The Archvillains fought their way to the great hall in the citadel, where the leaders of the house armed themselves.

Sumerlin shot red fire from his hands and burned members of House Gapylos to ashes. The foul beings overwhelmed their enemy with their special powers. Soldiers could not stand against the Archvillains, who began searching for Lordruingat in the fortress.

"What is this?" Darlesse asked

The Archvillains stood in a chamber around a stand with a red cube on it. The object glowed.

"Could this be the Cube of Power?" Foulbard asked.

Sumerlin grabbed it and felt power emanating from it. He put it back on the stand. "This is not Lordruingat. It's a source of energy and can supply much power."

"Destroy it," Namina said.

The other Archvillains stood back as the black magician shot red fire from his hands and reduced it to a useless form. Afterward, they joined the Nafreemen outside the main building.

"We have victory!" Amathis shouted.

The Nafreemen cheered. The Archvillains did not.

"Did you find Lordruingat?" Amathis asked the foul beings.

Sumerlin sighed. "We found something. But not what we were looking for."

The Archvillains decided to leave Nirobi. They said their goodbyes to the Nafreemen and got teleported back up to the *Slaughter*.

On the bridge, the Archvillains conferred. Next, they would travel to Fuscia. The ship engaged its teleport drive and telejumped to the Orion Sector of the Milky Way Galaxy.

The *Slaughter* established an orbit around Fuscia. It circled a yellow sun as the third planet. The tropical world was not a member of the Universal Federation of Planets, and it was inhabited by a race of humanoids. The Archvillains went to the teleporter room and beamed down to it.

Thick vegetation thrived all around them. Trees grew tall and featured dense crowns and big trunks. Heavy brush all around them. The planet teemed with animal life.

"This looks like a much better place to have the Cube of Power than Nirobi," Darlesse said.

The other Archvillains concurred. They began to travel west.

The foul beings heard birds singing. Many avian species perched in the trees. A small animal, like a wolverine but chubby and gray, crossed their path and ran off. A yellow and red snake slithered on their left. They could not tell if it was poisonous or nonpoisonous. On their right, they passed a stream with blue fish swimming in it.

"This seems so peaceful a setting," Tajanna remarked.

The temperature was hot. The Archvillains smelled warm vegetation. They stepped on twigs that snapped under their feet.

The Archvillains eventually arrived at a jungle city. People greeted them.

A tall male humanoid in a white outfit spoke. "Welcome to Ajumani. I am Corlass. How could we be of service?"

"We seek Lordruingat," Foulbard replied.

"The Cube of Power?" Corlass responded. "It's not on this world."

Sumerlin sensed the planet. "I don't feel the presence of Lordruingat here."

The Archvillains enjoyed the hospitality of the Fuscians as the humanoids treated them well. The foul beings stayed on the planet for a few days, then left. Next, they took the *Slaughter* to the world of Barexy, which proved to be uninhabited. After they searched for Lordruingat on it they took the *Slaughter* to Wolcoth, an industrial world habited by a race of humans.

Chapter 36

The *Constellation* and the other four battlecruisers received news about the prison ship attacked by space pirates from Federation authorities. By orders from the Federation, they hunted down the prison ship. Memfelice used her special powers to locate it. The Psychic Being employed clairvoyance to find it and did.

The Federation battlecruisers intercepted the prison ship, which gave up without a fight. They put a tractor beam on it and escorted it to the nearest Federation planet, Darwina, where the authorities took custody of the prisoners on board.

The *Constellation* and the other four battlecruisers resumed tracking the space pirates. They came across debris from a destroyed freighter.

"They have been busy with more plunder," Falatar said.

"They're leaving a trail of attacked vessels, cargo in nature," Hashrah remarked. "Except for the one prison ship."

"Plus bodies," Agwennel added.

Another freighter they found pirated. This time, the cargo vessel was not destroyed. It did have survivors. The Universal Marshals interviewed them.

The Enforcers gathered in the meeting room of the ship. Jeddriel sat before a control console. Across from the automatic doors hung a blank telescreen.

"We still have no idea where the Retreat is," Jarek said.

"Not a single clue to its whereabouts," Memfelice agreed. "I have been unable to see its location."

"Sooner or later, we will engage the space pirates in battle," Falatar stated. "They can't avoid us forever."

"True," Jeddriel said. "The question is when."

The Universal Marshals went over all the information on the space pirates they had, including everything they knew about the Incarnation of Piracy.

"The space pirates show no favoritism to which ships to attack," Jarek stated. "It doesn't matter to them if it is a Federation vessel or a non-Federation one. However, they mostly target freighters and trade ships."

Falatar frowned. "That is a pattern."

"Probably because cargo vessels and trade ships carry goods," Hashrah pointed out. "Plenty of plunder."

"Have they ever attacked a hospital ship?" Agwennel asked.

Jeddriel checked the information on the control console. "No. Not that we know of."

"If they would, they would steal the medicines aboard and likely sell it on the black markets," Memfelice interjected.

Jarek voiced a thought. "What about military vessels?"

Jeddriel checked the information on the control console again. "No. There is no record of them attacking military vessels. They tend to avoid them."

"What about diplomatic ships?" Agwennel asked.

Jeddriel checked once more the information on the control console. "No. They don't target them."

"Which means they don't take hostages of

ambassadors or envoys," Falatar said.

"They're not known to ransom people," Jeddriel added.

The meeting ended. The Universal Marshals returned to their individual quarters.

Later the five battlecruisers found another trade ship that had been pirated. The Universal Marshals interviewed the survivors of the raid. The vessel belonged to an alien race called the Watusu, their world a member of the Universal Federation of Planets.

"They just appeared out of nowhere," Vishnorr said, an official of the trade ship. "We had no warning of the attack."

"How many corsairs were there?" Falatar asked

"Three," Vishnorr replied.

"Did they identify themselves to you?" Jeddriel asked. "Learn any names?"

Vishnorr appeared dejected. "I heard the name Mahab as the captain. He had a parrot on his shoulder."

"How many people did they kill on your ship?" Falatar asked.

Vishnorr grimaced. "Eight, including two fellow officials."

"How much goods was your trade ship carrying?" Jeddriel asked.

"A large amount," Vishnorr responded. "We were on our way to the planet Glastour for a trade deal."

Glastour was another member of the Universal Federation of Planets. The Glastourans were a race of humanoids.

"Did you hear the pirates mention the Retreat?" Falatar asked.

"Yes," Vishnorr answered. "They were deciding

when to go back to it again."

The Universal Marshals needed to learn where the Retreat was. The trade official offered no clue as to what planet it was on.

"What else did you hear from the pirates?" Jeddriel asked.

"Something about doing a little more pirating," Vishnorr responded.

That was bad news. More ships would be victims of the buccaneers.

"Anything else?" Falatar asked.

Vishnorr shook his head. The trade official told them all he could. The Universal Marshals thanked him for all his help. After the interview, the trade ship returned to its planet.

"The pirate ships are operating freely in the galaxy," Hashrah remarked. "They don't seem to worry about being captured."

The Universal Marshals stood on the bridge. All five battlecruisers readied for the next move.

"Where to next?" Soberyn asked the Enforcers.

Falatar answered for them. "The planet Aveozah."

"Why there?" Soberyn asked.

"Because it is a spaceport for space pirates and other foul beings," Hashrah replied.

The captain ordered the helmsman to set course for the world. The *Constellation* and the other battlecruisers engaged teleport drives and telejumped to the Omega Sector of the Milky Way Galaxy. Then they engaged their cloaking mechanisms, and the ships became undetectable.

The Universal Marshals teleported down to the surface of the planet. They materialized outside a settlement where all kinds of beings could be found. Resigned, they entered the place.

Land speeders zoomed in and out of the settlement. A few of the residents owned strange animals. The place bustled with activity.

"This is a place I would rather not be," Agwennel remarked.

"Yeah," Falatar agreed.

The Universal Marshals came to a tavern. They entered the establishment. Inside, patrons of all the five basic races drank. Some ate. The Enforcers made their way to the bar. A male alien with a thick mustache and bald pate served customers behind the counter, the owner.

"What can I get for you?" the proprietor asked.

"A pink julip," Memfelice said.

"A white kalata," Falatar replied.

"An ale," Hashrah answered.

Jeddriel and Agwennel declined to order.

"If you're in here, you must order something," the proprietor stated.

Jeddriel normally did not drink alcoholic beverages. "All right. I'll take a wine."

"Blue or yellow?" the proprietor asked.

"Blue," Jeddriel responded.

Agwennel thought a moment. "A mead for me."

The owner got their drinks. All the Universal Marshals imbibed.

A fight broke out between two humanoids. The taller of the two punched the shorter one in the face. The smaller being fell to the floor, unconscious.

"Never a dull moment in here," Hashrah remarked. The Turbobeing drank more of her pink julip. She liked the taste of it—a bit sweet.

A tall male alien whispered to another one. Both were armed with blasters. They stepped over to the Universal Marshals. As they pulled their weapons, Jeddriel materialized a flaming sword as his wings appeared and sliced their ray guns to pieces. Before they could attack the Archangel-Enforcer with bare hands, Hashrah fired turbo blasts at the pair and sent them flying into a wall, knocked out.

The other patrons took notice. As one, they rose from their seats.

"We have a situation here," Falatar remarked.

The Lunar Being used his gravitic push and slammed into the mob, knocking them down. Memfelice employed her psychic ability of telekinesis and hurled them against another wall. Agwennel shot waves of water that materialized and blasted them. Jarek swung his hoe of power and cut them down as Jeddriel did the same with his flaming sword.

"Stop already!" the proprietor shouted.

The Universal Marshals halted after decimating the mob. The patrons did not attack anymore. They had been wiped out.

"Just who are you?" the proprietor asked.

Jeddriel made his flaming sword disappear. "We are Universal Marshals."

"What do you want?" the proprietor asked.

"We are on a mission to find space pirates," Hashrah replied.

The proprietor gasped. "There are patrons here that are space pirates."

"Could you point them out?" Jarek asked.

The proprietor seemed to look at the defeated

patrons, who did not move. He indicated a few with his hand. The Universal Marshals lifted those to their feet.

"Where is Mahab?" Falatar asked the space pirates.

One, a tall male humanoid in buccaneer clothes, spat at the Enforcers. "I ain't tellin' you nothin'."

Falatar used his special powers and caused mental pain in the head of the space pirate, who grabbed the sides of his head. "Ready to talk?"

"Make it stop!" the space pirate screamed.

"Not until you talk to us," Falatar responded.

The buccaneer gritted his teeth. "All right, all right!"

Falatar stopped the mental pain. "Good. Now answer the question."

The space pirate swallowed. "The captain will come here to pick some of us up here. We will then leave and find a freighter to plunder."

"Where is the Retreat?" Memfelice asked.

"I can't tell you that," the space pirate said.

Falatar used his special powers and again caused mental pain in the head of the buccaneer, who screamed in agony. "Tell us where the Retreat is."

"Make it stop!" the space pirate yelled.

Falatar halted the mental pain. "Well?"

The buccaneer almost fell to his knees. "I don't know exactly where it is. But the world it's on is swampy."

A new bit of information for the Universal Marshals. Two others there were space pirates. One of them told the buccaneer who spilled his guts he would suffer for it. The Lunar Being used his special powers on that fellow and caused him mental pain temporarily.

"What is the name of the planet the Retreat is on?" Memfelice asked the other two buccaneers.

Neither of them spoke and became silent. Falatar used his special powers and caused both of them mental pain. They grabbed the sides of their heads. The Lunar Being stopped after they pleaded with him.

"Answer the question," Falatar said.

Both space pirates talked at once. The Lunar Being told them one at a time.

The shorter of the two buccaneers spoke. "I don't know exactly the name of the planet. But it's the fourth world in its solar system."

Another bit of information. Still not what the Universal Marshals wanted.

The other space pirate spoke. "The pirate captains meet at the Retreat regularly."

That bit of information was more helpful to the Universal Marshals. If they could find out when the next meeting of the buccaneer leaders occurred, it would be one step closer to locating the Retreat.

The Universal Marshals could get nothing more out of the three space pirates, who did not know when the next meeting would occur. What the Enforcers learned drew them closer to the Incarnation of Piracy. They left the tavern and got teleported back up to the *Constellation*.

The Universal Marshals informed Soberyn what they learned. The captain listened intently to them. He frowned after they finished their report.

"What do you want to do?" Soberyn asked the Enforcers.

The Universal Marshals conferred among themselves. Eventually, they decided what to do next.

"We'll wait for the pirate ships a safe distance from the planet here," Falatar answered for them. "Stay cloaked. We will catch them by surprise."

The five battlecruisers moved a safe distance from Aveozah, still in stealth mode. They waited for the pirate ships to come.

The wait lasted awhile. No pirate ships appeared. The five battlecruisers readied their weapons systems for battle against the corsairs.

Memfelice used her special powers—specifically the psychic ability of precognition—to sense when the pirate ships would arrive. "I feel the presence of buccaneer vessels approaching Aveozah."

The battlecruisers decloaked as the pirate ships neared the planet. Three corsairs.

"Shields up," Soberyn ordered.

The pirate ships fired ion cannons at the battlecruisers. Shields deflected the shots.

"Return fire!" Soberyn commanded.

The battlecruisers fired lasers at the buccaneer vessels, whose own shields were raised. Both sides fired their weapons on the move.

"I feel the presence of Mahab aboard one of those pirate ships," Memfelice stated.

"Ready antimatter torpedoes," Soberyn said. "Fire when ready."

The *Constellation* launched antimatter torpedoes at one of the buccaneer vessels. The self-propelled, elongated missiles struck a pirate ship in the engineering section and disabled it. Both remaining corsairs continued firing their ion cannons. The battlecruisers pounded them with laser fire in return.

The battle lasted for a length of time. The two undamaged pirate ships decided they had had enough fighting and engaged their superluminal drives and tunneled through space to disappear. That left the remaining buccaneer vessel listing in space.

Soberyn spoke on the intercom from his command chair. "Prepare a boarding party armed." The captain addressed the Universal Marshals. "Do you wish to be with the boarding party?"

"Yes," Jeddriel answered for them.

The Enforcers joined the boarding party in the teleporter room. They all got teleported to the pirate ship.

The Universal Marshals led the boarding party. They met resistance. Space pirates opened fire on them with blasters and blast rifles. They returned fire.

The boarding party fought the space pirates near the engineering section. They advanced slowly against the enemy, who kept firing their laser weapons at them.

"We have to take them out quicker," Jarek said.

Hashrah shot turbo blasts at the buccaneers and took a few out. Falatar used his gravitic push and knocked out some more. Agwennel did the same by producing water waves to do it. Memfelice unleashed her pyrokinesis on them and set space pirates ablaze.

From a side corridor, buccaneers attacked them with scimitars. Jeddriel materialized his flaming sword and clashed with them. Jarek used his hoe of power and fought alongside the Archangel-Enforcer. Together, they slew a number of space pirates.

The boarding party took a few hits as members got wounded. They decimated the buccaneers more than they suffered injuries in the fight. The space pirates did not surrender but kept battling down to the last man.

"We must get to the bridge of the ship," Falatar said.

"They are making it hard on us," Hashrah commented.

"We need some of them alive so we can question them," Jeddriel stated.

The fighting continued on. It looked like it would be a long battle. The space pirates seemed to prefer death than to be captured.

"If we could reach the bridge, we could capture the captain and have him tell his men to surrender to us," Memfelice interjected.

"Good idea," Jarek agreed.

A blaster shot grazed the arm of Falatar. The Lunar Being winced but was not seriously hurt. He responded by causing mental pain to buccaneers, who dropped their weapons and grabbed the sides of their heads. Members of the boarding party cut them down with shots from blasters and blast rifles.

"How far are we from the bridge?" Jeddriel asked the Psychic Being.

Memfelice sensed it. "We are getting closer to it. I feel the presence of space pirates on the bridge, including the captain."

The boarding party pushed on. More buccaneers came at them. Some of the pirates charged at them with scimitars. Jeddriel and Jarek clashed with them with flaming sword and hoe of power, respectively.

The Archangel-Enforcer parried a strike by a buccaneer. He backhanded a swing with his flaming sword and wounded the space pirate in the shoulder, a deep cut. The man stumbled backward, then stabbed at the Universal Marshal with his blade. Jeddriel blocked it with his flaming sword and thrust it through the chest of his foe, who fell to the floor dead.

Jarek brought his hoe of power down on the head of a space pirate and split his skull. The buccaneer collapsed to the floor dead. The Incarnation of Life repeated his strike on another buccaneer and felled him as well.

"We're almost at the bridge," Memfelice informed the others of the boarding party.

Between the automatic doors to the bridge and them stood a dozen space pirates. The buccaneers fired blasters and blast rifles at them to keep them back.

"Final hurdle," Falatar remarked.

Memfelice used telekinesis on the space pirates and sent them flying against the automatic doors to the bridge. The entry opened. The boarding party proceeded to enter the bridge.

"You will never have this ship!" the captain, a male alien, shouted. He rushed to a control console and attempted to press the button to cause the pirate ship to self-destruct in a countdown.

Falatar used his gravitic push and knocked the captain away from the button before he could press it. The remaining buccaneers on the bridge surrendered.

A female member of the boarding party contacted the *Constellation* on a telecommunicator on her. She reported to Captain Soberyn that the buccaneer vessel was secured.

The boarding party rounded up all the surviving space pirates on the pirate ship. The buccaneers knelt on the floor on the bridge.

"Let's begin the interrogation," Jarek said. The Incarnation of Life addressed the head of the corsair. "What is your name?"

"I am Agyles, captain of the *Jolly Capcorn*."

"What is the name of the pirate ship captained by Mahab?" Jeddriel asked.

"The *Jolly Mercer*," Agyles answered

"What is the name of the other buccaneer vessel that fled?" Jarek asked.

"The *Jolly Vashon*," Agyles replied.

"Were you planning to raid another freighter before our battlecruisers engaged your ships in battle?" Falatar asked.

Agyles responded after pausing. "Yes."

The Universal Marshals talked among themselves. In a moment, they resumed questioning the space pirates.

"Where is the Retreat?" Hashrah asked.

"Nashotah?" Agyles said. "I cannot tell you that."

"Because it means death to anyone who reveals its location," Memfelice interjected.

"Yes." Agyles rubbed his hands together.

The Universal Marshals conversed among themselves again. It made the captured buccaneers uncomfortable.

"We'll ask again," Agwennel said. "Where is the Retreat?"

Agyles spat on the floor of the bridge. "I will never tell you."

Jeddriel addressed members of the boarding party. "Take the captain back to the *Constellation* and put him in the brig."

Two males of the boarding party escorted Agyles off the bridge. They contacted the *Constellation* via a telecommunicator and got teleported with the prisoner to the ship.

Jeddriel addressed the prisoners. "Do any of you wish to speak to us?"

None of the space pirates did. They knelt in silence and said nothing.

"Where is the Retreat?" Jarek asked the prisoners.

One buccaneer responded. "We'll never tell you where it is."

Falatar caused mental pain to the space pirate who spoke. The buccaneer grabbed the sides of his head in agony.

"Do you wish to tell us now?" Jeddriel asked.

"Screw you," another space pirate replied.

Falatar now caused mental pain to all the prisoners. They grabbed the sides of their heads in agony. The Lunar Being stopped after several minutes. All the buccaneers grimaced.

"Tell us where the Retreat is," Hashrah demanded.

"All right," a space pirate said. "It's on the planet Torbold."

"And?" Falatar prodded.

"In the Cancer Sector of the Milky Way Galaxy."

Members of the boarding party escorted the prisoners and got teleported to the *Constellation* and put in the brig. The Universal Marshals stayed a little longer on the pirate ship before beaming back to the *Constellation*. A battlecruiser used a tractor beam and towed the buccaneer vessel for Tellus.

The Enforcers contacted the Justiceplex on the Federation capital. They communicated with the High Enforcer. He instructed them to prepare a raid on the Retreat. More battlecruisers would be sent to join the mission.

Chapter 37

The Universal Marshals learned of another planet that might possibly have Lordruingat on it. Wolcoth, an industrial world in the Alpha Sector of the Milky Way Galaxy, inhabited by a race of humans. It was not a member of the Federation. Two moons orbited it.

The Enforcers sat in the meeting room. Nazzar sat before the control console.

"What else is known about Wolcoth?" Yevadne asked the Android-Enforcer.

Nazzar checked on the control console. "On the scientific level, it is progressive. On the occultic level, it is nonexistent. On the celestic level, it is nonexistent. The humans on the planet appear materialistic."

"Anything else?" Danbarrack asked.

"There have been no wars on it for several centuries," Nazzar replied. "Business has boomed on it since the last conflict. There are many merchants on the planet."

"What kind of government does it have?" Milantheus asked.

Nazzar checked on the control console again. "It is ruled by an oligarchy."

"Has it reached the point of spaceflight yet?" Apparis asked.

"No," Nazzar answered. "They have no space program at the moment."

"What about nuclear weapons?" Idyllion asked.

"They do not have a nuclear capability yet," Nazzar responded.

"Then they don't have satellites in space either," Kesharra said.

"Correct," Nazzar confirmed.

Ursanne voiced a question. "Does the Federation consider it as a potential candidate for membership?"

"Not at this time," Nazzar replied.

"What is their military like?" Kesharra asked.

"Reduced," Nazzar answered. "They still have armed forces. But their main concentration is on industry, not any military buildup."

"What about their practice of medicine?" Benethor asked.

"Advanced," Nazzar responded. "They have made strides in the field."

The Universal Marshals ended the meeting and returned to the bridge. They engaged the teleport drive of the *Horizon* and telejumped to the Alpha Sector of the Milky Way Galaxy. As the battlecruiser approached Wolcoth, they activated the cloaking mechanism and disappeared from sight.

The ship established orbit around the planet. They engaged its automated control. Hulkeme teleported them down to the industrial world. They materialized outside the city limits of a metropolitan area.

An overcast sky appeared above them. The humans of Wolcoth utilized transportation—cars, trucks, motorcycles, vans, buses, and airplanes—modern but primitive. Their technology lagged behind Tellus.

The Universal Marshals walked a distance before they entered the city. Vehicles sped by them. A few honked at them. The metropolitan area bustled with activity. Businesses flourished.

Tall buildings dotted the urban landscape. They passed through an industrial park. Manufacturers lined up and produced goods, such as an automobile assembly, a chemical plant, and a plastics factory. People went in and out of the places.

The Universal Marshals continued on. They came upon a warehouse district. Buildings in it stored merchandise such as clothes, household goods, hardware, and gardening supplies. People went in and out of the warehouses. Trucks parked to load or unload products.

"Nothing out of the ordinary here," Danbarrack remarked.

"No Archvillains stepped on this planet," Nazzar commented.

"A good thing," Yevadne said.

"We are the first Universal Marshals to visit this world," Kesharra pointed out. "Have they been visited before by any Federation members?"

"No," Nazzar said.

Hulkeme chimed in. "Do they have law enforcement here?"

"Yes," Nazzar replied. "But their crime rate is low."

"That is encouraging," Ursanne said.

The Universal Marshals left the warehouse district and came to a mall. It featured over a hundred stores. They decided to explore the shopping center.

"This would be an odd place for Lordruingat to be," Yevadne remarked.

"Who knows where the Cube of Power may be," Danbarrack said.

People went in and out of stores. Many shoppers visited the mall, a very busy place. The Universal Marshals went into a clothing store and looked around.

"Plenty of clothes for sale," Kesharra commented.

Apparis chimed in. "The citizens here are fashion-minded to a degree."

The Enforcers moved on. Next, they went into a sporting goods store. Plenty of gear for sale. A number of customers checked out the place.

Benethor picked up a large ball and looked at the price. "I wonder what kind of a game they use this for." He put it back.

On Tellus, they played sports. Some other planets of the Federation did so. None of the Universal Marshals involved themselves in them, though Enforcers could be athletes if they wanted to. The Federation Department of Justice did not bar them from such activities.

The Universal Marshals left the sporting goods store and entered a hardware store. It sold all kinds of products, from various tools to different paints. Customers bought items suited to their needs.

None of the Enforcers owned or worked for a business before they became Universal Marshals. But some of them were scientists, occultists, or celestists, permitted by the Federation Department of Justice.

Hulkeme looked over a bunch of different-sized screwdrivers; Phillips heads, and flat heads in packs. He saw the price for them.

"When you were granting wishes to individuals before you joined the Universal Marshals, did any of them wish to have a successful business?" Yevadne asked the Genie-Enforcer.

"Yes," Hulkeme replied. "But I granted so many

wishes for so many things." One of those wishes involved an old man who desired him to become a Universal Marshal. He became one twelve years ago.

The Enforcers left the hardware store and walked past a restaurant. People at lunch ate in the packed place. The business served all kinds of meals to its customers.

Ursanne stopped, and the others did likewise. She closed her eyes. The Norn-Enforcer sensed the planet. "I don't feel the presence of Lordruingat on this world. Just life teeming on it."

"The Cube of Power has eluded us thus far," Apparis remarked. "Finding it has been extremely difficult. No wonder why no one has been able to locate it."

"Wherever it is, it is safe and secure," Kesharra remarked.

"There must be a way to find it," Idyllion interjected.

"Yes," Benethor agreed. The Elf-Enforcer already used the blue Elfstone in his pouch to seek Lordruingat on worlds but to no avail. He felt the magic rock might work to discover where on a planet the Cube of Power rested once they found the right world,

The Universal Marshals went to a few more stores before leaving the mall. The trip to the city so far proved interesting. People of Wolcoth seemed contented with their lives to the Enforcers.

"Did any Archvillains ever visit this planet?" Kesharra asked the Android-Enforcer.

"There is no record of any of those foul beings ever coming here," Nazzar answered.

Benethor pulled out the blue Elfstone from his pouch and invoked it to seek the Cube of Power on

Wolcoth. Nothing happened. It meant either Lordruingat did not rest on the planet, or the magic rock was unable to detect it on this world.

The Universal Marshals spotted a stadium ahead. People filed into it. The Enforcers decided to go into the oval-shaped coliseum and see what transpired in it.

Fans sat on tiered seats in a crowded place. Below in the arena, two teams, each with nine members, played a game involving tossing a large ball into a net. The Universal Marshals asked a male fan what the sport was called.

"Land polo," the citizen responded.

"Interesting game," Apparis said.

"What is the name of this city?" Yevadne asked the male fan.

"Lannisville."

The Universal Marshals stayed a while to watch the game. Land polo was not played on any Federation planet.

****

The *Slaughter* neared Wolcoth at sublight speed. It engaged its cloaking mechanism and disappeared from sight, undetected in stealth mode. The Archvillains met in the meeting room.

"Wolcoth is a planet without magic," Sumerlin said. "It is not on the occultic level or the celestic level."

"Meaning it exists only on the scientific level," Foulbard remarked. "A place of science."

"True," Sumerlin responded. "It is heavy in industry."

"What kinds of arms do they wield?" Gnashboros asked.

Sumerlin checked that on the control console before

him. "They don't have any laser weapons. They do possess firearms that shoot bullets."

"What about swords and similar weapons?" Tajanna asked.

Sumerlin checked that on the control console. "No. Just guns that fire ammunition."

"Has any Federation planet ever visited this world?" Namina asked.

"None that is known of," Sumerlin replied.

Ripgarth chimed in. "So none of our kind has ever visited this world before."

"Yes," Sumerlin confirmed.

"What else?" Amyrielle asked.

"The Wolcothians have never ventured into space," Sumerlin stated. "Their planet has hardly been visited by other worlds. We may be the first extraterrestrials to come here."

"Not even the Enforcers have ever been here," Darlesse said.

"As far as we know," Sumerlin added.

The meeting ended. They retired to their private quarters. The next day, they gathered in the teleporter room and got teleported down to the planet.

They materialized outside the city limits of a metropolitan area. An overcast sky appeared above them. Vehicles sped by them as they began to walk for the city.

Sumerlin sensed Wolcoth for Lordruingat. The black magician shook his head. He still could not detect the presence of the Cube of Power anywhere. He felt a little frustrated.

The Archvillains came upon a sign. It read: *WELCOME TO LANNISVILLE.*

"Lousy sign," Xigan mumbled.

The Archvillains entered the city. Vehicles sped by them. A few honked horns at them. They smelled pollution and almost gagged.

"Give me fresher air," Daggermash remarked.

The Archvillains passed by a steel plant. Workers went in and out of the place. They heard a whistle sound from it. Farther on they came upon a clothing factory. Employees entered and exited the place. None of the foul beings ever worked for any manufacturers in their lives.

"This planet is not an advanced civilization," Foulbard stated.

"I would never want to live on it," Darlesse said.

"Not fit for our kind," Gnashboros added.

The Archvillains continued on. The industrial world featured many industries. They passed a recycling plant where materials were recycled regularly. Next they passed a junkyard filled with cars no longer driven. Then, they came to a scrap metal yard. Farther on they encountered a residential area where houses lined up. The homes were not automated.

"Primitive dwellings," Ripgarth commented.

Namina voiced a question to the black magician. "Does this world have robots?"

"Not that I know of," Sumerlin replied.

"Biocreation is not a science on the planet then?" Foulbard asked.

"Yes," Sumerlin answered. "The science on this world is advanced only to a degree."

Foulbard spoke again, "Then the Wolcothians have not yet entered the computer age."

"They have started using computers only a decade ago," Sumerlin responded. "They are not as sophisticated as the ones we use."

People watered their lawns with hoses. A few citizens did some gardening. Children played outside. It seemed like a good neighborhood the foul beings walked through.

In time, the Archvillains left the residential area and entered a commercial one. Businesses flourished, making huge profits. The foul beings decided to visit some of the shops. First, they entered a toy store. Inside, parents, some with their kids, shopped for objects their children could play with. It was a busy place. All kinds of toys filled shelves.

None of the Archvillains had offspring. After a little while, they left the toy store. Next to it stood a bicycle shop with a variety of two-wheeled vehicles driven by pedals. They checked it out briefly before moving on to a candy store.

"Sinful chocolate," Darlesse said. The Hellcat tasted a sample offered off a tray held by a female employee. "Delicious."

The Archvillains left the candy store and entered an electronics business. It featured such things for sale as radios, TVs, telephones, record players, and walkie-talkies. Customers scooped up merchandise as if there was no tomorrow.

"Nice items," Foulbard remarked. The Shocker picked up a set of walkie-talkies and looked them over. "Primitive communication devices." He put them back.

The Archvillains left the electronics business and continued on. They passed more stores like a shop that sold household goods, and a bookstore.

"This world seems prosperous," Amyrielle remarked.

The foul beings went into the bookstore. There were volumes that covered all kinds of subjects.

Sumerlin found no books on the occult in the place. Not even ones dealing with magic tricks. The black magician came across a volume on the world history of the planet that covered centuries. He looked through it.

Darlesse found books on martial arts. Some volumes dealt with striking systems, and others grappling ones. The Hellcat grabbed a book off a shelf and read about striking techniques. She smiled.

Foulbard located books on subjects dealing with the military. The Shocker picked up a volume on weapons and scanned through it.

Xigan went to the section that featured volumes on food. The Behemoth picked up randomly a book that covered making special dinners. He had a big appetite and loved to eat.

The Archvillains spent some time in the bookstore. Afterward, they continued on.

Soon, the Archvillains entered the downtown area of Lannisville. Tall buildings rose all around them like apartment ones and corporate headquarters. People walked on the sidewalks going about their business.

Sumerlin stiffened. The other foul beings halted.

"What is it?" Namina asked.

Sumerlin closed his eyes and sensed the downtown area. "I feel the presence of Enforcers."

"Universal Marshals are here?" Darlesse asked.

Sumerlin opened his eyes. "They are near." The black magician paused. He sensed again. "Now I feel the presence of other powerful beings in the area, not Enforcers."

"Can you identify them?" Tajanna asked.

Sumerlin let out a deep breath. "I will try." The black magician felt their presence. "I cannot detect exactly who they are. I have never before encountered such powerful beings."

****

The Watchers materialized outside the city limits of the metropolitan area after being beamed down. They started walking in the direction of the urban region.

"What is the name of this city?" Sorhea asked the leader.

"It is called Lannisville," Draegor replied.

The Watchers entered the city. Traffic was heavy. Some vehicles honked at them. They paid no attention and continued on. They looked up and saw an overcast sky.

"Are the Wolcothians a peaceful race?" Garion asked the leader.

"For the most part," Draegor answered. "There has been no war on this planet for several centuries."

"What kind of a world is this?" Narwyn asked the leader.

"It is an industrial one," Draegor responded. "Commerce is featured."

"Anything else?" Sorhea asked.

Draegor smiled. "It has a low crime rate."

The Watchers passed through a residential area full of nice-looking one- and two-story houses with people waving at them from front lawns.

"This appears to be a good neighborhood," Garion remarked. "A nice place to live."

The Watchers left the residential area in a while and entered a commercial one. People went in and out of businesses, from a department store to a supermarket.

The Wolcothians thrived.

The Watchers took it all in. Eventually, they reached the downtown area, which featured heavy traffic. They smelled pollution to a degree. Citizens walked on sidewalks in droves. Tall buildings surrounded them.

Draegor suddenly stopped. The other Watchers halted.

"What is it?" Sorhea asked the leader.

Draegor closed his eyes. "I sense other beings who are not Wolthians on this planet. I feel the presence of Enforcers and Archvillains."

"Where exactly?" Garion asked.

Draegor answered momentarily. "Close by."

"Are they aware of us?" Narwyn asked.

"Yes," Draegor replied.

****

The Universal Marshals left the stadium after the game. They enjoyed the land polo match. Many fans seemed happy because the home team won.

The Enforcers neared a park. Suddenly, the Norn-Enforcer stiffened.

"What is it?" Danbarrack asked.

Ursanne sensed the downtown area. "I feel the presence of Archvillains nearby. Also, the presence of other powerful beings."

"Can you identify those other powerful beings?" Kesharra asked.

"No," Ursanne responded.

"Could they be Watchers?" Idyllion asked.

"Maybe," Ursanne replied.

"That means Lordruingat could be on this planet," Yevadne interjected.

"I don't sense the Cube of Power on this world,"

Ursanne said.

The Universal Marshals continued on. They stopped at the park where Wolcothians relaxed. People sat on benches and picnicked on the cut grass. Others played, notably children.

The Enforcers spotted the Archvillains and the Watchers, who both saw the Universal Marshals. All three groups approached each other and halted when they were close enough.

"Give up your quest for Lordruingat," Draegor stated to the Enforcers and the Archvillains. "It is not for you to have."

Instead of talking, the Archvillains attacked the Universal Marshals and the Watchers. Sumerlin shot red fire from his hands at them both. Ripgarth did the same with a blue beam from his eye. Foulbard unleashed shock waves at them both.

Nazzar fired laser beams from his eyes. Kesharra shot solar rays from her hands. Idyllion unleashed nuclear blasts from his hands. Yevadne whipped cyclone winds at the other two groups. Benethor pulled the red Elfstone from his pouch and fired red beams from it. Apparis opened his beak and shot sonic blasts.

Draegor raised a force field to stop the attacks against the Watchers. Wolcothians scrambled for cover from the battle happening.

Milantheus used his special powers and froze the attacks against them by the Archvillains. So far the fight among the three parties remained a stalemate.

"This is getting us nowhere," Ursanne remarked.

The Watchers fired back at the other two with energy balls. The round projectiles did not reach their marks, destroyed by their opponents. Each side kept shooting at the others with everything they had. Explosions occurred when nuclear blasts from Idyllion hit shock waves from Foulbard.

"We're not making any ground against either of them," Darlesse said.

No civilians got hurt in the battle as collateral damage. But a few trees got hit and shattered. Shots from the three parties tore up the earth a bit in the park.

"This is a waste of time," Sorhea commented.

"No one is going to win this battle," Garion added.

Sirens could be heard as Lannisville police arrived at the chaotic scene in squad cars. Officers jumped out of their vehicles and drew their weapons.

"Stop what you're doing!" a police sergeant shouted. "You're all under arrest!"

Foulbard sent shock waves at the Lannesville police and caused the officers and their squad cars to fly backward, wiping them out. That made the Universal Marshals feel anguish for them. The Watchers did not have the same sentiment. Neither did the Archvillains, who experienced glee at the expense of the Lannisville police.

Benethor turned to the Genie-Enforcer. "Get us out of here."

"As you wish," Hulkeme responded.

The Genie-Enforcer teleported the Universal Marshals back to the *Horizon*. The Archvillains got the same idea and got teleported back to the *Slaughter*. As for the Watchers they escaped from Lannisville and returned to the *Galactic Star* as they got beamed up to the ship.

The Universal Marshals met in the meeting room. They felt exhausted from the battle.

"I read the minds of the Watchers," Ursanne said. "I know the location of Lordruingat."

"Where?" Apparis asked.

"The planet Drath," Ursanne replied.

Drath. Once visited by the Enforcers. Inhabited by a primitive race of humanoids. It orbited the white sun Azbruk as its fifth planet in the Rigellian Sector of the Milky Way Galaxy.

The Universal Marshals retired. The next morning, the *Horizon* set a course for Drath. The ship telejumped to the Rigellian Sector of the Milky Way Galaxy.

Chapter 38

The High Enforcer sent more battlecruisers to join the five waiting. Altogether, they formed a space fleet of twenty ships, ready to raid Nashotah, the Retreat. They kept a long distance from Aveozah. In the meeting room of the *Constellation*, the six Enforcers and the twenty captains of the combat vessels met to discuss the matter of the raid.

"Will the pirates be expecting us?" Kentu, a male alien and captain of the battlecruiser *Sunriser*, asked the Universal Marshals.

"They might," Memfelice answered for them.

"Is there an estimate of how many corsairs will meet us in battle?" Tolena, a female humanoid and captain of the battlecruiser *Telerider*, asked next.

Falatar replied this time. "Likely as many ships as we have."

Kalomas, a male human and captain of the battlecruiser *Pounder*, voiced the next question. "What is our main strategy against the pirates?"

"It is certain we will meet them in battle in space first," Hashrah said. "We will have to fight our way to get to the Retreat itself on Torbold."

"What about this Mahab?" Rothell, a male faerie and captain of the battlecruiser *Onager*, asked the Enforcers.

Jeddriel responded. "We Universal Marshals will

try to apprehend the Incarnation of Piracy if the opportunity presents itself. Under no circumstances is anyone else to try to capture him. He is an immortal with special powers on the celestic level."

The Archangel-Enforcer and the Incarnation of Life were the only ones of the Universal Marshals there with special powers on the celestic level. All six Enforcers possessed antipower handcuffs to cuff them on the Archvillain.

"Could the Fellowship of Darkness try and recruit Mahab to their side?" Soberyn asked. The captain of the *Constellation* sat before the control console.

"They could," Jarek replied. "We know the Archvillain organization grows in number as time passes. The Incarnation of Piracy might have joined it already."

Memfelice closed her eyes and used her psychic abilities. "I see that Mahab has not yet become a part of the Fellowship of Darkness." She opened her eyes.

"The question then is the Incarnation of Piracy aware of the Archvillain organization," Agwennel interjected.

"It is a possibility," Falatar added.

"Is there any chance that Mahab could recruit other Archvillains to his side?" Carryn, the male humanoid captain of the battlecruiser *Supernova*, asked the Enforcers.

Jeddriel frowned. "There is."

Memfelice closed her eyes again and used her psychic abilities once more. "I see no other Archvillains have joined the Incarnation of Piracy." She opened her eyes again.

"What other Archvillains would?" Soberyn asked.

"Spriggans," Agwennel said.

Spriggans were of the race of faerie. They were notorious thieves. They banded together to rob people and places. A few were imprisoned in the Universal Prisonplex until the invasion of Tellus.

'But my understanding is that the Incarnation of Piracy works alone as an Archvillain," Jeddriel stated. "He keeps company only with other pirates."

Memfelice spoke again. "I can see that."

"Is there a chance that other Archvillains are attacking vessels ?" Kentu asked the Enforcers.

"There is a chance," Jarek responded. "But it is highly unlikely."

Memfelice closed her eyes and used her psychic abilities a third time. "I do not see any other Archvillains attacking ships at present." She opened her eyes once more.

"What is the name of the corsair captained by Mahab?" Tolena asked.

"The *Jolly Mercer*," Falatar replied.

"If the Incarnation of Piracy is aboard the vessel when we battle the pirate ships in space near Nashotah," Jeddriel said, "then we should try and disable it instead of destroying it."

"You want to board the corsair and arrest him," Rothell interjected.

"Yes," Jarek confirmed.

"What if he flees to Torbold?" Kalomas asked.

"We pursue him to the planet," Hashrah replied.

"What is Torbold like?" Tolena asked.

"It is said to be a swampy world," Agwennel stated. The Undine-Enforcer knew about being on a swampy world. She lived on one for a while before she became a

Universal Marshal.

"Do the pirates have any combat vehicles other than corsairs?" Kentu asked. "Like laser tanks or photon artillery?"

Jeddriel answered the question. "None to our knowledge."

"What about fighting robots?" Tolenna asked.

"They are not known to employ battle droids," Hashrah explained.

"Do they usually attack prison ships to recruit new members?" Kentu asked. "I heard they intercepted one and swelled their ranks with prisoners they freed."

Jarek sighed. "They seem to occasionally do so. Records indicate that they rarely do it."

"Do they attack ships at random?" Rothell asked.

"There is no set pattern to their raiding vessels," Jeddriel responded. "Other than they plunder freighters and trade ships."

"What about the space pirates raiding penal colonies on planets to free their own kind?" Kalomas asked.

"Records indicate they rarely do so," Jarek said. "Typically, they go to worlds where buccaneers congregate and recruit new members there."

"Have they done so lately?" Rothell asked.

"No," Falatar replied. "But there is one instance of an attack on a penal colony with pirates as prisoners by corsairs that sailed seas." The Lunar Being explained that the Universal Marshals were there when it happened.

"When do we begin the raid?" Kentu asked the Enforcers.

Jeddriel stood up. "Tomorrow."

The Universal Marshals adjourned the meeting. The

captains returned to their battlecruisers. The fleet readied themselves for the upcoming battle.

****

In the meeting hall of the Retreat, the pirate captains held another meeting. They sat around the immense wooden table, perturbed, except the Incarnation of Piracy. On the right shoulder of Mahab perched Starly, his blue and yellow parrot.

"The *Jolly Capcorn* is lost to us," Hollis remarked. "Federation authorities have it."

Burrina spoke up. "Does the Federation know the location of Nashotah now?"

All eyes turned to the Incarnation of Piracy. He took a deep breath.

"Yes," Mahab replied. "They have learned where to find the Retreat."

All the other captains shouted in anger. The Incarnation calmed them down.

"That means the Federation will send a fleet of ships against us," Larcan stated.

"I have seen that they will," Mahab interjected.

Jayondu chimed in. "We have to prepare to defend ourselves against the Federation battlecruisers. They must not take the Retreat."

Borgan pounded the table with a fist. "Here, here."

Darwinona addressed the Incarnation of Piracy. "Have you seen when they will attack us?"

"Tomorrow," Mahab answered.

"That gives us little time to prepare against their raiding us," Gastov remarked.

Hollis voiced a thought. "Should we abandon Nashotah and find another world to establish a new Retreat on?"

"Not yet," Mahab said. "If the fight against the Federation fleet turns bad for us, then we might want to do that."

"Where would we go then?" Burrina asked the Incarnation of Piracy.

"That would need some thought," Mahab responded. "I will contemplate on it tonight."

Just then, two pirates on guard outside the meeting hall entered. The captains did not like being disturbed. One of the guards spoke.

"Sorry to interrupt your meeting, captains, but two strangers to our world have appeared and wish to talk with Captain Mahab."

"Who are they?" Larcan asked.

The other guard spoke. "They are beings like the Incarnation of Piracy."

Jayondu gasped. "Other Archvillains?"

"Yes," the guard replied.

"How did they find us?" Darwinona asked no one in particular.

"Through the use of their special powers," Mahab interjected.

"Do you want to talk with them?" the other guard asked the Incarnation of Piracy.

Mahab considered it. "I will listen to what they have to say. I will speak with them alone."

The Incarnation of Piracy excused himself and left the meeting hall. He met the other two Archvillains in a private chamber.

The first Archvillain was female. She was a tall oriental woman with black and white streaked red hair. Her nails were long, and her eyes were red. She wore a long black dress with a red shawl and white slippers.

The second Archvillain was male. He stood a muscular six and a half feet tall with blue eyes filled with intensity; his long hair and beard were blond. He wore a brown tunic with matching pants and boots. In his hand, he carried a battle-axe of power.

"Who and what are you?" Mahab asked the pair of foul beings.

The female Archvillain spoke first. "I am Wuminga, a Fox Maiden."

"And I am Ragnar, the Berserker," the male Archvillain answered.

"Why do you wish to see me?" Mahab asked.

"We are members of the Fellowship of Darkness," Wuminga explained. "An Archvillain organization."

Mahab seemed perplexed. "Never heard of you."

"We are recruiting others of our kind," Ragnar said. "Our numbers are growing steadily."

"Do you have a leader among you?" Mahab asked.

Wuminga smiled. "Yes. Professor Magnemus, the Scientific Being."

The parrot on the shoulder of the Incarnation of Piracy squawked. Mahab quieted him down.

"Have you heard about the invasion of Tellus?" Ragnar asked.

Mahab tried to recall. "I believe I heard something about a jailbreak on the planet."

"That was us," Wuminga responded. "We freed thousands of Archvillains. Now we are trying to recruit them all for the Fellowship of Darkness."

Mahab's eyes lit up. "Do you have a planet for your base of operations?"

"We have found a new home," Ragnar said. "The world of Murron."

The Incarnation of Piracy never heard of the planet.

"We are aware of an upcoming battle between your pirates and a fleet of Federation battlecruisers," Wuminga stated.

"How did you find out?" Mahab asked.

"One of our members foresaw the event," Ragnar replied. "She has the gift of foresight."

Mahab petted his parrot. "Did she also foresee the outcome of the battle between us and the Federation fleet?"

"No," Wuminga answered. "She did not look that far."

Mahab sighed. "You have given me a lot to think about."

"Do you wish to accept our invitation?" Ragnar asked.

Mahab fingered his beard. "I will seriously consider it. "

"When can we expect your answer?" Wuminga asked.

"After the battle against the Federation fleet," Mahab responded. "I want to see if we defeat it or not."

"All right," Ragnar said. "We shall return to our ship and await your answer."

"That is fair," Mahab commented.

Ragnar contacted their ship with a telecommunicator. The Berserker and the Fox Maiden got teleported up to the vessel, the *Marauder*. Mahab returned to the meeting hall and sat down again.

"What did they want with you?" Hollis asked the Incarnation of Piracy.

Mahab paused. "They want me to join an organization of my kind."

"Did you accept their invitation?" Burrina asked.

"I told them I would think about it," Mahab replied. "Anyway, back to the matter of the Federation fleet. We shall meet them with a fleet of our own. All our ships will meet them in battle. We will position ourselves between them and the planet."

The other captains agreed. They planned the defense of Torbold.

"They will not take Nashotah without a fight," Borgan swore.

The other captains seconded that. The Incarnation of Piracy feared they would lose the upcoming battle and was tempted to accept the offer by the Fellowship of Darkness. Mahab did not want to abandon the Retreat. He felt they might not have a choice. If the pirates lose the battle against the Federation fleet, all the stored loot on Torbold would be confiscated by their enemy.

The meeting adjourned. All the captains prepared for the attack by the Federation fleet, except the Incarnation of Piracy. He retired to his private quarters at the Retreat.

Mahab pondered the chance that the pirates would lose the battle against the Federation fleet. Where would the buccaneers go to establish a new home base? He knew about plenty of planets in the Milky Way Galaxy that could be the new Retreat.

Starly squawked. "Give us a kiss. Give us a kiss."

Mahab fed the parrot crackers. The bird ate the tasty snack with relish.

"Maybe I should accept their offer," Mahab mumbled.

"Accept their offer, accept their offer," Starly squawked.

Mahab petted his parrot. "I sense I should do it."

The Incarnation of Piracy never before experienced the company of other Archvillains, though he knew they existed. For thousands of years, he plundered in the galaxy with other pirates, who were all mortal. He was the only immortal buccaneer. Over the centuries he'd captained so many different crews, corsair after corsair.

The next morning, Mahab returned to his ship. He took his seat in the captain's chair. The crew on the bridge awaited his orders.

"Prepare for battle," Mahab commanded. "Arm all weapons."

"Aye, captain," Gaelor said.

The pirate ships positioned themselves before Torbold. Altogether, twenty buccaneer vessels formed their own fleet. Now, they waited for the Federation fleet to arrive.

****

The six Universal Marshals stood on the bridge of the *Constellation*. All twenty battlecruisers readied themselves for the upcoming battle.

Memfelice used her psychic abilities. "I sense the pirates are awaiting our arrival with a fleet of ships of their own."

"Not unexpected given the Incarnation of Piracy," Falatar remarked.

"Set course for Torbold," Soberyn ordered.

The Federation fleet plotted the coordinates for the planet. All battlecruisers engaged their teleport drives and telejumped to the Cancer Sector of the Milky Way Galaxy.

"This isn't going to be easy," Hashrah remarked.

The Federation fleet appeared a safe distance from

Torbold.

"Sensors detect a bunch of corsairs ahead, captain," Nymeron said.

"Prepare to engage the enemy," Soberyn commanded. "Ready all weapons. Shields up."

The Federation fleet raised their shields. All twenty battlecruisers readied their weapons. The corsairs raised their own shields and readied their weapons.

The distance closed between the two fleets. Soon, both were in range of their respective weapons.

"Fire lasers!" Soberyn ordered.

The Federation fleet fired lasers at the pirate fleet. The buccaneer vessels responded by shooting ion cannons. Both sides pounded each other with their weapons.

"Ready antimatter torpedoes!" Soberyn commanded.

"Ready, captain," Dolle said.

Soberyn sat forward in his captain's chair. "Fire!"

Federation ships launched antimatter torpedoes at the corsairs. Some struck the buccaneer vessels and damaged them. In turn the pirate ships struck Federation ships and damaged them in return.

"Keep firing!" Soberyn ordered.

A few Federation ships flanked the pirate fleet. The buccaneer vessels turned to meet the attack. Neither side used fighters in the battle. Nor would they employ battle droids.

Memfelice used her psychic abilities again. "I feel the presence of the Incarnation of Piracy on the lead ship of the pirate fleet."

"Target that vessel with antimatter torpedoes," Soeryn commanded. "Fire!"

The *Constellation* launched antimatter torpedoes at the *Jolly Mercer* and hit the engineering section of the pirate ship. They damaged the buccaneer vessel.

The tide of battle turned in favor of the Federation fleet. Pirate ships sustained more damage than theirs. The Federation fleet sent communications to the buccaneer vessels and asked them to surrender. The corsairs refused.

"I sense pirates beaming down to Torbold," Memfelice said.

"Sensors detect them on the surface of the planet," Nymeron confirmed.

A couple of corsairs imploded. Others decided to retreat and engaged superluminal drives to tunnel into space to disappear. Those that were left drifted into space.

"I sense the Incarnation of Piracy has gone to Torbold," Memfelice stated.

"You wish to pursue him?" Soberyn asked the Universal Marshals.

"Yes," Jeddriel answered for them.

The captain prepared a landing party of armed personnel to accompany the Enforcers down on the planet. They got teleported to the Retreat.

"They know we are coming," Memfelice remarked.

The Universal Marshals led the charge into Nashotah. Pirates opened fire on them with blasters and blast rifles. They returned fire against the buccaneers.

"I feel the presence of the Incarnation of Piracy," Memfelice said.

"We have to get through pirates to reach him," Falatar remarked.

From a corridor to their right, a bunch of buccaneers

charged them wielding scimitars. Jeddriel materialized his flaming sword and clashed with them. So did Jarek with his hoe of power. Both of them felled foes.

From a passageway to their left, more pirates attacked them. Hashrah fired turbo blasts from her hands at them. Memfelice used her psychic ability of telekinesis on them. Agwennel produced waves of water against them. Falatar employed his gravitic push on them. Together, they wiped out the buccaneers.

The fight continued. The Universal Marshals hoped the pirates would surrender, but the buccaneers refused. Onward, the Enforcers and the armed personnel from the Federation ships pressed against the enemy.

In space armed personnel from the Federation ships boarded the corsairs still around. The pirates refused to surrender, and battle ensued. Back and forth, both sides fired blasters and blast rifles. The buccaneers would not be taken alive.

In Nashotah, the Universal Marshals and the armed personnel from the Federation ships reached the meeting hall. The pirates keep shooting their weapons.

"No sign of the Incarnation of Piracy yet," Memfelice said.

"He has to be here somewhere," Falatar stated.

"He can't hide from us forever," Jarek remarked.

"Yes," Jeddriel agreed.

A few of the armed personnel from the Federation ships got wounded. In return, they took out some buccaneers. Each side took cover behind the immense table at opposite ends.

"Surrender!" Jeddriel shouted

"Never!" a pirate yelled.

"They're stubborn," Falatar remarked.

****

In his private quarters in the Retreat, Mahab wondered what to do now. The Federation forces overwhelmed the pirates. He felt they were going to lose the battle.

Just then, armed personnel from the Federation ships entered his room. The Incarnation of Piracy swung his scimitar of power and fought them. They tried taking him prisoner, but he slayed them all.

The next moment, Wuminga and Ragnar materialized in his private quarters. It caught him off guard.

"Do you wish to join us now?" Ragnar asked.

Mahab resigned to the fact that the buccaneers lost. He hated the idea of abandoning the Retreat. His corsair was also gone. All he had left was Starly. The parrot squawked a few times. Both of the other Archvillains waited for him to answer.

Mahab sighed. "Yes. I will join you."

"Welcome to the Fellowship of Darkness," Wuminga said.

Ragnar contacted the *Marauder* with a telecommunicator. All three foul beings got beamed up to the ship. Afterward, the vessel engaged its teleport drive and vanished from the Cancer Sector.

****

"The Incarnation of Piracy is no longer on Torbold," Memfelice said.

"Where did he go?" Falatar asked.

"Transported to another ship," Memfelice replied. "Not a corsair."

Eventually, the battle ended. The Federation forces took pirates as prisoners and confiscated buccaneer vessels and the stored loot in Nashotah.

The Universal Marshals interrogated pirates. They learned about the two Archvillains who had visited the Retreat to talk with Mahab.

Memfelice used her psychic abilities. "I sense that the Incarnation of Piracy has joined the Fellowship of Darkness."

"Another member of the Archvillain organization," Jeddriel remarked. "We don't know how many of the foul beings are in it currently."

The Federation ships fired antimatter torpedoes and destroyed the remaining corsairs. All the pirates still alive were taken to the penal colony on the planet Yhemene in the Libra Sector of the Milky Way Galaxy and imprisoned.

The Universal Marshals returned to Tellus and reported to the High Enforcer in the Justiceplex. The mission was deemed a success. All six Enforcers took time off before their next assignment.

Chapter 39

The Archvillains met in the meeting room of the *Slaughter*. The black magician sat before the control console. He shut off the telescreen on the wall right of him.

"The thoughts of the Watchers betrayed the location of Lordruingat to me," Sumerlin said. "The Cube of Power is on the world of Drath."

"Where is the planet located?" Darlesse asked.

Sumerlin checked the control console. "It is in the Rigellian Sector of the Milky Way Galaxy."

"What is known of Drath?" Ripgarth asked.

Surmerlin read what appeared on the control console. "The Drathians are a primitive race of humanoids. On the scientific level, they are low. On the occultic level, they are nonexistent. On the celestic level, they are nonexistent."

"What else?" Foulbard asked.

"They are ruled by clans," Sumerlin replied.

"Do the Enforcers know about Drath?" Namina asked.

"Yes," Sumerlin answered. "They also know the location of Lordruingat."

"Damn," Daggermash swore.

"So we're going to have to fight both Watchers and Enforcers to get the Cube of Power," Gnashboros remarked.

"It is unavoidable," Sumerlin said.

"What about the Drathians?" Darlesse asked. "Do we have to fight them, too?"

Sumerlin sensed the answer. "I feel they do not know about Lordruingat on their world. The Cube of Power is hidden from them."

"But it doesn't mean we will not encounter them," Tajanna stated.

"True," Sumerlin agreed. "We will try our best not to see them."

The meeting adjourned. They returned to their individual rooms. Later they met on the bridge of the ship. The *Slaughter* engaged its teleport drive and telejumped to the Rigellian Sector of the Milky Way Galaxy.

****

Draegor and the Watchers with him returned to the inactive volcano where Lordruingat rested. All the Watchers gathered together in the cave where the Cube of Power rested. Glow stones in cressets provided light.

"What is wrong, great leader?" Farianne asked.

"The Enforcers and the Archvillains know of the location of Lordruingat," Draegor replied. "We must protect the Cube of Power from falling in either of their hands."

"How did they both find out?" Garion asked.

"They used their special powers to discover the truth," Draegor explained. "I feared that this would happen."

"Should we take Lordruingat off this planet and find another to hide it on?" Maloras asked.

Draegor sighed. "I will consult with the Cube of Power."

The leader of the Watchers put his hands on the sides of Lordruingat. He closed his eyes and concentrated. Minutes later, he opened his eyes.

"What does the Cube of Power reveal, great leader?" Seuron asked.

"It is too late to take Lordruingat off of Drath," Draegor replied. "Ships of the Enforcers and Archvillains are here. There is no vessel for us to take the Cube of Power elsewhere."

"How unfortunate," Sorhea said.

"But neither the Enforcers nor the Archvillains know exactly where Lordruingat is on the planet," Draegor stated. "That is our only advantage."

"What about the Drathians?" Narwyn asked. "Could they help either the Enforcers or the Archvillains find the Cube of Power?"

Draegor grimaced. "The Drathians don't know about us or Lordruingat. They would be of little help to either side."

"Then what should we do, great leader?" Maloras asked.

"We must prepare to fight the Enforcers and the Archvillains," Draegor answered. "Hope that the Drathians don't get mixed up in this. I would hate to have to slay them if they help either the Enforcers or the Archvillains."

"How many do the Enforcers and the Archvillains number, great leader?" Garion asked.

"The Enforcers number ten," Draegor replied. "The Archvillains also number ten."

"There are twenty of us," Farianne said.

"An even fight," Maloras interjected.

The Watchers prepared to defend Lordruingat

against the Enforcers and the Archvillains. The Cube of Power glowed electric blue. They waited for the Universal Marshals and the foul beings to come.

****

The Universal Marshals met again in the meeting room. The *Horizon* orbited a safe distance from Drath, cloaked.

"Three of the Universal Marshals visited Drath a while ago," Benethor said.

The three that did were Zorrokin, the Thunderer, Chryssina, the Light Being, and Rorbash, the Dragonling. On the planet, they learned of the Fellowship of Darkness and the Archvillain organization on Earth. They established a friendship with the Drathians and helped them win the battle against the Archvillain Garrax and his minions.

Benethor continued. "Drath is also being considered to join the Federation. It is being debated by the Federation Assembly."

"Do the Drathians have a global government now?" Kesharra asked.

"The Drathians have a global council now," Benethor clarified. "It was facilitated by the war against the Beast and his warriors."

"Should we ask for the Drathians to help us get Lordruingat?" Danbarrack asked.

"I don't think that is a good idea," Apparis interjected. "They could get hurt in the fight against the Archvillains and the Watchers."

"I agree," Nazzar said. "We don't want their blood on our hands."

"But do they know about the Cube of Power?" Idyllion asked.

"Unlikely," Apparis said.

"And they would not know where it is on their world," Milantheus added.

"Still, we will have to talk with them," Benethor responded. "It is their world, and we don't want to seem like we're invaders to Drath."

"So we should meet with their global council," Yevadne interjected.

"Yes," Benethor said. "That we'll do first when we teleport down to the world."

The meeting adjourned. The Universal Marshals retired to their private quarters each. The next day, they went to the teleporter room and got beamed down to the surface of the planet.

Drathians met them outside a large settlement. The humanoids featured six fingers, six toes, and manes. They dressed in simple garb and were armed with spears, swords, and other weapons. They greeted the Universal Marshals as the white sun of Azbruk shined overhead.

"Welcome to Drath," a male Drathian with a golden mane said. "I am Sakiro, a member of the council. Who are you?"

"We are Universal Marshals from the Universal Federation of Planets," Nazzar replied. "We come in peace."

The Drathians talked among themselves. Then they quieted down.

"We remember the Enforcers who visited us once," Sakiro said. "Why are you here?"

Benethor answered. "We wish to speak with your council about an important matter."

"Very well," Sakiro responded.

The Drathians led the Universal Marshals into the

settlement. Around them rose stone houses and other structures. Children played, some with pets that resembled dogs. A river flowed west of the community. Outside the settlement to the east grew crops. Beyond the harvest stretched wilderness that also extended north and south. In the distance, north and south beyond the wilderness, rose mountains.

The Drathians put the Universal Marshals up in a guest dwelling. It was modestly furnished and the Enforcers made themselves at home. Later, they would be summoned before the council.

"We might as relax until they come for us," Benethor said.

A wooden table with wooden chairs sat in the middle of the guest dwelling, which featured three rooms. One a bedroom with four wooden beds, a living room, and the room they stood in.

Four Drathian women brought in food and drink for the Universal Marshals. Then they bowed to the Enforcers and left. The meal consisted of a light bread, cooked fish, raw vegetables, and fresh water.

Apparis took a piece of bread and ate it. "Tastes good."

The Universal Marshals relished the fare. The hospitality of the Drathians was decent.

"Do you think the Federation Assembly will accept Drath as a new member of the Federation?" Yevadne asked the other Enforcers.

Benethor drank a cup of water. "I think they will. The Drathians are a good people."

Danbarrack voiced a question. "What about Earth?"

"Maybe," Idyllion said. "The Federation Assembly is debating whether or not to make it a new member as well."

"Bolan is speaking on behalf of the Terran world," Milantheus interjected.

"That is logical," Nazzar added.

Enforcer Bolan Trevarre, the Noble Soldier, originally came from Earth. He fought in the war for Tellus when the Fellowship of Darkness sent a space fleet to invade the Federation capital to bust out the Archvillains imprisoned in the Universal Prisonplex. Since he became a Universal Marshal, he had not visited his native planet. He desired to see his homeworld again.

Eventually, the Drathians summoned the Universal Marshals before the council. Two male Drathians carrying spears escorted them to the council hall where the council awaited them. In twelve wooden chairs sat the members of the council on a stone dais. The Enforcers stood before the council, and behind them stood more Drathians. It was the middle of the afternoon.

"It has been a while since your kind has visited Drath," Sakiro stated. "We had not heard from the Federation about our joining it. Is there any news about that?"

"The Federation Assembly is debating about your membership into the Federation," Nazzar replied. "It is looking favorable that you will be accepted into it."

"That is excellent to hear," a female Drathian named Nurri, with a red mane, said.

The council talked among themselves. A commotion occurred among the Drathians behind the Universal Marshals. Sakiro quieted them down.

"You mentioned that there is an important matter you wish to discuss with the council," a male Drathian named Tamaric, with a brown mane, stated.

"Yes," Benethor acknowledged for the Enforcers.

Apparis spoke. "Do you know of Lordruingat, the Cube of Power?"

"We know of stories about a sacred object of magic that exists on our world," a female Drathian named Katanda, with a black mane, replied. "It is said to be guarded by higher beings."

"We know those higher beings as Watchers," Ursanne responded.

"You believe that this Lordruingat is on Drath?" Sakiro asked.

"Yes," Kesharra answered. "We have been questing for it for some time. We tracked it to your planet."

"How do you know it is here?" a male Drathian named Dellmar, with a tan mane, asked.

"Because we encountered the Watchers on another world who guard it," Ursanne explained. "I read their thoughts and it revealed to me where they are from and the location of Lordruingat."

The council talked among themselves again. More commotion from the Drathians behind the Universal Marshals. Sakiro quieted his people down once more.

"Do you know where exactly on our world where the Cube of Power rests?" a female Drathian named Ashirei, with an orange mane, asked.

Nazzar responded. "We don't know the exact location of Lordruingat on your planet. So we need to search for the Cube of Power here."

"What do you intend to do with it?" a male Drathian named Mared, with a blue mane, asked.

"Take it back to Tellus to study," Apparis answered.

Hulkeme spoke. "We're not the only ones looking for Lordruingat."

"Who else is searching for the Cube of Power?" Sakiro asked.

"A group of Archvillains," Kesharra replied. "Their number is the same as ours."

"We cannot let the foul beings get their hands on Lordruingat," Milantheus said. "They would use it for destructive purposes."

The council conversed among themselves still again. The Universal Marshals spoke among themselves.

"Do you wish us to go with you on your quest?" Dellmar asked the Enforcers.

"I don't think that would be a good idea," Apparis interjected. "We anticipate a battle against the Watchers and the Archvillains over the Cube of Power. If any of your people go with us, they could get hurt or killed in the fight."

"The Archvillains and the Watchers both have special powers to contend with," Idyllion added.

"Just like you," Nurri stated.

"Yes," Yevadne admitted for the Enforcers. "The last time an Archvillain came to your planet was when Garrax, the Beast, tried to conquer it."

The Drathians remembered the war against the foul being and his minions. It had united all the clans of Drath in a common cause. Drath became allies with the Universal Marshals and the Federation, which led to the defeat of the invaders.

"What is so special about Lordruingat?" Sakiro asked.

Nazzar explained. After he finished, the council conversed among themselves again.

"Do you know how to wield the Cube of Power?" Tamaric asked the Enforcers.

"No," Idyllion replied. "We have to figure that out."

"Where will you start looking for Lordruingat here?" Dellmar asked.

"The wilderness area," Nazzar answered.

Ursanne sensed the planet. "I feel the presence of Watchers on this world. But not the exact location yet of the Cube of Power."

"Go with the blessings of the gods," Sakiro said. "May you find what you seek."

The meeting with the council ended. The Universal Marshals stayed the night at the settlement. In the morning, they left the place after saying goodbye to the Drathians. Soon, they entered the wilderness area and began their search for Lordruingat.

****

The *Slaughter* established orbit a safe distance from Drath. The Archvillains went to the teleporter room and got beamed down to the surface of the planet. They found themselves in a wilderness area near a mountain range.

Sumerlin sensed the world. "I feel the presence of Watchers but not where Lordruingat rests here."

"Which way should we go?" Darlesse asked the black magician.

"Toward those peaks," Sumerlin replied.

The Archvillains headed north through the wilderness area. Birds sang in the trees. A herd of black-tailed deer crossed their path and ran off. To their left, a small mammal-like groundhog burrowed in the earth. To their right, a stream meandered east.

The Archvillains heard a howl. A huge creature with horns, four-legged, charged at them.

"I will take care of this animal," Foulbard said.

The Shocker blasted the large beast with shock waves and sent it flying through the trees. It landed on the ground dead.

The Archvillains continued on. Other fauna appeared. A small canine with yellow spots crossed their path and scampered away. To their right, a bear-like creature foraged in the brush for edible berries. Insects droned. The temperature felt hot.

"This world teems with nature," Tajanna remarked.

The Archvillains reached the mountain range. They began an ascent into the peaks. High overhead shined Azbruk in a cloudless sky.

"Where would a good place be for Lordruingat to hide in?" Namina asked no one in particular. The Siren felt like breaking out in song.

"The Cube of Power must be well hidden here," Ripgarth commented.

The Archvillains entered a mountain pass. They came upon some tracks.

"Whatever made these must be large," Gnashboros said.

Now, the foul beings heard roars. They stopped and waited. Over a ridge, a pack of big felines, mountain cats with black fur and long fangs, spotted them and dashed toward them.

The Archvillains defended themselves. Sumerlin shot red fire from his hands at the charging beasts. Ripgarth fired a blue beam from his eye into the four-legged creatures. Foulbard unleashed shock waves at the large animals. The Archvillains wiped out the pack of big felines, killing several of them. The rest of the mountain cats fled.

"Many dangers from nature here," Amyrielle

remarked.

"Are we any closer to finding Lordruingat?" Xigan asked the black magician.

Sumerlin sensed the mountains. "I feel the presence of beings in the mountains. Not Watchers, though."

The Archvillains came to a valley. In the elongated depression stood a village.

"Do they know we are here?" Daggermash asked the black magician.

"Not yet," Sumerlin replied. The black magician sensed the planet again. "I feel the presence of Watchers south of us."

The Archvillains returned the way they came. They descended the mountains and went through the wilderness area again. It took them days to travel through the uninhabited and uncultivated region. Their path brought them to an inactive volcano.

"I sense the Watchers are in there," Sumerlin said.

The Archvillains prepared to enter the lone mountain.

****

The Universal Marshals trekked through the wilderness area. They heard bird song. A stream appeared on their right with fish swimming in it. A female black-tailed deer and her fawn crossed their path and ran off. Insects buzzed.

"The scenery is nice," Kesharra remarked.

Benethor smiled. "There is beauty on this world."

Ahead, Universal Marshals heard howls. They halted. North of them, a pack of yellow wolves ran toward them. They defended themselves against it. Nazzar shot laser beams from his eyes to chase them off. Kehsarra did the same with solar rays from her hands.

Benethor grabbed the red Elfstone from his pouch and fired red beams from it into the pack of yellow wolves. The wild animals dispersed and fled from the Enforcers.

"I feel the presence of Watchers southwest of our position," Ursanne said.

The Universal Marshals changed course and went in the direction the Norn-Enforcer told them. No other wildlife threatened them. Days later, they reached an inactive volcano.

"The Watchers are in there," Ursanne stated.

The Universal Marshals prepared to enter the lone mountain.

****

"They will be here soon," Draegor informed the rest of the Watchers.

"We are ready for them," Maloras said.

The Watchers, willing to sacrifice their very lives for Lordruingat, marched to the mouth of a cavern leading outside, unarmed. Twenty of them were ready to do battle.

"Remember, if we have to slay them, then do so without hesitation," Draegor ordered. "The Cube of Power must not fall into either of their hands. Its great power must not be used by either side."

Lordruingat could not be destroyed by the Watchers. Its ulgnostic energy power would block any attempt to do so.

"We must not fail," Draegor stated. "We make this promise to the Cube of Power."

"We won't fail, great leader," Garion vowed.

****

The Universal Marshals spotted the Archvillains and the Watchers at the same time both saw the

Enforcers.

Sumerlin shot red fire from his hands at the Watchers. So did Ripgarth with a blue beam from his eye. Foulbard unleashed shock waves at the Universal Marshals.

The Watchers fired energy balls from their hands at the Archvillains and the Enforcers.

Nazzar shot laser beams from his eyes at the Archvillains. Benethor fired a red beam from the red Elfstone at the foul beings as Idyllion unleashed nuclear blasts from his hands at them. Kesharra shot solar rays from her hands at the Watchers as Apparis did with sonic blasts from his beak.

Milantheus froze energy balls from the Watchers in time and dispersed them. Yevadne launched a cyclone wind at the Archvillains. The nuclear blasts from Idyllion clashed with the shock waves of Foulbard and annihilated each other.

Attacks by the three parties canceled each other out. They fought on trying to gain an advantage over the other two.

The Watchers backed into the cavern behind them. They kept firing energy balls.

The Archvillains and the Enforcers moved forward toward the cavern. Neither stopped their attacks. They pressed the Watchers backward.

"I sense the presence of Lordruingat in the inactive volcano," Ursanne told the other Universal Marshals.

The Enforcers followed behind the Archvillains, who trailed the Watchers. Kesharra shined her body like a sun and provided light. All three groups kept up their attacks as they neared the Cube of Power.

The three parties entered the cavern where

Lordruingat rested. Glow stones in cressets provided illumination in the large cave. The Cube of Power glowed electric blue.

The Watchers surrounded Lordruingat. They still fired energy balls at the Archvillains and the Universal Marshals. The foul beings blocked the round projectiles as the Enforcers did the same.

"How do we get Lordruingat?" Yevadne asked the other Universal Marshals.

Danbarrack stretched out his right arm and arced it over the Archvillains and the Watchers. He reached the Cube of Power and grabbed it before the Archvillains and Watchers could stop him. The Rubber Being quickly drew his right arm back, holding Lordruingat.

"We got it," Idyllion remarked.

"Get us out of here," Benethor said to the Genie-Enforcer

Hulkeme teleported the Enforcers back up to the *Horizon*. The Watchers vanished and left the Archvillains alone in the cavern.

On the ship, the Enforcers set course for Tellus. The vessel engaged its teleport drive and telejumped to the Sagittarian Sector of the Milky Way Galaxy.

Chapter 40

The Fellowship of Darkness built a new and bigger Complex on Murron. The Archvillain organization made the forest world their new home base.

Magnemus grew another biolaboratory of a rain forest in the larger citadel. The Scientific Being transferred part of the biome on the *Technokado* to the huge fortress in Biolaboratory One. The professor walked through it. Loamy and earthy smells wafted to his nose. Many sounds of animals reverberated in the air, particularly bird cries and monkey chatter. He looked at the broad-leaved trees with high green canopies around him and smiled. Green ferns and bushes crowded underneath the treetops, vying for space to get the needed sustenance of sunlight, soil nutrients, and rainwater, which was provided by automated systems. Satisfied, Magnemus left the biolaboratory.

The Scientific Being went to Biolaboratory Three. It featured the building of robots. In it stood a half a dozen droids, inoperative at the moment. The professor stepped over to one and checked its circuits.

Someone buzzed him from outside the chamber. He told them to enter.

Asearse walked into the room. "There is news."

"What?" Magnemus asked.

"Our team looking for Lordruingat found the Cube of Power on the world of Drath. They encountered opposition from the Enforcers and the Watchers. The Universal Marshals managed to get Lordruingat."

Magnemus sighed. "Failure."

"There is other news," Asearse said. "Orlin has recruited the Incarnation of War, the Incarnation of Famine, and the Incarnation of Pestilence for our Fellowship."

The Four Horsemen of the Apocalypse reunited. That pleased Magnemus. The Scientific Being grinned.

"Also," Asearse added, "Wuminga and Ragnar recruited the Incarnation of Piracy to our cause."

"So we are steadily increasing our numbers," Magnemus remarked. "Excellent. How many members do we have now?"

"Fifty-seven."

"There are still plenty of other Archvillains out there to recruit to our organization. We will keep adding to our roll."

"War, Famine, and Pestilence are here. Do you wish to speak with them?"

Magnemus paused in thought. "Yes."

The Charybdian and the Scientific Being left Biolaboratory Three and went to a mess hall. Orlin waited with the other three Incarnations there.

The Grim Reaper introduced the Incarnation of War. Vidarius stood six feet eight with a muscular build. Red flecked his brown eyes, and his black hair was cut short. He wore chain mail over his red vest, brown trousers, and black boots. His sword of power, Warmaker, rested in a scabbard on his right side, and a war horn hung from his black belt on his left.

"It is good to be together again with my brothers of the Horsemen," Vidarius said. "Too long separated."

The Grim Reaper introduced the Incarnation of Famine next. Sallor appeared very thin with long red hair and blue eyes and stood six feet even. He wore a white tunic with red pants and matching shoes. He carried an iron pail of magic with him.

"Reunited at last," Sallor remarked. "Great to be the Horsemen once more."

The Grim Reaper introduced the Incarnation of Pestilence last. Jallar looked diseased with long white hair and white eyes and stood six feet two. He wore a white robe with leather sandals. In his hand, he held a steel poker of power.

"Yes, it is splendid to be the Four Horsemen again," Jallar said. "We shall rain terror on the galaxy once more."

"How many of our kind are in the Fellowship?" Vidarius asked.

"Fifty-seven at present," Asearse replied.

"It is wonderful not to be locked up in the Universal Prisonplex anymore," Sallor stated. "My special powers are free again."

"That was a terrible place for Archvillains to be imprisoned," Jallar added. "Not being able to use your special powers was quite painful."

"There are plenty more Archvillains to recruit to our organization," Magnemus said. "Thousands and thousands out there to join our cause."

"Do you want us to help you recruit others of our kind to the Fellowship?" Sallor asked. "It would be an honor."

"Yes," Magnemus answered.

"Have you made any plans?" Jallar asked.

Magnemus smiled. "We are working on something.

It is important that we finish construction on the new Complex. Right now, we are ahead of schedule."

Orlin showed the other three Incarnations to their private quarters. Wuminga and Ragnar entered with the Incarnation of Piracy. They introduced Mahab to the Scientific Being and the Charybdian.

"I have lost much thanks to the Enforcers and the Federation," Mahab said. On his shoulder, Starly squawked. He petted the parrot.

"But you gain by joining our Fellowship," Asearse pointed out.

Mahab nodded. "I look forward to paying them back for what they did to me."

"You will have your chance," Magnemus promised.

Mahab laughed. "Is there anything you want me to do?"

"You can help us recruit more Archvillains to our organization or help oversee the construction of the Complex," Magnemus responded.

"I will help oversee the construction of the Complex," Mahab said. "It looks nothing like the Retreat." He missed being at Nashotah with other pirate captains.

Magnemus returned to Biolaboratory One with a pocket recorder, a silver rectangular device activated, controlled, worked, and deactivated by voice commands. The Scientific Being began speaking into it.

"The biome has taken firm root in the biolaboratory. I will need to get specimens from it for scientific analysis."

The professor stopped at a small river in the biome. He studied schools of yellow, pancake-shaped sunfish swimming in the slow current. He spotted a group of freshwater turtles paddling underwater. A silver and red-scaled water snake glided through the clear water in a side-to-side motion. He spoke again into his pocket recorder.

"The aquatic life is flourishing quite well. I will introduce a few more species into the river."

Magnemus stayed awhile before leaving. The Scientific Being planned what to do next against the Federation and the Enforcers.

Chapter 41

Delveran entered the meeting room of the Justiceplex. At the table sat the six Universal Marshals who had been given the assignment on the matter of space piracy. The High Enforcer took his place before the control console. To his right, the telescreen shut off.

"Report," Delveran said.

"We defeated the pirates in battle," Jeddriel replied. "We found their homeworld of Nashotah, the Retreat. It exists no more."

"We arrested many buccaneers," Falatar added.

Delveran nodded. "Did you apprehend the Incarnation of Piracy?"

"Unfortunately, Mahab escaped from us," Memfelice answered. "We learn that the Fellowship of Darkness has recruited him."

That surprised Delveran a little. The High Enforcer was glad the problem of space piracy had taken a blow. Reports of attacks by buccaneers on freighters and other ships were much less now.

"We recovered many goods from the Retreat," Jarek interjected. "Their loot was a huge stockpile."

The Federation Department of Justice will be happy to know that the Universal Marshals curtailed space piracy in the galaxy. But not pleased that the Incarnation of Piracy eluded capture by the Enforcers. However, the recovery of stuff from the Retreat would satisfy them.

"Do you have new assignments for us?" Hashrah asked the High Enforcer.

"Yes," Delveran replied. "Jeddriel and Memfelice will investigate the black markets in the galaxy. It is rumored that Villains are operating them. Find out which foul beings are making profits from them."

"As you command," the Archangel-Enforcer and the Psychic Being responded.

Delveran continued. "Jarek and Hashrah will investigate the slave trade in the galaxy. Find out who is behind it and who is buying slaves."

"As you command," the Incarnation of Life and the Turbobeing responded.

Delveran resumed. "Agwennel and Falatar will investigate the sex trafficking problem in the galaxy. Find out who is behind it and those who are buying sex slaves."

"As you command," the Lunar Being and the Undine-Enforcer responded.

The meeting ended. The six Universal Marshals went about their assignments. Next, ten Enforcers entered the meeting room carrying Lordruingat.

"We have the Cube of Power," Benethor said.

Danbarrack laid it on the table. Lordruingat glowed electric blue.

"Have any of you tried using it?" Delveran asked.

"Yes," Nazzar replied. "So far, we have been unable to figure out how to wield it."

"We cannot fathom how to unlock its energy power," Ursanne added.

Delveran touched the Cube of Power. The High Enforcer could feel the power emanating from it. "Where did you locate Lordruingat?"

"On the planet, Drath," Yevadne answered.

"We had to fight for it against Watchers and Archvillains," Kesharra explained. "We found it in an inactive volcano."

"Did the Drathians know about the Cube of Power?" Delveran asked.

"They had stories about it and the Watchers," Milantheus interjected.

Delveran made a decision. "We will have teams of scientists, occultists, and celestists study Lordruingat. See if they can discover its secrets. Learn to use its ulgnostic power."

"The Drathians asked about the debate in the Federation Assembly about their membership into the Federation," Idyllion said.

Delveran smiled. "The Federation Assembly approved the membership of Drath into the Federation yesterday. Officials will contact the Drathians to send a delegation to Tellus to join the Federation Assembly."

"What about Earth?" Hulkeme asked.

Enforcer Bolan Trevarre spoke to the Federation Assembly on behalf of his homeworld. The Noble Soldier talked eloquently about his native planet and hoped the Federation Assembly would approve the Terran world for membership into the Federation.

"The Federation Assembly is still debating the matter," Delveran said. "It is divided on the issue."

"Have you new assignments for us?" Apparis asked.

"Yes," Delveran replied. "Nazzar and Yevadne will investigate the drug cartels in the galaxy. You will be members of a Federation task force to help stop the flow of illegal drugs in the sectors."

The   Android-Enforcer   and   the   Zephyr

acknowledged the High Enforcer. They left the meeting room to start their new assignment.

Delveran continued. "Idyllion and Ursanne will investigate the series of bank robberies in the Libra Sector. More than a billion credits have been stolen by the perpetrators. Find them and apprehend them."

The Nuclear Being and the Norn-Enforcer acknowledged the High Enforcer. They left the meeting room to begin their new assignment.

Delveran resumed. "Benethor and Apparis will investigate the theft of magical objects in the Orion Sector. These things of power are being misused against people on planets in the quadrant. Find the culprits and arrest them."

The Elf-Enforcer and the Roc acknowledged the High Enforcer. They left the meeting room to start their new assignment.

"I have foreseen the Fellowship of Darkness finding another planet to build a new home base on," Delveran stated. "Hulkeme and Kesharra will search the galaxy to see if they can find where the Archvillain organization has built their new Complex."

The Genie-Enforcer and the Solar Being acknowledged the High Enforcer. They left the meeting room to begin their new assignment.

"As for you, Danbarrack and Milantheus," Delveran said, "you will investigate the flow of illegal arms in the galaxy to renegade worlds. There are evil planets getting supplies of weapons to attack other worlds to rule them. You will join a Federation task force to stop this."

The Rubber Being and Father Time acknowledged the High Enforcer. They left the meeting room to start their new assignment.

Delveran left the meeting room and went to his office. The High Enforcer checked his messages. There were two. The first from the Warden of the Universal Prisonplex. The second was from the Federation Department of Justice. He answered both. The Warden informed the Grand Universal Marshal of a new batch of prisoners in the Universal Prisonplex. Officials from the Federation Department of Justice wanted to see him. He would go first to the Federationplex to speak with the officials. Then, he would go to the Universal Prisonplex.

The main concern of Delveran was the Fellowship of Darkness. He knew the Archvillain organization kept recruiting new members to their cause. They remained a threat to the Federation and the Enforcers. It needed to be dealt with, a top priority.

A word about the author...

Stephen M. T. Greene was born in Lowell, Massachusetts in 1959. He received his B.A. Degree in Liberal Arts/Writing from Vermont College of Norwich University and his M.S. Degree in Creative Writing from Columbus University. His publications include poems in three poetry anthologies and four stories in a fiction anthology, which he also edited, TALES OF THE UNKNOWN. In addition he writes plays, teleplays, and screenplays. He enjoys movies, music, sports, martial arts, video games, and reading. Currently he lives in Pennsylvania.

authorstephenmtgreenewebsite.godaddysites.com

Thank you for purchasing
this publication of The Wild Rose Press, Inc.

For questions or more information
contact us at
info@thewildrosepress.com.

The Wild Rose Press, Inc.
www.thewildrosepress.com